for [...]
iris[...]
city[...]

Bill

Christmas 2018

EVERYMAN,

I WILL GO WITH THEE,

AND BE THY GUIDE,

IN THY MOST NEED

TO GO BY THY SIDE

EVERYMAN'S POCKET CLASSICS

VENICE
STORIES

EDITED BY JONATHAN KEATES

EVERYMAN'S POCKET CLASSICS
Alfred A. Knopf New York London Toronto

THIS IS A BORZOI BOOK
PUBLISHED BY ALFRED A. KNOPF

This selection by Jonathan Keates first published in
Everyman's Library, 2019
Copyright © 2018 by Everyman's Library
A list of acknowledgments to copyright owners appears at the back
of this volume.

www.randomhouse.com/everymans
www.everymanslibrary.co.uk

ISBN: 978-1-101-90806-8 (US)
ISBN: 978-1-84159-625-9 (UK)

A CIP catalogue reference for this book is available from the
British Library

Library of Congress Cataloging-in-Publication Data

Names: Keates, Jonathan, 1946 – editor.
Title: Venice stories / edited by Jonathan Keates.
Description: New York: Everyman's Library, 2018. | Series: Everyman's
library pocket classics series
Identifiers: LCCN 2018031204 | ISBN 9781101908068 (hardback)
Subjects: LCSH: Venice (Italy)—In literature. | BISAC: FICTION /
Anthologies (multiple authors). | FICTION / Literary. | FICTION /
Classics.
Classification: LCC PN6071.V4 V45 2018 | DDC 808.8/
9324531—dc23 LC record available at https://lccn.loc.gov/2018031204

Typography by Peter B. Willberg

Typeset in the UK by Input Data Services Ltd, Isle Abbotts, Somerset

Printed and bound in Germany by GGP Media GmbH, Pössneck

Contents

PREFACE

LASTING A THOUSAND YEARS, the independent state of Venice liked to style itself 'The Most Serene Republic'. As a realm of fiction, however, the place has always been denied any sort of serenity. Writers have seized instead on the city as a domain of unease and moral decay, dwelling on the atmosphere of faded splendour, vanity and excess conveyed by the grandeur of its panoramas amid palaces, churches and canals. A built environment of unmatched architectural magnificence raised, as it seems, from nothing, in the middle of an Adriatic lagoon, has spurred the imagination of novelists and short-story writers to exploit its resonantly paradoxical qualities to the utmost.

Artists like Proust and Henry James meet this challenge by making Venice the natural backdrop for illusion, deceit and ambiguity. Vernon Lee, on the other hand, in 'A Wicked Voice', plays a variation on a unique local tradition of ghosts and haunting, while Baron Corvo takes merciless revenge on the city's expatriate British community for its pretentiousness, insularity and self-aggrandizement. Jeanette Winterson's *The Passion* shapes a fantasy Venice from a location not yet experienced at first hand and Daphne du Maurier, for whom the very name of the place was a code word for sexual unorthodoxy, invests the Venetian streetscape with a wondrously oblique menace.

And Casanova? Ah, Casanova . . . Those famous memoirs he wrote at the end of his life – how true exactly are they?

What his unique narratives seem to tell us is that Venice colours and fashions its special kind of truth and that we should enjoy this on his own terms, seductive and entrancing as these always are. Never mind reality when La Serenissima beckons.

Jonathan Keates

GIACOMO CASANOVA
CHEVALIER DE SEINGALT

From

HISTORY OF MY LIFE

Translated by William R. Trask

I receive an anonymous letter from a nun and I answer it.
Love intrigue.

1753.

ON ALL SAINTS' DAY, just as I was about to get into my
gondola to return to Venice after hearing mass, I met a
woman of the same type as Laura, who, after letting a letter
drop at my feet, walked on. I pick it up and I see the same
woman, satisfied that she had seen me do so, pursue her way.
The letter was white and sealed with wax the color of aven-
turine. The imprint represented a running knot. No sooner
have I entered the gondola than I unseal it and read the
following:

'A nun who has seen you in her church every feast day
for the past two and a half months wishes you to make her
acquaintance. A pamphlet which you lost and which has
come into her hands assures her that you understand French.
However, you may answer her in Italian, for she desires clarity and precision. She does not invite you to have her summoned to the visiting room, because before you obligate
yourself to speak with her she wishes you to see her. So she
will give you the name of a lady whom you can accompany
to the visiting room, who will not know you, and hence will
not be compelled to introduce you if by any chance you do
not wish to be known.

'If this seems to you unsuitable, the same nun who writes

you this letter will give you the address of a casino here in Murano where you will find her alone at the first hour of the night on the day you indicate to her; you can stay and sup with her, or leave a quarter of an hour later if you have business.

'Would you prefer to offer her supper in Venice? Let her know the day, the hour of the night, and the place to which she is to go, and you will see her leave a gondola masked, provided you are on the quay alone, without a servant, masked, and holding a candle.

'Being certain that you will answer me, and as impatient as you can imagine to read your answer, I beg you to deliver it tomorrow to the same woman who brought you this letter. You will find her an hour before noon in the Church of San Canziano at the first altar on the right.

'Consider that if I had not supposed you to be well disposed and honorable, I should never have resolved to take a step which might give you an unfavorable opinion of me.'

The tone of this letter, which I copy word for word, surprised me even more than its contents. I had business, but I dismissed everything to shut myself in my room and answer. Making such a request was sheer madness, yet I found a dignity in it which forced me to respect her. I was at first inclined to believe that the nun might be the one who was teaching C. C. French and who was beautiful, rich, and a flirt, and that my dear wife might have been indiscreet yet know nothing about this unheard-of step on her friend's part, and for that reason had been unable to notify me of it. But I dismissed the suspicion precisely because it pleased me. C. C. had written me that the nun who taught her French was not the only one who had a good command of the language. I could not doubt C. C.'s discretion and the candor with which she would have confessed it to me if she had confided anything at all to the nun. However, since the nun who had written me might be C. C.'s beautiful friend or might be someone else, I wrote her an answer in which I straddled the ditch as far as good manners permitted me to do so; here it is:

'I hope, Madame, that my answer in French will detract nothing from the clarity and precision which you demand and of which you set me an example.

'The subject is most interesting; it seems to me of the greatest moment under the circumstances, and obliged to give an answer without knowing to whom, do you not understand, Madame, that, not being a conceited fool, I must fear a snare? It is honor which obliges me to be on my guard. If it is true, then, that the pen which writes to me is that of a respectable lady who does me the justice to suppose me possessed of a soul as noble and a heart as well disposed as her own, she will find, I hope, that I can answer her only in the following terms:

'If you have thought me worthy, Madame, of making your acquaintance personally, your opinion of me being based only on my appearance, I consider it my duty to obey you if only to disabuse you should I by chance have involuntarily led you into error.

'Of the three arrangements which you have been so generous as to propose to me, I dare choose only the first, on the conditions which your very clear foresight has stipulated. I shall accompany to your visiting room a lady whom you will name to me and who will not know me. Hence there will be no question of introducing me. Be indulgent, Madame, to the specious reasons which oblige me not to name myself. In exchange, I promise you on my honor that your name will become known to me only that I may do you homage. If you see fit to speak to me I will answer you only with the most profound respect. Permit me to hope that you will be alone at the grating and to tell you for form's sake that I am a Venetian and free in the fullest sense of the word. The only reason which prevents me from deciding on the two other arrangements which you propose to me and which do me infinite honor is, permit me to repeat, my fear of being trapped. Those happy meetings can take place as soon as you have become better acquainted with me and no doubts trouble my soul, which abhors falsehood. Very impatient in my turn, I will go tomorrow at the same hour to San Canziano to receive your answer.'

Having found the woman at the appointed place, I gave her my letter and a zecchino. The next morning I returned there and she came up to me. After giving me back my zecchino she handed me the following answer, asking me to go and read it and to come back afterward to tell her if she should wait for an answer. After reading it I went and told her that I had no answer to give her. This is what the nun's letter to me said:

'I believe, Monsieur, that I have been mistaken in nothing. Like yourself, I abhor falsehood when it can have consequences; but I consider it only a trifle when it harms no one. Of my three proposals you have chosen the one which does most honor to your perception. Respecting the reasons you may have for concealing your name, I write the Countess S. what I ask you to read in the note herewith. You will seal it before having it delivered to her. She will be forewarned of it by another note. You will go to her house at your convenience; she will appoint an hour and you will accompany her here in her own gondola. She will not interrogate you, and you need give her no explanations. There will be no question of an introduction; but since you will learn my name, it will rest with you to come to see me masked whenever you wish, asking for me in the name of the same Countess. Thus we shall become acquainted without your being obliged to sacrifice any of the evening hours which may be precious to you. I have ordered the woman who brings this to wait for your answer in case you should be known to the Countess and hence unwilling to make this use of her. If my choice is agreeable to you tell the woman that you have no answer to send; whereupon she will take my note to the Countess. You may take the other to her at your convenience.'

I told the woman that I had no answer to send when I was certain that I was not known to the Countess, whose name I had never heard. Here is the wording of the note I was to deliver to her:

'I beg you, my dear friend, to come and speak with me when you have time, and to name your hour to the masker who brings you this note so that he can accompany you. He will be punctual. You will greatly oblige your loving friend.'

The address was to the Countess S., Riva del Rio Marin. I thought the note a masterpiece of the spirit of intrigue. There was something lofty in this way of proceeding. I was made to play the role of a person who was being granted a favor. I saw it all clearly.

In her last letter the nun, showing no interest in who I was, approved my choice and tried to appear indifferent to nocturnal meetings; but she expected, and even seemed certain, that I would come and have her called to the visiting room after I had seen her. Her certainty increased my curiosity. She had reason to hope that I would do it if she was young and pretty. It was perfectly possible for me to delay for three or four days and find out from C. C. who the nun might be; but aside from its being an underhanded action, I was afraid I should spoil my chances and be sorry. She told me to call on the Countess at my convenience; her dignity demanded that she should not seem eager; but she knew that I must be so. She seemed too much at home in intrigue for me to believe her a novice and inexperienced; I feared I would repent of having wasted my time; and I prepared to laugh if I found I was with some old woman. In short, it is certain that I would not have gone had I not felt curious to see what sort of face a woman of this kind would put upon a meeting with me after she had offered to come to supper with me in Venice. Then, too, I was much surprised at the great freedom enjoyed by these holy virgins, who could so easily violate their rule of enclosure.

At three in the afternoon I sent a note in to the Countess S. She came out a minute later from the room in which she was entertaining guests and said that she would be glad if I would call at her house the next day at the same hour; and after dropping me a fine curtsy she withdrew. She was a domineering woman, beginning to fade a little but still beautiful.

The next morning, which was a Sunday, I went to mass at my usual hour, in my finest clothes and with my hair elegantly dressed, and already unfaithful in imagination to my dear C. C., for I was more concerned with displaying myself to the nun, be she young or old, than to her.

After dinner I mask and at the appointed hour go to call on the Countess, who was waiting for me. We go down, get into a commodious two-oared gondola, we arrive at the convent of the XXX without having talked of anything but the beautiful autumn we were enjoying. She asks to see M. M. The name astonishes me, for the bearer of it was celebrated. We go into a small visiting room, and five minutes later I see M. M. appear, go straight to the grating, open four square sections of it by pressing a spring, embrace her friend, then close the ingenious window again. The four sections made an opening eighteen inches square. Any man of my stature could have passed through it. The Countess sat down facing the nun and I on the other side in a position from which I could examine this rare beauty of twenty-two or twenty-three years at my ease. I decide at once that she must be the same nun whom C. C. had praised to me, the one who loved her dearly and was teaching her French.

Very nearly beside myself with admiration, I heard nothing of what they said. As for me, not only did the nun not once speak to me, she did not condescend to give me a single look. She was a perfect beauty, tall, so white of complexion as to verge on pallor, with an air of nobility and decision but at the same time of reserve and shyness, large blue eyes; a sweet, smiling face, beautiful lips damp with dew, which allowed a glimpse of two magnificent rows of teeth; her nun's habit did not let me see any hair; but whether she had it or not, its color must be light chestnut; her eyebrows told me as much; but what I found admirable and surprising were her hand and forearm, which I saw to the elbow: it was impossible to see anything more perfect. No veins were visible, and instead of muscles I saw only dimples. Despite all this I did not regret having refused the two meetings over a supper which the divine beauty had offered me. Sure that I should possess her in a few days, I enjoyed the pleasure of paying her the tribute of desiring her. I could not wait to be alone with her at the grating, and I thought I should have committed the worst of offenses if I had waited any longer than the next day to assure her that I had accorded her qualities all the justice they deserved. She continued not to look at me; but in the end it pleased me.

Suddenly the two ladies lowered their voices and put their heads together; as this indicated that I was one too many, I slowly walked away from the grating and looked at a painting. A quarter of an hour later they bade each other good-by, after embracing at the movable window. The nun turned away without giving me an opportunity even to bow to her. On the way back to Venice the Countess, perhaps tiring of my silence, remarked with a smile:

'*M. M. is beautiful, but her mind is even more extraordinary.*'

'I have seen the one and I believe the other.'

'She did not say a word to you.'

'Since I did not wish to be introduced to her, she wished to ignore my being there. It was her way of punishing me.'

The Countess having made no reply, we arrived at her house without opening our mouths again. I left her at her door, because it was there that she dropped me the fine curtsy which means, 'Thank you. Good-by.' I went elsewhere to muse over the strange adventure, whose inevitable consequences I was eager to see.

Countess Coronini. Wounded feelings. Reconciliation.
First meeting. Philosophical digression.

THE NEXT MORNING I went to call on Countess Coronini, who chose to live in the convent of Santa Giustina. She was an old woman with a long experience of all the courts of Europe and who had made a reputation by taking a hand in their affairs. The desire for repose which follows disgust had made her choose the convent as her retreat. I had been introduced to her by a nun who was a relative of Signor Dandolo. This former beauty, finding that she no longer wished to exercise her considerable intelligence in the machinations of royal self-interest, kept it entertained with the frivolous gossip with which the city in which she lived supplied her. She knew everything and, as was only to be expected, always wanted to know more. She received all the ambassadors at her grating, and in consequence every foreigner was introduced to her and several grave Senators from time to time paid her long visits. Curiosity was always the mainspring of these visits on either side; but it was concealed under the veil of the interest which the nobility may be expected to take in whatever is going on. In short, Signora Coronini knew everything and took pleasure in giving me very entertaining lessons in morals when I went to see her. As I was to call on M. M. in the afternoon I thought that I should succeed in learning something about the nun from the well-informed Countess.

As I found it perfectly easy, after some other subjects, to bring the conversation around to that of the convents in Venice, we were soon discussing the intelligence and reputation of a nun of the Celsi family, who, though ugly, exercised great influence in whatever quarter she pleased. We then spoke of the young and charming nun of the Micheli family who had taken the veil to prove to her mother that she was the more intelligent of the two. Speaking of several other beauties who were said to indulge in love affairs, I named M. M. and said that she must be of the same stamp, but that she was an enigma. The Countess smiled and answered that she was not an enigma to everybody but that she must be so to people in general.

'But what really is an enigma,' she added, 'is her suddenly having taken the veil when she is rich, highly intelligent, very cultivated, and, so far as I know, a freethinker. She became a nun for no reason, either physical or moral. It was sheer caprice.'

'Do you think she is happy, Signora?'

'Yes, if she has not repented and if repentance does not overtake her – which, if she is wise, she will keep to herself.'

Convinced by the Countess's mysterious tone that M. M. must have a lover, but resolved not to let it trouble me, I mask after dining without appetite, I go to Murano, I ring at the gate, and, with my heart racing, I ask for M. M. in the name of Countess S. The small visiting room was closed. I am shown the one I am to enter. I take off my mask, put it on my hat, and sit down to wait for the goddess. She was long in coming, but instead of making me impatient the wait pleased me; I feared the moment of our interview and even its effect. But an hour having gone by very quickly, such a delay seemed to me unnatural. Surely she had not been informed. I rise, resuming my mask, go back to the gate, and ask if I have been announced to Mother M. M. A voice answers yes, and that I had only to wait. I returned to my chair, a little thoughtful, and a few minutes later I see a hideous lay sister, who says:

'*Mother M. M. is occupied the whole day.*'

The words were scarcely spoken before she was gone.

Such are the terrible moments to which a pursuer of women is exposed; there is nothing more cruel. They degrade, they distress, they kill. In my revulsion and humiliation, my first feeling was contempt for myself, a dark contempt which approached the limits of horror. The second was disdainful indignation toward the nun, on whom I passed the judgment she appeared to deserve. She was mad, a wretched creature, shameless. My only consolation was to think her such. She could not have acted toward me as she had done unless she was the most impudent of women, the most lacking in common sense; for her two letters, which were in my possession, were enough to dishonor her if I wanted to avenge myself, and what she had done cried for vengeance. She could only defy it if she was more than mad; her behavior was that of a raving maniac. I would already have thought her out of her mind, if I had not heard her talk rationally with the Countess.

Yet in the tumult which shame and anger aroused in my soul *affixa humo* ('fastened to the earth') I was encouraged by discerning lucid intervals. I saw clearly, laughing at myself, that if the nun's beauty and stately bearing had not dazzled me and made me fall in love, and if a certain amount of prejudice had not entered in as well, the whole thing would not amount to much. I saw that I could pretend to laugh at it, and that no one would be able to guess that I was only pretending.

Aware, despite all this, that I had been insulted, I saw that I must take my revenge, but that there must be nothing base in it; and no less aware that I must not give her the least opportunity to crow over having played a practical joke on me, I saw that I must not show any vexation. She had sent me word that she was engaged, and that was all. I must pretend indifference. Another time she would not be engaged; but I defied her to trap me another time. I thought I ought to convince her that her behavior had only made me laugh. I must, of course, send her back the originals of her letters, but enclosed in a short and sufficient one from me. What greatly annoyed me was that I must certainly stop going to mass at her church, for since she had no idea that I went there for C. C., she might have supposed that I would be going only in the hope that she would make some apology and would again offer me the opportunities to meet her which I had rejected. I wanted her to be certain that I scorned her. For a moment I believed that the meetings she had proposed were merely figments to deceive me.

I fell asleep about midnight with this plan in mind, and on waking in the morning I found it ripe. I wrote a letter and after writing it I put it aside for another twenty-four hours to see if, when I read it over, it would show even a trace of the wounded feelings which were tormenting me.

I did well, for when I read it over the next morning I thought it unworthy of me. I quickly tore it up. There were expressions in it which revealed that I was weak, pusillanimous, and in love, and so would have made her laugh. There were others which betrayed anger, and others which showed that I was sorry to have lost all hope of possessing her.

The next day I wrote her another, after writing to C. C.

that serious reasons forced me to stop going to hear mass at her church. But the next morning I thought my letter laughable, and I tore it up. It seemed to me that I had lost my ability to write, and I did not realize the reason for my difficulty until ten days after she had insulted me. I had one.

Sincerum est nisi vas, quodcumque in fundis acescit.

('Unless the vessel is clean, whatever is put in it turns sour.')

M. M.'s face had made an impression on me which could not be effaced by the greatest and most powerful of abstract beings – by Time.

In my ridiculous situation I was tempted again and again to go and tell my troubles to Countess S.; but – thank God! – I never went any farther than her door. The thought coming to me at last that the harebrained nun must be living in terror because of her letters, with which I could ruin her reputation and do the greatest harm to the convent, I resolved to send them to her with a note in the following terms. But it was not until ten or twelve days after the incident.

'I beg you to believe, Madame, that it was by an oversight that I did not immediately send you your two letters, which you will find herewith. I have never thought of departing from what I am by taking a base revenge. I am obliged to forgive you for two pieces of folly, whether you committed them naturally and unthinkingly or to mock me; but I advise you not to act in the same manner toward some other man in the future, for not everyone is like me. I know your name; but I assure you it is as if I did not know it. I tell you this though it is possible that you care nothing for my discretion; but if that is the case I am sorry for you.

'You will no longer see me in your church, Madame, and it will cost me nothing, for I will go to another; yet I think it proper that I should tell you the reason. I consider it likely that you have committed the third folly of boasting of your exploit to some of your friends, and so I am ashamed to put in an appearance. Forgive me if despite my being, as I suppose, five or six years older than you, I have not yet trampled upon all prejudices; believe me, Madame, there are some which should never be shaken off. Do not take it amiss if I give you this little lesson, after the only too substantial one which you apparently gave me only in mockery. Be certain that I will profit by it all the rest of my life.'

I felt that my letter was the gentlest treatment I could give the giddy nun. I went out and, calling aside a Friulian, who could not recognize me under my mask, I gave him my letter, which contained the two others, and gave him forty soldi to take it at once to its address in Murano, promising him another forty when he should come back to tell me he had faithfully done his errand. The instructions I gave him were that he should deliver the packet to the portress, then leave without waiting for an answer even if the portress told him to wait. But it would have been a mistake on my part to wait for him. In our city the Friulians are as reliable and trustworthy as the Savoyards were in Paris ten years ago.

Five or six days later, as I was coming out of the opera, I see the same Friulian carrying his lantern. I call him and, not taking off my mask, ask him if he knows me; after looking at me attentively he says he does not. I ask him if he had done the errand in Murano on which I sent him.

'Ah, Signore! God be praised! Since it is you I have something urgent to tell you. I took your letter as you ordered me to, and after delivering it to the portress I left despite her telling me to wait. When I got back I did not find you, but what of it? The next morning a Friulian of my acquaintance, who was at the gate when I delivered your letter, came and

24

woke me to tell me I must go to Murano, because the portress insisted on talking to me. I went, and after making me wait for a time she told me to go into the visiting room, where a nun wished to speak with me. The nun, who was as beautiful as the morning star, kept me for an hour and more, asking me countless questions all directed to learning, if not who you are, at least some way of my discovering where I could find you; but it was all to no avail since I knew nothing about you.

'She left, ordering me to wait, and two hours later she reappeared with a letter. She gave it to me and said that if I could manage to deliver it to you and bring her the answer she would give me two zecchini; but that if I did not find you I should go to Murano every day and show her her letter, promising me forty soldi for each trip I made. Up to now I have earned twenty lire; but I am afraid she will get tired of it. You have only to answer her letter and I will earn the two zecchini.'

'Where is it?'

'Locked up where I live, for I am always afraid of losing it.'

'Then how am I to answer it?'

'Wait for me here. You will see me back with the letter in a quarter of an hour.'

'I will not wait for you, for I have no interest in answering it; but tell me how you persuaded the nun to believe that you could find me. You are a rascal. It is not likely that she would have entrusted her letter to you if you had not given her reason to expect you to find me.'

'That is so. I described your coat to her, and your buckles, and your height. I assure you that for the last ten days I have looked carefully at every masker of your height, but in vain. It is your buckles there that I recognized; but I should not have recognized you by your coat. Alas, Signore! It will cost you nothing to answer only a line. Wait for me in that coffeehouse.'

Unable any longer to overcome my curiosity, I decide not to wait for him but to go with him to his lodging. I did not think I was obliged to answer more than: 'I have received your letter. Farewell.' The next morning I would have changed buckles and sold the coat. So I go to his door with the Friulian, he goes for the letter, hands it to me, and I take him with me to an inn where, to read the letter at leisure, I engage a room, have a fire lighted, and tell him to wait for me outside. I unseal the packet, and the first thing which surprises me is the two letters she had written me and which I had thought I should return to her to set her heart at rest. At the sight I am seized by a palpitation which already heralds my defeat. Besides the two letters I see a short one signed 'S.' It was addressed to 'M. M.' I read it, and I find:

'The masker who escorted me to the convent and home again would never have opened his lips to say a word to me if I had not taken it into my head to tell him that the charms of your mind are even more winning than those of your face. He answered that he wished to become acquainted with the former and that he was certain of the latter. I added that I did not understand why you had not spoken to him; and he answered with a smile that you wanted to punish him and that since he had not wished to be introduced to you, you in your turn wished to ignore his presence. I wanted to send you this note this morning; but I could not. Farewell. S. F.'

After reading the Countess's note, which neither added nor subtracted an iota from the truth, and which might be a piece of evidence for the defense, my heart beat less violently. Delighted to discover that I am on the verge of being convinced that I was wrong, I pluck up my courage, and this is what I find in the letter from M. M.:

'From a weakness which I consider thoroughly excusable, curious to know what you might have found to say about me to the Countess on your way to visit me and when you took her back home, I seized the moment when you were walking up and down in the visiting room to ask her to inform me. I told her to send me word at once, or at latest the next morning, for I foresaw that in the afternoon you would certainly come to pay me a duty call. Her note, which I send you and which I ask you to read, reached me a half hour after you were sent away. First fatal mishap. Not having received her letter when you asked to see me, I did not have the courage to receive you. Second fatal weakness, for which I can easily be forgiven. I ordered the lay sister to tell you that I was "ill the whole day." A perfectly legitimate excuse whether it is true or false, for it is a polite lie in which the words "the whole day" convey all. You had already left and I could not send someone running after you when the idiotic old woman came and reported to me what she had told you, not that I was "ill," but that I was "occupied." Third fatal mishap. You cannot imagine what I wanted to say, and to do, to the lay sister in my righteous anger; but here one can neither do nor say anything. One can only be patient, dissimulate, and thank God when mistakes arise from ignorance rather than from malice. I at once foresaw in part what did indeed happen, for human reason could never have foreseen it all. I guessed that, believing you had been duped, you would be disgusted, and I felt the blackest misery since I saw no way to let you know the truth until the feast day. I was certain that you would come to our church. Who could have guessed that you would take the thing with the extraordinary violence which your letter set before my eyes? When I did not see you appear in church my grief began to be unbearable, for it was mortal, but it drove me to despair and pierced

27

my heart when I read, ten days after the event, the cruel, barbarous, unjust letter which you wrote me. It made me wretched, and I will die of it unless you come to justify yourself immediately. You thought you had been duped – that is all you can say, and you are now convinced that you were mistaken. But even believing that you were duped, you must admit that to take the course you did and to write me the terrible letter you sent me, you must imagine me a monster not to be found among women who, like myself, are well born and have been well brought up. I send you back the two letters which you sent back to me to soothe my fears. Know that I am a better physiognomist than you are, and that what I did I did not do out of "folly." I have never thought you capable of a base action, even if you were certain that I had brazenly duped you; but in my countenance you have seen only the soul of shamelessness. You will perhaps be the cause of my death, or at least you will make me wretched for all the rest of my life, if you do not wish to justify yourself; since, for my part, I believe I am justified completely.

'Consider that, even if my life is of no concern to you, your honor demands that you come to talk with me at once. You must come in person to recant all that you have written me. If you do not realize the terrible effect your infernal letter must have on the soul of an innocent woman, and one who is not out of her mind, permit me to feel sorry for you. You would not have the slightest knowledge of the human heart. But I am sure you will come, if the man to whom I am entrusting this letter finds you. M. M.'

I did not need to read her letter twice to be in despair. M. M. was right. I at once masked to go out of the room and speak to the Friulian. I asked him if he had spoken with her that morning and if she looked ill. He replied that he thought she looked more dejected every day. I went back, telling him to wait.

I did not finish writing to her until daybreak. Here, word for word, is the letter which I wrote to the noblest of all women, whom, drawing the wrong conclusion, I had most cruelly insulted.

'I am guilty, Madame, and as unable to justify myself as I am completely convinced of your innocence. I cannot live except in the hope of your forgiveness, and you will grant it to me when you reflect upon what made me commit my crime. I saw you, you dazzled me, and, thinking of my honor, it seemed to me chimerical; I thought I was dreaming. I saw that I could not be rid of my doubt until twenty-four hours later, and God alone knows how long they seemed to me. They passed at last, and my heart palpitated when I was in the visiting room counting the minutes. At the end of sixty – which, however, as the result of a kind of impatience entirely new to me, went by very quickly – I see an ill-omened figure which, with odious brevity, tells me that you are "occupied" for the whole day; then it makes off. Imagine the rest! Alas, it was nothing short of a thunderbolt, *which did not kill me and did not leave me alive.* Dare I tell you, Madame, that if you had sent me, even by the hands of the same lay sister, two lines traced by your pen, you would have sent me away if not satisfied at least unperturbed. This is the fatal mishap, which you forgot to cite to me in your charming and most powerful justification. The effect of the thunderbolt was the fatal one which made me see myself as duped, mocked. It revolted me, my self-esteem cried out, dark shame overwhelmed me. I loathe myself and am forced to believe that under the countenance of an angel you fostered a fiendish soul. I leave in consternation, and in the course of eleven days I lose my common sense. I wrote you the letter of which you are a thousand times justified in complaining; but – can you believe it? – I thought it courteous. It is all over now. You will see me at your feet an hour before noon. I shall not go to bed. You shall pardon me, Madame, or I will avenge you. Yes, I myself will be your avenger. The only thing I ask of you, as a great favor, is that you will burn my letter or say nothing about it tomorrow. I sent it to you only after having written you four which I tore up after reading them, because I found expressions in them from which I feared you would read the passion which you have inspired in me. A lady who had duped me was not worthy of my love, were she an angel. I was not wrong but . . . wretched! Could I believe you capable of it after I had seen you? I will now lie down for three or four hours. My tears will flood my pillow. I order the bearer to go to your convent at once, so that I may be sure you will receive this letter when you wake. He would never have found me if I had not approached him as I left the opera. I shall have no more need of him. Do not answer me.'

After sealing my letter I gave it to him, ordering him to go to the convent gate and to deliver it only into the hands of the nun. He promised to do so, I gave him a zecchino, and he set off. After spending six hours in impatience I masked and went to Murano, where M. M. came down as soon as I was announced. I had been shown into the small visiting room in which I had seen her with the Countess. I went down on my knees before her; but she hurriedly told me to get up, for I could be seen. Her face was instantly suffused by a fiery blush. She sat down, I sat down before her; and so we spent a good quarter of an hour looking at each other. I finally broke the silence by asking her if I could count on being forgiven, and she put her beautiful hand out through the grating; I bathed it with my tears and kissed it a hundred times. She said that our acquaintance having begun with such a fierce storm should make us hope for an eternal calm.

'It is the first time,' she said, 'that we are talking together; but what has happened to us is enough for us to believe that we know each other perfectly. I hope that our friendship will be equally tender and sincere, and that we can be indulgent toward each other's failings.'

'When may I convince you of my feelings, Signora, outside these walls and in all the joy of my soul?'

'We will sup at my casino whenever you please – I need only know two days in advance – or with you in Venice, if that is not inconvenient for you.'

'It would only increase my happiness; I must tell you that I am in easy circumstances and that far from fearing to spend money I delight in it and that all I have belongs to the object I adore.'

'I welcome both the fact and the confidence. I, too, can tell you that I am tolerably rich and that I feel I could refuse nothing to my lover.'

'But you must have one.'

'Yes, I have; and it is he who makes me rich and who is completely my master. For this reason I never leave him in ignorance of anything. Day after tomorrow at my casino you shall know more.'

'But I hope that your lover—'

'Will not be there? You may be sure he will not. And have you a mistress?'

'Alas! I had one, but she has been torn from me. For six months I have lived in perfect celibacy.'

'But you still love her.'

'I cannot remember her without loving her; but I foresee that the seduction of your charms will make me forget her.'

'If you were happy I am sorry for you. She was torn from

you; and you have been consumed with grief, shunning society – I divined it. But if it falls out that I take her place, no one, my dear friend, shall tear me from your heart.'

'But what will your lover say?'

'He will be delighted to see me in love and happy with a lover like you. Such is his nature.'

'Admirable nature! Heroism beyond my strength.'

'What sort of life do you lead in Venice?'

'Theaters, society, casinos, where I defy Fortune and find her sometimes kind and sometimes not.'

'At the houses of foreign ambassadors too?'

'No, because I am too closely connected with certain patricians; but I know them all.'

'How can you know them if you do not see them?'

'I met them in foreign countries. In Parma I knew the Duke of Montealegre, the Spanish Ambassador; in Vienna Count Rosenberg; in Paris the French Ambassador, about two years ago.'

'My dear friend, I advise you to leave, for it is about to strike noon. Come day after tomorrow at the same hour, and I will give you the necessary instructions so that you can sup with me.'

'Alone?'

'Of course.'

'Dare I ask you for a pledge? For this good fortune is so great.'

'What pledge do you wish?'

'To see you stand at the small window, with myself in the place where Countess S. was.'

She rose and with the most gracious smile pressed the spring, and after a kiss whose harshness must have pleased her as much as its sweetness, I left her. She followed me to the door with her amorous eyes.

Joy and impatience absolutely prevented me from eating and sleeping during the whole two days. It seemed to me that I had never been so happy in love and that I was to be so for the first time. In addition to M. M.'s birth, her beauty, and her intelligence, which together constituted her true worth, bias entered in to make the extent of my happiness incomprehensible. She was a vestal. I was to taste a forbidden fruit. I was to infringe on the rights of an omnipotent husband, snatching from his seraglio the most beautiful of his sultanas.

If at the time my reason had not been enslaved I should have seen very well that my nun could not be essentially different from all the pretty women I had loved in the thirteen years I had been skirmishing on the fields of love; but what man in love dwells on such a thought? If it comes into his mind he rejects it with disdain. M. M. must be absolutely different from all the women in the universe and more beautiful.

Animal nature, which chemists call the 'animal kingdom,' instinctively secures the three means necessary to perpetuate itself. They are three real needs. It must feed itself; and in order that doing so shall not be a labor, it has the sensation called 'appetite'; and it finds pleasure in satisfying it. In the second place it must preserve its own species by generation, and certainly it would not peform that duty – despite what St. Augustine says – if it did not find pleasure in doing it. In the third place it has an unconquerable inclination to destroy its enemy; and nothing is better contrived, for since it must preserve itself it must hate whatever achieves or desires its destruction. Under this general law, however, each species acts independently. These three sensations – hunger, appetite for coitus, hate which tends to destroy the enemy – are habitual satisfactions in brute beasts, let us not call them pleasure; they can only be such comparatively speaking; for they do not reason about them. Man alone is capable of true pleasure, for, endowed with the faculty of reason, he foresees it, seeks it, creates it, and reasons about it after enjoying it. My dear reader, I beg you to follow me; if you drop me at this point, you are not polite. Let us examine the thing. Man is in the same condition as the beasts when he yields to these three instincts without his reason entering in. When our mind makes its contribution, these three satisfactions become pleasure, pleasure, pleasure: the inexplicable sensation which makes us taste what we call happiness, which we cannot explain either, although we feel it.

The voluptuary who reasons disdains greediness, lust, and the brutal vengeance which springs from a first impulse of anger; he is an epicure; he falls in love but he does not wish to enjoy the object he loves unless he is sure that he is loved; when he is insulted, he will not avenge himself until he has coldly arrived at the best way to relish the pleasure of his revenge. In the result he is more cruel, but he consoles himself by the knowledge that he is at least reasonable. These three operations are the work of the soul, which, to procure itself pleasure, becomes the minister of the passions *quae nisi parent imperant* ('which, if they do not obey, command'). We bear hunger in order to savor culinary concoctions better; we put off the pleasure of love in order to make it more intense; and we defer a vengeance in order to make it more deadly. Yet it is true that people often die of indigestion, that we deceive ourselves or allow ourselves to be deceived in love by sophisms, and that the object we wish to exterminate often escapes our vengeance; but we run these risks willingly.

Continuation of the preceding chapter. First assignation with M. M. Letter from C. C. My second assignation with the nun in my superb casino in Venice. I am happy.

NOTHING CAN BE dearer to the thinking man than life; yet the greatest voluptuary is he who best practices the difficult art of making it pass quickly. He does not want to make it shorter; but he wants amusement to render its passing insensible. He is right, if he has not failed in any duty. They who believe that they have no duty save that of pleasing their senses are wrong, and Horace may have been wrong too in the passage where he told Julius Florus: *Nec metuam quid de me judicet heres, Quod non plura datis inveniet* ('Nor will I fear my heir's judgment of me because he does not find more than I received').

The happiest of men is he who best knows the art of being happy without infringing on his duties; and the unhappiest is he who has adopted a profession in which he is under the sad necessity of foreseeing the future from dawn to dark of every day.

Certain that M. M. would not break her word, I went to the visiting room two hours before noon. My expression made her instantly ask me if I was ill.

'No,' I answered; 'but I may look so in the uneasy expectation of a happiness too great for me. I have lost appetite and sleep; if it is deferred I cannot answer to you for my life.'

'Nothing is deferred, my dear friend; but how impatient you are! Let us sit down. Here is the key to the casino to which you will go. There will be people there, for we have to be served; but no one will speak to you and you need speak to no one. You will be masked. You are not to go there until half past the first hour of night,* no sooner. You will go up the stairs opposite the street door and at the top of the stairs you will see, by the light of a lantern, a green door which you will open to enter an apartment which you will find lighted. In the second room you will find me, and if I am not there you will wait for me. I will not be more than a few minutes late. You may unmask, sit by the fire, and read. You will find books. The door to the casino is in such-and-such a place.'

Since her description could not be more precise, I express my delight that I cannot go wrong. I kiss the hand which gives the key and the key as well before putting it in my pocket. I ask her if I will see her in secular clothes or dressed as a saint as I now saw her.

'I leave here dressed in my habit, but at the casino I put on secular clothes. There I have everything I need in the way of masking attire too.'

'I hope that you will not put on secular clothes this evening.'

'Why, if I may ask?'

'I love you so much in your coif, as you are now.'

'Ah, I understand. You imagine that I have no hair, so I frighten you; but let me tell you that I have a wig which could not be better made.'

'Good God! What are you saying? The very name of "wig" undoes me. But no. No, no; never doubt it – I will think you

* According to the Italian reckoning this is two hours after sunset. (C.'s note.)

36

charming even so. Only be careful not to put it on in my presence. I see that you are mortified. Forgive me. I am in despair that I mentioned it to you. Are you certain that no one will see you leaving the convent?'

'You will be certain of it yourself when, making the circuit of the island in a gondola, you will see where the little quay is. It gives onto a room of which I have the key, and I am sure of the lay sister who waits on me.'

'And the gondola?'

'It is my lover who vouches to me for the fidelity of the gondoliers.'

'What a man your lover is! I imagine he is old.'

'Certainly not. I should be ashamed. I am sure he is not forty. He has everything, my dear friend, to deserve love. Good looks, wit, a gentle nature, and perfect manners.'

'And he forgives you your caprices.'

'What do you mean by "caprices"? He took me a year ago. Before him I knew no man, as before you I knew no one who inspired me with a fancy. When I told him everything he was rather surprised, then he laughed and only read me a short lecture on the risk I was running by putting myself in the power of a man who might be indiscreet. He wanted me to know who you are before I went any further; but it was too late. I vouched for you, and he laughed again at my vouching for someone I did not know.'

'When did you confide it all to him?'

'Day before yesterday; but completely truthfully. I showed him copies of my letters and of yours, reading which made him say he thought you were French despite your having told me that you were Venetian. He is curious to know who you are, and that is all; but since I am not curious about it you need have no fear. I give you my word of honor that I will never make the slightest attempt to find out.'

'Nor I to find out who this man is, who is as extraordinary as yourself. I am in despair when I think of the bitter sorrow I caused you.'

'Let us say no more about it; but console yourself; for when I think about it I conclude that you could have acted otherwise only if you were a conceited fool.'

When I left she repeated the pledge of her love to me at the little window and she remained there until I was out of the visiting room.

That night at the appointed hour I found the casino without any difficulty, I opened the door and, following her instructions, I found her dressed in secular clothes of the utmost elegance. The room was lighted by candles in girandoles in front of mirrors and by four other candelabra on a table on which there were some books. M. M. seemed to have a beauty entirely different from that which I had seen in the visiting room. Her hair appeared to have been done in a chignon which emphasized its abundance, but my eyes merely glanced at it for nothing would have been more stupid at the moment than a compliment on her fine wig. To fall on my knees before her to show her my boundless gratitude by constantly kissing her beautiful hands, were the forerunners of transports whose outcome ought to be a classical amorous combat; but M. M. thought her first duty was to defend herself. Ah! those charming refusals! The strength of two hands repelling the attacks of a respectful and tender lover who is at the same time bold and insistent, played very little part in them; the weapons she used to restrain my passion, to moderate my fire, were arguments delivered in words as amorous as they were energetic and reinforced every moment by loving kisses which melted my soul. In this struggle, as sweet as it was painful to us both, we spent two hours. At the end of the combat we congratulated ourselves

38

on each having carried off the victory; she in having been able to defend herself against all my attacks, I in having kept my impatience in check.

At four o'clock (I am still using the Italian reckoning) she said she was very hungry and that she hoped she would not find me differing from herself. She rang, and a well-dressed woman who was neither young nor old and whose appearance betokened respectability came in and laid a table for two, and after putting everything we needed on another beside us, she served us. The service was of Sèvres porcelain. Eight made dishes composed the supper; they were set on silver boxes filled with hot water which kept the food always hot. It was a choice and delicious supper. I exclaimed that the cook must be French, and she said I was right. We drank only Burgundy, and we emptied a bottle of 'oeil de perdrix' champagne and another of some sparkling wine for gaiety. It was she who dressed the salad; her appetite was equal to mine. She rang only to have the dessert brought, together with all the ingredients for making punch. In everything she did I could not but admire her knowledge, her skill, and her grace. It was obvious that she had a lover who had taught her. I was so curious to know who he was that I said I was ready to tell her my name if she would tell me that of the happy man whose heart and soul she possessed. She said we must leave it to time to satisfy our curiosity.

Among her watch charms she had a little rock-crystal flask exactly like the one I had on my watch chain. I showed it to her, praising the essence of rose which it contained and with which a small piece of cotton was soaked. She showed me hers, which was filled with the same essence in liquid form.

'I am surprised,' I said, 'for it is very rare and it costs a great deal.'

'And it is not for sale.'

39

'That is true. The creator of the essence is the King of France; he made a pound of it, which cost him ten thousand écus.'

'It was a present to my lover, who gave it to me.'

'Madame de Pompadour sent a small flask of it two years ago to Signor Mocenigo, the Venetian Ambassador in Paris, through the A. de B., who is now the French Ambassador here.'

'Do you know him?'

'I met him that day, having the honor to dine with him. As he was about to set out on his journey here, he had come to take his leave. He is a man whom Fortune has favored, but a man of merit and great wit and of distinguished birth, for he is a Count of Lyons. His handsome face has won him the nickname of "Belle-Babet"; we have a little collection of his poems, which do him honor.'

Midnight had struck and, since time was beginning to be precious, we leave the table, and before the fire I become insistent. I said that if she would not yield to love she could not refuse nature, which must be urging her to go to bed after such a fine supper.

'Are you sleepy, then?'

'Not in the least; but at this hour people go to bed. Let me put you to bed and sit by your side as long as you wish to stay there, or else permit me to retire.'

'If you leave me you will make me very unhappy.'

'No more unhappy than I shall feel at leaving you; but what are we to do here in front of the fire until dawn?'

'We can both sleep in our clothes on the sofa you see there.'

'In our clothes? So be it. I can even let you sleep; but if I do not sleep will you forgive me? Beside you, and uncomfortable in my clothes, how could I sleep?'

'Very well. Besides, this sofa is a real bed. You shall see.'

With that she rises, pulls the sofa out at an angle, arranges pillows, sheets, and a blanket, and I see a real bed. She tucks my hair under a large handkerchief and hands me another so that I can do her the same service, saying that she has no nightcap. I set to work, concealing my distaste for her wig, when something totally unexpected gives me the most agreeable surprise. Instead of a wig, I find the most beautiful head of hair. She tells me, after laughing heartily, that a nun's only obligation is not to let the outside world see her hair, and after saying so she throws herself down at full length on the couch. I quickly take off my coat, kick my feet out of my shoes, and fall more on her than beside her. She clasps me in her arms, and subjecting herself to a tyranny which insults nature, she considers that I must forgive her all the torments which her resistance cannot but inflict on me.

With a trembling and timid hand and looking at her with eyes which begged for charity, I undo six wide ribbons which fastened her dress in front and, ravished with joy because she does not stop me, I find myself the fortunate master of the most beautiful of bosoms. It is too late: she is obliged, after I have contemplated it, to let me devour it; I raise my eyes to her face, and I see the sweetness of love saying to me: 'Be content with that and learn from me to bear abstinence.' Driven by love and by omnipotent nature, in despair because she will not let my hands move elsewhere, I make every imaginable effort to guide one of hers to the place where she could have convinced herself that I deserved her mercy; but with a strength greater than mine she refuses to remove her hands from my chest, where she could have found nothing to interest her. Nevertheless, it was there that her mouth descended when it detached itself from mine.

Whether from need or from the effect of lassitude, having

passed so many hours unable to do anything but constantly swallow her saliva mixed with mine, I sleep in her arms, holding her clasped in mine. What woke me with a start was a loud chiming of bells.

'What is that?'

'Let us dress quickly, my dear, my love; I must get back to the convent.'

'Then dress. I am going to enjoy the spectacle of seeing you disguised as a saint again.'

'Gladly. If you are not in any hurry you can sleep here.'

She then rang for the same woman, who I realized must be the great confidante of all her amorous mysteries. After having her hair done up, she took off her dress, put her watches, her rings, and all her secular ornaments in a desk, which she locked, put on the shoes of her order, then a corset in which, as in a prison, she confined the pretty children which alone had fed me on their nectar, and finally put on her habit. Her confidante having gone out to summon the gondolier, she flung herself on my neck and said that she would expect me the next day but one to decide on the night she would come to spend with me in Venice, where, she said, we would make each other completely happy; and she left. Very well pleased with my good fortune, though full of unsatisfied desires, I put out the candles and slept deeply until noon.

I left the casino without seeing anyone, and, well masked, went to call on Laura, who gave me a letter from C. C. which ran as follows:

'Here, my dear husband, is a good example of my way of thinking. You will find me ever more worthy to be your wife. You must believe that, despite my age, I can keep a secret and that I am discreet enough not to take your silence in bad part. Sure of your heart, I am not jealous of what can divert your mind and help you to bear our separation patiently.

'I must tell you that yesterday, going through a corridor which is above the small visiting room and wanting to pick up a toothpick I had dropped, I had to take a stool away from the wall. Picking it up, I saw through an almost imperceptible crack where the floor meets the wall your own person very much interested in conversing with my dear friend Mother M. M. You cannot imagine either my surprise or my joy. Yet those two feelings instantly gave place to my fear of being seen and making some babbling nun curious. After quickly putting the stool back in its place, I left. Ah, my dear! I beg you to tell me everything. How could I love you and not be curious about the whole story of this remarkable occurrence? Tell me if she knows you, and how you made her acquaintance. She is my dear friend, of whom I told you, and whom I did not think it necessary to name to you. It is she who has taught me French and she has given me books in her room which have enlightened me on a very important matter of which few women have any knowledge. Know that but for her the terrible illness which almost killed me would have been discovered. She gave me linen and sheets; I owe her my honor; and so she learned that I have had a lover, as I have learned that she has had one too, but we were never curious about our respective secrets. Mother M. M. is an incomparable woman. I am certain, my dear, that you love her and that she loves you, and since I am not in the least jealous of her I deserve that you should tell me all about it. But I am sorry for you both, for all that either of you can do can only serve, I believe, to excite your mutual passion. The whole convent believes that you are ill; I am dying to see you. So come at least once. Farewell.'

The letter made me uneasy, for I felt very sure of C. C., but the crack might betray us to others. In addition, I now had to tell my darling a lie, for honor and love forbade me to tell her the truth. In the answer which I immediately sent her I said that she must at once inform her friend that she had seen her through the crack, talking to a masker. As for my having made the nun's acquaintance, I said that having heard of her rare qualities I had had her called to the grating, announcing myself under a false name, and that consequently she must refrain from talking about me, for she had recognized me as the same man who went to hear mass at her church. As for love, I assured her that there was no such thing between us, though I agreed that she was a charming woman.

On St. Catherine's Day, which was C. C.'s name day, I went to mass in her church. Going to the *traghetto* to take a gondola, I observe that I am followed. I needed to make sure of it. I see the same man also take a gondola and follow me; this could be natural; but to make certain I disembark in Venice at the Palazzo Morosini del Giardino, and I see the same man disembarking too. After that I am in no more doubt. I come out of the palace, I stop in a narrow street near the Flanders post, and, knife in hand, I force him into the corner of the street and putting the point to his throat, I insist on his telling me at whose order he is following me. He would perhaps have told me all if someone had not happened to enter the street. At that he got away, and I learned nothing. But seeing that it was only too easy for a busybody to know who I was if he persisted in trying to find out, I resolved not to go to Murano again except masked or at night.

The next day, which was the one on which M. M. was to let me know how she would arrange to come to supper with me, I went to the visiting room very early. I saw her before me, displaying on her face the signs of the contentment which flooded her soul. The first compliment she paid me was on my appearing at her church after three weeks during which I had not been seen there. She told me that the Abbess had been very pleased, because she said she was sure she knew who I was. I thereupon told her the story of the spy, and my resolve not to go to mass in her church again. She replied that I would do well to show myself in Murano as little as possible. She then told me the whole story of the crack in the old flooring and said that it had already been stopped up. She said she had been warned by a boarder at the convent who was fond of her, but she did not name her.

After these few remarks I asked her if my happiness was deferred, and she answered that it was deferred only for twenty-four hours because the new lay sister had invited her to supper in her room.

'Such invitations,' she said, 'come seldom, but when they do one cannot refuse except at the cost of making an enemy of the person who extends the invitation.'

'Can one not say one is ill?'

'Yes, but then one must receive visitors.'

'I understand, for if you refuse you may be suspected of slipping away.'

'No, no – slipping away is not considered possible.'

'Then you are the only one who can perform the miracle?'

'You may be sure that I am the only one, and that gold is the powerful god who performs it. So tell me where you will wait for me tomorrow precisely at the second hour of the night.'

'Could not I wait for you here at your casino?'

'No, for the person who will take me to Venice is my lover.'

'Your lover?'

'Himself.'

'That is something new! Well then, I will wait for you in the Piazza dei Santi Giovanni e Paolo, behind the pedestal of the equestrian statue of Bartolomeo da Bergamo.'

'I have never seen either the statue or the square except in an engraving; but I will not fail to be there. You have told me enough. Nothing but terribly bad weather could keep me from coming; but let us hope for good. So good-by. We will talk much tomorrow evening, and if we sleep we shall go to sleep more content.'

I had to act quickly, for I had no casino. I took a second rower, so that I was in the San Marco quarter in less than a quarter of an hour. After spending five or six hours looking at a number of them, I chose the most elegant and hence the most expensive. It had belonged to Lord Holderness, the English Ambassador, who had sold it cheaply to a cook on his departure. He rented it to me until Easter for a hundred zecchini in advance, on condition that he himself would cook the suppers and dinners I might give.

The casino had five rooms, furnished in exquisite taste. It contained nothing that was not made for the sake of love, good food, and every kind of pleasure. Meals were served through a blind window which was set back into the wall and filled by a revolving dumb-waiter which closed it completely. The masters and the servants could not see one another. The room was decorated with mirrors, chandeliers, and a magnificent pier glass above a white marble fireplace; and the walls were tiled with small squares of Chinese porcelain, all attracting interest by their representations of amorous couples in a state of nature, whose voluptuous attitudes fired the imagination. Some small armchairs matched the sofas which were placed to left and right. Another room was octagonal and walled with mirrors, with floor and ceiling of the same; the counterposed mirrors reflected the same objects from innumerable points of view. The room was next to an alcove, which gave by concealed doors onto a dressing room on one side and on the other a boudoir in which were a bathtub and an English-style water closet. All the wainscoting was embossed in ormolu or painted with flowers and arabesques. After telling him not to forget to put sheets on the bed and candles in all the chandeliers and in the candelabra in each room, I ordered him to prepare a supper for two for that evening, warning him that I wanted no wines except Burgundy and champagne and no more than eight made dishes, leaving the choice to him regardless of expense. He was to see to the dessert too. Taking the key to the street door I warned him that when I came in I wished to see no one. The supper was to be ready at the second hour of night and was to be served when I rang. I observed with pleasure that the clock in the alcove had an alarm, for despite my love I was beginning to succumb to the power of sleep.

After giving these orders I went to a milliner's to buy a pair of slippers and a nightcap trimmed with a double ruffle of Alençon point. I put it in my pocket. Since I was to give supper to the most beautiful of all the sultanas of the Master of the Universe, I wanted to make sure the evening before that everything would be in order. Having told her that I had a casino, I must not appear to be a novice in any respect.

It was the cook who was surprised when he saw me at the second hour all alone. I instantly berated him for not having lighted candles everywhere, when, as I had told him the hour, he could be in no doubt about it.

'I will not fail to do so another time.'

'Then light up and serve.'

'You told me it would be for two.'

'Serve for two. Remain present at my supper this first

47

time, so that I can point out to you everything I find good or bad.'

The supper came in the dumb-waiter in good order, two dishes at a time; I commented on everything; but I found everything excellent in Saxon porcelain. Game, sturgeon, truffles, oysters, and perfect wines. I only reproached him with having forgotten to set out hardboiled eggs, anchovies, and prepared vinegars on a dish, to make the salad. He rolled up his eyes with a contrite look, accusing himself of having committed a great crime. I also said that another time I wanted to have bitter oranges to give flavor to the punch and that I wanted rum, not arrack. After spending two hours at table I told him to bring me the account of all that he had spent. He brought it a quarter of an hour later, and I found it satisfactory. After paying him and ordering him to bring me coffee when I should ring, I retired to the excellent bed which was in the alcove. The bed and the good supper won me the most perfect sleep. But for them, I should not have been able to sleep for thinking that on the next night I should have my goddess in my arms in that very bed. On leaving in the morning I told my man that for dessert I wanted all the fresh fruits he could find and, above all, ices. To keep the day from seeming long I gambled until nightfall and I did not find Fortune different from my love. Everything went just as I wished. In the depths of my soul I gave thanks for it to the powerful Genius of my beautiful nun.

It was at the first hour of night that I took up my post by the statue of the heroic Colleoni. She had told me to be there at the second hour, but I wanted to have the sweet pleasure of waiting for her. The night was cold, but magnificent, and without the least wind.

Exactly at the second hour I saw a gondola with two rowers arrive and disembark a masker, who, after speaking to the gondolier at the prow, came toward the statue. Seeing a male masker, I am alarmed, I slip away, and I regret not having pistols. The masker walks around the statue, comes up to me, and offers me a peaceable hand which leaves me in no more doubt. I recognize my angel dressed as a man. She laughs at my surprise, clings to my arm, and without a word between us we make our way to the Piazza San Marco, cross it, and go to the casino, which was only a hundred paces from the Teatro San Moisè.

Everything is as I have ordered. We go upstairs, I quickly unmask, but M. M. gives herself the pleasure of walking slowly through every corner of the delicious place in which she was being received, delighted that I should see all the graces of her person in every profile and often in full face and admire in her clothing what kind of man the lover who possessed her must be. She was surprised at the magic which everywhere showed her her person from a hundred different points of view at the same time even when she stood still. The multiplied portraits of her which the minors offered her by the light of all the candles expressly placed for the purpose were a new spectacle which made her fall in love with herself. Sitting on a stool I attentively examined all the elegance of her attire. A coat of short-napped rose velvet edged with an embroidery of gold spangles, a matching hand-embroidered waistcoat, than which nothing could be richer, black satin breeches, needle-lace ruffles, buckles set with brilliants, a solitaire of great value on her little finger and on her other hand a ring which showed only a surface of white taffeta covered by convex crystal. Her *bautta* of black blond-lace was as beautiful as possible in both design and fineness. So that I could see her better she came and stood in front of me. I search her pockets and I find a snuffbox, a comfit box, a phial, a case of toothpicks, a pair of opera glasses, and

49

handkerchiefs exhaling scents which sweetened the air. I attentively examine the richness and workmanship of her two watches and of her fine seals hung as pendants from chains covered with small diamonds. I search her side pockets and I find flintlock pistols with a spring firing mechanism, of the finest English manufacture.

'All that I see,' I say, 'is beneath you, but permit my astonished soul to do homage to the adorable being who wishes to convince you that you are really his mistress.'

'That is what he said when I asked him to take me to Venice and leave me there, adding that his wish was that I should enjoy myself there and become ever more convinced that he whom I was about to make happy deserved it.'

'It is unbelievable, my dear. Such a lover is one of a kind, and I can never deserve a happiness by which I am already dazzled.'

'Let me go and unmask by myself.'

A quarter of an hour later she appeared before me with her beautiful hair dressed like a man's but unpowdered and with side locks in long curls which came down to the bottom of her cheeks. A black ribbon tied it behind, and it fell to her knees in a hanging plait. M. M. as a woman resembled Henriette, and as a man a Guards officer named *L'Étorière* whom I had known in Paris; or rather she resembled the youth Antinoüs, whose statues are still to be seen, if her French clothes had permitted the illusion.

Overwhelmed by so many charms, I thought I felt ill. I threw myself on the sofa to support my head.

'I have lost all my confidence,' I said; 'you will never be mine; this very night some fatal mishap will tear you from my desires; perhaps a miracle performed by your divine spouse in his jealousy of a mortal. I feel prostrated. In a quarter of an hour I may no longer exist.'

'Are you mad? I am yours this moment if you wish. Though I have not eaten I do not care about supper. Let us go to bed.'

She felt cold. We sit down before the fire. She tells me that she has no vest on. I unfasten a diamond brooch in the shape of a heart which kept her ruffle closed, and my hands feel before my eyes see what only her shirt defended against the air, the two springs of life which ornamented her bosom. I become ardent; but she needs only a single kiss to calm me, and two words: 'After supper.'

I ring, and seeing her alarm I show her the dumb-waiter.

'No one will see you,' I say; 'you must tell your lover, who may not know of this device.'

'He knows of it; but he will admire your thoughtfulness and will say that you are no novice in the art of pleasing and that clearly I am not the only woman who enjoys the delights of this little house with you.'

'And he will be wrong. I have neither supped nor slept here except alone; and I hate deceit. You are not my first passion, my divine love; but you will be my last.'

'I am happy, my dear, if you will be faithful. My lover is so; he is kind, he is gentle; but he has always left my heart empty.'

'His must be so too, for if his love were like mine he would not permit you an absence of this kind. He could not put up with it.'

'He loves me, as I love you; do you believe that I love you?'

'I must believe it; but you would not put up with—'

'Say no more; for I feel that, if you will not keep anything from me, I will forgive you everything. The joy which I feel in my soul at this moment is due more to my certainty that I shall leave you wanting nothing than to my certainty that I shall spend a delicious night with you. It will be the first in my life.'

'Then you have not spent nights with your worthy lover?'

'Yes, but those nights were inspired only by friendship, gratitude, and compliance. Love is what counts. Despite that, my lover is like you. He has a natural vivacity and his wit is always ready, like yours; besides which both his face and his person are attractive, though he does not resemble you in looks. I also think he is richer than you are, though this casino might make one conclude the opposite. But do not imagine that I consider you less deserving than he because you confess that you are incapable of the heroism of permitting me an absence; on the contrary, if you told me that you would be as indulgent as he is to one of my caprices, I should know that you do not love me as I am very glad that you do love me.'

'Will he wish to know the details of this night?'

'He will believe that it will please me if he asks me about it, and I shall tell him everything except some circumstances which might humiliate him.'

After the supper, which she found choice and exquisite, as she did the ices and the oysters, she made punch, and in my amorous impatience, after drinking several glasses of it, I begged her to consider that we had only seven hours before us and that we should be doing very wrong not to spend them in bed. So we went into the alcove, which was lighted by twelve flaming candles, and from there to the dressing room, where, presenting her with the fine lace cap, I asked her to dress her hair like a woman. After saying that the cap was magnificent she told me to go and undress in the outer room, promising that she would call me as soon as she was in bed.

It took only two minutes. I flung myself into her burning

arms, on fire with love and giving her the most lively proofs of it for seven continuous hours which were interrupted only by as many quarters of an hour devoted to the most feeling talk. She taught me nothing new so far as the physical side of the performance was concerned, but any quantity of new things in the way of sighs, ecstasies, transports, and unfeigned sentiments which find scope only at such moments. Each discovery I made elevated my soul to Love, who furnished me with fresh strength to show him my gratitude. She was astonished to find herself capable of so much pleasure, for I had shown her many things which she thought were fictions. I did what she did not think she was entitled to ask me to do to her, and I taught her that the slightest constraint spoils the greatest of pleasures. When the alarm chimed she raised her eyes to the Third Heaven like an idolator, to thank the Mother and the Son for having so well rewarded her for the effort it had cost her to declare her passion to me.

We dressed in haste, and seeing me put the beautiful cap in her pocket she assured me that it would always be most dear to her. After taking coffee we hurried to the Piazza dei Santi Giovanni e Paolo, where I left her, assuring her that she would see me on the next day but one. After watching her get into her gondola I went home, where ten hours of sleep restored me to my normal state.

Continuation of the preceding chapter. Visit to the convent and conversation with M. M. Letter which she writes me and my answer. Another meeting at the casino in Murano in the presence of her lover.

ON THE NEXT DAY but one I went to the visiting room after dinner. I send for her, and she comes at once and tells me to leave, for she is expecting her lover, but that I must come without fail on the following day. I leave. At the end of the bridge I see a poorly masked masker getting out of a gondola the gondolier of which I knew and had good reason to believe was then in the service of the French Ambassador. He was not in livery, and the gondola was plain, like all gondolas belonging to Venetians. I turn and see the masker going to the convent. I feel no more doubt, and I go back to Venice delighted to have made the discovery and pleased that the Ambassador was my senior partner. I resolve to say nothing about it to M. M.

I go to see her the next day and she tells me that her friend had come to take leave of her until the Christmas holidays.

'He is going to Padua,' she says, 'but everything is arranged for us to sup at his casino if we wish.'

'Why not in Venice?'

'No, not in Venice, until he is back. He asked me not to. He has great judgment.'

'Very well. When shall we sup at the casino?'

'Sunday, if you like.'

'Let it be Sunday; I will go to the casino at dusk and will read while I wait for you. Did you tell your friend that you were not uncomfortable in my casino?'

'My dear, I told him everything; but one thing greatly troubles him. He wants me to beg you not to expose me to the danger of a big belly.'

'May I die if it ever entered my mind. But don't you run the same risk with him?'

'Never.'

'Then we must be very careful in future. I think, since there is no masking during the nine days before Christmas, I shall have to go to your casino by water, for if I go by land I could easily be recognized as the same man who went to your church.'

'That is very prudent. I can easily point out the quay to you. I think you can come during Lent too, when God wants us to mortify our senses. Isn't it odd that there is a time when God approves of our amusing ourselves and another when we can only please him by abstinence! What can an anniversary have in common with the divinity? I do not understand how the action of the creature can influence the creator, whom my reason can only conceive as independent. It seems to me that if God had created man with the power to offend him, man would be justified in doing everything he forbade him to do, if only to teach him how to create. Can one imagine God being sad during Lent?'

'My divine one, you reason perfectly; but may I ask you where you learned to reason, and how you managed to break away?'

'My friend gave me good books, and the light of truth quickly dissipated the clouds of superstition which were oppressing my reason. I assure you that when I reflect on myself I think I am more fortunate in having found someone who has enlightened my mind than unfortunate in having taken the veil, for the greatest happiness of all is to live and die at peace, which we cannot hope to do if we believe what the priests tell us.'

'You are very right; but permit me to wonder at you, for enlightening an extremely prejudiced mind such as yours must have been could not be the work of a few months.'

'I should have seen the light much less quickly if I had been less steeped in error. What separated the true from the false in my mind was only a curtain; reason alone could draw it; but I had been taught to scorn reason. As soon as I was shown that I should set the greatest store by it I put it to work; it drew the curtain. The evidence of truth appeared with the utmost clarity, my stupid notions disappeared; and I have no reason to fear that they will reappear, for I strengthen my defenses every day. I can say that I did not begin to love God until after I had rid myself of the idea of him which religion had given me.'

'I congratulate you. You were more fortunate than I. You have gone further in a year than I in ten.'

'Then you did not begin by reading what Lord Bolingbroke has written. Five or six months ago I was reading Charron's *La Sagesse*, and I don't know how our confessor found it out. He dared to tell me at confession that I must stop reading it, I answered that since my conscience was not troubled by it, I could not obey him. He said that he would not absolve me, and I answered that I would go to communion nevertheless. The priest went to Bishop Diedo to ask what he should do, and the Bishop came to talk with me and gave me to understand that I should be guided by my confessor. I answered that my confessor's business was to absolve me, and that he did not even have the right to advise me unless I asked him for advice. I told him outright that, since it was my duty not to scandalize the entire convent, if he persisted in refusing me absolution I would go to communion nevertheless. The Bishop ordered him to leave me to my conscience. But I was not satisfied. My lover procured me a brief from the Pope which authorizes me to confess to anyone I choose. All my sisters are jealous of the privilege; but I used it only once, for the thing is not worth the trouble. I always confess to the same priest, who has no difficulty in absolving me, for I tell him absolutely nothing of any importance.'

So it was that I came to know her as an adorable freethinker; but it could not be otherwise, for she had an even greater need to quiet conscience than to satisfy her senses.

After assuring her that she would find me at the casino I went back to Venice. On Sunday after dinner I had myself rowed around the island of Murano in a two-oared gondola, to see where the quay for the casino was and also the small one by which she left the convent; but I could make out nothing. I did not find the quay for the casino until during the novena, and the small quay for the convent six months later at the risk of my life. We shall speak of it when we come to that time.

About the first hour of night I went to the temple of my love and, waiting for my idol to arrive, I amused myself by looking at the books which made up a small library in the boudoir. They were few but choice. They included all that the wisest philosophers have written against religion and all that the most voluptuous pens have written on the subject which is the sole aim of love. Seductive books, whose incendiary style drives the reader to seek the reality, which alone can quench the fire he feels running through his veins. Beside the books there were folios containing only lascivious engravings. Their great merit lay in the beauty of the drawing far more than in the lubricity of the poses. I saw engravings for the *Portier des Chartreux*, made in England, and others for Meursius, or Aloisia Sigea Toletana, than which I had never seen anything finer. In addition the small pictures which decorated the room were so well painted that the figures seemed to be alive. An hour went by in an instant.

The appearance of M. M. in her nun's habit wrung a cry from me. I told her, springing to embrace her, that she could not have come in better time to prevent a schoolboy masturbation to which all that I had seen during the past hour would have driven me.

'But in that saintly dress you surprise me. Let me adore you here and now, my angel.'

'I will put on secular clothes at once. It will take me only a quarter of an hour. I do not like myself in these woolens.'

'No, no. You shall receive the homage of love dressed as you were when you brought it to birth.'

She answered only with a *Fiat voluntas tua* ('Thy will be done') delivered with the most devout expression as she let herself fall on the commodious sofa, where I treated her with caution despite herself. After the act I helped her take off her habit and put on a plain robe of Pekin muslin which was the height of elegance. I then played the role of chambermaid while she dressed her hair and put on a nightcap.

After supper, before going to bed we agreed not to meet again until the first day of the novena when, the theaters being closed for ten days, masks are not worn. She then gave me the keys to the door giving onto the quay. A blue ribbon fastened to the window above it was to be the signal which would show it to me by day, so that I could later go there by night. But what filled her with joy was that I went to stay in the casino and never left it until her lover returned. During the ten days I stayed there I had her four times and thereby convinced her that I lived only for her. I amused myself reading, or writing to C. C., but my love for the latter had grown calm. The chief thing which interested me in the letters she wrote me was what she told me about her dear friend Mother M. M. She said that I had done wrong not to cultivate her acquaintance, and I answered that I had not pursued it for fear of being recognized. In this way I made her even more obliged to keep my secret inviolably.

It is not possible to love two objects at once, and it is not possible to keep love vigorous if one either gives it too much food or none at all. What kept my passion for M. M. always at the same pitch was that I could never have her except with the greatest fear of losing her. I told her it was impossible that, one time or another, some nun would not need to speak with her at a time when she was neither in her room nor in the convent. She maintained that it could not happen, since nothing was more respected in the convent than a nun's privilege of shutting herself up in her room and denying herself even to the Abbess. She had nothing to fear but the fatal circumstance of a fire, for then, when everything was in confusion and it was not natural that a nun would remain calm and indifferent, her absence must become known. She congratulated herself on having been able to win over the lay sister, the gardener, and another nun whom she always refused to name. Her lover's tact and his money had done it all, and he vouched for the fidelity of the cook and his wife, who together took care of the casino. He was sure of his gondoliers, too, despite the fact that one of them must certainly be a spy for the State Inquisitors.

On Christmas Eve she told me that her lover was about to arrive, that she was to go with him to the opera on St. Stephen's Day and sup with him at the casino on the third day of Christmas. After saying that she would expect me for supper on the last day of the year she gave me a letter, asking me not to read it until I was at home.

An hour before dawn I packed my things and went to the Palazzo Bragadin, where, impatient to read the letter she had given me, I immediately locked myself in my room. It ran as follows:

'You nettled me a little, my dear, when day before yesterday, on the subject of my having to keep everything about my lover from you, you said that, satisfied with possessing my heart, you leave me mistress of my mind. Dividing heart and mind is a sophistical distinction, and if it does not seem so to you, you must admit that you do not love the whole of me, for it is impossible that I can exist without a mind and that you can cherish my heart if it is not in accord with it. If your love can be content with the contrary, it does not excel in delicacy.

'But since circumstances may arise in which you could convict me of not having acted toward you with all the sincerity which true love demands, I have resolved to reveal a secret concerning my lover to you, despite the fact that I know he is certain I will never reveal it, for it is treachery. Yet you will not love me the less for it. Reduced to choosing between the two of you, and obliged to deceive one or the other, love has conquered in me; but not blindly. You shall weigh the motives which had the power to tip the scales to your side.

'When I could no longer resist my desire to know you intimately I could not satisfy it except by confiding in my friend. I had no doubt of his willingness. He conceived a very favorable idea of your character when he read your first letter, in which you chose the visiting room, and he thought you showed yourself a man of honor when, after we became

60

acquainted, you chose the casino in Murano in preference to your own. But as soon as he learned of it he also asked me to do him the favor of allowing him to be present at our first interview ensconced in a perfect hiding place from which he would not only see all that we did without himself being seen but also hear all that we said. It is a closet whose existence cannot even be guessed. You did not see it during the ten days you spent in the casino; but I will show it to you on the last day of the year. Tell me if I could refuse him the favor. I granted it; and nothing was more natural than to keep it a secret from you. So now you know that my friend witnessed all that we said and did the first time we were together. But do not take it amiss, my darling; you pleased him, not only by everything you did but also by all the amusing things you said to me. I felt very anxious when our conversation turned to the nature my lover must have to be so excessively tolerant; but fortunately all that you said could only be flattering to him. This is the complete confession of my treachery, which, as a sensible lover, you must forgive me, and the more so since it did you no harm. I can assure you that my friend is most curious to know who you are. That night you were natural and very likable; if you had known that you were being watched God knows what you would have been. If I had told you the thing it is even possible that you would not have consented, and you would perhaps have been right.

'But now I must risk everything for the sake of everything and make myself easy, knowing that I have done nothing for which I can be reproached. Know, my dear, that on the last day of the year my friend will be at the casino, and that he will not leave it until the next day. You will not see him, and he will see everything. Since you are not supposed to know, you understand how natural you must be in everything, for if you were not, my friend, who is very intelligent, might

61

suspect that I have betrayed the secret. The principal thing you must be careful about is what you say. He has all the virtues except the theological one called faith, and on that subject you have free rein. You can talk of literature, travel, politics, and tell as many anecdotes as you please, and be sure of his approval.

'The question remains whether you are willing to let a man see you during the moments when you surrender to the furies of love. This uncertainty is now my torment. Yes or no: there is no middle course. Do you understand how painful my fear is? Do you feel how difficult it must have been for me to take this step? I shall not sleep tomorrow night. I shall have no rest until I have read your answer. I will then decide on a course in case you answer that you cannot be affectionate in someone's presence, especially if the "someone" is unknown to you. Yet I hope that you will come nevertheless, and that if you cannot play the role of lover as you did the first time no bad consequences will ensue. He will believe, and I will let him believe, that your love has cooled.'

Her letter surprised me greatly; then, after thinking it over, I laughed. But it would not have made me laugh if I had not known what sort of man it was who would witness my amorous exploits. Certain that M. M. must be very uneasy until she received my answer, I answered her at once, in the following terms:

'My divine angel, I want you to receive my answer to your letter before noon. You shall dine perfectly easy.

'I will spend the night of the last day of the year with you and I assure you that your friend, as our spectator, will see and hear nothing which can lead him to suppose that you have revealed his secret to me. Be sure that I will play my role perfectly. If man's duty is to be ever the slave of his reason, if he must, so far as he is able, permit himself nothing without

62

taking reason as his guide, I can never understand how a man can be ashamed of letting a friend see him at a moment when he is giving the greatest proofs of love to a very beautiful woman. Such is my situation. Yet I must tell you that if you had forewarned me the first time you would have done wrong. I would have refused absolutely. I should have thought that my honor was involved; I should have thought that, in inviting me to supper, you were only the willing accomplice of a friend, a strange man dominated by this strange taste, and I would have formed such an unfavorable opinion of you that it would perhaps have cured me of my love, which at that time was only beginning to bud. Such, my charmer, is the human heart; but at present the case is different. Everything you have told me about your worthy friend has shown me his character, I consider him my friend too, and I love him. If a feeling of shame does not keep you from letting him see you fond and loving with me, how – far from being ashamed of it – can I fail to be proud of it? Can a man blush at what makes him proud? I cannot, my dear, either blush over having conquered you or over letting myself be seen in moments when I flatter myself I shall not appear unworthy of your conquest. Yet I know that, by a natural feeling which reason cannot disapprove, most men feel a repugnance to letting themselves be seen at such moments. Those who cannot give good reasons for their repugnance must have something of the cat in their nature; but they can have good reasons for it and yet feel under no obligation to explain them to anyone. The chief reason is probably that a third person who is looking on and whom they see cannot but distract them, and that any distraction can only lessen the pleasure of intercourse. Another important reason could also be considered legitimate, that is, if the actors knew that their means of obtaining pleasure would appear pitiable to those who should witness them. Such unfortunates are right in not wishing to arouse feelings of pity in the performance of an act which would seem more properly to arouse jealousy. But we know, my dear, that we certainly do not arouse feelings of pity. Everything you have told me makes me certain that your friend's angelic soul must, in seeing us, share our pleasures. But do you know what will happen, and what I shall be very sorry for, since your lover can only be a most likable man? Seeing us will drive him frantic, and he will either run away or have to come out of his hiding place and go down on his knees to me, begging me to give you up to the violence of his amorous desires in his need to calm the fire which our transports will have kindled in his soul. If that happens I will laugh and give you up to him; but I will leave, for I feel that I could not remain the unmoved spectator of what some other man might do to you. So good-by, my angel; all will be well. I hasten to seal this letter, and I will take it to your casino this instant.'

I spent these six holidays with my friends and at the Ridotto, which at that period was opened on St. Stephen's Day. As I could not deal, since only patricians wearing the official robe were allowed to make bank there, I played day and night, and I constantly lost. Whoever punts cannot but lose. The loss of four or five thousand zecchini, which was my entire wealth, only made my love stronger.

At the end of the year 1774 a law issued by the Great Council forbade all games of chance and caused the closing of the Ridotto, as it was called. The Great Council was amazed when it saw, on counting the ballots, that it had passed a law which it could not pass, for at least three quarters of those who had cast ballots had not wanted it, and yet three quarters of the ballot proved that they had wanted it. The voters looked at one another in astonishment. It was a visible miracle of the glorious Evangelist St. Mark, who had been invoked by Signor Flangini, then First Corrector, now a Cardinal, and by the three State Inquisitors.

On the appointed day I arrived at the casino at the usual hour, and there was the beautiful M. M. dressed as a woman of fashion, standing with her back to the fireplace.

'My friend,' she said, 'has not yet come; but as soon as he is here I will give you a wink.'

'Where is the place?'

'There. Look at the back of that sofa against the wall. All the flowers in relief which you see have holes in their centers which go through to the closet behind. There is a bed, a table, and everything a man needs to stay there for seven or eight hours entertaining himself by watching what is done here. You shall see it when you wish.'

'Did he have it built himself?'

'Certainly not, for he could not foresee that it might be of use to him.'

'I understand that the spectacle may give him great pleasure; but since he cannot have you when nature will give him the greatest need of you, what will he do?'

'That is his concern. Besides, he is free to go if he is bored, and he can sleep, but if you are natural he will enjoy it.'

'I shall be, except that I shall be more polite.'

'No politeness, my dear, for you will at once become unnatural. Where did you ever hear of two lovers in the fury of love thinking of being polite?'

'You are right, dear heart; but I will be delicate.'

'That you may, just as you always are. Your letter pleased me. You treated the subject thoroughly.'

M. M. was wearing nothing over her hair, but it was negligently dressed. A sky-blue quilted dress was her only attire. She had on ear-buttons studded with brilliants; her neck was

65

completely bare. A fichu of silk gauze and silver thread, arranged in haste, half revealed the beauty of her bosom and displayed its whiteness where her dress opened in front. She had on slippers. Her shy and modestly smiling face seemed to be saying: 'This is the person you love.' What I found most unusual and what pleased me excessively was her rouge, which was applied as the court ladies apply it in Versailles. The charm of such painting lies in the carelessness with which it is placed on the cheeks. The rouge is not meant to look natural, it is put on to please the eyes, which see in it the tokens of an intoxication which promises them amorous transports and furies. She said that she had put on rouge to please her lover, who liked it. I answered that such a taste led me to think him French. When I said this she winked at me: her friend had arrived. So it was then that the comedy was to begin.

'The more I look at your face, the more angry I am at your spouse.'

'They say he was ugly.'

'It has been said: so he deserves to be cuckolded, and we shall work at it all night. I have lived in celibacy for the past week, but I need to eat, for I have nothing in my stomach but a cup of chocolate and the whites of six fresh eggs which I ate in a salad dressed with Lucca oil and Four Thieves vinegar.'

'You must be ill.'

'Yes; but I shall be well when I have distilled them one by one into your amorous soul.'

'I did not know that you were in need of *frustratoires*.'

'Who could need them with you? But my fear is reasonable, for if I miss you, I will blow out my brains.'

'What does "miss" mean?'

'In the figurative sense it means "fail in one's purpose."

66

Literally it means that when I want to shoot my pistol at my enemy, the priming doesn't catch. I *miss* him.'

'Now I understand you. And it would be a misfortune, my dark-haired love, but not enough to make you blow out your brains.'

'What are you doing?'

'I am taking off your cloak. Give me your muff, too.'

'That will be difficult, for it is nailed.'

'Nailed?'

'Put your hand in it. Try.'

'Oh, the wretch! Is it the egg whites that gave you such a nail?'

'No, my angel, it is your whole charming person.'

At that I picked her up, she held me around the shoulders to make less weight for me, and, having dropped my muff, I grasped her by the thighs and she steadied herself on the nail; but after a turn around the room, fearing what would follow I set her down on the carpet, then sat down myself and made her sit on me, whereupon she had the kindness to finish the job with her beautiful hand, collecting the white of the first egg in the palm of it.

'Five to go,' she said; and after cleaning her beautiful hand in a potpourri of aromatic herbs, she gave it to me to kiss again and again. Calmed, I spent an hour telling her amusing stories; then we sat down at table.

She ate for two, but I for four. The service was of porcelain but at dessert of silver gilt, as were the candelabra, each of which held four candles. Seeing that I admired their beauty she said they were a present her friend had made her.

'Did he give you snuffers too?'

'No.'

'Then I conclude that your lover must be a great lord, for great lords know nothing of snuffing.'

'The wicks of our candles do not need snuffing.'

'Tell me who taught you French, for you speak it too well for me not to be curious to know.'

'Old La Forêt, who died last year. I was his pupil for six years; he taught me to compose verses too; but I have learned words from you which I never heard pass his lips: *à gogo, frustratoire, dorloter.* Who taught them to you?'

'Good society in Paris, Madame de Boufflers for example, a woman of profound intelligence who one day asked me why the Italian alphabet contained *con rond*. I laughed, and did not know how to answer.'

'I think they are abbreviations used in the old days.'

After making punch we amused ourselves eating oysters, exchanging them when we already had them in our mouths. She offered me hers on her tongue at the same time that I put mine between her lips; there is no more lascivious and voluptuous game between two lovers, it is even comic, but comedy does no harm, for laughter is only for the happy. What a sauce that is which dresses an oyster I suck in from the mouth of the woman I love! It is her saliva. The power of love cannot but increase when I crush it when I swallow it.

She said that she was going to change her dress and come back with her hair ready for the night. Not knowing what to do I amused myself looking at what she had in her desk, which was open. I did not touch her letters but, opening a box and seeing some condoms, I quickly wrote the following verses and substituted them for what I had stolen:

Enfants de l'amitié, ministres de la peur,
Je suis l'amour, tremblez, respectez le voleur,
Et toi, femme de Dieu, ne crains pas d'être mère
Car si tu fais un fils, il se dira son père.

S'il est dit cependant que tu veux te barrer
Parle; je suis tout prêt, je me ferai châtrer.

('Children of friendship, ministers of fear, I am Love,
tremble, and respect the thief. And you, wife of God, do
not fear to become a mother, for if you bear a son he will
say he is its father. Yet if you are determined to bar your
door, speak; I am ready, I will have myself gelded.')

M. M. reappeared in a new guise. She had on a dressing
gown of India muslin embroidered with flowers in gold
thread, and her nightcap was worthy of a queen.

I threw myself at her feet to beg her to yield to my desires
then and there; but she ordered me to hold my fire until we
were in bed.

'I do not want,' she said with a smile, 'to be bothered with
keeping your quintessence from falling on the carpet. You
shall see.'

With that she goes to her desk, and instead of the condoms she finds my six verses. After reading them, then reading them over again aloud, she calls me a thief and, giving
me kiss after kiss, she tries to persuade me to restore the
stolen goods. After reading my verses slowly aloud once
more, pretending to reflect on them, she goes out on the pretext of looking for a better pen, then comes back and writes
the following answer:

Dès qu'un ange me f . . ., je deviens d'abord sûre
Que mon seul époux est l'auteur de la nature.
Mais pour rendre sa race exempt des soupçons
L'amour doit dans l'instant me rendre mes condoms.
Ainsi toujours soumise à sa volonté sainte
J'encourage l'ami de me f . . . sans crainte.

69

('When an angel f . . . s me I am at once sure that my only husband is the author of nature. But to make his lineage free from suspicion Love must instantly give me back my condoms. Thus always obedient to his sacred will, I encourage my friend to f . . . me without fear.')

I thereupon returned them to her, giving a very natural imitation of surprise; for really it was too much.

Midnight had struck, I showed her her little Gabriel, who was sighing for her, and she made the sofa ready, saying that as the alcove was too cold, we would sleep there. The reason was that in the alcove her friend could not see us.

While waiting I tied up my hair in a Masulipatam kerchief which, going round my head four times, gave me the redoubtable look of an Asiatic despot in his seraglio. After imperiously putting my sultana in the state of nature and doing the same to myself, I laid her down and subjugated her in the classic manner, delighting in her swoons. A pillow which I had fitted under her buttocks and one of her knees bent away from the back of the sofa must have afforded a most voluptuous vision for our hidden friend. After the frolic, which lasted an hour, she took off the sheath and rejoiced to see my quintessence in it; but finding, even so, that she was wet with her own distillations, we agreed that a brief ablution would restore us *in statu quo*. After that we stood side by side in front of a large upright mirror, each putting one arm around the other's back. Admiring the beauty of our images and becoming eager to enjoy them, we engaged in every kind of combat, still standing. After the last bout she fell onto the Persian carpet which covered the floor. With her eyes closed, her head to one side, lying on her back, her arms and legs as if she had just been taken down from a St. Andrew's cross, she would have looked like a corpse if the beating of her heart had not been visible. The last bout had exhausted her. I made her do the 'straight tree,' and in that position I lifted her up to devour her chamber of love, which I could not reach otherwise since I wanted to make it possible for her, in turn, to devour the weapon which wounded her to death without taking her life.

Reduced after this exploit to asking her to grant me a truce, I set her on her feet again; but a moment later she challenged me to give her her revenge. It was my turn to do the 'straight tree' and hers to grasp me by the hips and lift me up. In this position, steadying herself on her two diverging pillars, she was horrified to see her breasts splattered with my soul distilled in drops of blood.

'What do I see?' she cried, letting me fall and herself falling with me. Just then the alarm chimed.

I called her back to life by making her laugh.

'Have no fear, my angel,' I said, 'it is the yolk of the last egg, which is often red.'

I myself washed her beautiful breasts, which human blood had never soiled before that moment. She was very much afraid that she had swallowed some drops of it; but I easily persuaded her that even if it were so, it would do no harm. She dressed in her habit and then left, after imploring me to go to bed there and to write and tell her how I was before I went back to Venice. She promised to do as much for me the next day. The caretaker would have her letter. I obeyed. She did not leave until a half hour later, which she certainly spent with her friend.

ANTHONY TROLLOPE

THE LAST AUSTRIAN
WHO LEFT VENICE

IN THE SPRING and early summer of the year last past, – the year 1866, – the hatred felt by Venetians towards the Austrian soldiers who held their city in thraldom, had reached its culminating point. For years this hatred had been very strong; how strong can hardly be understood by those who never recognise the fact that there had been, so to say, no mingling of the conquered and the conquerors, no process of assimilation between the Italian vassals and their German masters.

Venice as a city was as purely Italian as though its barracks were filled with no Hungarian long-legged soldiers, and its cafés crowded with no white-coated Austrian officers. And the regiments which held the town, lived as completely after their own fashion as though they were quartered in Pesth, or Prague, or Vienna, – with this exception, that in Venice they were enabled, and, indeed, from circumstances were compelled, – to exercise a palpable ascendancy which belonged to them nowhere else. They were masters, daily visible as such to the eye of every one who merely walked the narrow ways of the city or strolled through the open squares; and, as masters, they were as separate as the gaoler is separate from the prisoner.

The Austrian officers sat together in the chief theatre, – having the best part of it to themselves. Few among them spoke Italian. None of the common soldiers did so. The Venetians seldom spoke German; and could hold no intercourse whatever with the Croats, Hungarians, and Bohemians, of whom the garrison was chiefly composed. It could not be otherwise than that there should be intense hatred in a city so ruled. But the hatred which had been intense for years had reached its boiling point in the May preceding the outbreak of the war.

Whatever other nations might desire to do, Italy, at any rate, was at this time resolved to fight. It was not that the King and the Government were so resolved. What was the purpose just then of the powers of the state, if any purpose had then been definitely formed by them, no one now knows. History, perhaps, may some day tell us. But the nation was determined to fight. Hitherto all had been done for the Italians by outside allies, and now the time had come in which Italians would do something for themselves.

The people hated the French aid by which they had been allowed to live, and burned with a desire to prove that they could do something great without aid. There was an enormous army, and that army should be utilised for the enfranchisement of Venetia and to the great glory of Italy. The King and the ministers appreciated the fact that the fervour of the people was too strong to be repressed, and were probably guided to such resolutions as they did make by that appreciation.

The feeling was as strong in Venice as it was in Florence or in Milan; but in Venice only, – or rather in Venetia only – all outward signs of such feeling were repressible, and were repressed. All through Lombardy and Tuscany any young man who pleased might volunteer with Garibaldi; but to volunteer with Garibaldi was not, at first, so easy for young men in Verona or in Venice. The more complete was this repression, the greater was this difficulty, the stronger, of course, arose the hatred of the Venetians for the Austrian soldiery.

I have never heard that the Austrians were cruel in what they did; but they were determined; and, as long as they had any intention of holding the province, it was necessary that they should be so.

During the past winter there had been living in Venice a certain Captain von Vincke, – Hubert von Vincke, – an Austrian officer of artillery, who had spent the last four or five years among the fortifications of Verona, and who had come to Venice, originally, on account of ill health. Some military employment had kept him in Venice, and he remained there till the outbreak of the war; going backwards and forwards, occasionally, to Verona, but still having Venice as his head-quarters.

Now Captain von Vincke had shown so much consideration for the country which he assisted in holding under subjection as to learn its language, and to study its manners; and had, by these means, found his way more or less, into Italian society. He was a thorough soldier, good-looking, perhaps eight-and-twenty or thirty years of age, well educated, ambitious, very free from the common vice of thinking that the class of mankind to which he belonged was the only class in which it would be worth a man's while to live; but nevertheless imbued with a strong feeling that Austria ought to hold her own, that an Austrian army was indomitable, and that the quadrilateral fortresses, bound together as they were now bound by Austrian strategy, were impregnable. So much Captain von Vincke thought and believed on the part of his country; but in thinking and believing this, he was still desirous that much should be done to relieve Austrian-Italy from the grief of foreign rule. That Italy should think of succeeding in repelling Austria from Venice was to him an absurdity.

He had become intimate at the house of a widow lady,

who lived in the Campo San Luca, one Signora Pepé, whose son had first become acquainted with Captain von Vincke at Verona.

Carlo Pepé was a young advocate, living and earning his bread at Venice, but business had taken him for a time to Verona; and when leaving that city he had asked his Austrian friend to come and see him in his mother's house.

Both Madame Pepé and her daughter Nina, Carlo's only sister, had somewhat found fault with the young advocate's rashness in thus seeking the close intimacy of home-life with one whom, whatever might be his own peculiar virtues, they could not but recognise as an enemy of their country.

'That would be all very fine if it were put into a book,' said the Signora to her son, who had been striving to show that an Austrian, if good in himself, might be as worthy a friend as an Italian; 'but it is always well to live on the safe side of the wall. It is not convenient that the sheep and the wolves should drink at the same stream.'

This she said with all that caution which everywhere forms so marked a trait in the Italian character. 'Who goes softly goes soundly.' Half of the Italian nature is told in that proverb, though it is not the half which was becoming most apparent in the doings of the nation in these days. And the Signorina was quite of one mind with her mother.

'Carlo,' she said, 'how is it that one never sees one of these Austrians in the house of any friend? Why is it that I have never yet found myself in a room with one of them?'

'Because men and women are generally so pigheaded and unreasonable,' Carlo had replied. 'How am I, for instance, ever to learn what a German is at the core, or a Frenchman, or an Englishman, if I refuse to speak to one?'

It ended by Captain von Vincke being brought to the house in the Campo San Luca, and there becoming as intimate with the Signora and the Signorina as he was with the advocate.

Our story must be necessarily too short to permit us to see how the affair grew in all its soft and delicate growth; but by the beginning of April Nina Pepé had confessed her love to Hubert von Vincke, and both the captain and Nina had had a few words with the Signora on the subject of their projected marriage.

'Carlo will never allow it,' the old lady had said, trembling as she thought of the danger that was coming upon the family.

'He should not have brought Captain von Vincke to the house, unless he was prepared to regard such a thing as possible,' said Nina proudly.

'I think he is too good a fellow to object to anything that you will ask him,' said the captain, holding by the hand the lady whom he hoped to call his mother-in-law.

Throughout January and February Captain von Vincke had been an invalid. In March he had been hardly more than convalescent, and had then had time and all that opportunity which convalescence gives for the sweet business of love-making.

During this time, through March and in the first weeks of April, Carlo Pepé had been backwards and forwards to Verona, and had in truth had more business on hand than that which simply belonged to him as a lawyer. Those were the days in which the Italians were beginning to prepare for the great attack which was to be made, and in which correspondence was busily carried on between Italy and Venetia as to the enrolment of Venetian Volunteers.

It will be understood that no Venetian was allowed to go into Italy without an Austrian passport, and that at this time the Austrians were becoming doubly strict in seeing that the order was not evaded. Of course it was evaded daily, and twice in that April did young Pepé travel between Verona and Bologna in spite of all that Austria could say to the contrary.

When at Venice he and von Vincke discussed very freely the position of the country, nothing of course being said as to those journeys to Bologna. Indeed, of them no one in the Campo San Luca knew aught. They were such journeys that a man says nothing of them to his mother or his sister, or even to his wife, unless he has as much confidence in her courage as he has in her love. But of politics he would talk freely, as would also the German; and though each of them would speak of the cause as though they two were simply philosophical lookers-on, and were not and could not become actors, and though each had in his mind a settled resolve to bear with the political opinion of the other, yet it came to pass that they now and again were on the verge of quarrelling.

The fault, I think, was wholly with Carlo Pepé, whose enthusiasm of course was growing as those journeys to Bologna were made successfully, and who was beginning to feel assured that Italy at last would certainly do something for herself. But there had not come any open quarrel, – not as yet, when Nina, in her lover's presence, was arguing as to the impropriety of bringing Captain von Vincke to the house, if Captain von Vincke was to be regarded as altogether unfit for matrimonial purposes. At that moment Carlo was absent at Verona, but was to return on the following morning. It was decided at this conference between the two ladies and the lover, that Carlo should be told on his return of Captain von Vincke's intentions. Captain von Vincke himself would tell him.

There is a certain hotel or coffee-house, or place of general public entertainment in Venice, kept by a German, and called the Hotel Bauer, probably from the name of the German who keeps it. It stands near the church of St. Moses, behind the grand piazza, between that and the great canal, in a narrow intricate throng of little streets, and is approached by a close dark water-way which robs it of any attempt at hotel grandeur. Nevertheless it is a large and commodious house, at which good dinners may be eaten at prices somewhat lower than are compatible with the grandeur of the Grand Canal. It used to be much affected by Germans, and had, perhaps, acquired among Venetians a character of being attached to Austrian interests.

There was not much in this, or Carlo Pepé would not have frequented the house, even in company with his friend Von Vincke. He did so frequent it, and now, on this occasion of his return home, Von Vincke left word for him that he would breakfast at the hotel at eleven o'clock. Pepé by that time would have gone home after his journey, and would have visited his office. Von Vincke also would have done the greatest part of his day's work. Each understood the habits of the other, and they met at Bauer's for breakfast.

It was the end of April, and Carlo Pepé had returned to Venice full of schemes for that revolution which he now regarded as imminent. The alliance between Italy and Prussia was already discussed. Those Italians who were most eager said that it was a thing done, and no Italian was more eager than Carlo Pepé. And it was believed at this time, and more thoroughly believed in Italy than elsewhere, that Austria and Prussia would certainly go to war. Now, if ever, Italy must do something for herself.

Carlo Pepé was in this mood, full of these things, when he sat down to breakfast at Bauer's with his friend Captain von Vincke.

'Von Vincke,' he said, 'in three months' time you will be out of Venice.'

'Shall I?' said the other; 'and where shall I be?'

'In Vienna, as I hope; or at Berlin if you can get there. But you will not be here, or in the Quadrilatere, unless you are left behind as a prisoner.'

The captain went on for a while cutting his meat and drinking his wine, before he made any reply to this. And Pepé said more of the same kind, expressing strongly his opinion that the empire of the Austrians in Venice was at an end. Then the captain wiped his moustaches carefully with his napkin, and did speak.

'Carlo, my friend,' he said, 'you are rash to say all this.'

'Why rash?' said Carlo; 'you and I understand each other.'

'Just so, my friend; but we do not know how far that long-eared waiter may understand either of us.'

'The waiter has heard nothing, and I do not care if he did.'

'And beyond that,' continued the captain, 'you make a difficulty for me. What am I to say when you tell me these things? That you should have one political opinion and I another is natural. The question between us, in an abstract point of view, I can discuss with you willingly. The possibility of Venice contending with Austria I could discuss, if no such rebellion were imminent. But when you tell me that it is imminent, that it is already here, I cannot discuss it.'

'It is imminent,' said Carlo.

'So be it,' said Von Vincke.

And then they finished their breakfast in silence. All this was very unfortunate for our friend the captain, who had come to Bauer's with the intention of speaking on quite another subject. His friend Pepé had evidently taken what he had said in a bad spirit, and was angry with him. Nevertheless, as he had told Nina and her mother that he would declare his purpose to Carlo on this morning, he must do it. He was not a man to be frightened out of his purpose by his friend's ill-humour.

'Will you come into the piazza, and smoke a cigar?' said Von Vincke, feeling that he could begin upon the other subject better as soon as the scene should be changed.

'Why not let me have my cigar and coffee here?' said Carlo.

'Because I have something to say which I can say better walking than sitting. Come along.'

Then they paid the bill and left the house, and walked in silence through the narrow ways to the piazza. Von Vincke said no word till he found himself in the broad passage leading into the great square. Then he put his hand through the other's arm and told his tale at once.

'Carlo,' said he, 'I love your sister, and would have her for my wife. Will you consent?'

'By the body of Bacchus, what is this you say?' said the other, drawing his arm away, and looking up into the German's face.

'Simply that she has consented and your mother. Are you willing that I should be your brother?'

'This is madness,' said Carlo Pepé.

'On their part, you mean?'

'Yes, and on yours. Were there nothing else to prevent it, how could there be marriage between us when this war is coming?'

'I do not believe in the war; that is, I do not believe in war between us and Italy. No war can affect you here in Venice. If there is to be a war in which I shall be concerned, I am quite willing to wait till it be over.'

'You understand nothing about it,' said Carlo, after a pause; 'nothing! You are in the dark altogether. How should it not be so, when those who are over you never tell you anything? No, I will not consent. It is a thing out of the question.'

'Do you think that I am personally unfit to be your sister's husband?'

'Not personally, but politically and nationally. You are not one of us; and now, at this moment, any attempt at close union between an Austrian and a Venetian must be ruinous. Von Vincke, I am heartily sorry for this. I blame the women, and not you.'

Then Carlo Pepé went home, and there was a rough scene between him and his mother, and a scene still rougher between him and his sister.

And in these interviews he told something, though not the whole of the truth as to the engagements into which he had entered. That he was to be the officer second in command in a regiment of Venetian volunteers, of those volunteers whom it was hoped that Garibaldi would lead to victory in the coming war, he did not tell them; but he did make them understand that when the struggle came he would be away from Venice, and would take a part in it. 'And how am I to do this,' he said, 'if you here are joined hand and heart to an Austrian? A house divided against itself must fall.'

Let the reader understand that Nina Pepé, in spite of her love and of her lover, was as good an Italian as her brother, and that their mother was equally firm in her political desires and national antipathies. Where would you have found the Venetian, man or woman, who did not detest Austrian rule, and look forward to the good day coming when Venice should be a city of Italia?

The Signora and Nina had indeed, some six months before this, been much stronger in their hatred of all things German, than had the son and brother. It had been his liberal feeling, his declaration that even a German might be good, which had induced them to allow this Austrian to come among them.

Then the man and the soldier had been two; and Von Vincke had himself shown tendencies so strongly at variance with those of his comrades that he had disarmed their fears. He had read Italian, and condescended to speak it; he knew the old history of their once great city, and would listen to them when they talked of their old Doges. He loved their churches, and their palaces, and their pictures. Gradually he had come to love Nina Pepé with all his heart, and Nina loved him too with all her heart.

But when her brother spoke to her and to her mother with more than his customary vehemence of what was due from them to their country, of the debt which certainly should be paid by him, of obligations to him from which they could not free themselves; and told them also, that by that time six months not an Austrian would be found in Venice, they trembled and believed him, and Nina felt that her love would not run smooth.

'You must be with us or against us,' said Carlo.

'Why then did you bring him here?' Nina replied.

'Am I to suppose that you cannot see a man without falling in love with him?'

'Carlo, that is unkind, almost unbrotherly. Was he not your friend, and were not you the first to tell us how good he is? And he is good; no man can be better.'

'He is a honest young man,' said the Signora.

'He is Austrian to the backbone,' said Carlo.

'Of course he is,' said Nina. 'What should he be?'

'And will you be Austrian?' her brother asked.

'Not if I must be an enemy of Italy,' Nina said. 'If an Austrian may be a friend to Italy, then I will be an Austrian.

I wish to be Hubert's wife. Of course I shall be an Austrian if he is my husband.'

'Then I trust that you may never be his wife,' said Carlo.

By the middle of May Carlo Pepé and Captain von Vincke had absolutely quarrelled. They did not speak, and Von Vincke had been ordered by the brother not to show himself at the house in the Campo San Luca.

Every German in Venice had now become more Austrian than before, and every Venetian more Italian. Even our friend the captain had come to believe in the war.

Not only Venice but Italy was in earnest, and Captain von Vincke foresaw, or thought that he foresaw, that a time of wretched misery was coming upon that devoted town. He would never give up Nina, but perhaps it might be well that he should cease to press his suit till he might be enabled to do so with something of the éclat of Austrian success.

And now at last it became necessary that the two women should be told of Carlo's plans, for Carlo was going to leave Venice till the war should be over and he could re-enter the city as an Italian should enter a city of his own.

'Oh! my son, my son,' said the mother; 'why should it be you?'

'Many must go, mother. Why not I as well as another?'

'In other houses there are fathers; and in other families more sons than one.'

'The time has come, mother, in which no woman should grudge either husband or son to the cause. But the thing is settled. I am already second colonel in a regiment which will serve with Garibaldi. You would not ask me to desert my colours?'

There was nothing further to be said. The Signora threw herself on her son's neck and wept, and both mother and sister felt that their Carlo was already a second Garibaldi. When a man is a hero to women, they will always obey him. What could Nina do at such a time, but promise that she would not see Hubert von Vincke during his absence. Then there was a compact made between the brother and sister.

During three weeks past, that is, since the breakfast at Bauer's, Nina had seen Hubert von Vincke but once, and had then seen him in the presence of her mother and brother. He had come in one evening in the old way, before the quarrel, to take his coffee, and had been received, as heretofore, as a friend, Nina sitting very silent during the evening, but with a gracious silence; and after that the mother had signified to the lover that he had better come no more for the present. He therefore came no more.

I think it is the fact that love, though no doubt it may run as strong with an Italian or with an Austrian as it does with us English, is not allowed to run with so uncontrollable a stream. Young lovers, and especially young women, are more subject to control, and are less inclined to imagine that all things should go as they would have them. Nina, when she was made to understand that the war was come, that her brother was leaving her and her mother and Venice, that he might fight for them, that an Austrian soldier must for the time be regarded as an enemy in that house, resolved with a slow, melancholy firmness that she would accept the circumstances of her destiny.

'If I fall,' said Carlo, 'you must then manage for yourself. I would not wish to bind you after my death.'

'Do not talk like that, Carlo.'

'Nay, my child, but I must talk like that; and it is at least well that we should understand each other. I know that you will keep your promise to me.'

'Yes,' said Nina; 'I will keep my promise.'

'Till I come back, or till I be dead, you will not again see Captain von Vincke; or till the cause be gained.'

'I will not see him, Carlo, till you come back, or till the cause be gained.'

'Or till I be dead. Say it after me.'

'Or till you be dead, if I must say it.'

But there was a clause in the contract that she was to see her lover once before her brother left them. She had acknowledged the propriety of her brother's behests, backed as they came to be at last by their mother; but she declared through it all that she had done no wrong, and that she would not be treated as though she were an offender. She would see her lover and tell him what she pleased. She would obey her brother, but she would see her lover first. Indeed, she would make no promise of obedience at all, would promise disobedience instead, unless she were allowed to see him. She would herself write to him and bid him come.

This privilege was at last acceded to her, and Captain von Vincke was summoned to the Campo San Luca. The morning sitting-room of the Signora Pepé was up two pairs of stairs, and the stairs were not paved as are the stairs of the palaces in Venice. But the room was large and lofty, and seemed to be larger than its size from the very small amount of furniture which it contained. The floor was of hard, polished cement, which looked like variegated marble, and the amount of carpet upon it was about four yards long, and was extended simply beneath the two chairs in which sat habitually the Signora and her daughter. There were two large mirrors and a large gold clock, and a large table and a small table, a small sofa and six chairs, and that was all. In England the room would have received ten times as much furniture, or it would not have been furnished at all. And there were in it no more than two small books, belonging both to Nina, for the Signora read but little. In England, in such a sitting-room, tables, various tables, would have been strewed with books; but then, perhaps, Nina Pepé's eye required the comfort of no other volumes than those she was actually using.

Nina was alone in the room when her lover came to her. There had been a question whether her mother should or should not be present; but Nina had been imperative, and she received him alone.

'It is to bid you good-bye, Hubert,' she said, as she got up and touched his hand, – just touched his hand.

'Not for long, my Nina.'

'Who can say for how long, now that the war is upon us? As far as I can see, it will be for very long. It is better that you should know it all. For myself, I think, I fear that it will be for ever.'

'For ever! why for ever?'

'Because I cannot marry an enemy of Italy. I do not think that we can ever succeed.'

'You can never succeed.'

'Then I can never be your wife. It is so, Hubert; I see that it must be so. The loss is to me, not to you.'

'No, no – no. The loss is to me, – to me.'

'You have your profession. You are a soldier. I am nothing.'

'You are all in all to me.'

'I can be nothing, I shall be nothing, unless I am your wife. Think how I must long for that which you say is so impossible. I do long for it; I shall long for it. Oh, Hubert! go and lose your cause; let our men have their Venice. Then come to me, and your country shall be my country, and your people my people.'

As she said this she gently laid her hand upon his arm, and

the touch of her fingers thrilled through his whole frame. He put out his arms as though to grasp her in his embrace.

'No, Hubert – no; that must not be till Venice is our own.'

'I wish it were,' he said; 'but it will never be so. You may make me a traitor in heart, but that will not drive out fifty thousand troops from the fortresses.'

'I do not understand these things, Hubert, and I have felt your country's power to be so strong, that I cannot now doubt it.'

'It is absurd to doubt it.'

'But yet they say that we shall succeed.'

'It is impossible. Even though Prussia should be able to stand against us, we should not leave Venetia. We shall never leave the fortresses.'

'Then, my love, we may say farewell for ever. I will not forget you. I will never be false to you. But we must part.'

He stood there arguing with her, and she argued with him, but they always came round to the same point. There was to be the war, and she would not become the wife of her brother's enemy. She had sworn, she said, and she would keep her word. When his arguments became stronger than hers, she threw herself back upon her plighted word.

'I have said it, and I must not depart from it. I have told him that my love for you should be eternal, and I tell you the same. I told him that I would see you no more, and I can only tell you so also.'

He could ask her no questions as to the cause of her resolution, because he could not make inquiries as to her brother's purpose. He knew that Carlo was at work for the Venetian cause; or, at least, he thought that he knew it. But it was essential for his comfort that he should really know as little of this as might be possible. That Carlo Pepé was coming and going in the service of the cause he could not but surmise: but should authenticated information reach him as to whither Carlo went, and how he came, it might become his duty to put a stop to Carlo's comings and Carlo's goings. On this matter, therefore, he said nothing, but merely shook his head, and smiled with a melancholy smile when she spoke of the future struggle. 'And now, Hubert, you must go. I was determined that I would see you, that I might tell you that I would be true to you.'

'What good will be such truth?'

'Nay; it is for you to say that. I ask you for no pledge.'

'I shall love no other woman. I would if I could. I would if I could – to-morrow.'

'Let us have our own, and then come and love me. Or you need not come. I will go to you, though it be to the furthest end of Galicia. Do not look like that at me. You should be proud when I tell you that I love you. No, you shall not kiss me. No man shall ever kiss me till Venice is our own. There, – I have sworn it. Should that time come, and should a certain Austrian gentleman care for Italian kisses then, he will know where to seek for them. God bless you now, and go.'

She made her way to the door and opened it, and there was nothing for him but that he must go. He touched her hand once more as he went, but there was no other word spoken between them.

'Mother,' she said, when she found herself again with the Signora, 'my little dream of life is over. It has been very short.'

'Nay, my child, life is long for you yet. There will be many dreams, and much of reality.'

'I do not complain of Carlo,' Nina continued. 'He is sacrificing much, perhaps everything, for Venice. And why should his sacrifice be greater than mine? But I feel it to be severe, – very severe. Why did he bring him here if he felt thus?'

June came, that month of June that was to be so fatal to Italian glory, and so fraught with success for the Italian cause, and Carlo Pepé was again away.

Those who knew nothing of his doings, knew only that he had gone to Verona – on matters of law. Those who were really acquainted with the circumstances of his present life were aware that he had made his way out of Verona, and that he was already with his volunteers near the lakes waiting for Garibaldi, who was then expected from Caprera. For some weeks to come, for some months probably, during the war perhaps, the two women in the Campo San Luca would know nothing of the whereabouts or of the fate of him whom they loved. He had gone to risk all for the cause, and they too must be content to risk all in remaining desolate at home without the comfort of his presence; – and she also, without the sweeter comfort of that other presence.

It is thus that women fight their battles. In these days men by hundreds were making their way out of Venice, and by thousands out of the province of Venetia, and the Austrians were endeavouring in vain to stop the emigration. Some few were caught, and kept in prison; and many Austrian threats were uttered against those who should prove themselves to be insubordinate. But it is difficult for a garrison to watch a whole people, and very difficult indeed when there is a war on hand.

It at last became a fact, that any man from the province could go and become a volunteer under Garibaldi if he pleased, and very many did go. History will say that they were successful, – but their success certainly was not glorious.

It was in the month of June that all the battles of that short war were fought. Nothing will ever be said or sung in story to the honour of the volunteers who served in that campaign with Garibaldi, amidst the mountains of the Southern Tyrol; but nowhere, probably, during the war was there so much continued fighting, or an equal amount endured of the hardships of military life.

The task they had before them, of driving the Austrians from the fortresses amidst their own mountains, was an impossible one, impossible even had Garibaldi been supplied with ordinary military equipments, – but ridiculously impossible for him in all the nakedness in which he was sent. Nothing was done to enable him to succeed. That he should be successful was neither intended nor desired. He was, in fact, – then, as he has been always, since the days in which he gave Naples to Italy, – simply a stumbling-block in the way of the king, of the king's ministers, and of the king's generals. 'There is that Garibaldi again, – with volunteers flocking to him by thousands: – what shall we do to rid ourselves of Garibaldi and his volunteers? How shall we dispose of them?' That has been the feeling of those in power in Italy, – and not unnaturally their feeling, – with regard to Garibaldi. A man so honest, so brave, so patriotic, so popular, and so impracticable, cannot but have been a trouble to them. And here he was with twenty-five thousand volunteers, all armed after a fashion, all supplied, at least, with a red shirt. What should be done with Garibaldi and his army? So they sent him away up into the mountains, where his game of play might at any rate detain him for some weeks; and in the meantime everything might get itself arranged by the benevolent and omnipotent interference of the emperor.

Things did get themselves arranged while Garibaldi was up among the mountains, kicking with unarmed toes against Austrian pricks – with sad detriment to his feet. Things did get themselves arranged very much to the advantage of Venetia, but not exactly by the interference of the emperor.

The facts of the war became known more slowly in Venice than they did in Florence, in Paris, or in London. That the battle of Custozza had been fought and lost by the Italian troops was known. And then it was known that the battle of Lissa also had been fought and lost by Italian ships. But it was not known, till the autumn was near at hand that Venetia had, in fact, been surrendered. There were rumours; and women, who knew that their husbands had been beaten, could not believe that success was to be the result of such calamities.

There were weeks in which came no news from Carlo Pepé to the women in the Campo San Luca, and then came simply tidings that he had been wounded.

'I shall see my son never again,' said the widow in her ecstasy of misery.

And Nina was able to talk to her mother only of Carlo. Of Hubert von Vincke she spoke not then a word. But she repeated to herself over and over again the last promise she had given him. She had sent him away from her, and now she knew nothing of his whereabouts. That he would be fighting she presumed. She had heard that most of the soldiers from Venice had gone to the fortresses. He, too, might be wounded, – might be dead. If alive at the end of the war, he would hardly return to her after what had passed between them. But if he did not come back no lover should ever take a kiss from her lips.

Then there was the long truce, and a letter from Carlo reached Venice. His wound had been slight, but he had been very hungry. He wrote in great anger, abusing, not the Austrians, but the Italians. There had been treachery, and the Italian general-in-chief had been the head of the traitors. The king was a traitor! The emperor was a traitor! All concerned were traitors, but yet Venetia was to be surrendered to Italy.

I think that the two ladies in the Campo San Luca never really believed that this would be so until they received that angry letter from Carlo.

'When I may get home, I cannot tell,' he said. 'I hardly care to return, and I shall remain with the General as long as he may wish to have any one remaining with him. But you may be sure that I shall never go soldiering again. Venetia, may, perhaps, prosper, and become a part of Italy; but there will be no glory for us. Italy has been allowed to do nothing for herself.' The mother and sister endeavoured to feel some sympathy for the young soldier who spoke so sadly of his own career, but they could hardly be unhappy because his fighting was over and the cause was won.

The cause was won. Gradually there came to be no doubt about that.

It was now September, and as yet it had not come to pass that shop-windows were filled with wonderful portraits of Victor Emmanuel and Garibaldi, cheek by jowl – they being the two men who at that moment were perhaps, in all Italy, the most antagonistic to each other; nor were there as yet fifty different new journals cried day and night under the arcades of the Grand Piazza, all advocating the cause of Italy, one and indivisible, as there came to be a month afterwards; but still it was known that Austria was to cede Venetia, and that Venice would henceforth be a city of Italy. This was known; and it was also known in the Campo San Luca that Carlo Pepé, though very hungry up among the mountains, was still safe.

Then Nina thought that the time had come in which it would become her to speak of her lover. 'Mother,' she said, 'I must know something of Hubert.'

'But how, Nina? how will you learn? Will you not wait till Carlo comes back?'

95

'No,' she said. 'I cannot wait longer. I have kept my promise. Venice is no longer Austrian, and I will seek him. I have kept my word to Carlo, and now I will keep my word to Hubert.'

But how to seek him? The widow, urged by her daughter, went out and asked at barrack doors; but new regiments had come and gone, and everything was in confusion. It was supposed that any officer of artillery who had been in Venice and had left it during the war must be in one of the four fortresses.

'Mother,' she said, 'I shall go to Verona.'

And to Verona she went, all alone, in search of her lover. At that time the Austrians still maintained a sort of rule in the province; and there were still current orders against private travelling, orders that passports should be investigated, orders that the communication with the four fortresses should be specially guarded; but there was an intense desire on the part of the Austrians themselves that the orders should be regarded as little as possible. They had to go, and the more quietly they went the better. Why should they care now who passed hither and thither? It must be confessed on their behalf that in their surrender of Venetia they gave as little trouble as it was possible in them to cause.

The chief obstruction to Nina's journey she experienced in the Campo San Luca itself. But in spite of her mother, in spite of the not yet defunct Austrian mandates, she did make her way to Verona. 'As I was true in giving him up,' she said to herself, 'so will I be true in clinging to him.'

Even in Verona her task was not easy, but she did at last find all that she sought. Captain von Vincke had been in command of a battery at Custozza, and was now lying wounded in an Austrian hospital. Nina contrived to see an old grey-haired surgeon before she saw Hubert himself.

Captain von Vincke had been terribly mauled; so the surgeon told her; his left arm had been amputated, and – and – and –

It seemed as though wounds had been showered on him. The surgeon did not think that his patient would die; but he did think that he must be left in Verona when the Austrians were marched out of the fortress. 'Can he not be taken to Venice?' said Nina Pepé.

At last she found herself by her lover's bedside; but with her there were two hospital attendants, both of them worn-out Austrian soldiers, – and there was also there the grey-haired surgeon. How was she to tell her love, all that she had in her heart before such witnesses? The surgeon was the first to speak. 'Here is your friend, Captain,' he said; but as he spoke in German, Nina did not understand him.

'Is it really you, Nina?' said her lover. 'I could hardly believe that you should be in Verona.'

'Of course it is I. Who could have so much business to be in Verona as I have? Of course I am here.'

'But, – but – what has brought you here, Nina?'

'If you do not know I cannot tell you.'

'And Carlo?'

'Carlo is still with the General; but he is well.'

'And the Signora?'

'She also is well; well, but not easy in mind while I am here.'

'And when do you return?'

'Nay; I cannot tell you that. It may be to-day. It may be to-morrow. It depends not on myself at all.'

He spoke not a word of love to her then, nor she to him, unless there was love in such greeting as has been here repeated. Indeed, it was not till after that first interview that he fully understood that she had made her journey to

Verona, solely in quest of him. The words between them for the first day or two were very tame, as though neither had full confidence in the other; and she had taken her place as nurse by his side, as a sister might have done by a brother, and was established in her work, – nay, had nearly completed her work, before there came to be any full understanding between them. More than once she had told herself that she would go back to Venice and let there be an end of it. 'The great work of the war,' she said to herself, 'has so filled his mind, that the idleness of his days in Venice and all that he did then, are forgotten. If so, my presence here is surely a sore burden to him, and I will go.' But she could not now leave him without a word of farewell. 'Hubert,' she said, for she had called him Hubert when she first came to his bedside, as though she had been his sister, 'I think I must return now to Venice. My mother will be lonely without me.'

At that moment it appeared almost miraculous to her that she should be sitting there by his bedside, that she should have loved him, that she should have had the courage to leave her home and seek him after the war, that she should have found him, and that she should now be about to leave him, almost without a word between them.

'She must be very lonely,' said the wounded man.

'And you, I think, are stronger than you were?'

'For me, I am strong enough. I have lost my arm, and I shall carry this gaping scar athwart my face to the grave, as my cross of honour won in the Italian war; but otherwise I shall soon be well.'

'It is a fair cross of honour.'

'Yes; they cannot rob us of our wounds when our service is over. And so you will go, Signorina?'

'Yes; I will go. Why should I remain here? I will go, and

Carlo will return, and I will tend upon him. Carlo also was wounded.'

'But you have told me that he is well again.'

'Nevertheless, he will value the comfort of a woman's care after his sufferings. May I say farewell to you now, my friend?' And she put her hand down upon the bed so that he might reach it. She had been with him for days, and there had been no word of love. It had seemed as though he had understood nothing of what she had done in coming to him; that he had failed altogether in feeling that she had come as a wife goes to a husband. She had made a mistake in this journey, and must now rectify her error with as much of dignity as might be left to her.

He took her hand in his, and held it for a moment before he answered her. 'Nina,' he said, 'why did you come hither?'

'Why did I come?'

'Why are you here in Verona, while your mother is alone in Venice?'

'I had business here; a matter of some moment. It is finished now, and I shall return.'

'Was it other business than to sit at my bedside?'

She paused a moment before she answered him.

'Yes,' she said; 'it was other business than that.'

'And you have succeeded?'

'No; I have failed.'

He still held her hand; and she, though she was thus fencing with him, answering him with equivoques, felt that at last there was coming from him some word which would at least leave her no longer in doubt.

'And I too, have I failed?' he said. 'When I left Venice I told myself heartily that I had failed.'

'You told yourself, then,' said she, 'that Venetia never would be ceded. You know that I would not triumph over you, now that your cause has been lost. We Italians have not much cause for triumphing.'

'You will admit always that the fortresses have not been taken from us,' said the sore-hearted soldier.

'Certainly we shall admit that?'

'And my own fortress, – the stronghold that I thought I had made altogether mine, – is that, too, lost for ever to the poor German?'

'You speak in riddles, Captain von Vincke,' she said.

She had now taken back her hand; but she was sitting quietly by his bedside, and made no sign of leaving him.

'Nina,' he said, 'Nina, – my own Nina. In losing a single share of Venice, – one soldier's share of the province, – shall I have gained all the world for myself? Nina, tell me truly, what brought you to Verona?'

She knelt slowly down by his bedside, and again taking his one hand in hers, pressed it first to her lips and then to her bosom. 'It was an unmaidenly purpose,' she said. 'I came to find the man I loved.'

'But you said you had failed?'

'And I now say that I have succeeded. Do you not know that success in great matters always trembles in the balance before it turns the beam, thinking, fearing, all but knowing that failure has weighed down the scale?'

'But now – ?'

'Now I am sure that – Venice has been won.'

It was three months after this, and half of December had passed away, and all Venetia had in truth been ceded, and Victor Emmanuel had made his entry into Venice and exit out of it, with as little of real triumph as ever attended a king's progress through a new province, and the Austrian army had moved itself off very quietly, and the city had become as thoroughly Italian as Florence itself, and was in a way to be equally discontented, when a party of four, two ladies and two gentlemen, sat down to breakfast in the Hôtel Bauer.

The ladies were the Signora Pepé and her daughter, and the men were Carlo Pepé and his brother-in-law, Hubert von Vincke. It was but a poor fête, this family breakfast at an obscure inn, but it was intended as a gala feast to mark the last day of Nina's Italian life.

To-morrow, very early in the morning, she was to leave Venice for Trieste, – so early that it would be necessary that she should be on board this very night.

'My child,' said the Signora, 'do not say so; you will never cease to be Italian. Surely, Hubert, she may still call herself Venetian?'

'Mother,' she said, 'I love a losing cause. I will be Austrian now. I told him that he could not have both. If he kept his Venice, he could not have me; but as he has lost his province, he shall have his wife entirely.'

'I told him that it was fated that he should lose Venetia,' said Carlo, 'but he would never believe me.'

'Because I knew how true were our soldiers,' said Hubert, 'and could not understand how false were our statesmen.'

'See how he regrets it,' said Nina; 'what he has lost, and what he has won, will, together, break his heart for him.'

'Nina,' he said, 'I learned this morning in the city, that I shall be the last Austrian soldier to leave Venice, and I hold that of all who have entered it, and all who have left it, I am the most successful and the most triumphant.'

CAMILLO BOITO

SENSO

Translated by Christine Donougher

YESTERDAY IN MY yellow drawing-room, the young lawyer Gino, his voice thick with long-repressed passion, was whispering in my ear, 'Contessa, take pity on me. Drive me away, instruct the servants not to let me in any more, but in God's name release me from this deadly uncertainty. Tell me whether there's any hope for me, or not ...' The poor boy threw himself at my feet, while I stood there, unperturbed, looking at myself in the mirror.

I was examining my face in search of a wrinkle. My forehead, framed with pretty little curls, is smooth and clear as a baby's. There is not a line to be seen on either side of my flared nostrils, or above my rather full, red lips. I have never found a single white strand in my long hair, which, when loose, falls in lovely glossy waves, blacker than ink, over my snow-white shoulders.

Thirty-nine! I shudder as I write this horrible figure.

I gave a light slap with my tapering fingers to the hot hand groping towards me, and was on my way out of the room. I do not know what prompted me – surely some laudable sense of compassion or friendship – but on the threshold I turned and whispered, I think, these words: 'There's hope ...'

I must curb my vanity. The anxiety that gnaws at my mind, leaving virtually no trace on my body, alternates with overconfidence in my beauty, leaving me no other comfort but this: my mirror.

I hope to find further comfort in writing of what happened to me sixteen years ago, an experience I look back on with bitter delight. This notebook, which I keep triple-locked in my secret safe, away from all prying eyes, and as soon as I have reached the end of my story I shall throw it on the fire, dispersing the ashes, but confiding my old memories to paper should help to abate their persistently caustic edge. Every word and deed, and above all every humiliation, of that feverish period in my past remains etched in my mind. And I am always testing and probing the lesions of this unhealed wound, not really knowing whether what I feel is actually pain or an itch of pleasure.

What a joy it is, to confide in no one but yourself, free from scruples, hypocrisy and reserve, respecting the truth in your recollections, even with regard to what ridiculous social conventions make it most difficult to speak of publicly: the depths to which you have sunk! I have read of holy anchorites who lived in the midst of vermin and putrefaction (filth, that is), but who believed that the more they wallowed in the mire, the higher they elevated themselves. So my spirit exalts in self-humiliation. I take pride in the sense of being utterly different from other women. There is no sight whatsoever that daunts me. There is, in my weakness, a daring strength: I am like the women of ancient Rome who gave the thumbs-down, those women that Parini mentions in one of his odes – I don't remember it exactly, but I know that when I read it I really thought that the poet could have been referring to me.

Were it not for the feverishness of vivid memories on the one hand and dread of old age on the other, I should be a happy woman. My husband, who is old and infirm, and utterly dependent on me, allows me to spend as much as I want and to do as I please. I am one of the first ladies of Trento. I have no lack of admirers, and, far from lessening, the kind envy of my dear women friends is ever mounting.

I was of course more beautiful at the age of twenty. Not that my features have changed, or that my body seems any less slender and supple, but there was in my eyes a flame, which now, alas, is dying. The very blackness of my pupils seems to me on close inspection a little less intense. They say that the purpose of philosophy is to know yourself. I have studied myself with so much trepidation for so many years, hour by hour, minute by minute, that I believe I know myself through and through, and can declare myself an excellent philosopher.

I would say that I was at my most beautiful (there is always in a woman's blossoming a brief period of consummate loveliness), when I had just turned twenty-two, in Venice. It was July of the year 1865. I had been married for only a few days and was on my honeymoon. For my husband, who could have been my grandfather, I felt indifference mingled with pity and contempt. He bore his sixty-two years and his ample paunch with seeming vigour. He dyed his sparse hair and thick moustaches with a rank ointment that stained his pillows with big yellowish blotches. Otherwise, he was an amiable man, in his own way full of attentions for his young wife, inclined to gluttony, an occasional blasphemer, an indefatigable smoker, a haughty aristocrat, a bully towards the meek and himself timorous in the face of aggression, a lively raconteur of lewd stories that he would tell at every opportunity, neither tight-fisted nor a spendthrift. He would strut like a peacock when holding me on his arm, yet eyed with a smile of lascivious connivance the women of easy virtue who passed us in Piazza San Marco. And from one point of view I was pleased by this, since

I would happily have banished him into the arms of any other woman, just to be rid of him; and from another, it vexed me.

I had taken him of my own free will. Indeed, I had actually wanted him. My family were opposed to so ill-assorted a match. Nor, if truth be told, was the poor man ardently seeking my hand. But I was bored with my position as an unmarried woman. I wanted to have my own carriages, jewels, velvet gowns, a title, and above all my freedom. It took a few flirtatious glances to inflame the desire of the pot-bellied Count, but once inflamed, he could not rest until I was his, neither did he mind about the small dowry, nor give any thought to the future. Before the priest, I answered with a firm and resounding 'I do'. I was pleased with what I had done, and I do not regret it now, after all these years. Even in those days, when I suddenly lost my heart and surrendered myself to the frenzy of a first blind passion, I did not really think I had anything to regret. Until the age of twenty-two, my heart had remained impervious. My women friends, who weakened when confronted with the allurements of romantic love, envied and respected me. To them, my coolness, in my disdainful indifference to fond words and languishing glances showed common sense and strength of character. I had already established my reputation at sixteen, by trifling with the affections of a good-looking young fellow from my home town, and then afterwards spurning him, with the result that the poor boy tried to kill himself. And when he had recovered, he left Trento and ran away to Piedmont to join up as a volunteer. He died in one of the battles of '59 – I don't remember which. I was too young then to feel any remorse. And besides, my parents, relatives and acquaintances, all of them devoted to the Austrian government, which they served loyally as soldiers and administrators, had nothing else to say about the young hot-head's death but, 'Serves him right!'

In Venice, I was reborn. My beauty came into full bloom. Men's eyes would light up with a gleam of desire whenever they looked at me. Even without seeing them looking, I could feel their burning gaze on my body. The women, too, would openly stare at me, then admiringly examine me from head to toe. I would smile like a queen, like a goddess. In the gratification of my vanity, I became kind, indulgent, natural, carefree, witty: the greatness of my triumph made me appear almost modest.

I was invited with my husband, a representative of the Tyrolese nobility at the Diet of Innsbruck, to the Imperial Lord-Lieutenant's dinners and soirées. Whenever I entered a room, with my arms bare, in a *décolleté* gown of velvet and lace with a very long train, wearing a great flower of rubies with leaves of emeralds in my hair, I would sense a murmur running all around me. A blush of satisfaction would colour my cheeks. I would unassumingly take a few slow, solemn steps, without looking at anybody, and as the hostess came towards me and invited me to sit next to her, I would wave my fan in front of my face as if to hide modestly from the eyes of the astonished guests.

I never missed an occasion for a gondola-ride on the Grand Canal, in the cool of a summer's evening, when serenades were sung. At Quadri's café in Piazza San Marco I was surrounded by a host of satellites, as if I were the sun of a new planetary system. I would laugh, mock and tease those who tried to win me with their sighs or verses. I gave the impression of being an impregnable fortress, yet I did not try too hard to appear truly impregnable lest I discouraged anyone. My court of admirers consisted largely of junior officers and Tyrolese officials who were rather dull and very self-satisfied, which meant that the most fun were the most irresponsible; those who from their dissolute life had acquired, if nothing else, the insolent boldness of their own follies. There was one I knew who stood out from the crowd for two reasons. According to his own friends, he combined reckless profligacy with such a cynical lack of moral principles that nothing in this world seemed to him worthy of respect, save the penal code and military regulations. Besides which, he really was extremely handsome and extraordinarily strong: a cross between Adonis and Alcides. His complexion was white and rosy, he had blond curly hair, a beardless chin, ears so small they were like a girl's, and big restless-looking eyes of sky-blue. The expression on his face was sometimes mild, and sometimes fierce, but of a fierceness and mildness tempered by signs of a constant, almost cruel, irony. His head was set magnificently on his sturdy neck. His shoulders were not square and heavy, but sloped down gracefully. A close-fitting, white uniform of an Austrian officer showed off to perfection his muscular physique, which brought to mind those Roman statues of gladiators.

This infantry lieutenant, who was only twenty-four, two years older than me, had already succeeded in squandering the large estate inherited from his father, and still he continued to gamble, and whore, and to live like a lord – nobody could understand how he managed it. Yet no one excelled him in swimming, gymnastics, or physical strength. He had never had occasion to take part in battle, and he did not care for duelling. In fact, two young officers told me one evening that rather than fight, he had more than once swallowed the most appalling insults. Strong, handsome, degenerate, reprobate – I was attracted by him. I did not let him know it, because I took delight in teasing and riling this latter-day Hercules.

Venice, which I had never seen and so longed to see, spoke more to my senses than my intellect: I cared less for its monuments, whose history I did not know and beauty I did not understand, than for its green waters, starry skies, silvery moon, golden sunsets, and above all the black gondola in which I would recline, abandoning myself to the most voluptuous caprices of my imagination. In the intense heat of July, after a blazing-hot day, the fresh breeze would caress my brow as I travelled by boat from the Piazzetta to the island of Sant'Elena, or beyond, to Sant'Elisabetta and San Nicolo on the Lido: that west wind impregnated with a sharp salty tang would revive my limbs and my spirits, and seemed to whisper in my ears the passionate secrets of true love. I would trail my bare arm up to the elbow in the water, letting the lace trim on my short sleeve get wet; and then I watched the drops of water falling from my fingernails one by one, like the purest diamonds. One evening I took a ring from my finger – a ring my husband had given me, set with a big sparkling solitaire – and threw it far from the boat into the lagoon: I felt I had married the sea.

One day the Lord-Lieutenant's wife insisted on taking me to see the Accademia Gallery: I understood next to nothing. Since then, from travelling, and from talking to artists (there was one, as handsome as Raphael, who desperately wanted to teach me to paint), I have learned a few things; but at the time, although I did not know anything, the brightness of those colours, the richness of those reds, yellows, greens, blues, and whites – like painted music, rendered with such sensual passion – seemed to me not art but a Venetian aspect of Nature. And in the presence of Titian's golden *Assumption*, Paolo Veronese's magnificent *Feast*, or Bonifazio's fleshy, carnal, gleaming faces, I would be put in mind of the uninhibited songs I had heard the common people singing.

My husband smoked, snored, spoke ill of Piedmont, and bought himself cosmetics; I needed someone to love.

Now, this is how my terrible passion began for the Alcides, the white-uniformed Adonis with a name not much to my liking: Remigio. I was in the habit of going to Rima's floating baths, situated between the gardens of the Royal Palace and the Customs House Point. I had hired for one hour, from seven till eight, the Sirena, one of the two women's baths big enough to swim around in a little, and my maid came along to undress and dress me. But since no one else could enter, I did not bother to put on bathing clothes. The bath was screened round with wooden panels and covered with a grey awning with broad red stripes. The slated bottom was fixed at a depth to allow women of small stature to stand with their heads above the water, which did not even cover my shoulders.

O that lovely, clear, emerald-green water, in which I could see the shape of my body gracefully undulating, right down to my slender feet! And a few tiny, silvery fish darted around me. I swam the length of the Sirena; I beat the water with the flat of my hand until that diaphanous green was covered with white spray; I lay on my back, letting my long hair soak in the water, and trying to keep afloat for a moment without moving; I splashed my maid, who ran away; I laughed like a child.

A number of large openings, just below the surface, let the water flow in and out freely, and if you put your eye to the gaps in the ill-fitted screens you could see something of what was outside: the red campanile of San Giorgio, a stretch of the lagoon with boats swiftly sailing past, a thin strip of the military baths floating a little way off from my Sirena.

I knew that Lieutenant Remigio went swimming there. He cut such an heroic figure in the water: he would dive in head first, pick up a bottle from the bottom, and emerge from the bathing area by swimming out underneath the dressing rooms. I found his strength and agility so alluring, I would have given anything to be able to see him.

One morning while I was examining a bluish mark on my right thigh, probably a slight bruise, which marred a little the rosy whiteness of my skin, I heard a noise outside that sounded like someone swimming very fast. The disturbance of the water made cool waves that sent a shiver down my limbs, and all of a sudden, through one of the large gaps between the bottom of the pool and the screens, a man came into the Sirena. I did not cry out; I was not afraid. He was so white and handsome, he looked as if he were made of marble, but his broad chest rose and fell as he took deep breaths, and his blue eyes shone, and drops of water fell from his fair hair like a shower of lustrous pearls. He stood upright, half covered by the still unsettled water, and raised his limber, muscular arms aloft; he seemed to be rendering thanks to the gods, and saying, 'At last!'

So began our relationship. And from then on I saw him every day, whether out for a walk, or at a café or restaurant – for my husband had taken a liking to him, and often invited him. I also saw him in secret, and gradually our clandestine meetings became a positively daily occurrence. We were often alone for one or two hours, while the count slept between luncheon and dinner or went wandering off on his own round the city; then we would spend two or three hours together in public, exchanging the occasional fleeting hand-clasp. Sometimes he would step on my foot, often hurting me so much I became quite red in the face, but this very pain gave me pleasure. Never had I looked so beautiful, to others and to myself, never so healthy and light-hearted and happy – with myself, with life, with everything and everybody. The wicker chair that I sat on in Piazza San Marco became a throne. I thought that the military band that played Strauss waltzes and Meyerbeer melodies in front of the Old Procurators' Building were performing their music solely for me, and the blue sky and ancient monuments seemed to rejoice in my happiness.

Our meeting-place was not always the same. Sometimes Remigio would be waiting for me in a closed gondola on the filthy quayside of some long, dark alley leading to a narrow canal, lined with poor houses so decrepit and crooked they looked as if they were falling down, with rags of every colour hanging from the windows. And there were other times when, throwing caution to the winds, we would take a boat in some busy part of the city, even from the landing in front of the Piazzetta. Wearing a thick veil to cover my face, I would visit him in a house by the barracks at San Sepolcro, encountering in the dark shadows of its winding staircase officers and men who would not let me pass without some show of gallantry. In that house, where the sun never shone, the musty smell of dampness was combined with the nauseating stench of stale tobacco smoke hanging in the air in those unventilated rooms.

This young lawyer Gino irritates me. He looks at me with those wildly staring eyes that often make me laugh, but sometimes make my blood run cold. He says he cannot go on living without some kind word of affection from me; he begs, weeps, sobs. He keeps saying, 'Contessa, do you remember that day when you turned to me, there in the doorway, and said in the voice of an angel, "There's hope for you."' And he goes on and on, begging for pity, sobbing and weeping. I cannot stand any more of it. A few days ago I let him take my hand. He kissed it repeatedly, so hard that he left bruises on my skin. The fact is, I am tired of him! Yesterday I lost my temper. I shouted at him, and told him not to bother me any more, and said that he was never to attempt to set foot in my house again, and if he ever dared to show his face I would have him thrown out by the servants, and would tell the count the whole story. He turned so pale that his black eyes looked like two holes in a wall of plaster. He rose from the sofa and staggered out, without looking at me. He'll be back, he'll be back, I bet he will. But the sad truth is, the only thing capable of affecting me deeply is the memory of a man of whose total degeneracy I was, to the shame of raging passion for him, perfectly aware.

Every so often Remigio would ask me for money. At first he did so in a roundabout way: he had some gambling debt, or there was a dinner to which he had to treat his companions for some special occasion – he would return the money in a few days' time. In the end he was asking for a hundred florins here, two hundred florins there, without any excuse. Once he asked me for a thousand lire. I gave it to him, and was pleased to give it. I had some savings of my own and, besides, my husband was generous towards me, indeed he was happy when I asked him for something. But there came a point when he thought I was spending too much. I took offence and became furiously angry; as a rule easy-going and compliant, he held out for a whole day.

That was the day that Remigio urgently needed two hundred and fifty florins, straightaway. He was so loving, and said so many sweet things, in a voice so passionate that I was glad to be able to give him a diamond hairpin, which, if I remember rightly, cost forty gold napoleons.

The next day Remigio failed to keep our appointment. I spent a good hour pacing up and down some of those little alleyways on the far side of the Rialto Bridge, causing people to eye me with sly curiosity, and prompting jokes at my expense. In the end, my cheeks were burning with shame and tears of anger filled my eyes. Despairing by then of meeting my lover, and imagining God knows what might have happened to him, I ran to his house, panting for breath and almost out of my mind.

His batman, who was polishing his sabre, told me that there had been no sight of the lieutenant since the day before.

'Out all night?' I asked, not quite understanding.

Whistling, the soldier nodded.

'For God's sake, run and find out what's happened to him. He must have had some dreadful accident – he may have been injured, or killed!'

The soldier shrugged, with a sarcastic laugh.

'Well, tell me, where is the lieutenant?' As he continued to laugh, I had grabbed the soldier by the arm, and I shook him hard. He brought his moustache right up close to my face. I leapt back, but said again, 'For pity's sake, tell me.'

He finally growled, 'Dining with Gigia, or Cate, or Nana, or with all three together. A dreadful accident? Hah!'

I realized then that Lieutenant Remigio was my life. My blood froze. I collapsed almost unconscious on the bed in that dingy room, and had he not at that moment appeared in the doorway my heart would have burst in a fit of rage and suspicion. I was insanely jealous; if need be, I was capable of becoming criminally jealous.

* * *

116

It was the very depravity of the man that attracted me.

When he declared, 'I swear to you, Livia, I shall never love or embrace any other woman but you ...', I believed him. And when he knelt before me, I looked at him adoringly, as though he were a god. If anyone had asked me, 'Would you have Remigio become a hero?', I would have replied no. What use would I have had for a hero? Perfect virtue would have seemed dull and worthless compared with his vices. To me, his infidelity, dishonesty, wantonness and lack of restraint constituted a mysterious but powerful strength to which I was happy, and proud, to enslave myself. The more depraved his heart appeared, the more wonderfully hand-some his body.

Twice only, and only momentarily, I would have wished him to be different. We were walking one day along the quayside of a canal marking the perimeter of the Arsenal. It was a blindingly bright, sunny morning. On our left, the tall chimneys, their tops like upturned bells, the white cornices and red roofs stood against the turquoise-blue sky, whilst on our right, austere and forbidding, ran the long boundary wall round the shipyards. We rested our dazzled eyes upon dark patches of shade, in the gloom of an archway or narrow alley. And the water glistened with every shade of green, reflecting every colour, disappearing here and there into cavernous holes and strips of dense blackness. There were ten or twelve young urchins running and jumping along the canalside, which had no barrier of any kind on the waterfront, and shouting at the tops of their voices. Some of them were very small, some were a bit older. One of the younger ones – a tubby little fellow, practically naked, with blond curls crown-ing his pink, chubby face – was making a fiendish racket, cuffing and pinching his companions, then running off like streaked lightning.

I stopped to watch, while Remigio was telling me of his past extravagances. All of a sudden, in his headlong rush, that little demon of a child was unable to stop himself at the edge of the quay and went flying into the canal. There was a yell and a splash, then at once the air was ringing with the cries of all the children and all the women who had been talking in the street or looking out of their windows. But above the clamour rose the shrill, desperate, piercing shriek of the young mother, who threw herself at Remigio's feet – he being the only man on the scene – screaming, 'Save him, please, save him!'

With icy coldness Remigio said to the woman, 'I can't swim.'

Meanwhile, one of the older boys had jumped into the water, grabbed the youngster by his blond curls and dragged him to the bank. It all happened in an instant. The screeching turned into enthusiastic cheers; women and children wept with joy; people came running from all around to see; and the fair-haired child looked around with his big blue eyes, amazed at such a fuss. With a violent tug Remigio drew me away from the crowd.

The other time that my lover somewhat disappointed me, the reason was as follows. He had been overheard, at Quadri's, speaking German with some Tyrolese officials, loudly disparaging the Venetians. A gentleman sitting in a corner leapt to his feet, and planting himself in front of Remigio, who was in uniform, he shouted, 'Soldier, you're a coward!' And he threw three or four visiting cards in his face. Pandemonium broke out. The next day the seconds were supposed to arrange the duel, but having noticed that his adversary was a small thin man, and not very strong, Remigio refused pistols, and he refused swords; although the choice of weapons should have been the challenger's, being confident of the strength of his own arm, he insisted on sabres. The Venetian gave way to his high-handedness, but was imprisoned before the duel could take place, and Remigio received orders to proceed immediately to a new posting in Croatia.

When I learned of this I was in despair: I could not live without that man. I so prevailed upon the Lord-Lieutenant's wife, and my husband, at my entreaty, so lobbied the Governor and the Generals, that Remigio managed to get himself transferred to Trento, just when the count and I were due to return there. Everything thus far had favoured my blind passion.

I have not set eyes on this notebook of mine for the past three months. I dared not take it away with me, and, I confess, I regretted leaving it behind in Trento. Going back in my mind over those events of so long ago, my heartbeat starts to quicken again, and I feel the hot breath of youth blowing around me.

My manuscript has been kept under triple lock in my secret safe at the back of the alcove in my bedroom; and it was sealed, with five seals, inside a big envelope, on which I had written in large letters, before going away, 'I entrust to my husband's honour the secret of these pages, which he is to burn without opening, after my death.'

I went away without the slightest misgiving. I was sure that, whatever his suspicions, the count would have religiously carried out his wife's wishes.

My maid has just told me something that has annoyed me: the young lawyer Gino is getting married.

So much for the faithfulness of men, so much for undying passion! 'Contessa Livia, I shall die, I shall kill myself. Not until I've shed the very last drop of my blood will your image fade from my heart. Treat me like a slave, but allow me to adore you like a goddess.' Melodramatic words, but a few months later and there is nothing left to show for them: love, frenzy, vows, tears, sobs – all gone without trace. How contemptible is human nature! And seeing those black eyes in that pallid face, anyone would have said that they gleamed with the deep sincerity of an impassioned soul. How his lips stammered and his arteries throbbed and his hands trembled and his whole body grovelled at my feet. That despicable, scrofulous wretch of a lawyer richly deserved to be sent packing. The dolt!

And whom is he marrying? An eighteen-year-old ninny whose parents would not bring her to my house because Contessa Livia is known to be too risquée. A vapid creature with two red apples for cheeks; short, fat, pink hands; a stable-boy's feet; and the pert air of a little saint, as a consolation. And the man who is taking such a goose for his wife dared to love me and to tell me so! It makes my face burn . . .

Even if he was no gentleman, that officer of mine, sixteen years ago, was at least a real man. When he put his arms around my waist, he used to squeeze the breath out of me, and he would bite my shoulders until they bled.

Vague rumours of war began to circulate, and then came the usual contradictory announcements and the usual denials: they're arming, they're not arming, yes, no. Meanwhile, a certain mood, at once feverish and mysterious, spread, from the military to civilians. The trains began to run late, and to bring in more soldiers and horses and carriages and cannons, while the newspapers kept denying that there was even the slightest mobilization going on at all. Ignoring the evidence of my own eyes, I believed the newspapers, so scared I was by the thought of a war. I feared for my lover's life; but I feared even more the long inevitable separation that it would surely have meant for us. And indeed, on the last day of March, Remigio was ordered to report to Verona. Before his departure, he was given two days' leave, which we spent together, never for one moment apart, in the shabby room of an inn on Lake Cavedine. And he swore to come and see me soon, and I swore to go to Verona if he could not get away. As I kissed him for the last time, I thrust into his pocket a purse containing fifty napoleons.

When the count returned from the country, ten or twelve days after Remigio had gone, he found me thin and pale. I really was suffering horribly. Every so often my head would start to swim and I would feel dizzy, and three or four times I was so unsteady I had to lean against the wall or a piece of furniture so as not to fall. The doctors that my husband, concerned and worried, insisted on consulting kept shrugging their shoulders and saying, 'It's a matter of nerves.' They told me to take exercise, to eat, sleep and cheer up.

It was mid April and by then the preparations for war were undisguised. All types of soldiers filled the streets; battalions marched to the sound of brass bands and drums; aides-de camp went flying past on their horses; old generals, a little bent in the saddle, rode at a trot, followed by the General Staff, looking bold and splendid on their prancing mounts. These preparations filled me with grotesque fears. The Italians wanted to kill all the Austrians; Garibaldi and his hordes of red devils wanted to butcher every prisoner taken captive: there was clearly going to be a bloodbath.

I was in a complete state of frenzy. In six weeks I had received only four letters from Verona. The postal service was virtually non-existent: letters had to be entrusted, after much begging and bribing, to anybody willing to face the difficulties and interminable delays the journey entailed; someone who needed, and dared, to travel from one place to another. Unable any longer to bear the anguish to which Remigio's silence, whether deliberate or innocent, condemned me night and day, I had determined to attempt the journey. But how was I to manage, a beautiful young woman alone amid the brutality of soldiers made bolder by loose discipline and by the thought of the very dangers they were about to meet.

One morning at daybreak, having fallen asleep after an endless night spent tossing and turning, I was suddenly awakened by a noise. I opened my eyes and saw Remigio at my bedside. I thought I was dreaming.

The soft, rosy light of dawn already brightened the room. I leapt out of bed to close the alcove curtains, and we began to talk in lowered voices. I was worried: the count, who was sleeping in the next room but one, might hear us, and appear; the servants might have seen my lover stealing in at this early hour. He reassured me with a few impatient words: as on previous occasions he had knocked at the ground-floor window where the chambermaid slept. She had opened the door to him very quietly and he had entered without anyone having the least suspicion. I was not much bothered about the maid, since she already knew everything; but the worst part was getting out: he had to be quick. I jumped out of bed again and went to listen at the door of my husband's room: he was snoring.

'You're stopping in Trento, aren't you?'
'You've taken leave of your senses.'
'A few days at least?'
'Impossible.'
'A day?'
'I'm leaving in an hour.'

I was devastated. Brimming with bright hope the moment before, my heart was now filled with anguish and fear.

'And don't try to keep me. War is no time for playing games.'

'Damn the war!'

'You're right. By all accounts, it's going to be terrible.'

'Listen, couldn't you run away, couldn't you hide? I'll help you. I don't want your life to be in danger.'

'Don't be silly. I'd be found and captured, and shot as a deserter.'

'Shot!'

'There's something I need from you.'

'My life, anything.'

'No, two thousand five hundred florins.'

'My God, how am I to manage that?'

'Do you want to save me?'

'At whatever the price.'

'Then listen. For two thousand five hundred florins two doctors from the military hospital and two with the brigade will issue me with a genuine sickness certificate, and come and visit me occasionally in order to confirm to HQ that I have some complaint which makes me totally unfit for service. I don't lose rank, I don't lose any pay, I'm out of any danger, able to stay quietly at home, limping a little, it's true, because of a bad attack of sciatica or a damaged leg-bone, but safe and happy. I'll find some petty clerk to play cards with; I'll eat and drink and sleep in late. It will be a bore having to be at home all day, but at night, still taking care to limp slightly, I'll be able to get out and have some fun. How do you like that?'

'I'd like it, if you were in Trento. I'd see you every day, twice a day. Once they believe you're ill, it's all the same whether you're in Verona or Trento, isn't it?'

'No, the regulations are that a sick soldier has to remain where Headquarters are based, under the doctors' constant and scrupulous supervision. But I shall return as soon as the war is over – the fighting will be bitter, but brief.'

'Will you love me always, will you always be faithful, will you never look at another woman? Do you swear?'

'Yes, yes, I swear. But it's getting late and I need those two thousand five hundred florins.'

'Right away?'

'Of course. I must take them with me.'

'But I doubt that there are even fifty gold napoleons in my safe. I never keep much money.'

'Well, find some.'

'What do you mean, find some? How do you expect me to ask my husband, now, at this hour – with what excuse, to give to whom?'

'The proof of love is making sacrifices. You don't love me then.'

'Not love you? When I'd willingly give you every drop of my blood.'

'That's just talk. If you haven't the money, give me jewellery.'

I did not answer, and felt myself turn pale.

Realizing the effect his last words had had upon me, Remigio clasped me in his arms of iron, and in a different tone of voice repeated several times, 'You know I love you, Livia darling, and that I'll love you as long as there's a breath of life in me. But save my life, I beg you, save it for yourself, if you love me.'

He took my hands and kissed them.

I was already persuaded. I went over to my writing-table to fetch the three little keys to my safe. I was afraid of making a noise, and walked on tiptoe even though I was barefooted.

Remigio came with me into the study behind the alcove. I locked the door lest the count should hear, then opened the safe with some difficulty, for I was in such a state, and took out a complete set of diamonds, murmuring, 'Here, take them. They cost almost twelve thousand lire. Will you manage to sell them?'

Remigio took the jewellery case from my hand. He looked at the jewels and said, 'There are money-lenders everywhere.'

'It would be a shame to part with them for too little. Try and find some way of getting them back again.'

I was heartbroken. The tiara especially suited me so well.

'And will you give me the money as well?' asked Remigio. 'It would be useful.'

I searched in the safe for the gold napoleons, which I had stacked in a pile, and handed them to him, without counting them. He kissed me, and was about to rush off. I held him back. He pushed me away impatiently, saying, 'If you value my life, let me go.'

'Take care, can't you hear your boots squeak? In any case, wait. I need to see if the maid's there. She'll have to let you out.'

Sure enough, the maid was waiting in a nearby room.

'You'll write to me soon?'

'Yes.'

'Every other day?'

I wanted to give my lover, the man I loved so much, one last kiss; he was already gone.

I opened the windows and looked out into the street. The sun shone golden on the high mountainpeaks. The stable-boy and the scullery lad were standing in front of the gate-way, talking. They looked up and saw me. Then they saw Remigio emerging from the house and hurrying away with his coat pockets bulging.

I went back to bed and cried all day long. I felt drained of energy. The next morning the doctor found that I had a temperature and was running a high fever. He prescribed quinine, which I did not take. I wanted to die. A whole week after Remigio's visit, the maid, as calm as ever, brought me a letter. As soon as I saw it, I snatched it from her hand. I had guessed it was from him – the first since his departure – and I sat down to read it with such frantic eagerness that when I came to the end I had to read it all over again; I had not taken any of it in.

I still remember it word for word, so often did the terrible events that followed give me cause to recall them:

'Beloved Livia,
You've saved my life. I sold the set of diamonds to some Shylock, for not much, to tell the truth, but in these times of fear and turmoil it was impossible to get more than two thousand florins – enough to fill the doctors' voracious bellies. Before taking ill, I found a comfortable room near the Adige, in Via Santo Stefano 147 (write to me at this address). It is big and clean, with its own hallway leading directly onto the stairs. I have stocked up with tobacco, rum, playing cards and the entire works of Charles-Paul de Kock and Dumas. I've no lack of agreeable company, all male (don't panic), and all of them scroungers, and were it not for having to appear lame, and being unable to leave the house during the day, I would say that I was the happiest man in the world. Of course, there's one thing missing – your self, darling Livia, that I adore and would like to hold in my arms day and night. Well, now, don't worry about a thing. I shall read the news of the war, while having a smoke; and the more Italians and Austrians go to hell, the more I shall enjoy it. Love me always, as I love you. As soon as the war is over and these wretched

126

doctors, who are costing me a tidy sum, leave me in peace, I shall come running to embrace you, more passionate than ever.

Yours,

Remigio'

The letter left me disconcerted and shocked, so vulgar did it seem. But then, poring over it, I gradually persuaded myself that the tone in which it was written was affectedly light and gay, and that my lover had made a painful but very noble effort to contain the violence of his own feelings, so as not to fan the flames of my already blazing passion, and in order to calm my mind a little, knowing how terribly anxious I was. I studied every phrase, every syllable of the letter. I had burned all the others almost as soon as I received them: this one I kept in a little pocket of my purse, and often took it out when I was alone, after locking myself in the room. Everything confirmed me in my wishful thinking: these expressions of love seemed all the more heartfelt for being hasty, and these coarse cynical remarks, I fancied, were sublime in their generous self-sacrifice. I so badly needed to believe in his infatuation, as an excuse for my own; and his cowardice thrilled my heart because I believed myself to be the cause of it. But my overheated imagination did not stop there. Who knows, I thought to myself, who knows whether this letter might not be all a well-intentioned deceit. Perhaps he has already gone to the battlefield, perhaps he is even now facing the enemy. But caring more for me than for himself, not wanting me to die of terror and dismay, he was allaying my fears by telling a white lie. The idea had no sooner occurred to me than I became obsessed with it. The insomnia, aversion to food, and physical ailments I was suffering contributed to a state of acute mental feverishness.

I was living in virtual solitude. My social circle had already been getting gradually more restricted, because for some time now the noble families of Trentino, opposed to the count's political opinions, had very politely but firmly been keeping their distance. The young people, being fervently nationalist, unceremoniously avoided us, indeed hated us. Local officials, not knowing how the war would end, and wary of compromising themselves one way or another, now avoided setting foot in our house. So, we were seeing a few pro-Austrian aristocrats, all of them penniless and parasitic, and a few high-ranking Tyrolese officials, who were crass, pig-headed and stank of beer and cheap tobacco. Army officers no longer had any free time to spare, nor any desire to spend it in my company.

My relationship with Remigio, which everybody but my husband knew about, had increased my isolation – an isolation that I actually welcomed, indeed needed, given the state of mind I had been living in for some while. Remigio had not written again since that memorable letter. I imagined him facing perils that seemed all the more horrible for being uncertain. I could perhaps have lived with the sure risks of battle, but the suspense of not knowing whether my lover was fighting or not was driving me mad. I wrote to Verona to a general I knew, to two colonels, then to one of those junior officers who had so long courted me in Venice: I received no reply. I sent Remigio countless letters: he never answered.

Meanwhile, hostilities began: civilian life was overridden; the railways and roads were solely for the use of munitions wagons, ambulance carts and supply trucks; of cavalry brigades that went by amid clouds of dust, artillery units that made the houses shake, and infantry regiments that kept coming, one after another, in an endless winding column, creeping along like a snake trying to encompass the whole world within its enormous coils.

One breathlessly hot morning, 26th June, came the first news of a dreadful battle: Austria was defeated, with ten thousand dead, twenty thousand wounded, the standards lost, and Verona, still ours, but, like the other strongholds, close to surrendering to the Italians' diabolical onslaught.

My husband was in the country and was to be away for a week.

I rang furiously; the maid did not come. I rang again; the butler appeared in the doorway.

'Are you all asleep? Lazy wretches! Send me the coachman, at once, do you hear?'

A few minutes later an apprehensive-looking Giacomo arrived, buttoning up his livery.

'How many miles is it from here to Verona?'

He thought for a moment.

'Well?' I said, losing my temper.

Giacomo made his calculations. 'From here to Rovereto, about fourteen. From Rovereto to Verona must be . . . I don't know . . . with two good horses it would be ten hours, give or take a little, without counting the stops.'

'You've never driven with the horses from Trento to Verona?'

'No, signora contessa. I've done the journey from Rovereto to Verona.'

'It doesn't matter. I know myself that it's two hours to Rovereto from here.'

'Forgive me, signora contessa, two and a half.'

'So two and ten makes twelve in total.'

'Let's say thirteen, signora contessa, and going at a good pace.'

'How many horses has the count taken with him?'

'His usual black mare.'

'So there are four in the stables.'

'Yes, signora contessa: Fanny, Candida, Lampo and the stallion.'

'Could you harness all four of them?'

'Together?'

'Yes, together.'

Giacomo smiled with a benevolently pitying look. 'I'm sorry, signora contessa, that can't be done. The stallion . . .'

'Well, then, harness the other three.'

'Poor Lampo is lame, and can't even manage a brisk walk.'

'Then for God's sake, harness Fanny and Candida as usual,' I shouted, stamping my feet. Then I added, 'For tomorrow morning, at four.'

'As you wish, signora contessa. And, forgive me, so that I know how much fodder to take, where are we going?'

'To Verona.'

'Verona! God help us! In how many days?'

'By evening.'

'Forgive me, signora contessa, but that's just not possible.'

'And I insist on it, do you understand?'

I replied in such an imperious tone that the poor man scarcely had the courage to stammer out, 'Have a heart, signora contessa. It'll be the death of both horses, and the master will throw me out into the street.'

'I take full responsibility. Do as you're told and don't worry about anything else.' And I gave him four gold coins. 'I'll give you twice as much on our return, on condition that you don't breathe a word to anybody.'

'There's no danger of that. But what about the chaos on the roads – the wagons and cannons, unruly soldiers, trouble from the police?'

'I'll worry about that.'

Giacomo bowed his head, resigned but not convinced.

'What time will we get to Verona?'

'That's in the hands of Providence, signora contessa. And it'll be a miracle if we all get there alive – you, signora contessa, me, and the two poor beasts. For me, it doesn't matter, but for you and the horses!'

'Well, at four o'clock then, and not a word. If you hold your tongue, you shall have what I promised. If you talk, I'll sack you on the spot, with no wages. Is that clear? See to it that everyone, including the chambermaid, thinks we're going to see Marchesa Giulia at San Michele.'

Wearing a gloomy expression, Giacomo bowed and left the room.

At dawn I was in the carriage, and on my way. I had drawn the curtains over the windows, and out of a corner I watched the gasping dusty foot-soldiers, who lined up along the ditches, thinking there was some important person in the coach; some of them gave a military salute.

From time to time, to my intense annoyance, we had to slow down, or actually stop for a few minutes to wait for heavy swaying wagons to get out of our way. However, things went much better than Giacomo had predicted. A mounted police patrol stopped the carriage, but when the sergeant saw there was a lady inside he contented himself with calling out chivalrously, 'Safe journey!' After Rovereto, at Pieve, we stopped to rest a little. Then, having unhitched the mares at Borghetto, for they could take no more, we spent a good three hours there that to me felt like three years, being cooped up inside the carriage as I was, listening to the complaining and swearing of the squads of soldiers who would collapse on the ground near the inn for a few moments, beneath the meagre shade of the stunted trees, to eat a crust of bread and take a swig of water. I must have called Giacomo ten times. He came to the window looking extremely disgruntled, forcing himself to appear calm. Then raising his hat, he kept saying, 'Another ten minutes, signora contessa.'

Eventually, we set off again, thank God. The River Adige, which we drove alongside, was almost dry; the fields looked parched; the road gleamed with a blinding whiteness; there was not a cloud to be seen in the blue skies. The sides of the carriage were burning hot and I felt suffocated in that oppressive heat and thick dust. My forehead was beaded with sweat, and I drummed my feet with impatience. I did not spare Chiusa a glance, but listened for the crack of Giacomo's whip. At Pescantina we stopped again for fresh horses: it was another ten long miles to Verona and the poor beasts could hardly walk. The sun had gone down in a fiery blaze. And still there were wagons and soldiers, police patrols, and the dust, with a deafening din and a screech of metal at times, and at other times a confused and fearful murmur, in which it was possible to distinguish groans and curses and verses of lewd songs sung by muffled voices. So far, we had been travelling with the tide of men and vehicles, now we passed a number of ambulance carts coming towards us, and several companies of walking wounded; soldiers with their arms in slings, and with bandages round their heads, pale-faced, stooped, limping, and in tatters. And Remigio? Remigio? I shouted to Giacomo to use the whip-handle on the horses. It was beginning to get dark.

We reached the walls of Verona at about nine. And so great was the panic, so great the confusion, that no one paid any attention to the carriage, and we were able to get to the Torre di Londra hotel without further hindrance. There was not a room to be had, not so much as a corner to sleep in, either in the hotel, or, so I was assured, in any other lodging house in the city: they had all been requisitioned for officers. The horses were tied up in the courtyard, more dead than alive; Giacomo was to attend to them. I jumped out of the carriage at last.

I had some young ragamuffin take me to number 147 in Via Santo Stefano. We had to walk up and down the street several times, looking above the doorways, before we were able to discern the number of the house by the glimmer of the few streetlights.

If Remigio was at home, I wanted to surprise him. My limbs were all atremble with impatience and desire, but he might be in bed, he might be with someone, and although I desperately wanted to see him at once, yet I felt I ought to send the boy on ahead as a scout. He was crafty and understood immediately: he was to ring and ask for the lieutenant on a matter of the utmost urgency, insist that he open the door, go upstairs and tell him some story – for instance, that a gentleman whose name he had forgotten, who was staying at the Torre di Londra hotel, wanted news of his health, without delay. As the boy came out he was to leave open the door to Remigio's lodgings, as well as the street door. I hid by the side of the house, in an alleyway running from the road down to the river.

The boy rang the bell.

An angry voice came from the top floor.

'Who is it?'

'Is Lieutenant Ruz there?'

'It's the other bell, the middle one. Damn you!'

The boy rang the other bell. A minute went by that seemed to last for ever, and no one appeared. The boy rang again. Then from the second floor a woman's voice called out, 'Who is it?'

'Is Lieutenant Ruz there?'

133

'Yes, but he won't see anybody.'

'I need to speak to him.'

'Tomorrow morning, after nine.'

'No, this evening. Are you afraid of burglars?'

Another minute went by, and at last the door opened.

There was Remigio! My heart was bursting with joy. My eyes grew clouded and I had to lean against the wall for support. Shortly afterwards the boy returned. Remigio had sent him packing, but he had managed to leave both doors ajar. I regained control of myself, gave the cunning lad a few coins, and slipped into the house. I had thought to bring some matches with me: on the second floor landing there were two doors, with Remigio's visiting card pinned above one of them. I pushed it and it swung open, and without making a sound I entered a room that was practically dark. This was the culmination of all my hopes: I could already feel the arms of my lover – the man for whom I would unhesitatingly have given everything I owned, including my life – crushing me to his broad chest. I could feel his teeth biting into my skin, and I was overwhelmed in anticipation with ineffable bliss.

I felt weak with relief, and had to sit down on a chair in the hall. Hearing and seeing as if in a deep dream, I had lost all sense of reality. But someone nearby was laughing and laughing: it was a woman's laughter, shrill, coarse and boisterous, and it gradually roused me. I listened, rising from my seat, and, holding my breath, approached a door that stood wide open, through which I could see into a huge, brightly lit room. I was standing in shadow, out of sight. Oh, why did God not strike me blind at that moment? There was a table with the remains of a meal on it. Beyond the table was a big green sofa: there lay Remigio, playfully tickling a girl's armpit. She was hooting and shrieking with laughter,

134

wriggling and writhing all over, trying in vain to free herself from his clutches, and he was kissing her on the arms, the neck, the nape – wherever he could.

I was incapable of moving: I was nailed to the spot, my eyes transfixed, my ears straining to hear, my throat dry.

The man, tiring of this game, grabbed the girl by the wrist and sat her on his lap. Then they began talking, often breaking off for caresses and playfulness. I heard the words, but their meaning escaped me. Suddenly the woman said my name.

'Show me the pictures of Contessa Livia.'

'You've seen them so many times already.'

'Show them to me, please.'

Without getting up from the sofa, the man lifted the edge of the tablecloth, opened the drawer of the table, and took out some papers. The girl, who had now turned serious, searched through them for the photographs and gazed at them for a long time.

Then she said, 'Is Contessa Livia beautiful?'

'You can see she is.'

'You don't understand: I want to know whether you think she's more beautiful than I am.'

'To me, no woman could be more beautiful than you.'

'Look, in this photograph, her ballgown leaves her arms and shoulders completely bare, right down to here.' And the young girl rearranged her blouse, holding up the picture for comparison.

'Look, do you think I'm more beautiful?'

The man kissed her between her breasts. 'A thousand times more beautiful!' he exclaimed.

The girl stood by the lamp, staring at the man, who smiled at her, and she picked up the four pictures one by one and very slowly tore each of them into four pieces and let the shreds drop on to the table, amid the plates and glasses. The man kept smiling.

'But you also tell her that you love her, you devil.'

'You know I say it to her as little as possible. But I need her, and we would not be here together, darling, if she hadn't given me that money I told you about. Those wretched doctors made me pay dearly for my life.'

'How much were you left with?'

'Five hundred florins, some of which is already spent. I need to write to my treasure-house in Trento: one gold coin for every sweet word.'

'And yet,' said the woman, her eyes filled with tears, 'and yet it upsets me.'

The man drew her very close to him on the green sofa, murmuring, 'Now, I don't want any tears.'

At that point I had a complete change of heart: love turned to loathing. I found myself in the street, not knowing where I was going. I was jostled by groups of soldiers that passed me in the darkness. Stretchers went by, from which came long drawn-out groans or shrill cries of pain, and I saw a few scuttling townsfolk, a few frightened peasants. No one paid any attention to me, as I hugged close to the walls of the houses, dressed all in black with a thick veil over my face. I came to a broad avenue planted with shadowy trees, where the river, flowing on my right, cooled the breathless air a little. The water was almost lost in the shadows, but I was not tempted, even for one second, to commit suicide. Although I was not in the least aware of it, an ugly idea, as yet vague and indistinct, had already germinated within me, and it gradually invaded my heart and mind entirely: the idea of revenge.

I had given everything to that man. He had been my life.

Without him, I had felt as though I would die; with him, I had been in heaven. And he gave his heart and kisses to another woman! The entire scene I had just witnessed was conjured up before me; I could still see that wanton lust before my very eyes. It was intolerable! For his sake I had come running, surmounting every obstacle, scorning every danger, casting my good name into the mud. I had come running to help him, to comfort him, and I find him safe and sound, more handsome than ever, in someone else's arms! And the pair of them – he who owes me everything, and his sweetheart – insult my dignity and love, and deride and ridicule me. And it is I who am paying for their orgies! That blonde minx brazenly boasts of being more beautiful than me, and (this was the supreme insult that really rankled) he himself proclaims her more beautiful!

All this emotion had left me weak: the anger boiling inside me had afflicted my whole body with a burning fever that made my legs tremble. I did not know where I was. I would not, could not, ask some passer-by to take me back to the inn, to be shut up inside the carriage again. I sat down on the riverbank, staring up at the dark sky. Unable to rest, I went back into the city-streets. I was going out of my mind. I was dropping with exhaustion, and had not eaten for eighteen hours. I happened to find myself outside a modest coffee-house. I passed in front of the window several times; it looked empty, so I went inside and sat down in the farthest and darkest corner, and ordered something.

In the opposite corner, lying stretched out on the narrow red banquette that ran all the way round that huge, damp, dimly lit, low-ceilinged room were two soldiers, smoking and yawning. Shortly afterwards another two officers came in: a tall, thin young man of maybe nineteen, with a neat moustache; and a stocky, thick-set fellow of about forty, who had a purple face, all lumps and warts, and coal-black, bushy eyebrows, while the moustaches under his big nose were so thick and coarse they looked like horsehair. He had in his mouth a short-stemmed Bohemian pipe with an enormous bowl that issued great clouds of smoke, rising one after the other, to darken the ceiling.

The young man went straight over to greet the officers in the corner. I heard him say, 'In the space of two hours I've seen forty men die on the operating table under the knife – the surgeons were tossing aside arms and legs as though playing ball, and they were trepanning and mending heads . . .'

'They should mend the heads of our generals,' growled the pipe-smoker sarcastically.

No one took any notice of me.

A girl came in, alone, who looked like a shop-girl, and she sat down beside the thin young officer. 'Will you buy me a coffee?' she asked him aloud.

After some conversation, to which I paid no attention, one of the two soldiers lying down said to the girl, without moving, 'You know, I saw that Lieutenant Remigio of yours, Costanza.'

'When?' asked the woman.

'Today. I went to visit him. He was with Giustina. Do you know her?'

'Yes, that fair-haired girl with three false teeth.'

'I've never noticed.'

'Take a good look at her. And how is Remigio?'

'He has the odd twinge in his leg that makes him yelp every now and then, and he limps a bit, that's all. A truly providential illness, that was. Other men are risking their lives, wearing themselves out with hunger and exhaustion in this infernal heat, suffering all the calamities of this war, while he has fun, eating and drinking, with someone to pay his keep.'

'Who on earth is keeping a wastrel like that?'

'A lady.'

'An old crone.'

'No, my dear, a beautiful young woman, a millionairess and a countess, what's more, who's madly in love with him.'

'And she pays for the Lieutenant's amusements?'

'She gives him money – a lot of money.'

'Poor fool!'

'Remigio calls her his Messalina. He hasn't told me her family name, but he did say that she was from Trento and that her first name was Livia. Is there anyone here who knows Trento?'

The thin officer said, 'I'll ask round and let you know whatever I find out, tomorrow evening, assuming we're still in Verona by then. Contessa Silvia, was that it?'

'Livia, Contessa Livia, and don't forget,' shouted the recumbent officer.

Costanza spoke up again. 'But is Remigio really unwell then?'

'That's for sure. You see, no one can fool four doctors: one from Remigio's own regiment; one, selected by the general, from another regiment; and two from the military hospital. Every three days they go and visit him. They squeeze and tap and tug his leg, and make him yell. Once he fainted. He's better now.'

'He'll be cured as soon as the war's over,' Costanza insisted.

'Don't even say that as a joke,' said the other officer lying stretched out, who had not spoken till then. 'Let me tell you that if there were the least suspicion of chicanery the lieutenant and the doctors would be shot within twenty-four hours, one as a deserter from the field of battle, the others as accomplices and accessories.'

'And they would deserve it, by God!' roared the Bohemian without removing the pipe from his mouth.

The young officer added, 'General Hauptmann wouldn't even wait twenty-four hours.'

At these words the hazy idea already in my mind became vividly clear: I had found the solution.

'General Hauptmann,' I repeated to myself.

Overcome, as the blood rushed to my head, I was obliged to remove the veil completely from my face. I felt parched, and called for some water. Alerted to my presence, the officers immediately came crowding round me.

'Ah, what a beautiful woman!'

'Is there anything you need?'

'Would you like a glass of Marsala?'

'May we keep you company?'

'Are you waiting for someone?'

'What wonderful eyes!'

'Such lips were meant for kissing!'

The thin young officer had insinuated himself onto the banquette, next to me. Being the youngest, he wanted to prove himself the boldest. I freed myself from his clutches and tried to get up to leave, but two others held me back. The ugly Bohemian looked on, smoking his pipe. I turned to him and cried, 'Sir, I am a lady. Help me, and escort me back to the Torre di Londra.'

The Bohemian pushed his way over, and practically sent the young officer flying. Then, looking stern and serious, he put his pipe in his pocket and offered me his arm.

We left together. On the way to the hotel, which was not far, he said little, but spoke to me with respect. I asked him who General Hauptmann was, where he had his office, and further information that I had my own good reasons for wanting to know.

I learned that the General was commander-in-chief of this stronghold, and that his Headquarters was based in Castel San Pietro.

The carriage entrance to the inn was still wide open although it was long past one in the morning. There was a great coming and going of soldiers and civilians. I thanked the officer, who reeked of infernal tobacco, and I made myself as comfortable as I could on the cushions in my carriage that stood in a corner of the yard. Being dead tired, I soon dozed off, but the sound of someone banging on the window woke me with a start.

The rough, coarse voice of the Bohemian was saying repeatedly, 'It's me, signora contessa. With all due respect, I'd just like a word with you.'

I lowered the window and the officer handed me something: it was my purse, which I had left behind on the table in the coffee-house in the confusion that had arisen when I was about to pay. His three companions had found it and given it to him.

He said solemnly, 'There's not a piece of paper or a single coin missing.'

'But were the papers read?' I was thinking of Remigio's letter, the only one I had kept and that, not for anything in the world, would I have wanted to let out of my hands.

'No, signora contessa. Your visiting-cards were seen, and the portrait of Lieutenant Remigio. Nothing else, on my honour.'

The following morning before nine I had Giacomo drive me in the carriage up to the Headquarters of the stronghold. It seemed an endless climb. I shouted to Giacomo to whip the horses. The square in front of the castle was crowded with all kinds of soldiers, casualties, and townspeople, but I reached the entrance to the offices unhindered. There, an old disabled soldier took my visiting-card. He returned a few minutes later, saying that General Hauptmann invited me to enter his private quarters, and that he would come and pay his respects as soon as he had dealt with some matters of the utmost urgency.

I was led through loggias, along corridors and across terraces to a room with three windows that looked out over the whole city. Broken into sections by its bridges, the Adige traced an S-shape, with one of its loops winding round the foot of the little hill on which Castel San Pietro stood, and the other round the foot of another dark, crenellated castle. And rising above the houses were the rooftops and towers of the ancient basilicas; and marked by a large open space was the vast oval of the Arena. The morning sun shone brightly on the town and hills, on one side turning the mountains golden, and on the other casting a serene light over the endless green plain scattered with white villages, houses, churches, and bell-towers.

Two little girls, with pink faces and straw-blonde hair, burst into the room, with great peals of laughter. When they saw me, they were shy at first, but then suddenly plucked up courage and came over to me.

The older one said, 'Please take a seat. Shall I fetch Mama?'

'No, my child, I'm waiting for your Papa.'

'We haven't seen Papa this morning. He's so busy.'

'I want to see Papa,' cried the little one. 'I love my Papa.'

At that point the General came in, and the little girls went running up to him, and clung to his legs, and tried to climb on to his shoulders. He picked up each child in turn and kissed her; and his two madcap daughters laughed, while two tears of blissful tenderness welled up in the General's eyes. He turned to me, saying, 'Forgive me, signora. If you have children, you'll understand.'

He sat down opposite me and added, 'I know the count by name, and should be delighted to be of any service to the signora contessa.'

I made it clear to the General that the children should leave us, and in a voice full of gentleness he said to them, 'Run along now, girls, run along, the contessa and I have things to discuss.'

The children took a step towards me as if they were about to kiss me. I turned away. They finally went off, looking a little upset.

'General,' I murmured, 'I've come to do my duty as a loyal citizen.'

'Is the signora contessa German?'

'No, I'm from the Trentino.'

'Ah, very well, then!' he exclaimed, gazing at me with a somewhat astonished and impatient air.

'Read this.' And with a decisive gesture I handed him Remigio's letter, which I had found again in the pocket of my purse.

Having read the letter, the General said, 'I don't understand. Is the letter addressed to you?'

'Yes, General.'

'So the man who wrote it is your lover.'

I did not reply. The General drew a cigar from his pocket and lit it. He leapt up and began to pace round the room. All of a sudden he planted himself in front of me, and staring into my face, he said, 'Well, be quick, I'm in a hurry.'

'The letter is from Remigio Ruz, Lieutenant of the 3rd Grenadiers.'

'And?'

'The letter is clear. He passed himself off as sick, by paying the four doctors.' And in a voice quickened with hatred, I added, 'He is a deserter from the field of battle.'

'I see. The Lieutenant was your lover and he has jilted you. You're taking your revenge by having him shot, and the doctors along with him. Is that it?'

'I don't care about the doctors.'

The General stood there for a while, thinking, with a frown on his face, then he handed back the letter I had given him.

'Signora, consider this carefully: it's dishonourable to act as an informer, and what you are doing is murder.'

'General,' I exclaimed, looking up at him haughtily, 'carry out your duty.'

At about nine o'clock that evening a soldier delivered a note to me at the Torre di Londra hotel, where a room had finally been found for me. It read as follows:

'Tomorrow morning, at four thirty precisely, Lieutenant Ruz and his regiment's doctor will be shot in the second courtyard of Castel San Pietro. This letter will grant you access to witness the execution. The undersigned regrets that he cannot also offer the signora contessa the spectacle of the other two doctors' execution. For reasons that it would be futile to explain here, they have been referred to another court martial.

General Hauptmann'

At three thirty I left the hotel on foot, in the pitch dark, accompanied by Giacomo. I told him to leave me at the bottom of the hill of Castel San Pietro, and I began to climb the steep road alone. I was hot, I could not breathe. I did not want to remove the veil from my face. Instead I undid the top buttons of my dress and tucked the flaps inside. With the air on my breast I was able to breathe more easily.

The stars were growing pale, as dawn came, diffusing its yellow light. I followed some soldiers round the side of the castle and into a courtyard enclosed within high, forbidding outer walls. Two squads of grenadiers were already lined up, motionless. No one took any notice of me, in the semi-darkness, amid the silent throng of soldiers.

I could hear the bells ringing down in the city, and a con-fusion of sound rising from below. A low door in the castle creaked open and two men came out, with their hands tied behind their backs. One of them, a thin, dark-haired fellow, stepped forward boldly, with his head held high. The other, flanked by two soldiers supporting him with great difficulty by the armpits, dragged his feet, sobbing.

What happened next, I do not know. Something was read out, I think. Then there was a deafening noise and I saw the dark young man fall to the ground, and in the same instant I noticed that Remigio was stripped to the waist, and I was blinded by those arms, shoulders, neck, and limbs that I had so loved. Into my mind flashed a picture of my lover, full of ardour and joy, when he held me for the first time in his steely embrace, in Venice at the Sirena. I was startled by a second burst of sound. On his chest that still quivered, whiter than marble, a blonde woman had thrown herself, and was spattered with spurting blood.

At the sight of that shameless hussy all my anger and resentment returned to me, and with them came dignity and strength. I had acted within my rights, and I turned to leave, serene in the self-respect that came from having fulfilled a difficult duty.

As I was going through the gate I felt the veil being torn from my face. I turned and saw before me the unsightly features of the Bohemian officer. He removed the stem of his pipe from his huge mouth, and with his moustaches coming at me, he spat on my cheek ...

Did I not say that young lawyer Gino would be back? All it took was one line – 'Come, let's be friends again' – to bring him running. He jilted that child-bride of his a week to the day before the marriage was to take place. And embracing me almost with Lieutenant Remigio's strength, he keeps telling me over and over again, 'Livia, you're an angel!'

VERNON LEE

A WICKED VOICE

IN REMEMBRANCE OF THE LAST SONG
AT PALAZZO BARBARO,
Chi ha inteso, intenda.

THEY HAVE BEEN congratulating me again today upon being the only composer of our days – of these days of deafening orchestral effects and poetical quackery – who has despised the newfangled nonsense of Wagner, and returned boldly to the traditions of Handel and Gluck and the divine Mozart, to the supremacy of melody and the respect of the human voice.

O cursed human voice, violin of flesh and blood, fashioned with the subtle tools, the cunning hands, of Satan! O execrable art of singing, have you not wrought mischief enough in the past, degrading so much noble genius, corrupting the purity of Mozart, reducing Handel to a writer of high-class singing-exercises, and defrauding the world of the only inspiration worthy of Sophocles and Euripides, the poetry of the great poet Gluck? Is it not enough to have dishonoured a whole century in idolatry of that wicked and contemptible wretch the singer, without persecuting an obscure young composer of our days, whose only wealth is his love of nobility in art, and perhaps some few grains of genius?

And then they compliment me upon the perfection with

which I imitate the style of the great dead masters; or ask me very seriously whether, even if I could gain over the modern public to this bygone style of music, I could hope to find singers to perform it. Sometimes, when people talk as they have been talking to-day, and laugh when I declare myself a follower of Wagner, I burst into a paroxysm of unintelligble, childish rage, and exclaim, 'We shall see that some day!'

Yes; some day we shall see! For, after all, may I not recover from this strangest of maladies? It is still possible that the day may come when all these things shall seem but an incredible nightmare; the day when *Ogier the Dane* shall be completed, and men shall know whether I am a follower of the great master of the Future or the miserable singing-masters of the Past. I am but half-bewitched, since I am conscious of the spell that binds me. My old nurse, far off in Norway, used to tell me that were-wolves are ordinary men and women half their days, and that if, during that period, they become aware of their horrid transformation they may find the means to forestall it. May this not be the case with me? My reason, after all, is free, although my artistic inspiration be enslaved; and I can despise and loathe the music I am forced to compose, and the execrable power that forces me.

Nay, is it not because I have studied with the doggedness of hatred this corrupt and corrupting music of the Past, seeking for every little peculiarity of style and every biographical trifle merely to display its vileness, is it not for this presumptuous courage that I have been overtaken by such mysterious, incredible vengeance?

And meanwhile, my only relief consists in going over and over again in my mind the tale of my miseries. This time I will write it, writing only to tear up, to throw the manuscript unread into the fire. And yet, who knows? As the last charred pages shall crackle and slowly sink into the red embers, perhaps the spell may be broken, and I may possess once more my long-lost liberty, my vanished genius.

It was a breathless evening under the full moon, that implacable full moon beneath which, even more than beneath the dreamy splendour of noontide, Venice seemed to swelter in the midst of the waters, exhaling, like some great lily, mysterious influences, which make the brain swim and the heart faint – a moral malaria, distilled, as I thought, from those languishing melodies, those cooing vocalisations which I had found in the musty music-books of a century ago. I see that moonlight evening as if it were present. I see my fellow-lodgers of that little artists' boarding-house. The table on which they lean after supper is strewn with bits of bread, with napkins rolled in tapestry rollers, spots of wine here and there, and at regular intervals chipped pepper-pots, stands of toothpicks, and heaps of those huge hard peaches which nature imitates from the marble-shops of Pisa. The whole *pension*-full is assembled, and examining stupidly the engraving which the American etcher has just brought for me, knowing me to be mad about eighteenth century music and musicians, and having noticed, as he turned over the heaps of penny prints in the square of San Polo, that the portrait is that of a singer of those days.

Singer, thing of evil, stupid and wicked slave of the voice, of that instrument which was not invented by the human intellect, but begotten of the body, and which, instead of moving the soul, merely stirs up the dregs of our nature! For what is the voice but the Beast calling, awakening that other Beast sleeping in the depths of mankind, the Beast which all great art has ever sought to chain up, as the archangel chains up, in old pictures, the demon with his woman's face? How could the creature attached to this voice, its owner and its victim, the singer, the great, the real singer who once ruled over every heart, be otherwise than wicked and contempt-ible? But let me try and get on with my story.

I can see all my fellow-boarders, leaning on the table, con-templating the print, this effeminate beau, his hair curled into *ailes de pigeon*, his sword passed through his embroid-ered pocket, seated under a triumphal arch somewhere among the clouds, surrounded by puffy Cupids and crowned with laurels by a bouncing goddess of fame. I hear again all the insipid exclamations, the insipid questions about this singer: – 'When did he live? Was he very famous? Are you sure, Magnus, that this is really a portrait,' &c. &c. And I hear my own voice, as if in the far distance, giving them all sorts of information, biographical and critical, out of a battered little volume called *The Theatre of Musical Glory; or, Opinions upon the most Famous Chapel-masters and Virtuosi of this Century*, by Father Prosdocimo Sabatelli, Barnalite, Professor of Eloquence at the College of Modena, and Mem-ber of the Arcadian Academy, under the pastoral name of Evander Lilybæan, Venice, 1785, with the approbation of the Superiors. I tell them all how this singer, this Balthasar Cesari, was nicknamed Zaffirino because of a sapphire engraved with cabalistic signs presented to him one evening by a masked stranger, in whom wise folk recognised that great cultivator of the human voice, the devil; how much more wonderful had been this Zaffirino's vocal gifts than those of any singer of ancient or modern times; how his brief life had been but a series of triumphs, petted by the greatest kings, sung by the most famous poets, and finally, adds Father Prosdocimo, 'courted (if the grave Muse of history may incline her ear to the gossip of gallantry) by the most charming nymphs, even of the very highest quality.'

My friends glance once more at the engraving; more insipid remarks are made; I am requested – especially by the

American young ladies – to play or sing one of this Zaffirino's favourite songs – 'For of course you know them, dear Maestro Magnus, you who have such a passion for all old music. Do be good, and sit down to the piano.' I refuse, rudely enough, rolling the print in my fingers. How fearfully this cursed heat, these cursed moonlight nights, must have unstrung me! This Venice would certainly kill me in the long-run! Why, the sight of this idiotic engraving, the mere name of that coxcomb of a singer, have made my heart beat and my limbs turn to water like a love-sick hobbledehoy.

After my gruff refusal, the company begins to disperse; they prepare to go out, some to have a row on the lagoon, others to saunter before the *cafés* at St. Mark's; family discussions arise, gruntings of fathers, murmurs of mothers, peals of laughing from young girls and young men. And the moon, pouring in by the wide-open windows, turns this old palace ballroom, nowadays an inn dining-room, into a lagoon, scintillating, undulating like the other lagoon, the real one, which stretches out yonder furrowed by invisible gondolas betrayed by the red prow-lights. At last the whole lot of them are on the move. I shall be able to get some quiet in my room, and to work a little at my opera of *Ogier the Dane.* But no! Conversation revives, and, of all things, about that singer, that Zaffirino, whose absurd portrait I am crunching in my fingers.

The principal speaker is Count Alvise, an old Venetian with dyed whiskers, a great check tie fastened with two pins and a chain; a threadbare patrician who is dying to secure for his lanky son that pretty American girl, whose mother is intoxicated by all his mooning anecdotes about the past glories of Venice in general, and of his illustrious family in particular. Why, in Heaven's name, must he pitch upon Zaffirino for his mooning, this old duffer of a patrician?

'Zaffirino, – ah yes, to be sure! Balthasar Cesari, called Zaffirino,' snuffles the voice of Count Alvise, who always repeats the last word of every sentence at least three times. 'Yes, Zaffirino, to be sure! A famous singer of the days of my forefathers; yes, of my forefathers, dear lady!' Then a lot of rubbish about the former greatness of Venice, the glories of old music, the former Conservatoires, all mixed up with anecdotes of Rossini and Donizetti, whom he pretends to have known intimately. Finally, a story, of course containing plenty about his illustrious family: – 'My great grand-aunt, the Procuratessa Vendramin, from whom we have inherited our estate of Mistrà, on the Brenta' – a hopelessly muddled story, apparently, fully of digressions, but of which that singer Zaffirino is the hero. The narrative, little by little, becomes more intelligible, or perhaps it is I who am giving it more attention.

'It seems,' says the Count, 'that there was one of his songs in particular which was called the "Husbands' Air" – *L'Aria dei Mariti* – because they didn't enjoy it quite as much as their better-halves. ... My grand-aunt, Pisana Renier, married to the Procuratore Vendramin, was a patrician of the old school, of the style that was getting rare a hundred years ago. Her virtue and her pride rendered her unapproachable. Zaffirino, on his part, was in the habit of boasting that no woman had ever been able to resist his singing, which, it appears, had its foundation in fact – the ideal changes, my dear lady, the ideal changes a good deal from one century to another! – and that his first song could make any woman turn pale and lower her eyes, the second make her madly in love, while the third song could kill her off on the spot, kill her for love, there under his very eyes, if he only felt inclined. My grand-aunt Vendramin laughed when this story was told her, refused to go to hear this insolent dog, and added that

154

it might be quite possible by the aid of spells and infernal pacts to kill a *gentildonna*, but as to making her fall in love with a lackey – never! This answer was naturally reported to Zaffirino, who piqued himself upon always getting the better of any one who was wanting in deference to his voice. Like the ancient Romans, *parcere subjectis et debellare superbos.* You American ladies, who are so learned, will appreciate this little quotation from the divine Virgil. While seeming to avoid the Procuratessa Vendramin, Zaffirino took the opportunity, one evening at a large assembly, to sing in her presence. He sang and sang and sang until the poor grand-aunt Pisana fell ill for love. The most skilful physicians were kept unable to explain the mysterious malady which was visibly killing the poor young lady; and the Procuratore Vendramin applied in vain to the most venerated Madonnas, and vainly promised an altar of silver, with massive gold candlesticks, to Saints Cosmas and Damian, patrons of the art of healing. At last the brother-in-law of the Procuratessa, Monsignor Almorò Vendramin, Patriarch of Aquileia, a prelate famous for the sanctity of his life, obtained in a vision of Saint Justina, for whom he entertained a particular devotion, the information that the only thing which could benefit the strange illness of his sister-in-law was the voice of Zaffirino. Take notice that my poor grand-aunt had never condescended to such a revelation.

'The Procuratore was enchanted at this happy solution; and his lordship the Patriarch went to seek Zaffirino in person, and carried him in his own coach to the Villa of Mistrà, where the Procuratessa was residing. On being told what was about to happen, my poor grand-aunt went into fits of rage, which were succeeded immediately by equally violent fits of joy. However, she never forgot what was due to her great position. Although sick almost unto death, she had herself arrayed with the greatest pomp, caused her face to be painted, and put on all her diamonds: it would seem as if she were anxious to affirm her full dignity before this singer. Accordingly she received Zaffirino reclining on a sofa which had been placed in the great ballroom of the Villa of Mistrà, and beneath the princely canopy; for the Vendramins, who had intermarried with the house of Mantua, possessed imperial fiefs and were princes of the Holy Roman Empire. Zaffirino saluted her with the most profound respect, but not a word passed between them. Only, the singer inquired from the Procuratore whether the illustrious lady had received the Sacraments of the Church. Being told that the Procuratessa had herself asked to be given extreme unction from the hands of her brother-in-law, he declared his readiness to obey the orders of His Excellency, and sat down at once to the harpsichord.

'Never had he sung so divinely. At the end of the first song the Procuratessa Vendramin had already revived most extraordinarily; by the end of the second she appeared entirely cured and beaming with beauty and happiness; but at the third air – the *Aria dei Mariti*, no doubt – she began to change frightfully; she gave a dreadful cry, and fell into the convulsions of death. In a quarter of an hour she was dead! Zaffirino did not wait to see her die. Having finished his song, he withdrew instantly, took post-horses, and travelled day and night as far as Munich. People remarked that he had presented himself at Mistrà dressed in mourning, although he had mentioned no death among his relatives; also that he had prepared everything for his departure, as if fearing the wrath of so powerful a family. Then there was also the extraordinary question he had asked before beginning to sing, about the Procuratessa having confessed and received extreme unction. . . . No, thanks, my dear lady, no cigarettes for me. But if it does not distress you or your charming daughter, may I humbly beg permission to smoke a cigar?'

And Count Alvise, enchanted with his talent for narrative, and sure of having secured for his son the heart and the dollars of his fair audience, proceeds to light a candle, and at the candle one of those long black Italian cigars which require preliminary disinfection before smoking.

... If this state of things goes on I shall just have to ask the doctor for a bottle; this ridiculous beating of my heart and disgusting cold perspiration have increased steadily during Count Alvise's narrative. To keep myself in countenance among the various idiotic commentaries on this cock-and-bull story of a vocal coxcomb and a vapouring great lady, I begin to unroll the engraving, and to examine stupidly the portrait of Zaffirino, once so renowned, now so forgotten. A ridiculous ass, this singer, under his triumphal arch, with his stuffed Cupids and the great fat winged kitchenmaid crowning him with laurels. How flat and vapid and vulgar it is, to be sure, all this odious eighteenth century!

But he, personally, is not so utterly vapid as I had thought. That effeminate, fat face of his is almost beautiful, with an odd smile, brazen and cruel. I have seen faces like this, if not in real life, at least in my boyish romantic dreams, when I read Swinburne and Baudelaire, the faces of wicked, vindictive women. Oh yes! he is decidedly a beautiful creature, this Zaffirino, and his voice must have had the same sort of beauty and the same expression of wickedness. ...

'Come on, Magnus,' sound the voices of my fellow-boarders, 'be a good fellow and sing us one of the old chap's songs; or at least something or other of that day, and we'll make believe it was the air with which he killed that poor lady.'

'Oh yes! the *Aria dei Mariti*, the "Husbands' Air,"' mumbles old Alvise, between the puffs at his impossible black cigar. 'My poor grand-aunt, Pisana Vendramin; he went and killed her with those songs of his, with that *Aria dei Mariti.*'

I feel senseless rage overcoming me. Is it that horrible palpitation (by the way, there is a Norwegian doctor, my fellow-countryman, at Venice just now) which is sending the blood to my brain and making me mad? The people round the piano, the furniture, everything together seems to get mixed and to turn into moving blobs of colour. I set to singing; the only thing which remains distinct before my eyes being the portrait of Zaffirino, on the edge of that boarding-house piano; the sensual, effeminate face, with its wicked, cynical smile, keeps appearing and disappearing as the print wavers about in the draught that makes the candles smoke and gutter. And I set to singing madly, singing I don't know what. Yes; I begin to identify it: 'tis the *Biondina in Gondoleta*, the only song of the eighteenth century which is still remembered by the Venetian people. I sing it, mimicking every old-school grace; shakes, cadences, languishingly swelled and diminished notes, and adding all manner of buffooneries, until the audience, recovering from its surprise, begins to shake with laughing; until I begin to laugh myself, madly, frantically, between the phrases of the melody, my voice finally smothered in this dull, brutal laughter. . . . And then, to crown it all, I shake my fist at this long-dead singer, looking at me with his wicked woman's face, with his mocking, fatuous smile.

'Ah! you would like to be revenged on me also!' I exclaim. 'You would like me to write you nice roulades and flourishes, another nice *Aria dei Mariti*, my fine Zaffirino!'

* * *

That night I dreamed a very strange dream. Even in the big half-furnished room the heat and closeness were stifling. The air seemed laden with the scent of all manner of white flowers, faint and heavy in their intolerable sweetness: tube-roses, gardenias, and jasmines drooping I know not where in neglected vases. The moonlight had transformed the marble floor around me into a shallow, shining pool. On account of the heat I had exchanged my bed for a big old-fashioned sofa of light wood, painted with little nosegays and sprigs, like an old silk; and I lay there, not attempting to sleep, and letting my thoughts go vaguely to my opera of *Ogier the Dane*, of which I had long finished writing the words, and for whose music I had hoped to find some inspiration in this strange Venice, floating, as it were, in the stagnant lagoon of the past. But Venice had merely put all my ideas into hopeless confusion; it was as if there arose out of its shallow waters a miasma of long-dead melodies, which sickened but intoxicated my soul. I lay on my sofa watching that pool of whitish light, which rose higher and higher, little trickles of light meeting it here and there, wherever the moon's rays struck upon some polished surface; while huge shadows waved to and fro in the draught of the open balcony.

I went over and over that old Norse story: how the Paladin, Ogier, one of the knights of Charlemagne, was decoyed during his homeward wanderings from the Holy Land by the arts of an enchantress, the same who had once held in bondage the great Emperor Cæsar and given him King Oberon for a son; how Ogier had tarried in that island only one day and one night, and yet, when he came home to his kingdom, he found all changed, his friends dead, his family dethroned, and not a man who knew his face; until at last, driven hither and thither like a beggar, a poor minstrel had taken compassion of his sufferings and given him all he could give – a song, the song of the prowess of a hero dead for hundreds of years, the Paladin Ogier the Dane.

The story of Ogier ran into a dream, as vivid as my waking thoughts had been vague. I was looking no longer at the pool of moonlight spreading round my couch, with its trickles of light and looming, waving shadows, but the frescoed walls of a great saloon. It was not, as I recognised in a second, the dining-room of that Venetian palace now turned into a boarding-house. It was a far larger room, a real ballroom, almost circular in its octagon shape, with eight huge white doors surrounded by stucco mouldings, and, high on the vault of the ceiling, eight little galleries or recesses like boxes at a theatre, intended no doubt for musicians and spectators. The place was imperfectly lighted by only one of the eight chandeliers, which revolved slowly, like huge spiders, each on its long cord. But the light struck upon the gilt stuccoes opposite me, and on a large expanse of fresco, the sacrifice of Iphigenia, with Agamemnon and Achilles in Roman helmets, lappets, and knee-breeches. It discovered also one of the oil panels let into the mouldings of the roof, a goddess in lemon and lilac draperies, foreshortened over a great green peacock. Round the room, where the light reached, I could make out big yellow satin sofas and heavy gilded consoles; in the shadow of a corner was what looked like a piano, and farther in the shade one of those big canopies which decorate the anterooms of Roman palaces. I looked about me, wondering where I was: a heavy, sweet smell, reminding me of the flavour of a peach, filled the place.

Little by little I began to perceive sounds; little, sharp, metallic, detached notes, like those of a mandoline; and there was united to them a voice, very low and sweet, almost a whisper, which grew and grew and grew, until the whole place was filled with that exquisite vibrating note, of a strange, exotic, unique quality. The note went on, swelling and swelling. Suddenly there was a horrible piercing shriek, and the thud of a body on the floor, and all manner of smothered exclamations. There, close by the canopy, a light suddenly appeared; and I could see, among the dark figures moving to and fro in the room, a woman lying on the ground, surrounded by other women. Her blond hair, tangled, full of diamond-sparkles which cut through the half-darkness, was hanging dishevelled; the laces of her bodice had been cut, and her white breast shone among the sheen of jewelled brocade; her face was bent forwards, and a thin white arm trailed, like a broken limb, across the knees of one of the women who were endeavouring to lift her. There was a sudden splash of water against the floor, more confused exclamations, a hoarse, broken moan, and a gurgling, dreadful sound. . . . I awoke with a start and rushed to the window.

Outside, in the blue haze of the moon, the church and belfry of St. George loomed blue and hazy, with the black hull and rigging, the red lights, of a large steamer moored before them. From the lagoon rose a damp sea-breeze. What was it all? Ah! I began to understand: that story of old Count Alvise's, the death of his grand-aunt, Pisana Vendramin. Yes, it was about that I had been dreaming.

I returned to my room; I struck a light, and sat down to my writing-table. Sleep had become impossible. I tried to work at my opera. Once or twice I thought I had got hold of what I had looked for so long. . . . But as soon as I tried to lay hold of my theme, there arose in my mind the distant echo of that voice, of that long note swelled slowly by insensible degrees, that long note whose tone was so strong and so subtle.

* * *

There are in the life of an artist moments when, still unable to seize his own inspiration, or even clearly to discern it, he becomes aware of the approach of that long-invoked idea. A mingled joy and terror warn him that before another day, another hour have passed, the inspiration shall have crossed the threshold of his soul and flooded it with its rapture. All day I had felt the need of isolation and quiet, and at nightfall I went for a row on the most solitary part of the lagoon. All things seemed to tell that I was going to meet my inspiration, and I awaited its coming as a lover awaits his beloved.

I had stopped my gondola for a moment, and as I gently swayed to and fro on the water, all paved with moonbeams, it seemed to me that I was on the confines of an imaginary world. It lay close at hand, enveloped in luminous, pale blue mist, through which the moon had cut a wide and glistening path; out to sea, the little islands, like moored black boats, only accentuated the solitude of this region of moonbeams and wavelets; while the hum of the insects in orchards hard by merely added to the impression of untroubled silence. On some such seas, I thought, must the Paladin Ogier have sailed when about to discover that during that sleep at the enchantress's knees centuries had elapsed and the heroic world had set, and the kingdom of prose had come.

While my gondola rocked stationary on that sea of moonbeams, I pondered over that twilight of the heroic world. In the soft rattle of the water on the hull I seemed to hear the rattle of all that armour, of all those swords swinging rusty on the walls, neglected by the degenerate sons of the great champions of old. I had long been in search of a theme which I called the theme of the 'Prowess of Ogier;' it was to appear from time to time in the course of my opera, to develop at last into that song of the Minstrel, which reveals to the hero

162

that he is one of a long-dead world. And at this moment I seemed to feel the presence of that theme. Yet an instant, and my mind would be overwhelmed by that savage music, heroic, funereal.

Suddenly there came across the lagoon, cleaving, chequering, and fretting the silence with a lace-work of sound even as the moon was fretting and cleaving the water, a ripple of music, a voice breaking itself in a shower of little scales and cadences and trills.

I sank back upon my cushions. The vision of heroic days had vanished, and before my closed eyes there seemed to dance multitudes of little stars of light, chasing and interlacing like those sudden vocalisations.

'To shore! Quick!' I cried to the gondolier.

But the sounds had ceased; and there came from the orchards, with their mulberry-trees glistening in the moonlight, and their black swaying cypress-plumes, nothing save the confused hum, the monotonous chirp, of the crickets.

I looked around me: on one side empty dunes, orchards, and meadows, without house or steeple; on the other, the blue and misty sea, empty to where distant islets were profiled black on the horizon.

A faintness overcame me, and I felt myself dissolve. For all of a sudden a second ripple of voice swept over the lagoon, a shower of little notes, which seemed to form a little mocking laugh.

Then again all was still. This silence lasted so long that I fell once more to meditating on my opera. I lay in wait once more for the half-caught theme. But no. It was not that theme for which I was waiting and watching with baited breath. I realised my delusion when, on rounding the point of the Giudecca, the murmur of a voice arose from the midst of the waters, a thread of sound slender as a moonbeam, scarce audible, but exquisite, which expanded slowly, insensibly, taking volume and body, taking flesh almost and fire, an ineffable quality, full, passionate, but veiled, as it were, in a subtle, downy wrapper. The note grew stronger and stronger, and warmer and more passionate, until it burst through that strange and charming veil, and emerged beaming, to break itself in the luminous facets of a wonderful shake, long, superb, triumphant.

There was a dead silence.

'Row to St. Mark's!' I exclaimed. 'Quick!'

The gondola glided through the long, glittering track of moonbeams, and rent the great band of yellow, reflected light, mirroring the cupolas of St. Mark's, the lace-like pinnacles of the palace, and the slender pink belfry, which rose from the lit-up water to the pale and bluish evening sky.

In the larger of the two squares the military band was blaring through the last spirals of a *crescendo* of Rossini. The crowd was dispersing in this great open-air ballroom, and the sounds arose which invariably follow upon out-of-door music. A clatter of spoons and glasses, a rustle and grating of frocks and of chairs, and the click of scabbards on the pavement. I pushed my way among the fashionable youths contemplating the ladies while sucking the knob of their sticks; through the serried ranks of respectable families, marching arm in arm with their white frocked young ladies close in front. I took a seat before Florian's, among the customers stretching themselves before departing, and the waiters hurrying to and fro, clattering their empty cups and trays. Two imitation Neapolitans were slipping their guitar and violin under their arm, ready to leave the place.

'Stop!' I cried to them; 'don't go yet. Sing me something – sing *La Camesella* or *Funiculì, funiculà* – no matter what, provided you make a row;' and as they screamed and scraped their utmost, I added, 'But can't you sing louder, d——n you! – sing louder, do you understand?'

I felt the need of noise, of yells and false notes, of something vulgar and hideous to drive away that ghost-voice which was haunting me.

Again and again I told myself that it had been some silly prank of a romantic amateur, hidden in the gardens of the shore or gliding unperceived on the lagoon; and that the sorcery of moonlight and sea-mist had transfigured for my excited brain mere humdrum roulades out of exercises of Bordogni or Crescentini.

But all the same I continued to be haunted by that voice. My work was interrupted ever and anon by the attempt to catch its imaginary echo; and the heroic harmonies of my Scandinavian legend were strangely interwoven with voluptuous phrases and florid cadences in which I seemed to hear again that same accursed voice.

To be haunted by singing-exercises! It seemed too ridiculous for a man who professedly despised the art of singing. And still, I preferred to believe in that childish amateur, amusing himself with warbling to the moon.

One day, while making these reflections the hundredth time over, my eyes chanced to light upon the portrait of Zaffirino, which my friend had pinned against the wall. I pulled it down and tore it into half a dozen shreds. Then, already ashamed of my folly, I watched the torn pieces float down from the window, wafted hither and thither by the sea-breeze. One scrap got caught in a yellow blind below me; the others fell into the canal, and were speedily lost to sight in the dark water. I was overcome with shame. My heart beat like bursting. What a miserable, unnerved worm I had become in this cursed Venice, with its languishing moon-lights, its atmosphere as of some stuffy boudoir, long unused, full of old stuffs and pot-pourri!

That night, however, things seemed to be going better. I was able to settle down to my opera, and even to work at it. In the intervals my thoughts returned, not without a certain pleasure, to those scattered fragments of the torn engraving fluttering down to the water. I was disturbed at my piano by the hoarse voices and the scraping of violins which rose from one of those music-boats that station at night under the hotels of the Grand Canal. The moon had set. Under my balcony the water stretched black into the distance, its dark-ness cut by the still darker outlines of the flotilla of gondolas in attendance on the music-boat, where the faces of the singers, and the guitars and violins, gleamed reddish under the unsteady light of the Chinese-lanterns.

'*Jammo, jammo; jammo, jammo jà,*' sang the loud, hoarse voices; then a tremendous scrape and twang, and the yelled-out burden, '*Funiculì, funiculà; funiculì, funiculà; jammo, jammo, jammo, jammo, jammo jà.*'

Then came a few cries of '*Bis, Bis!*' from a neighbouring hotel, a brief clapping of hands, the sound of a handful of coppers rattling into the boat, and the oar-stroke of some gondolier making ready to turn away.

'Sing the *Camesella*,' ordered some voice with a foreign accent.

'No, no! *Santa Lucia.*'

'I want the *Camesella.*'

'No! *Santa Lucia.* Hi! sing *Santa Lucia* – d'you hear?'

The musicians, under their green and yellow and red lamps, held a whispered consultation on the manner of con-ciliating these contradictory demands. Then, after a minute's hesitation, the violins began the prelude of that once famous air, which has remained popular in Venice – the words written, some hundred years ago, by the patrician Gritti, the music by an unknown composer – *La Biondina in Gondoleta*.

That cursed eighteenth century! It seemed a malignant fatality that made these brutes choose just this piece to interrupt me.

At last the long prelude came to an end; and above the cracked guitars and squeaking fiddles there arose, not the expected nasal chorus, but a single voice singing below its breath.

My arteries throbbed. How well I knew that voice! It was singing, as I have said, below its breath, yet none the less it sufficed to fill all that reach of the canal with its strange quality of tone, exquisite, far-fetched.

They were long-drawn-out notes, of intense but peculiar sweetness, a man's voice which had much of a woman's, but more even of a chorister's, but a chorister's voice without its limpidity and innocence; its youthfulness was veiled, muffled, as it were, in a sort of downy vagueness, as if a passion of tears withheld.

There was a burst of applause, and the old palaces re-echoed with the clapping. 'Bravo, bravo! Thank you, thank you! Sing again – please, sing again. Who can it be?'

And then a bumping of hulls, a splashing of oars, and the oaths of gondoliers trying to push each other away, as the red prow-lamps of the gondolas pressed round the gaily lit singing-boat.

But no one stirred on board. It was to none of them that this applause was due. And while every one pressed on, and clapped and vociferated, one little red prow-lamp dropped away from the fleet; for a moment a single gondola stood forth black upon the black water, and then was lost in the night.

For several days the mysterious singer was the universal topic. The people of the music-boat swore that no one besides themselves had been on board, and that they knew as little as ourselves about the owner of that voice. The gondoliers, despite their descent from the spies of the old Republic, were equally unable to furnish any clue. No musical celebrity was known or suspected to be at Venice; and every one agreed that such a singer must be a European celebrity. The strangest thing in this strange business was, that even among those learned in music there was no agreement on the subject of this voice: it was called by all sorts of names and described by all manner of incongruous adjectives; people went so far as to dispute whether the voice belonged to a man or to a woman: every one had some new definition.

In all these musical discussions I, alone, brought forward no opinion. I felt a repugnance, an impossibility almost, of speaking about that voice; and the more or less commonplace conjectures of my friend had the invariable effect of sending me out of the room.

Meanwhile my work was becoming daily more difficult, and I soon passed from utter impotence to a state of inexplicable agitation. Every morning I arose with fine resolutions and grand projects of work; only to go to bed that night without having accomplished anything. I spent hours leaning on my balcony, or wandering through the network of lanes with their ribbon of blue sky, endeavouring vainly to expel the thought of that voice, or endeavouring in reality to reproduce it in my memory; for the more I tried to banish it from my thoughts, the more I grew to thirst for that extraordinary tone, for those mysteriously downy, veiled notes; and no sooner did I make an effort to work at my opera than my head was full of scraps of forgotten eighteenth-century airs, of frivolous or languishing little phrases; and I fell to wondering with a bitter-sweet longing how those songs would have sounded if sung by that voice.

At length it became necessary to see a doctor, from whom, however, I carefully hid away all the stranger symptoms of my malady. The air of the lagoons, the great heat, he answered cheerfully, had pulled me down a little; a tonic and a month in the country, with plenty of riding and no work, would make me myself again. That old idler, Count Alvise, who had insisted on accompanying me to the physician's, immediately suggested that I should go and stay with his son, who was boring himself to death superintending the maize harvest on the mainland: he could promise me excellent air, plenty of horses, and all the peaceful surroundings and the delightful occupations of a rural life – 'Be sensible, my dear Magnus, and just go quietly to Mistrà.'

Mistrà – the name sent a shiver all down me. I was about to decline the invitation, when a thought suddenly loomed vaguely in my mind.

'Yes, dear Count,' I answered; 'I accept your invitation with gratitude and pleasure. I will start to-morrow for Mistrà.'

The next day found me at Padua, on my way to the Villa of Mistrà. It seemed as if I had left an intolerable burden behind me. I was, for the first time since how long, quite light of heart. The tortuous, rough-paved streets, with their empty, gloomy porticoes; the ill-plastered palaces, with closed, discoloured shutters; the little rambling square, with meagre trees and stubborn grass; the Venetian garden-houses reflecting their crumbling graces in the muddy canal; the gardens without gates and the gates without gardens, the avenues leading nowhere; and the population of blind and legless beggars, of whining sacristans, which issued as by magic from between the flagstones and dust-heaps and weeds under the fierce August sun, all this dreariness merely amused and pleased me. My good spirits were heightened by a musical mass which I had the good fortune to hear at St. Anthony's.

Never in all my days had I heard anything comparable, although Italy affords many strange things in the way of sacred music. Into the deep nasal chanting of the priests there had suddenly burst a chorus of children, singing absolutely independent of all time and tune; grunting of priests answered by squealing of boys, slow Gregorian modulation interrupted by jaunty barrel-organ pipings, an insane, insanely merry jumble of bellowing and barking, mewing and cackling and braying, such as would have enlivened a witches' meeting, or rather some mediæval Feast of Fools. And, to make the grotesqueness of such music still more fantastic and Hoffmannlike, there was, besides, the magnificence of the piles of sculptured marbles and gilded bronzes, the tradition of the musical splendour for which St. Anthony's had been famous in days gone by. I had read in old travellers, Lalande and Burney, that the Republic of St. Mark had squandered immense sums not merely on the monuments and decoration, but on the musical establishment of its great cathedral of Terra Firma. In the midst of this ineffable concert of impossible voices and instruments, I tried to imagine the voice of Guadagni, the soprano for whom Gluck had written *Che farò senza Euridice*, and the fiddle of Tartini, that Tartini with whom the devil had once come and made music. And the delight in anything so absolutely, barbarously, grotesquely, fantastically incongruous as such a performance in such a place was heightened by a sense of profanation: such were the successors of those wonderful musicians of that hated eighteenth century!

The whole thing had delighted me so much, so very much more than the most faultless performance could have done, that I determined to enjoy it once more; and towards vesper-time, after a cheerful dinner with two bagmen at the inn of the Golden Star, and a pipe over the rough sketch of a possible cantata upon the music which the devil made for Tartini, I turned my steps once more towards St. Anthony's.

The bells were ringing for sunset, and a muffled sound of organs seemed to issue from the huge, solitary church; I pushed my way under the heavy leathern curtain, expecting to be greeted by the grotesque performance of that morning.

I proved mistaken. Vespers must long have been over. A smell of stale incense, a crypt-like damp filled my mouth; it was already night in that vast cathedral. Out of the darkness glimmered the votive-lamps of the chapels, throwing wavering lights upon the red polished marble, the gilded railing, and chandeliers, and plaqueing with yellow the muscles of some sculptured figure. In a corner a burning taper put a halo about the head of a priest, burnishing his shining bald skull, his white surplice, and the open book before him. 'Amen' he chanted; the book was closed with a snap, the light moved up the apse, some dark figures of women rose from their knees and passed quickly towards the door; a man saying his prayers before a chapel also got up, making a great clatter in dropping his stick.

The church was empty, and I expected every minute to be turned out by the sacristan making his evening round to close the doors. I was leaning against a pillar, looking into the greyness of the great arches, when the organ suddenly burst out into a series of chords, rolling through the echoes of the church: it seemed to be the conclusion of some service. And above the organ rose the notes of a voice; high, soft, enveloped in a kind of downiness, like a cloud of incense, and which ran through the mazes of a long cadence. The voice dropped into silence; with two thundering chords the organ closed in. All was silent. For a moment I stood leaning against one of the pillars of the nave: my hair was clammy, my knees sank beneath me, an enervating heat spread through my body; I tried to breathe more largely, to suck in the sounds with the incense-laden air. I was supremely happy, and yet as if I were dying; then suddenly a chill ran through me, and with it a vague panic. I turned away and hurried out into the open.

The evening sky lay pure and blue along the jagged line of roofs; the bats and swallows were wheeling about; and from the belfries all around, half-drowned by the deep bell of St. Anthony's, jangled the peel of the *Ave Maria*.

'You really don't seem well,' young Count Alvise had said the previous evening, as he welcomed me, in the light of a lantern held up by a peasant, in the weedy back-garden of the Villa of Mistrà. Everything had seemed to me like a dream: the jingle of the horse's bells driving in the dark from Padua, as the lantern swept the acacia-hedges with their wide yellow light; the grating of the wheels on the gravel; the supper-table, illumined by a single petroleum lamp for fear of attracting mosquitoes, where a broken old lackey, in an old stable jacket, handed round the dishes among the fumes of onion; Alvise's fat mother gabbling dialect in a shrill, bene-volent voice behind the bullfights on her fan; the unshaven village priest, perpetually fidgeting with his glass and foot, and sticking one shoulder up above the other. And now, in the afternoon, I felt as if I had been in this long, rambling, tumble-down Villa of Mistrà – a villa three-quarters of which was given up to the storage of grain and garden tools, or to the exercise of rats, mice, scorpions, and centipedes – all my life; as if I had always sat there, in Count Alvise's study, among the pile of undusted books on agriculture, the sheaves of accounts, the samples of grain and silkworm seed, the ink-stains and the cigar-ends; as if I had never heard of anything save the cereal basis of Italian agriculture, the diseases of maize, the peronospora of the vine, the breeds of bullocks, and the iniquities of farm labourers; with the blue cones of the Euganean hills closing in the green shimmer of plain out-side the window.

After an early dinner, again with the screaming gabble of the fat old Countess, the fidgeting and shoulder-raising of the unshaven priest, the smell of fried oil and stewed onions, Count Alvise made me get into the cart beside him, and whirled me along among clouds of dust, between the endless glister of poplars, acacias, and maples, to one of his farms.

In the burning sun some twenty or thirty girls, in coloured skirts, laced bodices, and big straw-hats, were threshing the maize on the big red brick threshing-floor, while others were winnowing the grain in great sieves. Young Alvise III. (the old one was Alvise II.: every one is Alvise, that is to say, Lewis, in that family; the name is on the house, the carts, the bar-rows, the very pails) picked up the maize, touched it, tasted it, said something to the girls that made them laugh, and something to the head farmer that made him look very glum; and then led me into a huge stable, where some twenty or thirty white bullocks were stamping, switching their tails, hitting their horns against the mangers in the dark. Alvise III. patted each, called him by his name, gave him some salt or a turnip, and explained which was the Mantuan breed, which the Apulian, which the Romagnolo, and so on. Then he bade me jump into the trap, and off we went again through the dust, among the hedges and ditches, till we came to some more brick farm buildings with pinkish roofs smoking against the blue sky. Here there were more young women threshing and winnowing the maize, which made a great golden Danaë cloud; more bullocks stamping and lowing in the cool darkness; more joking, fault-finding, explaining; and thus through five farms, until I seemed to see the rhythmical rising and falling of the flails against the hot sky, the shower of golden grains, the yellow dust from the winnowing-sieves on to the bricks, the switching of innumerable tails and plunging of innumerable horns, the glistening of huge white flanks and foreheads, whenever I closed my eyes.

'A good day's work!' cried Count Alvise, stretching out his long legs with the tight trousers riding up over the Wellington boots. 'Mamma, give us some aniseed-syrup after dinner; it is an excellent restorative and precaution against the fevers of this country.'

'Oh! you've got fever in this part of the world, have you? Why, your father said the air was so good!'

'Nothing, nothing,' soothed the old Countess. 'The only thing to be dreaded are mosquitoes; take care to fasten your shutters before lighting the candle.'

'Well,' rejoined young Alvise, with an effort of conscience, 'of course there *are* fevers. But they needn't hurt you. Only, don't go out into the garden at night, if you don't want to catch them. Papa told me that you have fancies for moonlight rambles. It won't do in this climate, my dear fellow; it won't do. If you must stalk about at night, being a genius, take a turn inside the house; you can get quite exercise enough.'

After dinner the aniseed-syrup was produced, together with brandy and cigars, and they all sat in the long, narrow, half-furnished room on the first floor; the old Countess knitting a garment of uncertain shape and destination, the priest reading out the newspaper; Count Alvise puffing at his long, crooked cigar, and pulling the ears of a long, lean dog with a suspicion of mange and a stiff eye. From the dark garden outside rose the hum and whirr of countless insects, and the smell of the grapes which hung black against the starlit, blue sky, on the trellis. I went to the balcony. The garden lay dark beneath; against the twinkling horizon stood out the tall poplars. There was the sharp cry of an owl; the barking of a dog; a sudden whiff of warm, enervating perfume, a perfume that made me think of the taste of certain peaches, and suggested white, thick, wax-like petals. I seemed to have smelt that flower once before: it made me feel languid, almost faint.

'I am very tired,' I said to Count Alvise. 'See how feeble we city folk become!'

But, despite my fatigue, I found it quite impossible to sleep. The night seemed perfectly stifling. I had felt nothing like it at Venice. Despite the injunctions of the Countess I opened the solid wooden shutters, hermetically closed against mosquitoes, and looked out.

The moon had risen; and beneath it lay the big lawns, the rounded tree-tops, bathed in a blue, luminous mist, every leaf glistening and trembling in what seemed a heaving sea of light. Beneath the window was the long trellis, with the white shining piece of pavement under it. It was so bright that I could distinguish the green of the vine-leaves, the dull red of the catalpa-flowers. There was in the air a vague scent of cut grass, of ripe American grapes, of that white flower (it must be white) which made me think of the taste of peaches all melting into the delicious freshness of falling dew. From the village church came the stroke of one: Heaven knows how long I had been vainly attempting to sleep. A shiver ran through me, and my head suddenly filled as with the fumes of some subtle wine; I remembered all those weedy embankments, those canals full of stagnant water, the yellow faces of the peasants; the word malaria returned to my mind. No matter! I remained leaning on the window, with a thirsty longing to plunge myself into this blue moon-mist, this dew and perfume and silence, which seemed to vibrate and quiver like the stars that strewed the depths of heaven. ... What music, even Wagner's, or of that great singer of starry nights, the divine Schumann, what music could ever compare with this great silence, with this great concert of voiceless things that sing within one's soul?

As I made this reflection, a note, high, vibrating, and sweet, rent the silence, which immediately closed around it. I leaned out of the window, my heart beating as though it must burst. After a brief space the silence was cloven once more by that note, as the darkness is cloven by a falling star or a firefly rising slowly like a rocket. But this time it was plain that the voice did not come, as I had imagined, from the garden, but from the house itself, from some corner of this rambling old villa of Mistrà.

Mistrà – Mistrà! The name rang in my ears, and I began at length to grasp its significance, which seems to have escaped me till then. 'Yes,' I said to myself, 'it is quite natural.' And with this odd impression of naturalness was mixed a feverish, impatient pleasure. It was as if I had come to Mistrà on purpose, and that I was about to meet the object of my long and weary hopes.

Grasping the lamp with its singed green shade, I gently opened the door and made my way through a series of long passages and of big, empty rooms, in which my steps re-echoed as in a church, and my light disturbed whole swarms of bats. I wandered at random, farther and farther from the inhabited part of the buildings.

This silence made me feel sick; I gasped as under a sudden disappointment.

All of a sudden there came a sound – chords, metallic, sharp, rather like the tone of a mandoline – close to my ear. Yes, quite close: I was separated from the sounds only by a partition. I fumbled for a door; the unsteady light of my lamp was insufficient for my eyes, which were swimming like those of a drunkard. At last I found a latch, and, after a moment's hesitation, I lifted it and gently pushed open the door. At first I could not understand what manner of place I was in. It was dark all round me, but a brilliant light blinded me, a light coming from below and striking the opposite wall. It was as if I had entered a dark box in a half-lighted theatre. I was, in fact, in something of the kind, a sort of dark hole with a high balustrade, half-hidden by an up-drawn curtain. I remembered those little galleries or recesses for the use of musicians or lookers-on which exist under the ceiling of the ballrooms in certain old Italian palaces. Yes; it must have been one like that. Opposite me was a vaulted ceiling covered with gilt mouldings, which framed great time-blackened canvases; and lower down, in the light thrown up from below, stretched a wall covered with faded frescoes. Where had I seen that goddess in lilac and lemon draperies fore-shortened over a big, green peacock? For she was familiar to me, and the stucco Tritons also who twisted their tails round her gilded frame. And that fresco, with warriors in Roman cuirasses and green and blue lappets, and knee-breeches – where could I have seen them before? I asked myself these questions without experiencing any surprise. Moreover, I was very calm, as one is calm sometimes in extraordinary dreams – could I be dreaming?

I advanced gently and leaned over the balustrade. My eyes were met at first by the darkness above me, where, like gigantic spiders, the big chandeliers rotated slowly, hanging from the ceiling. Only one of them was lit, and its Murano-glass pendants, its carnations and roses, shone opalescent in the light of the guttering wax. This chandelier lighted up the opposite wall and that piece of ceiling with the goddess and the green peacock; it illumined, but far less well, a corner of the huge room, where, in the shadow of a kind of canopy, a little group of people were crowding round a yellow satin sofa, of the same kind as those that lined the walls. On the sofa, half-screened from me by the surrounding persons, a woman was stretched out: the silver of her embroidered dress and the rays of her diamonds gleamed and shot forth as she moved uneasily. And immediately under the chandelier, in the full light, a man stooped over a harpsichord, his head bent slightly, as if collecting his thoughts before singing.

He struck a few chords and sang. Yes, sure enough, it was the voice, the voice that had so long been persecuting me! I recognised at once that delicate, voluptuous quality, strange, exquisite, sweet beyond words, but lacking all youth and clearness. That passion veiled in tears which had troubled my brain that night on the lagoon, and again on the Grand Canal singing the *Biondina*, and yet again, only two days since, in the deserted cathedral of Padua. But I recognised now what seemed to have been hidden from me till then, that this voice was what I cared most for in all the wide world.

The voice wound and unwound itself in long, languishing phrases, in rich, voluptuous *rifiorituras*, all fretted with tiny scales and exquisite, crisp shakes; it stopped ever and anon, swaying as if panting in languid delight. And I felt my body melt even as wax in the sunshine, and it seemed to me that I too was turning fluid and vaporous, in order to mingle with these sounds as the moonbeams mingle with the dew.

Suddenly, from the dimly lighted corner by the canopy, came a little piteous wail; then another followed, and was lost in the singer's voice. During a long phrase on the harpsichord, sharp and tinkling, the singer turned his head towards the dais, and there came a plaintive little sob. But he, instead of stopping, struck a sharp chord; and with a thread of voice so hushed as to be scarcely audible, slid softly into a long *cadenza.* At the same moment he threw his head backwards, and the light fell full upon the handsome, effeminate face, with its ashy pallor and big, black brows, of the singer Zaffirino. At the sight of that face, sensual and sullen, of that smile which was cruel and mocking like a bad woman's, I understood – I knew not why, by what process – that his singing *must* be cut short, that the accursed phrase *must* never be finished. I understood that I was before an assassin, that he was killing this woman, and killing me also, with his wicked voice.

I rushed down the narrow stair which led down from the box, pursued, as it were, by that exquisite voice, swelling, swelling by insensible degrees. I flung myself on the door which must be that of the big saloon. I could see its light between the panels. I bruised my hands in trying to wrench the latch. The door was fastened tight, and while I was struggling with that locked door I heard the voice swelling, swelling, rending asunder that downy veil which wrapped it, leaping forth clear, resplendent, like the sharp and glittering blade of a knife that seemed to enter deep into my breast. Then, once more, a wail, a death-groan, and that dreadful noise, that hideous gurgle of breath strangled by a rush of blood. And then a long shake, acute, brilliant, triumphant.

The door gave way beneath my weight, one half crashed in. I entered. I was blinded by a flood of blue moonlight. It poured in through four great windows, peaceful and diaphanous, a pale blue mist of moonlight, and turned the huge room into a kind of submarine cave, paved with moonbeams, full of shimmers, of pools of moonlight. It was as bright as at midday, but the brightness was cold, blue, vaporous, supernatural. The room was completely empty, like a great hay-loft. Only, there hung from the ceiling the ropes which had once supported a chandelier; and in a corner, among stacks of wood and heaps of Indian-corn, whence spread a sickly smell of damp and mildew, there stood a long, thin harpsichord, with spindle-legs, and its cover cracked from end to end.

I felt, all of a sudden, very calm. The one thing that mattered was the phrase that kept moving in my head, the phrase of that unfinished cadence which I had heard but an instant before. I opened the harpsichord, and my fingers came down boldly upon its keys. A jingle-jangle of broken strings, laughable and dreadful, was the only answer.

Then an extraordinary fear overtook me. I clambered out of one of the windows; I rushed up the garden and wandered through the fields, among the canals and the embankments, until the moon had set and the dawn began to shiver, followed, pursued for ever by that jangle of broken strings.

People expressed much satisfaction at my recovery. It seems that one dies of those fevers.

Recovery? But have I recovered? I walk, and eat and drink and talk; I can even sleep. I live the life of other living creatures. But I am wasted by a strange and deadly disease. I can never lay hold of my own inspiration. My head is filled with music which is certainly by me, since I have never heard it before, but which still is not my own, which I despise and abhor: little, tripping flourishes and languishing phrases, and long-drawn, echoing cadences.

O wicked, wicked voice, violin of flesh and blood made by the Evil One's hand, may I not even execrate thee in peace; but is it necessary that, at the moment when I curse, the longing to hear thee again should parch my soul like hell-thirst? And since I have satiated thy lust for revenge, since thou hast withered my life and withered my genius, is it not time for pity? May I not hear one note, only one note of thine, O singer, O wicked and contemptible wretch?

HENRY JAMES

From

THE WINGS OF THE DOVE

I

IT WAS AFTER they had gone that he truly felt the difference, which was most to be felt moreover in his faded old rooms. He had recovered from the first a part of his attachment to this scene of contemplation, within sight, as it was, of the Rialto bridge, on the hither side of that arch of associations and the left going up the Canal; he had seen it in a particular light, to which, more and more, his mind and his hands adjusted it; but the interest the place now wore for him had risen at a bound, becoming a force that, on the spot, completely engaged and absorbed him, and relief from which – if relief was the name – he could find only by getting away and out of reach. What had come to pass within his walls lingered there as an obsession importunate to all his senses; it lived again, as a cluster of pleasant memories, at every hour and in every object; it made everything but itself irrelevant and tasteless. It remained, in a word, a conscious watchful presence, active on its own side, for ever to be reckoned with, in face of which the effort at detachment was scarcely less futile than frivolous. Kate had come to him; it was only once – and this not from any failure of their need, but from such impossibilities, for bravery alike and for subtlety, as there was at the last no blinking; yet she had come, that once, to stay, as people called it; and what survived of her, what reminded and insisted, was something he couldn't have banished if he had wished. Luckily he didn't wish, even though there might be for a man almost a shade of the awful in so unqualified a consequence of his act. It had simply *worked*, his idea, the idea he had made her accept; and all erect before him, really covering the ground as far as he could see, was the fact of the gained success that this represented. It was, otherwise, but the fact of the idea as directly applied, as converted from a luminous conception into an historic truth. He had known it before but as desired and urged, as convincingly insisted on for the help it would render; so that at present, *with* the help rendered, it seemed to acknowledge its office and to set up, for memory and faith, an insistence of its own. He had in fine judged his friend's pledge in advance as an inestimable value, and what he must now know his case for was that of a possession of the value to the full. Wasn't it perhaps even rather the value that possessed *him*, kept him thinking of it and waiting on it, turning round and round it and making sure of it again from this side and that?

It played for him – certainly in this prime after-glow – the part of a treasure kept at home in safety and sanctity, something he was sure of finding in its place when, with each return, he worked his heavy old key in the lock. The door had but to open for him to be with it again and for it to be all there; so intensely there that, as we say, no other act was possible to him than the renewed act, almost the hallucination, of intimacy. Wherever he looked or sat or stood, to whatever aspect he gave for the instant the advantage, it was in view as nothing of the moment, nothing begotten of time or of chance could be, or ever would; it was in view as, when the curtain has risen, the play on the stage is in view, night after night, for the fiddlers. He remained thus, in his own theatre, in his single person, perpetual orchestra to the ordered drama, the confirmed 'run'; playing low and slow, moreover, in the regular way, for the situations of most importance. No other visitor was to come to him; he met, he bumped occasionally, in the Piazza or in his walks, against claimants to acquaintance, remembered or forgotten, at present mostly effusive, sometimes even inquisitive; but he gave no address and encouraged no approach; he couldn't for his life, he felt, have opened his door to a third person. Such a person would have interrupted him, would have profaned his secret or perhaps have guessed it; would at any rate have broken the spell of what he conceived himself – in the absence of anything 'to show' – to be inwardly doing. He was giving himself up – that was quite enough – to the general feeling of his renewed engagement to fidelity. The force of the engagement, the quantity of the article to be supplied, the special solidity of the contract, the way, above all, as a service for which the price named by him had been magnificently paid, his equivalent office was to take effect – such items might well fill his consciousness when there was nothing from outside to interfere. Never was a consciousness more rounded and fastened down over what filled it; which is precisely what we have spoken of as, in its degree, the oppression of success, the somewhat chilled state – tending to the solitary – of supreme recognition. If it was slightly awful to feel so justified, this was by the loss of the warmth of the element of mystery. The lucid reigned instead of it, and it was into the lucid that he sat and stared. He shook himself out of it a dozen times a day, tried to break by his own act his constant still communion. It wasn't still communion she had meant to bequeath him; it was the very different business of that kind of fidelity of which the other name was careful action.

Nothing, he perfectly knew, was less like careful action

than the immersion he enjoyed at home. The actual grand
queerness was that to be faithful to Kate he had positively to
take his eyes, his arms, his lips straight off her – he had to let
her alone. He had to remember it was time to go to the palace
– which in truth was a mercy, since the check was not less
effectual than imperative. What it came to, fortunately, as
yet, was that when he closed the door behind him for an
absence he always shut her in. Shut her out – it came to that
rather, when once he had got a little away; and before he
reached the palace, much more after hearing at his heels the
bang of the greater *portone*, he felt free enough not to know
his position as oppressively false. As Kate was *all* in his poor
rooms, and not a ghost of her left for the grander, it was only
on reflexion that the falseness came out; so long as he left it
to the mercy of beneficent chance it offered him no face and
made of him no claim that he couldn't meet without aggravation of his inward sense. This aggravation had been his original horror; yet what – in Milly's presence, each day – was
horror doing with him but virtually letting him off? He
shouldn't perhaps get off to the end; there was time enough
still for the possibility of shame to pounce. Still, however, he
did constantly a little more what he liked best, and that kept
him for the time more safe. What he liked best was, in any
case, to know *why* things were as he felt them; and he knew
it pretty well, in this case, ten days after the retreat of his
other friends. He then fairly perceived that – even putting
their purity of motive at its highest – it was neither Kate nor
he who made his strange relation to Milly, who made her
own, so far as it might be, innocent; it was neither of them
who practically purged it – if practically purged it was. Milly
herself did everything – so far at least as he was concerned –
Milly herself, and Milly's house, and Milly's hospitality, and
Milly's manner, and Milly's character, and, perhaps still more

than anything else, Milly's imagination, Mrs Stringham and Sir Luke indeed a little aiding: whereby he knew the blessing of a fair pretext to ask himself what more he had to do. Something incalculable wrought for them – for him and Kate; something outside, beyond, above themselves, and doubtless ever so much better than they: which wasn't a reason, however – its being so much better – for them not to profit by it. Not to profit by it, so far as profit could be reckoned, would have been to go directly against it; and the spirit of generosity at present engendered in Densher could have felt no greater pang than by his having to go directly against Milly.

To go *with* her was the thing, so far as she could herself go; which, from the moment her tenure of her loved palace stretched on, was possible but by his remaining near her. This remaining was of course on the face of it the most 'marked' of demonstrations – which was exactly why Kate had required it; it was so marked that on the very evening of the day it had taken effect Milly herself hadn't been able not to reach out to him, with an exquisite awkwardness, for some account of it. It was as if she had wanted from him some name that, now they were to be almost alone together, they could, for their further ease, know it and call it by – it being, after all, almost rudimentary that his presence, of which the absence of the others made quite a different thing, couldn't but have for himself some definite basis. She only wondered about the basis it would have for himself, and how he would describe it; that would quite do for her – it even would have done for her, he could see, had he produced some reason merely trivial, had he said he was waiting for money or clothes, for letters or for orders from Fleet Street, without which, as she might have heard, newspaper-men never took a step. He hadn't in the event quite sunk to that; but he had none the less had there with her, that night, on Mrs Stringham's leaving them alone – Mrs Stringham proved really prodigious – his acquaintance with a shade of awkwardness darker than any Milly could know. He had supposed himself beforehand, on the question of what he was doing or pretending, in possession of some tone that would serve; but there were three minutes of his feeling incapable of promptness quite in the same degree in which a gentleman whose pocket has been picked feels incapable of purchase. It even didn't help him, oddly, that he was sure Kate would in some way have spoken for him – or rather not so much in some way as in one very particular way. He hadn't asked her, at the last, what she might, in the connexion, have said; nothing would have induced him to put such a question after she had been to see him: his lips were so sealed by that passage, his spirit in fact so hushed, in respect to any charge upon her freedom. There was something he could only therefore read back into the probabilities, and when he left the palace an hour afterwards it was with a sense of having breathed there, in the very air, the truth he had been guessing.

Just this perception it was, however, that had made him for the time ugly to himself in his awkwardness. It was horrible, with this creature, to *be* awkward; it was odious to be seeking excuses for the relation that involved it. Any relation that involved it was by the very fact as much discredited as a dish would be at dinner if one had to take medicine as a sauce. What Kate would have said in one of the young women's last talks was that – if Milly absolutely must have the truth about it – Mr Densher was staying because she had really seen no way but to require it of him. If he stayed he didn't follow her – or didn't appear to her aunt to be doing so; and when she kept him from following her Mrs Lowder couldn't pretend, in scenes, the renewal of which at this time of day was painful, that she after all didn't snub him as she might. She did nothing in fact *but* snub him – wouldn't that have been part of the story? – only Aunt Maud's suspicions were of the sort that had repeatedly to be dealt with. He had been, by the same token, reasonable enough – as he now, for that matter, well might; he had consented to oblige them, aunt and niece, by giving the plainest sign possible that he could exist away from London. To exist away from London was to exist away from Kate Croy – which was a gain, much appreciated, to the latter's comfort. There was a minute, at this hour, out of Densher's three, during which he knew the terror of Milly's uttering some such allusion to their friend's explanation as he must meet with words that wouldn't destroy it. To destroy it was to destroy everything, to destroy probably Kate herself, to destroy in particular by a beauty of faith still uglier than anything else the beauty of their own last passage. He had given her his word of honour that if she would come to him he would act absolutely in her sense, and he had done so with a full enough vision of what her sense implied. What it implied for one thing was that to-night in the great saloon, noble in its half-lighted beauty, and straight in the white face of his young hostess, divine in her trust, or at any rate inscrutable in her mercy – what it implied was that he should lie with his lips. The single thing, of all things, that could save him from it would be Milly's letting him off after having thus scared him. What made her mercy inscrutable was that if she had already more than once saved him it was yet apparently without knowing how nearly he was lost.

These were transcendent motions, not the less blest for being obscure; whereby yet once more he was to feel the pressure lighten. He was kept on his feet in short by the felicity of her not presenting him with Kate's version as a version to adopt. He couldn't stand up to lie – he felt as if he should have to go down on his knees. As it was he just sat there shaking a little for nervousness the leg he had crossed over the other. She was sorry for his suffered snub, but he had nothing more to subscribe to, to perjure himself about, than the three or four inanities he had, on his own side, feebly prepared for the crisis. He scrambled a little higher than the reference to money and clothes, letters and directions from his manager; but he brought out the beauty of the chance for him – there before him like a temptress painted by Titian – to do a little quiet writing. He was vivid for a moment on the difficulty of writing quietly in London; and he was precipitate, almost explosive, on his idea, long cherished, of a book.

The explosion lighted her face. 'You'll do your book here?'

'I hope to begin it.'

'It's something you haven't begun?'

'Well, only just.'

'And since you came?'

She was so full of interest that he shouldn't perhaps after all be too easily let off. 'I tried to think a few days ago that I had broken ground.'

Scarcely anything, it was indeed clear, could have let him in deeper. 'I'm afraid we've made an awful mess of your time.'

'Of course you have. But what I'm hanging on for now is precisely to repair that ravage.'

'Then you mustn't mind me, you know.'

'You'll see,' he tried to say with ease, 'how little I shall mind anything.'

'You'll want' – Milly had thrown herself into it – 'the best part of your days.'

He thought a moment: he did what he could to wreathe it in smiles. 'Oh I shall make shift with the worst part. The best will be for *you*.' And he wished Kate could hear him. It didn't help him moreover that he visibly, even pathetically, imaged to her by such touches his quest for comfort against discipline. He was to bury Kate's so signal snub, and also the hard law she had now laid on him, under a high intellectual effort. This at least was his crucifixion – that Milly was so interested. She was so interested that she presently asked him if he found his rooms propitious, while he felt that in just decently answering her he put on a brazen mask. He should need it quite particularly were she to express again her imagination of coming to tea with him – an extremity that he saw he was not to be spared. 'We depend on you, Susie and I, you know, not to forget we're coming' – the extremity was but to face that remainder, yet it demanded all his tact. Facing their visit itself – to that, no matter what he might have to do, he would never consent, as we know, to be pushed; and this even though it might be exactly such a demonstration as would figure for him at the top of Kate's list of his proprieties. He could wonder freely enough, deep within, if Kate's view of that especial propriety had not been modified by a subsequent occurrence; but his deciding that it was quite likely not to have been had no effect on his own preference for tact. It pleased him to think of 'tact' as his present prop in doubt; that glossed his predicament over, for it was of application among the sensitive and the kind. He wasn't inhuman, in fine, so long as it would serve. It had to serve now, accordingly, to help him not to sweeten Milly's hopes. He didn't want to be rude to them, but he still less wanted them to flower again in the particular connexion; so that, casting about him in his anxiety for a middle way to meet her, he put his foot, with unhappy effect, just in the wrong place. 'Will it be safe for you to break into your custom of not leaving the house?'

'"Safe"—?' She had for twenty seconds an exquisite pale

glare. Oh but he didn't need it, by that time, to wince; he had winced for himself as soon as he had made his mistake. He had done what, so unforgettably, she had asked him in London not to do; he had touched, all alone with her here, the supersensitive nerve of which she had warned him. He had not, since the occasion in London, touched it again till now; but he saw himself freshly warned that it was able to bear still less. So for the moment he knew as little what to do as he had ever known it in his life. He couldn't emphasise that he thought of her as dying, yet he couldn't pretend he thought of her as indifferent to precautions. Meanwhile too she had narrowed his choice. 'You suppose me so awfully bad?'

He turned, in his pain, within himself; but by the time the colour had mounted to the roots of his hair he had found what he wanted. 'I'll believe whatever you tell me.'

'Well then, I'm splendid.'

'Oh I don't need you to tell me that.'

'I mean I'm capable of life.'

'I've never doubted it.'

'I mean,' she went on, 'that I want so to live—!'

'Well?' he asked while she paused with the intensity of it.

'Well, that I know I *can*.'

'Whatever you do?' He shrank from solemnity about it.

'Whatever I do. If I want to.'

'If you want to do it?'

'If I want to live. I *can*,' Milly repeated.

He had clumsily brought it on himself, but he hesitated with all the pity of it. 'Ah then *that* I believe.'

'I will, I will,' she declared; yet with the weight of it somehow turned for him to mere light and sound.

He felt himself smiling through a mist. 'You simply must!'

It brought her straight again to the fact. 'Well then, if you say it, why mayn't we pay you our visit?'

'Will it help you to live?'

'Every little helps,' she laughed; 'and it's very little for me, in general, to stay at home. Only I shan't want to miss it—!'

'Yes?' – she had dropped again.

'Well, on the day you give us a chance.'

It was amazing what so brief an exchange had at this point done with him. His great scruple suddenly broke, giving way to something inordinately strange, something of a nature to become clear to him only when he had left her. 'You can come,' he said, 'when you like.'

What had taken place for him, however – the drop, almost with violence, of everything but a sense of her own reality – apparently showed in his face or his manner, and even so vividly that she could take it for something else. 'I see how you feel – that I'm an awful bore about it and that, sooner than have any such upset, you'll go. So it's no matter.'

'No matter? Oh!' – he quite protested now.

'If it drives you away to escape us. We want you not to go.'

It was beautiful how she spoke for Mrs Stringham. Whatever it was, at any rate, he shook his head. 'I won't go.'

'Then *I* won't go!' she brightly declared.

'You mean you won't come to me?'

'No – never now. It's over. But it's all right. I mean, apart from that,' she went on, 'that I won't do anything I oughtn't or that I'm not forced to.'

'Oh who can ever force you?' he asked with his hand-to-mouth way, at all times, of speaking for her encouragement. 'You're the least coercible of creatures.'

'Because, you think, I'm so free?'

'The freest person probably now in the world. You've got everything.'

'Well,' she smiled, 'call it so. I don't complain.'

On which again, in spite of himself, it let him in. 'No I know you don't complain.'

As soon as he had said it he had himself heard the pity in it. His telling her she had 'everything' was extravagant kind humour, whereas his knowing so tenderly that she didn't complain was terrible kind gravity. Milly felt, he could see, the difference; he might as well have praised her outright for looking death in the face. This was the way she just looked *him* again, and it was of no attenuation that she took him up more gently than ever. 'It isn't a merit – when one sees one's way.'

'To peace and plenty? Well, I dare say not.'

'I mean to keeping what one has.'

'Oh that's success. If what one has is good,' Densher said at random, 'it's enough to try for.'

'Well, it's my limit. I'm not trying for more.' To which then she added with a change: 'And now about your book.'

'My book—?' He had got in a moment so far from it.

'The one you're now to understand that nothing will induce either Susie or me to run the risk of spoiling.'

He cast about, but he made up his mind. 'I'm not doing a book.'

'Not what you said?' she asked in a wonder. 'You're not writing?'

He already felt relieved. 'I don't know, upon my honour, what I'm doing.'

It made her visibly grave; so that, disconcerted in another way, he was afraid of what she would see in it. She saw in fact exactly what he feared, but again his honour, as he called it, was saved even while she didn't know she had threatened it. Taking his words for a betrayal of the sense that he, on his side, *might* complain, what she clearly wanted was to urge on him some such patience as he should be perhaps able to arrive at with her indirect help. Still more clearly, however, she wanted to be sure of how far she might venture; and he could see her make out in a moment that she had a sort of test.

'Then if it's not for your book—?'

'What *am* I staying for?'

'I mean with your London work – with all you have to do. Isn't it rather empty for you?'

'Empty for me?' He remembered how Kate had held that she might propose marriage, and he wondered if this were the way she would naturally begin it. It would leave him, such an incident, he already felt, at a loss, and the note of his finest anxiety might have been in the vagueness of his reply. 'Oh well—!'

'I ask too many questions?' She settled it for herself before he could protest. 'You stay because you've got to.'

He grasped at it. 'I stay because I've got to.' And he couldn't have said when he had uttered it if it were loyal to Kate or disloyal. It gave her, in a manner, away; it showed the tip of the ear of her plan. Yet Milly took it, he perceived, but as a plain statement of his truth. He was waiting for what Kate would have told her of – the permission from Lancaster Gate to come any nearer. To remain friends with either niece or aunt he mustn't stir without it. All this Densher read in the girl's sense of the spirit of his reply; so that it made him feel he was lying, and he had to think of something to correct that. What he thought of was, in an instant, 'Isn't it enough, whatever may be one's other complications, to stay after all for *you*?'

'Oh you must judge.'

He was by this time on his feet to take leave, and was also at last too restless. The speech in question at least wasn't disloyal to Kate; that was the very tone of their bargain. So was it, by being loyal, another kind of lie, the lie of the uncandid profession of a motive. He was staying so little 'for' Milly that he was staying positively against her. He didn't, none the less, know, and at last, thank goodness, didn't care. The only thing he could say might make it either better or worse. 'Well then, so long as I don't go, you must think of me all *as* judging!'

2

HE DIDN'T GO home, on leaving her – he didn't want to; he walked instead, through his narrow ways and his *campi* with gothic arches, to a small and comparatively sequestered café where he had already more than once found refreshment and comparative repose, together with solutions that con- sisted mainly and pleasantly of further indecisions. It was a literal fact that those awaiting him there to-night, while he leaned back on his velvet bench with his head against a florid mirror and his eyes not looking further than the fumes of his tobacco, might have been regarded by him as a little less limp than usual. This wasn't because, before getting to his feet again, there was a step he had seen his way to; it was simply because the acceptance of his position took sharper effect from his sense of what he had just had to deal with. When half an hour before, at the palace, he had turned about to Milly on the question of the impossibility so inwardly felt, turned about on the spot and under her eyes, he had acted, by the sudden force of his seeing much further, seeing how little, how not at all, impossibilities mattered. It wasn't a case for pedantry; when people were at *her* pass everything was allowed. And her pass was now, as by the sharp click of a spring, just completely his own – to the extent, as he felt, of her deep dependence on him. Anything he should do or shouldn't would have close reference to her life, which was thus absolutely in his hands – and ought never to have reference to anything else. It was on the cards for him that he might kill her – that was the way he read the cards as he sat in his customary corner. The fear in this thought made him let everything go, kept him there actually, all motionless, for three hours on end. He renewed his consumption and smoked more cigarettes than he had ever done in the time. What had come out for him had come out, with this first intensity, as a terror; so that action itself, of any sort, the right as well as the wrong – if the difference even survived – had heard in it a vivid 'Hush!' the injunction to keep from that moment intensely still. He thought in fact while his vigil lasted of several different ways for his doing so, and the hour might have served him as a lesson in going on tiptoe.

What he finally took home, when he ventured to leave the place, was the perceived truth that he might on any other system go straight to destruction. Destruction was represented for him by the idea of his really bringing to a point, on Milly's side, anything whatever. Nothing so 'brought', he easily argued, but *must* be in one way or another a catastrophe. He was mixed up in her fate, or her fate, if that should be better, was mixed up in *him*, so that a single false motion might either way snap the coil. They helped him, it was true, these considerations, to a degree of eventual peace, for what they luminously amounted to was that he was to do nothing, and that fell in after all with the burden laid on him by Kate. He was only not to budge without the girl's leave – not, oddly enough at the last, to move without it, whether further or nearer, any more than without Kate's. It was to this his wisdom reduced itself – to the need again simply to be kind.

That was the same as being still – as studying to create the minimum of vibration. He felt himself as he smoked shut up to a room on the wall of which something precious was too precariously hung. A false step would bring it down, and it must hang as long as possible. He was aware when he walked away again that even Fleet Street wouldn't at this juncture successfully touch him. His manager might wire that he was wanted, but he could easily be deaf to his manager. His money for the idle life might be none too much; happily, however, Venice was cheap, and it was moreover the queer fact that Milly in a manner supported him. The greatest of his expenses really was to walk to the palace to dinner. He didn't want, in short, to give that up, and he should probably be able, he felt, to stay his breath and his hand. He should be able to be still enough through everything.

He tried that for three weeks, with the sense after a little of not having failed. There had to be a delicate art in it, for he wasn't trying – quite the contrary – to be either distant or dull. That would not have been being 'nice', which in its own form was the real law. That too might just have produced the vibration he desired to avert; so that he best kept everything in place by not hesitating or fearing, as it were, to let himself go – go in the direction, that is to say, of staying. It depended on where he went; which was what he meant by taking care. When one went on tiptoe one could turn off for retreat without betraying the manœuvre. Perfect tact – the necessity for which he had from the first, as we know, happily recognised – was to keep all intercourse in the key of the absolutely settled. It was settled thus for instance that they were indissoluble good friends, and settled as well that her being the American girl was, just in time and for the relation they found themselves concerned in, a boon inappreciable. If, at least, as the days went on, she was to fall short of her prerogative of the great national, the great maidenly ease, if she didn't diviningly and responsively desire and labour to record herself as possessed of it, this wouldn't have been for want of Densher's keeping her, with his idea, well up to it – wouldn't have been in fine for want of his encouragement and reminder. He didn't perhaps in so many words speak to her of the quantity itself as of the thing she was least to intermit; but he talked of it, freely, in what he flattered himself was an impersonal way, and this held it there before her – since he was careful also to talk pleasantly. It was at once their idea, when all was said, and the most marked of their conveniences. The type was so elastic that it could be stretched to almost anything; and yet, not stretched, it kept down, remained normal, remained properly within bounds. And he *had* meanwhile, thank goodness, without being too much disconcerted, the sense, for the girl's part of the business, of the queerest conscious compliance, of her doing very much what he wanted, even though without her quite seeing why. She fairly touched this once in saying: 'Oh yes, you like us to be as we are because it's a kind of facilitation to you that we don't quite measure: I think one would have to be English to measure it!' – and that too, strangely enough, without prejudice to her good nature. She might have been conceived as doing – that is of being – what he liked in order perhaps only to judge where it would take them. They really as it went on *saw* each other at the game; she knowing he tried to keep her in tune with his conception, and he knowing she thus knew it. Add that he again knew she knew, and yet that nothing was spoiled by it, and we get a fair impression of the line they found most completely workable. The strangest fact of all for us must be that the success he himself thus promoted was precisely what figured to his gratitude as the something above and beyond him, above and beyond Kate, that made for daily decency. There would scarce have been felicity – certainly too little of the right lubricant – had not the national character so invoked been, not less inscrutable than entirely, in Milly's chords. It made up her unity and was the one thing he could unlimitedly take for granted.

He did so then, daily, for twenty days, without deepened fear of the undue vibration that was keeping him watchful. He knew in his nervousness that he was living at best from day to day and from hand to mouth; yet he had succeeded, he believed, in avoiding a mistake. All women had alternatives, and Milly's would doubtless be shaky too; but the national character was firm in her, whether as all of her, practically, by this time, or but as a part; the national character that, in a woman still so young, made of the air breathed a virtual non-conductor. It wasn't till a certain occasion when the twenty days had passed that, going to the palace at teatime, he was met by the information that the signorina padrona was not 'receiving'. The announcement met him, in the court, on the lips of one of the gondoliers, met him, he thought, with such a conscious eye as the knowledge of his freedoms of access, hitherto conspicuously shown, could scarce fail to beget. Densher had not been at Palazzo Leporelli among the mere receivable, but had taken his place once for all among the involved and included, so that on being so flagrantly braved he recognised after a moment the propriety of a further appeal. Neither of the two ladies, it appeared, received, and yet Pasquale was not prepared to say that either was *poco bene.* He was yet not prepared to say that either was anything, and he would have been blank, Densher mentally noted, if the term could ever apply to members of a race in whom vacancy was but a nest of darknesses – not a vain surface, but a place of withdrawal in which something obscure, something always ominous, indistinguishably lived. He felt afresh indeed at this hour the force of the veto laid within the palace on any mention, any cognition, of the liabilities of its mistress. The state of her health was never confessed to there as a reason. How much it might deeply be taken for one was another matter; of which he grew fully aware on carrying his question further. This appeal was to his friend Eugenio, whom he immediately sent for, with whom, for three rich minutes, protected from the weather, he was confronted in the gallery that led from the water-steps to the court, and whom he always called, in meditation, his friend; seeing it was so elegantly presumable he would have put an end to him if he could. That produced a relation which required a name of its own, an intimacy of consciousness in truth for each – an intimacy of eye, of ear, of general sensibility, of everything but tongue. It had been, in other words, for the five weeks, far from occult to our young man that Eugenio took a view of him not less finely formal than essentially vulgar, but which at the same time he couldn't himself raise an eyebrow to prevent. It was all in the air now again; it was as much between them as ever while Eugenio waited on him in the court.

The weather, from early morning, had turned to storm, the first sea-storm of the autumn, and Densher had almost invidiously brought him down the outer staircase – the massive ascent, the great feature of the court, to Milly's *piano nobile*. This was to pay him – it was the one chance – for all imputations; the imputation in particular that, clever, *tanto bello* and not rich, the young man from London was – by the obvious way – pressing Miss Theale's fortune hard. It was to pay him for the further ineffable intimation that a gentleman must take the young lady's most devoted servant (interested scarcely less in the high attraction) for a strangely casual appendage if he counted in such a connexion on impunity and prosperity. These interpretations were odious to Densher for the simple reason that they might have been so true of the attitude of an inferior man, and three things alone, accordingly, had kept him from righting himself. One of these was that his critic sought expression only in an impersonality, a positive inhumanity, of politeness; the second was that refinements of expression in a friend's servant were not a thing a visitor could take action on; and the third was the fact that the particular attribution of motive did him after all no wrong. It was his own fault if the vulgar view, the view that might have been taken of an inferior man, happened so incorrigibly to fit him. He apparently wasn't so different from inferior men as that came to. If therefore, in fine, Eugenio figured to him as 'my friend' because he was conscious of his seeing so much of him, what he made him see on the same lines in the course of their present interview was ever so much more. Densher felt that he marked himself, no doubt, as insisting, by dissatisfaction with the gondolier's answer, on the pursuit taken for granted in him; and yet felt it only in the augmented, the exalted distance that was by this time established between them. Eugenio had of course reflected that a word to Miss Theale from such a pair of lips would cost him his place; but he could also bethink himself that, so long as the word never came – and it was, on the basis he had arranged, impossible – he enjoyed the imagination of mounting guard. He had never so mounted guard, Densher could see, as during these minutes in the damp *loggia* where the storm-gusts were strong; and there came in fact for our young man, as a result of his presence, a sudden sharp sense that everything had turned to the dismal. Something had happened – he didn't know what; and it wasn't Eugenio who would tell him. What Eugenio told him was that he thought the ladies – as if their liability had been equal – were a 'leetle' fatigued, just a 'leetle leetle', and without any cause named for it. It was one of the signs of what Densher felt in him that, by a profundity, a true deviltry of resources, he always met the latter's Italian with English and his English with Italian. He now, as usual, slightly smiled at him in the process – but ever so slightly this time, his manner also being attuned, our young man made out, to the thing, whatever it was, that constituted the rupture of peace.

This manner, while they stood a long minute facing each other over all they didn't say, played a part as well in the sudden jar to Densher's protected state. It was a Venice all of evil that had broken out for them alike, so that they were together in their anxiety, if they really could have met on it; a Venice of cold lashing rain from a low black sky, of wicked wind raging through narrow passes, of general arrest and interruption, with the people engaged in all the water-life huddled, stranded and wageless, bored and cynical, under archways and bridges. Our young man's mute exchange with his friend contained meanwhile such a depth of reference that, had the pressure been but slightly prolonged, they might have reached a point at which they were equally weak. Each had verily something in mind that would have made a hash of mutual suspicion and in presence of which, as a possibility, they were more united than disjoined. But it was to have been a moment for Densher that nothing could ease off – not even the formal propriety with which his interlocutor finally attended him to the *portone* and bowed upon his retreat. Nothing had passed about his coming back, and the air had made itself felt as a non-conductor of messages. Densher knew of course, as he took his way again, that Eugenio's invitation to return was not what he missed; yet he knew at the same time that what had happened to him was part of his punishment. Out in the square beyond the *fondamenta* that gave access to the land-gate of the palace, out where the wind was higher, he fairly, with the thought of it, pulled his umbrella closer down. It couldn't be, his consciousness, unseen enough by others – the base predicament of having, by a concatenation, just to *take* such things: such things as the fact that one very acute person in the world, whom he couldn't dispose of as an interested scoundrel, enjoyed an opinion of him that there was no attacking, no disproving, no (what was worst of all) even noticing. One had come to a queer pass when a servant's opinion so mattered. Eugenio's would have mattered even if, as founded on a low vision of appearances, it had been quite wrong. It was the more disagreeable accordingly that the vision of appearances was quite right, and yet was scarcely less low.

Such as it was, at any rate, Densher shook it off with the more impatience that he was independently restless. He had to walk in spite of weather, and he took his course, through crooked ways, to the Piazza, where he should have the shelter of the galleries. Here, in the high arcade, half Venice was crowded close, while, on the Molo, at the limit of the expanse, the old columns of the Saint Theodore and of the Lion were the frame of a door wide open to the storm. It was odd for him, as he moved, that it should have made such a difference – if the difference wasn't only that the palace had for the first time failed of a welcome. There was more, but it came from that; that gave the harsh note and broke the spell. The wet and the cold were now to reckon with and it was to Densher precisely as if he had seen the obliteration, at a stroke, of the margin on a faith in which they were all living. The margin had been his name for it – for the thing that, though it had held out, could bear no shock. The shock, in some form, had come, and he wondered about it while, threading his way among loungers as vague as himself, he dropped his eyes sightlessly on the rubbish in shops. There were stretches of the gallery paved with squares of red marble, greasy now with the salt spray; and the whole place, in its huge elegance, the grace of its conception and the beauty of its detail, was more than ever like a great drawing-room, the drawing-room of Europe, profaned and bewildered by some reverse of fortune. He brushed shoulders with brown men whose hats askew, and the loose sleeves of whose pendent jackets, made them resemble melancholy maskers. The tables and chairs that overflowed from the cafés were gathered, still with a pretence of service, into the arcade, and here and there a spectacled German, with his coat-collar up, partook publicly of food and philosophy. These were impressions for Densher too, but he had made the whole circuit thrice before he stopped short, in front of Florian's, with the force of his sharpest. His eye had caught a face within the café – he had spotted an acquaintance behind the glass. The person he had thus paused long enough to look at twice was seated, well within range, at a small table on which a tumbler, half-emptied and evidently neglected, still remained; and though he had on his knee, as he leaned back, a copy of a French newspaper – the heading of the *Figaro* was visible – he stared straight before him at the little opposite rococo wall. Densher had him for a minute in profile, had him for a time during which his identity produced, however quickly, all the effect of establishing connexions – connexions startling and direct; and then, as if it were the one thing more needed, seized the look, determined by a turn of the head, that might have been a prompt result of the sense of being noticed. This wider view showed him *all* Lord Mark – Lord Mark as encountered, several weeks before, the day of the first visit of each to Palazzo Leporelli. For it had been all Lord Mark that was going out, on that occasion, as he came in – he had felt it, in the hall, at the time; and he was accordingly the less at a loss to recognise in a few seconds, as renewed meeting brought it to the surface, the same potential quantity.

It was a matter, the whole passage – it could only be – but of a few seconds; for as he might neither stand there to stare nor on the other hand make any advance from it, he had presently resumed his walk, this time to another pace. It had been for all the world, during his pause, as if he had caught his answer to the riddle of the day. Lord Mark had simply faced him – as he had faced *him*, not placed by him, not at first – as one of the damp shuffling crowd. Recognition, though hanging fire, had then clearly come; yet no light of salutation had been struck from these certainties. Acquaintance between them was scant enough for neither to take it up. That neither had done so was not, however, what now mattered, but that the gentleman at Florian's should be in the place at all. He couldn't have been in it long; Densher, as inevitably a haunter of the great meeting-ground, would in that case have seen him before. He paid short visits; he was on the wing; the question for him even as he sat there was of his train or of his boat. He had come back for something – as a sequel to his earlier visit; and whatever he had come back for it had had time to be done. He might have arrived but last night or that morning; he had already made the difference. It was a great thing for Densher to get this answer. He held it close, he hugged it, quite leaned on it as he continued to circulate. It kept him going and going – it made him no less restless. But it explained – and that was much, for with explanations he might somehow deal. The vice in the air, otherwise, was too much like the breath of fate. The weather had changed, the rain was ugly, the wind wicked, the sea impossible, *because* of Lord Mark. It was because of him, *a fortiori*, that the palace was closed. Densher went round again twice; he found the visitor each time as he had found him first. Once, that is, he was staring before him; the next time he was looking over his *Figaro*, which he had opened out. Densher didn't again stop, but left him apparently unconscious of his passage – on another repetition of which Lord Mark had disappeared. He had spent but the day; he would be off that night; he had now gone to his hotel for arrangements. These things were as plain to Densher as if he had had them in words. The obscure had cleared for him – if cleared it was; there was something he didn't see, the great thing; but he saw so round it and so close to it that this was almost as good. He had been looking at a man who had done what he had come for, and for whom, as done, it temporarily sufficed. The man had come again to see Milly, and Milly had received him. His visit would have taken place just before or just after luncheon, and it was the reason why he himself had found her door shut.

He said to himself that evening, he still said even on the morrow, that he only wanted a reason, and that with this perception of one he could now mind, as he called it, his business. His business, he had settled, as we know, was to keep thoroughly still; and he asked himself why it should prevent this that he could feel, in connexion with the crisis, so remarkably blameless. He gave the appearances before him all the benefit of being critical, so that if blame were to accrue he shouldn't feel he had dodged it. But it wasn't a bit he who, that day, had touched her, and if she was upset it wasn't a bit his act. The ability so to think about it amounted for Densher during several hours to a kind of exhilaration. The exhilaration was heightened fairly, besides, by the visible conditions – sharp, striking, ugly to him – of Lord Mark's return. His constant view of it, for all the next hours, of which there were many, was as a demonstration on the face of it sinister even to his own actual ignorance. He didn't need, for seeing it as evil, seeing it as, to a certainty, in a high degree 'nasty', to know more about it than he had so easily and so wonderfully picked up. You couldn't drop on the poor girl that way without, by the fact, being brutal. Such a visit was a descent, an invasion, an aggression, constituting precisely one or other of the stupid shocks he himself had so decently sought to spare her. Densher had indeed drifted by the next morning to the reflexion – which he positively, with occasion, might have brought straight out – that the only delicate and honourable way of treating a person in such a state was to treat her as *he*, Merton Densher, did. With time, actually – for the impression but deepened – this sense of the contrast, to the advantage of Merton Densher, became a sense of relief, and that in turn a sense of escape. It was for all the world – and he drew a long breath on it – as if a special danger for him had passed. Lord Mark had, without in the least intending such a service, got it straight out of the way. It was *he*, the brute, who had stumbled into just the wrong inspiration and who had therefore produced, for the very person he had wished to hurt, an impunity that was comparative innocence, that was almost like purification. The person he had wished to hurt could only be the person so unaccountably hanging about. To keep still meanwhile was, for this person, more comprehensively, to keep it all up; and to keep it all up was, if that seemed on consideration best, not, for the day or two, to go back to the palace.

The day or two passed – stretched to three days; and with the effect, extraordinarily, that Densher felt himself in the course of them washed but the more clean. Some sign would come if his return should have the better effect; and he was at all events, in absence, without the particular scruple. It wouldn't have been meant for him by either of the women that he was to come back but to face Eugenio. That was impossible – the being again denied; for it made him practically answerable, and answerable was what he wasn't. There was no neglect either in absence, inasmuch as, from the moment he didn't get in, the one message he could send up would be some hope on the score of health. Since accordingly that sort of expression was definitely forbidden him he had only to wait – which he was actually helped to do by his feeling with the lapse of each day more and more wound up to it. The days in themselves were anything but sweet; the wind and the weather lasted, the fireless cold hinted at worse; the broken charm of the world about was broken into smaller pieces. He walked up and down his rooms and listened to the wind – listened also to tinkles of bells and watched for some servant of the palace. He might get a note, but the note never came; there were hours when he stayed at home not to miss it. When he wasn't at home he was in circulation again as he had been at the hour of his seeing Lord Mark. He strolled about the Square with the herd of refugees; he raked the approaches and the cafés on the chance the brute, as he now regularly imaged him, *might* be still there. He could only be there, he knew, to be received afresh; and that – one had but to think of it – would be indeed stiff. He had gone, however – it was proved; though Densher's care for the question either way only added to what was most acrid in the taste of his present ordeal. It all came round to what he was doing for Milly – spending days that neither relief nor escape could purge of a smack of the abject. What was it but abject for a man of his parts to be reduced to such pastimes? What was it but sordid for him, shuffling about in the rain, to have to peep into shops and to consider possible meetings? What was it but odious to find himself wondering what, as between him and another man, a possible meeting would produce? There recurred moments when in spite of everything he felt no straighter than another man. And yet even on the third day, when still nothing had come, he more than ever knew that he wouldn't have budged for the world.

He thought of the two women, in their silence, at last – he at all events thought of Milly – as probably, for her reasons, now intensely wishing him to go. The cold breath of her reasons was, with everything else, in the air; but he didn't care for them any more than for her wish itself, and he would stay in spite of her, stay in spite of odium, stay in spite perhaps of some final experience that would be, for the pain of it, all but unbearable. That would be his one way, purified though he was, to mark his virtue beyond any mistake. It would be accepting the disagreeable, and the disagreeable would be a proof; a proof of his not having stayed for the thing – the agreeable, as it were – that Kate had named. The thing Kate had named was not to have been the odium of staying in spite of hints. It was part of the odium as actual too that Kate was, for her comfort, just now well aloof. These were the first hours since her flight in which his sense of what she had done for him on the eve of that event was to incur a qualification. It was strange, it was perhaps base, to be thinking such things so soon; but one of the intimations of his solitude was that she had provided for herself. She was out of it all, by her act, as much as he was in it; and this difference grew, positively, as his own intensity increased. She had said in their last sharp snatch of talk – sharp though thickly muffled, and with every word in it final and deep, unlike even the deepest words they had ever yet spoken: 'Letters? Never – *now*. Think of it. Impossible.' So that as he had sufficiently caught her sense – into which he read, all the same, a strange inconsequence – they had practically wrapped their understanding in the breach of their correspondence. He had moreover, on losing her, done justice to her law of silence; for there was doubtless a finer delicacy in his not writing to her than in his writing as he must have written had he spoken of themselves. That would have been a turbid strain, and her idea had been to be noble; which, in a degree, was a manner. Only it left her, for the pinch, comparatively at ease. And it left *him*, in the conditions, peculiarly alone. He was alone, that is, till, on the afternoon of his third day, in gathering dusk and renewed rain, with his shabby rooms looking doubtless, in their confirmed dreariness, for the mere eyes of others, at their worst, the grinning padrona threw open the door and introduced Mrs Stringham. That made at a bound a difference, especially when he saw that his visitor was weighted. It appeared part of her weight that she was in a wet waterproof, that she allowed her umbrella to be taken from her by the good woman without consciousness or care, and that her face, under her veil, richly rosy with the driving wind, was – and the veil too – as splashed as if the rain were her tears.

3

THEY CAME TO it almost immediately; he was to wonder afterwards at the fewness of their steps. 'She has turned her face to the wall.'

'You mean she's worse?'

The poor lady stood there as she had stopped; Densher had, in the instant flare of his eagerness, his curiosity, all responsive at sight of her, waved away, on the spot, the padrona, who had offered to relieve her of her mackintosh. She looked vaguely about through her wet veil, intensely alive now to the step she had taken and wishing it not to have been in the dark, but clearly, as yet, seeing nothing. 'I don't know *how* she is – and it's why I've come to you.'

'I'm glad enough you've come,' he said, 'and it's quite – you make me feel – as if I had been wretchedly waiting for you.'

She showed him again her blurred eyes – she had caught at his word. 'Have you been wretched?'

Now, however, on his lips, the word expired. It would have sounded for him like a complaint, and before something he already made out in his visitor he knew his own trouble as small. Hers, under her damp draperies, which shamed his lack of a fire, was great, and he felt she had brought it all with her. He answered that he had been patient and above all that he had been still. 'As still as a mouse – you'll have seen it for yourself. Stiller, for three days together, than I've ever been in my life. It has seemed to me the only thing.'

This qualification of it as a policy or a remedy was straightway for his friend, he saw, a light that her own light could answer. 'It has been best. I've wondered for you. But it has been best,' she said again.

'Yet it has done no good?'

'I don't know. I've been afraid you were gone.' Then as he gave a headshake which, though slow, was deeply mature: 'You *won't* go?'

'Is to "go",' he asked, 'to be still?'

'Oh I mean if you'll stay for me.'

'I'll do anything for you. Isn't it for you alone now I can?'

She thought of it, and he could see even more of the relief she was taking from him. His presence, his face, his voice, the old rooms themselves, so meagre yet so charged, where Kate had admirably been to him – these things counted for her, now she had them, as the help she had been wanting: so

that she still only stood there taking them all in. With it however popped up characteristically a throb of her conscience.
What she thus tasted was almost a personal joy. It told Densher of the three days she on her side had spent. 'Well, anything you do for me – is for her too. Only, only—!'

'Only nothing now matters?'

She looked at him a minute as if he were the fact itself that
he expressed. 'Then you know?'

'Is she dying?' he asked for all answer.

Mrs Stringham waited – her face seemed to sound him.
Then her own reply was strange. 'She hasn't so much as
named you. We haven't spoken.'

'Not for three days?'

'No more,' she simply went on, 'than if it were all over.
Not even by the faintest allusion.'

'Oh,' said Densher with more light, 'you mean you haven't
spoken about *me*?'

'About what else? No more than if you were dead.'

'Well,' he answered after a moment, 'I *am* dead.'

'Then *I* am,' said Susan Shepherd with a drop of her arms
on her waterproof.

It was a tone that, for the minute, imposed itself in its dry
despair; it represented, in the bleak place, which had no life
of its own, none but the life Kate had left, – the sense of
which, for that matter, by mystic channels, might fairly be
reaching the visitor – the very impotence of their extinction.
And Densher had nothing to oppose it withal, nothing but
again: 'Is she dying?'

It made her, however, as if these were crudities, almost
material pangs, only say as before: 'Then you know?'

'Yes,' he at last returned, 'I know. But the marvel to me is
that *you* do. I've no right in fact to imagine or to assume that
you do.'

'You may,' said Susan Shepherd, 'all the same. I know.'

'Everything?'

Her eyes, through her veil, kept pressing him. 'No – not everything. That's why I've come.'

'That I shall really tell you?' With which, as she hesitated and it affected him, he brought out in a groan a doubting 'Oh, oh!' It turned him from her to the place itself, which was a part of what was in him, was the abode, the worn shrine more than ever, of the fact in possession, the fact, now a thick association, for which he had hired it. *That* was not for telling, but Susan Shepherd was, none the less, so decidedly wonderful that the sense of it might really have begun, by an effect already operating, to be a part of her knowledge. He saw, and it stirred him, that she hadn't come to judge him; had come rather, so far as she might dare, to pity. This showed him her own abasement – that, at any rate, of grief; and made him feel with a rush of friendliness that he liked to be with her. The rush had quickened when she met his groan with an attenuation.

'We shall at all events – if that's anything – be together.'

It was his own good impulse in herself. 'It's what I've ventured to feel. It's much.' She replied in effect, silently, that it was whatever he liked; on which, so far as he had been afraid for anything, he knew his fear had dropped. The comfort was huge, for it gave back to him something precious, over which, in the effort of recovery, his own hand had too imperfectly closed. Kate, he remembered, had said to him, with her sole and single boldness – and also on grounds he hadn't then measured – that Mrs Stringham was a person who *wouldn't*, at a pinch, in a stretch of confidence, wince. It was but another of the cases in which Kate was always showing. 'You don't think then very horridly of me?'

And her answer was the more valuable that it came

without nervous effusion – quite as if she understood what he might conceivably have believed. She turned over in fact what she thought, and that was what helped him. 'Oh you've been extraordinary!'

It made him aware the next moment of how they had been planted there. She took off her cloak with his aid, though when she had also, accepting a seat, removed her veil, he recognised in her personal ravage that the words she had just uttered to him were the one flower she had to throw. They were all her consolation for him, and the consolation even still depended on the event. She sat with him at any rate in the grey clearance, as sad as a winter dawn, made by their meeting. The image she again evoked for him loomed in it but the larger. 'She has turned her face to the wall.'

He saw with the last vividness, and it was as if, in their silences, they were simply so leaving what he saw. 'She doesn't speak at all? I don't mean not of me.'

'Of nothing – of no one.' And she went on, Susan Shepherd, giving it out as she had had to take it. 'She doesn't *want* to die. Think of her age. Think of her goodness. Think of her beauty. Think of all she is. Think of all she *has*. She lies there stiffening herself and clinging to it all. So I thank God—!' the poor lady wound up with a wan inconsequence.

He wondered. 'You thank God—?'

'That she's so quiet.'

He continued to wonder. '*Is* she so quiet?'

'She's more than quiet. She's grim. It's what she has never been. So you see – all these days. I can't tell you – but it's better so. It would kill me if she *were* to tell me.'

'To tell you?' He was still at a loss.

'How she feels. How she clings. How she doesn't want it.'

'How she doesn't want to die? Of course she doesn't want it.' He had a long pause, and they might have been thinking together of what they could even now do to prevent it. This, however, was not what he brought out. Milly's 'grimness' and the great hushed palace were present to him; present with the little woman before him as she must have been waiting there and listening. 'Only, what harm have *you* done her?'

Mrs Stringham looked about in her darkness. 'I don't know. I come and talk of her here with you.'

It made him again hesitate. 'Does she utterly hate me?'

'I don't know. How *can* I? No one ever will.'

'She'll never tell?'

'She'll never tell.'

Once more he thought. 'She must be magnificent.'

'She *is* magnificent.'

His friend, after all, helped him, and he turned it, so far as he could, all over. 'Would she see me again?'

It made his companion stare. 'Should you like to see her?'

'You mean as you describe her?' He felt her surprise, and it took him some time. 'No.'

'Ah then!' Mrs Stringham sighed.

'But if she could bear it I'd do anything.'

She had for the moment her vision of this, but it collapsed. 'I don't see what you can do.'

'I don't either. But *she* might.'

Mrs Stringham continued to think. 'It's too late.'

'Too late for her to see—?'

'Too late.'

The very decision of her despair – it was after all so lucid – kindled in him a heat. 'But the doctor, all the while—?'

'Tacchini? Oh he's kind. He comes. He's proud of having been approved and coached by a great London man. He hardly in fact goes away; so that I scarce know what becomes of his other patients. He thinks her, justly enough, a great personage; he treats her like royalty; he's waiting on events.

But she has barely consented to see him, and, though she has told him, generously – for she *thinks* of me, dear creature – that he may come, that he may stay, for my sake, he spends most of his time only hovering at her door, prowling through the rooms, trying to entertain me, in that ghastly saloon, with the gossip of Venice, and meeting me, in doorways, in the sala, on the staircase, with an agreeable intolerable smile. We don't,' said Susan Shepherd, 'talk of her.'

'By her request?'

'Absolutely. I don't do what she doesn't wish. We talk of the price of provisions.'

'By her request too?'

'Absolutely. She named it to me as a subject when she said, the first time, that if it would be any comfort to me he might stay as much as we liked.'

Densher took it all in. 'But he isn't any comfort to you!'

'None whatever. That, however,' she added, 'isn't his fault. Nothing's any comfort.'

'Certainly,' Densher observed, 'as I but too horribly feel, *I'm* not.'

'No. But I didn't come for that.'

'You came for *me*.'

'Well then call it that.' But she looked at him a moment with eyes filled full, and something came up in her the next instant from deeper still. 'I came at bottom of course—'

'You came at bottom of course for our friend herself. But if it's, as you say, too late for me to do anything?'

She continued to look at him, and with an irritation, which he saw grow in her, from the truth itself. 'So I did say. But, with you here' – and she turned her vision again strangely about her – 'with you here, and with everything, I feel we mustn't abandon her.'

'God forbid we should abandon her.'

219

'Then you *won't*?' His tone had made her flush again.

'How do you mean I "won't", if she abandons *me*? What can I do if she won't see me?'

'But you said just now you wouldn't like it.'

'I said I shouldn't like it in the light of what you tell me. I shouldn't like it only to see her as you make me. I should like it if I could help her. But even then,' Densher pursued without faith, 'she would have to want it first herself. And there,' he continued to make out, 'is the devil of it. She *won't* want it herself. She *can't*!'

He had got up in his impatience of it, and she watched him while he helplessly moved. 'There's one thing you can do. There's only that, and even for that there are difficulties. But there *is* that.' He stood before her with his hands in his pockets, and he had soon enough, from her eyes, seen what was coming. She paused as if waiting for his leave to utter it, and as he only let her wait they heard in the silence, on the Canal, the renewed downpour of rain. She had at last to speak, but, as if still with her fear, she only half-spoke. 'I think you really know yourself what it is.'

He did know what it was, and with it even, as she said – rather! – there were difficulties. He turned away on them, on everything, for a moment; he moved to the other window and looked at the sheeted channel, wider, like a river, where the houses opposite, blurred and belittled, stood at twice their distance. Mrs Stringham said nothing, was as mute in fact, for the minute, as if she had 'had' him, and he was the first again to speak. When he did so, however, it was not in straight answer to her last remark – he only started from that. He said, as he came back to her, 'Let me, you know, *see* – one must understand,' almost as if he had for the time accepted it. And what he wished to understand was where, on the essence of the question, was the voice of Sir Luke Strett. If they talked of not giving up shouldn't *he* be the one least of all to do it? 'Aren't we, at the worst, in the dark without him?'

'Oh,' said Mrs Stringham, 'it's he who has kept me going. I wired the first night, and he answered like an angel. He'll come like one. Only he can't arrive, at the nearest, till Thursday afternoon.'

'Well then that's something.'

She considered. 'Something – yes. She likes him.'

'Rather! I can see it still, the fact with which, when he was here in October – that night when she was in white, when she had people there and those musicians – she committed him to my care. It was beautiful for both of us – she put us in relation. She asked me, for the time, to take him about; I did so, and we quite hit it off. That proved,' Densher said with a quick sad smile, 'that she liked him.'

'He liked *you*,' Susan Shepherd presently risked.

'Ah I know nothing about that.'

'You ought to then. He went with you to galleries and churches; you saved his time for him, showed him the choicest things, and you perhaps will remember telling me myself that if he hadn't been a great surgeon he might really have been a great judge. I mean of the beautiful.'

'Well,' the young man admitted, 'that's what he is – in having judged *her*. He hasn't,' he went on, 'judged her for nothing. His interest in her – which we must make the most of – can only be supremely beneficent.'

He still roamed, while he spoke, with his hands in his pockets, and she saw him, on this, as her eyes sufficiently betrayed, trying to keep his distance from the recognition he had a few moments before partly confessed to. 'I'm glad,' she dropped, 'you like him!'

There was something for him in the sound of it. 'Well,

I do no more, dear lady, than you do yourself. Surely *you* like him. Surely, when he was here, we all liked him.'

'Yes, but I seem to feel I know what he thinks. And I should think, with all the time you spent with him, you'd know it,' she said, 'yourself.'

Densher stopped short, though at first without a word. 'We never spoke of her. Neither of us mentioned her, even to sound her name, and nothing whatever in connexion with her passed between us.'

Mrs Stringham stared up at him, surprised at this picture. But she had plainly an idea that after an instant resisted it. 'That was his professional propriety.'

'Precisely. But it was also my sense of that virtue in him, and it was something more besides.' And he spoke with sudden intensity. 'I couldn't *talk* to him about her!'

'Oh!' said Susan Shepherd.

'I can't talk to any one about her.'

'Except to *me*,' his friend continued.

'Except to you.' The ghost of her smile, a gleam of significance, had waited on her words, and it kept him, for honesty, looking at her. For honesty too – that is for his own words – he had quickly coloured: he was sinking so, at a stroke, the burden of his discourse with Kate. His visitor, for the minute, while their eyes met, might have been watching him hold it down. And he *had* to hold it down – the effort of which, precisely, made him red. He couldn't let it come up; at least not yet. She might make what she would of it. He attempted to repeat his statement, but he really modified it. 'Sir Luke, at all events, had nothing to tell me, and I had nothing to tell him. Make-believe talk was impossible for us, and—'

'And *real*' – she had taken him right up with a huge emphasis – 'was more impossible still.' No doubt – he didn't deny it; and she had straightway drawn her conclusion. 'Then that proves what I say – that there were immensities between you. Otherwise you'd have chattered.'

'I dare say,' Densher granted, 'we were both thinking of her.'

'You were neither of you thinking of any one else. That's why you kept together.'

Well, that too, if she desired, he took from her; but he came straight back to what he had originally said. 'I haven't a notion, all the same, of what he thinks.' She faced him, visibly, with the question into which he had already observed that her special shade of earnestness was perpetually flowering, right and left – 'Are you *very* sure?' – and he could only note her apparent difference from himself. 'You, I judge, believe that he thinks she's gone.'

She took it, but she bore up. 'It doesn't matter what I believe.'

'Well, we shall see' – and he felt almost basely superficial. More and more, for the last five minutes, had he known she had brought something with her, and never in respect to anything had he had such a wish to postpone. He would have liked to put everything off till Thursday; he was sorry it was now Tuesday; he wondered if he were afraid. Yet it wasn't of Sir Luke, who was coming; nor of Milly, who was dying; nor of Mrs Stringham, who was sitting there. It wasn't, strange to say, of Kate either, for Kate's presence affected him suddenly as having swooned or trembled away. Susan Shepherd's, thus prolonged, had cast on it some influence under which it had ceased to act. She was as absent to his sensibility as she had constantly been, since her departure, absent, as an echo or a reference, from the palace; and it was the first time, among the objects now surrounding him, that his sensibility so noted her. He knew soon enough that it was of himself he was afraid, and that even, if he didn't take care, he should infallibly be more so. 'Meanwhile,' he added for his companion, 'it has been everything for me to see you.'

She slowly rose at the words, which might almost have conveyed to her the hint of his taking care. She stood there as if she had in fact seen him abruptly moved to dismiss her. But the abruptness would have been in this case so marked as fairly to offer ground for insistence to her imagination of his state. It would take her moreover, she clearly showed him she was thinking, but a minute or two to insist. Besides, she had already said it. 'Will you do it if *he* asks you? I mean if Sir Luke himself puts it to you. And will you give him' – oh she was earnest now! – 'the opportunity to put it to you?'

'The opportunity to put what?'

'That if you deny it to her, that may still do something.'

Densher felt himself – as had already once befallen him in the quarter of an hour – turn red to the top of his forehead. Turning red had, however, for him, as a sign of shame, been, so to speak, discounted: his consciousness of it at the present moment was rather as a sign of his fear. It showed him sharply enough of what he was afraid. 'If I deny what to her?'

Hesitation, on the demand, revived in her, for hadn't he all along been letting her see that he knew? 'Why, what Lord Mark told her.'

'And what did Lord Mark tell her?'

Mrs Stringham had a look of bewilderment – of seeing him as suddenly perverse. 'I've been judging that you yourself know.' And it was she who now blushed deep.

It quickened his pity for her, but he was beset too by other things. 'Then *you* know—'

'Of his dreadful visit?' She stared. 'Why it's what has done it.'

'Yes – I understand that. But you also know—'

He had faltered again, but all she knew she now wanted to say. 'I'm speaking,' she said soothingly, 'of what he told her. It's *that* I've taken you as knowing.'

'Oh!' he sounded in spite of himself.

It appeared to have for her, he saw the next moment, the quality of relief, as if he had supposed her thinking of something else. Thereupon, straightway, that lightened it. 'Oh you thought I've known it for *true*!'

Her light had heightened her flush, and he saw that he had betrayed himself. Not, however, that it mattered, as he immediately saw still better. There it was now, all of it at last, and this at least there was no postponing. They were left with her idea – the one she was wishing to make him recognise. He had expressed ten minutes before his need to understand, and she was acting after all but on that. Only what he was to understand was no small matter; it might be larger even than as yet appeared.

He took again one of his turns, not meeting what she had last said; he mooned a minute, as he would have called it, at a window; and of course she could see that she had driven him to the wall. She did clearly, without delay, see it; on which her sense of having 'caught' him became as promptly a scruple, which she spoke as if not to press. 'What I mean is that he told her you've been all the while engaged to Miss Croy.'

He gave a jerk round; it was almost – to hear it – the touch of a lash; and he said – idiotically, as he afterwards knew – the first thing that came into his head. 'All *what* while?'

'Oh it's not I who say it.' She spoke in gentleness. 'I only repeat to you what he told her.'

Densher, from whom an impatience had escaped, had already caught himself up. 'Pardon my brutality. Of course

I know what you're talking about. I saw him, toward the evening,' he further explained, 'in the Piazza; only just saw him – through the glass at Florian's – without any words. In fact I scarcely know him – there wouldn't have been occasion. It was but once, moreover – he must have gone that night. But I knew he wouldn't have come for nothing, and I turned it over – what he would have come for.'

Oh so had Mrs Stringham. 'He came for exasperation.'

Densher approved. 'He came to let her know that he knows better than she for whom it was she had a couple of months before, in her fool's paradise, refused him.'

'How you *do* know!' – and Mrs Stringham almost smiled.

'I know that – but I don't know the good it does him.'

'The good, he thinks, if he has patience – not too much – may be to come. He doesn't know what he has done to her. Only *we*, you see, do that.'

He saw, but he wondered. 'She kept from him – what she felt?'

'She was able – I'm sure of it – not to show anything. He dealt her his blow, and she took it without a sign.' Mrs Stringham, it was plain, spoke by book, and it brought into play again her appreciation of what she related. 'She's magnificent.'

Densher again gravely assented. 'Magnificent!'

'And *he*,' she went on, 'is an idiot of idiots.'

'An idiot of idiots.' For a moment, on it all, on the stupid doom in it, they looked at each other. 'Yet he's thought so awfully clever.'

'So awfully – it's Maud Lowder's own view. And he was nice, in London,' said Mrs Stringham, 'to *me*. One could almost pity him – he has had such a good conscience.'

'That's exactly the inevitable ass.'

'Yes, but it wasn't – I could see from the only few things

she first told me – that he meant *her* the least harm. He intended none whatever.'

'That's always the ass at his worst,' Densher returned. 'He
only of course meant harm to me.'

'And good to himself – he thought that would come. He
had been unable to swallow,' Mrs Stringham pursued, 'what
had happened on his other visit. He had been then too
sharply humiliated.'

'Oh I saw that.'

'Yes, and he also saw you. He saw you received, as it were,
while he was turned away.'

'Perfectly,' Densher said – 'I've filled it out. And also that
he has known meanwhile for *what* I was then received. For
a stay of all these weeks. He had had it to think of.'

'Precisely – it was more than he could bear. But he has it,'
said Mrs Stringham, 'to think of still.'

'Only, after all,' asked Densher, who himself somehow, at
this point, was having more to think of even than he had yet
had – 'only, after all, how has he happened to know? That
is, to know enough.'

'What do you call enough?' Mrs Stringham enquired.

'He can only have acted – it would have been his sole
safety – from full knowledge.'

He had gone on without heeding her question; but, face
to face as they were, something had none the less passed
between them. It was this that, after an instant, made her
again interrogative. 'What do you mean by full knowledge?'

Densher met it indirectly. 'Where has he been since
October?'

'I think he has been back to England. He came in fact,
I've reason to believe, straight from there.'

'Straight to do this job? All the way for his half-hour?'

'Well, to try again – with the help perhaps of a new fact.

To make himself possibly right with her – a different attempt from the other. He had at any rate something to tell her, and he didn't know his opportunity would reduce itself to half an hour. Or perhaps indeed half an hour would be just what was most effective. It *has* been!' said Susan Shepherd.

Her companion took it in, understanding but too well; yet as she lighted the matter for him more, really, than his own courage had quite dared – putting the absent dots on several i's – he saw new questions swarm. They had been till now in a bunch, entangled and confused; and they fell apart, each showing for itself. The first he put to her was at any rate abrupt. 'Have you heard of late from Mrs Lowder?'

'Oh yes, two or three times. She depends naturally upon news of Milly.'

He hesitated. 'And does she depend, naturally, upon news of *me*?'

His friend matched for an instant his deliberation.

'I've given her none that hasn't been decently good. This will have been the first.'

'"This"?' Densher was thinking.

'Lord Mark's having been here, and her being as she is.'

He thought a moment longer. 'What has Mrs Lowder written about him? Has she written that he has been with them?'

'She has mentioned him but once – it was in her letter before the last. Then she said something.'

'And what did she say?'

Mrs Stringham produced it with an effort. 'Well it was in reference to Miss Croy. That she thought Kate was thinking of him. Or perhaps I should say rather that he was thinking of her – only it seemed this time to have struck Maud that he was seeing the way more open to him.'

Densher listened with his eyes on the ground, but he presently raised them to speak, and there was that in his face which proved him aware of a queerness in his question. 'Does she mean he has been encouraged to *propose* to her niece?'

'I don't know what she means.'

'Of course not' – he recovered himself; 'and I oughtn't to seem to trouble you to piece together what I can't piece myself. Only I "guess",' he added, 'I *can* piece it.'

She spoke a little timidly, but she risked it. 'I dare say I can piece it too.'

It was one of the things in her – and his conscious face took it from her as such – that from the moment of her coming in had seemed to mark for him, as to what concerned him, the long jump of her perception. They had parted four days earlier with many things, between them, deep down. But these things were now on their troubled surface, and it wasn't he who had brought them so quickly up. Women were wonderful – at least this one was. But so, not less, was Milly, was Aunt Maud; so, most of all, was his very Kate. Well, he already knew what he had been feeling about the circle of petticoats. They were all *such* petticoats! It was just the fineness of his tangle. The sense of that, in its turn, for us too, might have been not unconnected with his putting to his visitor a question that quite passed over her remark. 'Has Miss Croy meanwhile written to our friend?'

'Oh,' Mrs Stringham amended, '*her* friend also. But not a single word that I know of.'

He had taken it for certain she hadn't – the thing being after all but a shade more strange than his having himself, with Milly, never for six weeks mentioned the young lady in question. It was for that matter but a shade more strange than Milly's not having mentioned her. In spite of which, and however inconsequently, he blushed anew for Kate's silence. He got away from it in fact as quickly as possible, and the furthest he could get was by reverting for a minute to the man they had been judging. 'How did he manage to get *at* her? She had only – with what had passed between them before – to say she couldn't see him.'

'Oh she was disposed to kindness. She was easier,' the good lady explained with a slight embarrassment, 'than at the other time.'

'Easier?'

'She was off her guard. There was a difference.'

'Yes. But exactly not *the* difference.'

'Exactly not the difference of her having to be harsh. Perfectly. She could afford to be the opposite.' With which, as he said nothing, she just impatiently completed her sense. 'She had had *you* here for six weeks.'

'Oh!' Densher softly groaned.

'Besides, I think he must have written her first – written I mean in a tone to smooth his way. That it would be a kindness to himself. Then on the spot—'

'On the spot,' Densher broke in, 'he unmasked? The horrid little beast!'

It made Susan Shepherd turn slightly pale, though quickening, as for hope, the intensity of her look at him. 'Oh he went off without an alarm.'

'And he must have gone off also without a hope.'

'Ah that, certainly.'

'Then it *was* mere base revenge. Hasn't he known her, into the bargain,' the young man asked – 'didn't he, weeks before, see her, judge her, feel her, as having for such a suit as his not more perhaps than a few months to live?'

Mrs Stringham at first, for reply, but looked at him in silence; and it gave more force to what she then remarkably added. 'He has doubtless been aware of what you speak of, just as you have yourself been aware.'

'He has wanted her, you mean, just *because*—?'

'Just because,' said Susan Shepherd.

'The hound!' Merton Densher brought out. He moved off, however, with a hot face, as soon as he had spoken, conscious again of an intention in his visitor's reserve. Dusk was now deeper, and after he had once more taken counsel of the dreariness without he turned to his companion. 'Shall we have lights – a lamp or the candles?'

'Not for me.'

'Nothing?'

'Not for me.'

He waited at the window another moment and then faced his friend with a thought. 'He *will* have proposed to Miss Croy. That's what has happened.'

Her reserve continued. 'It's you who must judge.'

Well, I do judge. Mrs Lowder will have done so too – only *she*, poor lady, wrong. Miss Croy's refusal of him will have struck him' – Densher continued to make it out – 'as a phenomenon requiring a reason.'

'And you've been clear to him *as* the reason?'

'Not too clear – since I'm sticking here and since that has been a fact to make his descent on Miss Theale relevant. But clear enough. He has believed,' said Densher bravely, 'that I may have been a reason at Lancaster Gate, and yet at the same time have been up to something in Venice.'

Mrs Stringham took her courage from his own. ' "Up to" something? Up to what?'

'God knows. To some "game", as they say. To some deviltry. To some duplicity.'

'Which of course,' Mrs Stringham observed, 'is a monstrous supposition.' Her companion, after a stiff minute

– sensibly long for each – fell away from her again, and then added to it another minute, which he spent once more looking out with his hands in his pockets. This was no answer, he perfectly knew, to what she had dropped, and it even seemed to state for his own ears that no answer was possible. She left him to himself, and he was glad she had declined, for their further colloquy, the advantage of lights. These would have been an advantage mainly to herself. Yet she got her benefit too even from the absence of them. It came out in her very tone when at last she addressed him – so differently, for confidence – in words she had already used. 'If Sir Luke himself asks it of you as something you can do for *him*, will you deny to Milly herself what she has been made so dreadfully to believe?'

Oh how he knew he hung back! But at last he said: 'You're absolutely certain then that she does believe it?'

'Certain?' She appealed to their whole situation. 'Judge!'

He took his time again to judge. 'Do *you* believe it?'

He was conscious that his own appeal pressed her hard; it eased him a little that her answer must be a pain to her discretion. She answered none the less, and he was truly the harder pressed. 'What I believe will inevitably depend more or less on your action. You can perfectly settle it – if you care. I promise to believe you down to the ground if to save her life, you consent to a denial.'

'But a denial, when it comes to that – confound the whole thing, don't you see! – of exactly what?'

It was as if he were hoping she would narrow; but in fact she enlarged. 'Of everything.'

Everything had never even yet seemed to him so incalculably much. 'Oh!' he simply moaned into the gloom.

4

THE NEAR THURSDAY, coming nearer and bringing Sir Luke Strett, brought also blessedly an abatement of other rigours. The weather changed, the stubborn storm yielded, and the autumn sunshine, baffled for many days, but now hot and almost vindictive, came into its own again and, with an almost audible pæan, a suffusion of bright sound that was one with the bright colour, took large possession. Venice glowed and plashed and called and chimed again; the air was like a clap of hands, and the scattered pinks, yellows, blues, sea-greens, were like a hanging-out of vivid stuffs, a laying-down of fine carpets. Densher rejoiced in this on the occasion of his going to the station to meet the great doctor. He went after consideration, which, as he was constantly aware, was at present his imposed, his only, way of doing anything. That was where the event had landed him – where no event in his life had landed him before. He had thought, no doubt, from the day he was born, much more than he had acted; except indeed that he remembered thoughts – a few of them – which at the moment of their coming to him had thrilled him almost like adventures. But anything like his actual state he had not, as to the prohibition of impulse, accident, range – the prohibition in other words of freedom – hitherto known. The great oddity was that if he had felt his arrival, so few weeks back, especially as an adventure, nothing could now less resemble one than the fact of his staying. It would be an adventure to break away, to depart, to go back, above all, to London, and tell Kate Croy he had done so; but there was something of the merely, the almost meanly, obliged and involved sort in his going on as he was. That was the effect in particular of Mrs Stringham's visit, which had left him as with such a taste in his mouth of what he couldn't do. It had made this quantity clear to him, and yet had deprived him of the sense, the other sense, of what, for a refuge, he possibly *could*.

It was but a small make-believe of freedom, he knew, to go to the station for Sir Luke. Nothing equally free, at all events, had he yet turned over so long. What then was his odious position but that again and again he was afraid? He stiffened himself under this consciousness as if it had been a tax levied by a tyrant. He hadn't at any time proposed to himself to live long enough for fear to preponderate in his life. Such was simply the advantage it had actually got of him. He was afraid for instance that an advance to his distinguished friend might prove for him somehow a pledge or a committal. He was afraid of it as a current that would draw him too far; yet he thought with an equal aversion of being shabby, being poor, through fear. What finally prevailed with him was the reflexion that, whatever might happen, the great man had, after that occasion at the palace, their young woman's brief sacrifice to society – and the hour of Mrs Stringham's appeal had brought it well to the surface – shown him marked benevolence. Mrs Stringham's comments on the relation in which Milly had placed them made him – it was unmistakeable – feel things he perhaps hadn't felt. It was in the spirit of seeking a chance to feel again adequately whatever it was he had missed – it was, no doubt, in that spirit, so far as it went a stroke for freedom, that Densher, arriving betimes, paced the platform before the train came in. Only, after it had come and he had presented himself at the door of Sir Luke's compartment with everything that followed – only, as the situation developed, the sense of an anti-climax to so many intensities deprived his apprehensions and hesitations even of the scant dignity they might claim. He could scarce have said if the visitor's manner less showed the remembrance that might have suggested expectation, or made shorter work of surprise in presence of the fact.

Sir Luke had clean forgotten – so Densher read – the rather remarkable young man he had formerly gone about with, though he picked him up again, on the spot, with one large quiet look. The young man felt himself so picked, and the thing immediately affected him as the proof of a splendid economy. Opposed to all the waste with which he was now connected the exhibition was of a nature quite nobly to admonish him. The eminent pilgrim, in the train, all the way, had used the hours as he needed, thinking not a moment in advance of what finally awaited him. An exquisite case awaited him – of which, in this queer way, the remarkable young man was an outlying part; but the single motion of his face, the motion into which Densher, from the platform, lightly stirred its stillness, was his first renewed cognition. If, however, he had suppressed the matter by leaving Victoria he would at once suppress now, in turn, whatever else suited. The perception of this became as a symbol of the whole pitch, so far as one might one's self be concerned, of his visit. One saw, our friend further meditated, everything that, in contact, he appeared to accept – if only, for much, not to trouble to sink it: what one missed was the inward use he made of it. Densher began wondering, at the great water-steps outside, what use he would make of the anomaly of their having there to separate. Eugenio had been on the platform, in the respectful rear, and the gondola from the palace, under his direction, bestirred itself, with its attaching mixture of alacrity and dignity, on their coming out of the station together. Densher didn't at all mind now that, he himself of necessity refusing a seat on the deep black cushions beside the guest of the palace, he had Milly's three emissaries for spectators; and this susceptibility, he also knew, it was something to have left behind. All he did was to smile down vaguely from the steps – they could see him, the donkeys, as shut out as they would. 'I don't,' he said with a sad headshake, 'go there now.'

'Oh!' Sir Luke Strett returned, and made no more of it; so that the thing was splendid, Densher fairly thought, as an inscrutability quite inevitable and unconscious. His friend appeared not even to make of it that he supposed it might be for respect to the crisis. He didn't moreover afterwards make much more of anything – after the classic craft, that is, obeying in the main Pasquale's inimitable stroke from the poop, had performed the manœuvre by which it presented, receding, a back, so to speak, rendered positively graceful by the high black hump of its *felze*. Densher watched the gondola out of sight – he heard Pasquale's cry, borne to him across the water, for the sharp firm swerve into a side-canal, a short cut to the palace. He had no gondola of his own; it was his habit never to take one; and he humbly – as in Venice it *is* humble – walked away, though not without having for some time longer stood as if fixed where the guest of the palace had left him. It was strange enough, but he found himself as never yet, and as he couldn't have reckoned, in presence of the truth that was the truest about Milly. He couldn't have reckoned on the force of the difference instantly made – for it was all in the air as he heard Pasquale's cry and saw the boat disappear – by the mere visibility, on the spot, of the personage summoned to her aid. He hadn't only never been near the facts of her condition – which counted so as a blessing for him; he hadn't only, with all the world, hovered outside an impenetrable ring fence, within which there reigned a kind of expensive vagueness made up of smiles and silences and beautiful fictions and priceless arrangements, all strained to breaking; but he had also, with every one else, as he now

236

felt, actively fostered suppressions which were in the direct interest of every one's good manner, every one's pity, every one's really quite generous ideal. It was a conspiracy of silence, as the *cliché* went, to which no one had made an exception, the great smudge of mortality across the picture, the shadow of pain and horror, finding in no quarter a surface of spirit or of speech that consented to reflect it. 'The mere æsthetic instinct of mankind—!' our young man had more than once, in the connexion, said to himself; letting the rest of the proposition drop, but touching again thus sufficiently on the outrage even to taste involved in one's having to *see*. So then it had been – a general conscious fool's paradise, from which the specified had been chased like a dangerous animal. What therefore had at present befallen was that the specified, standing all the while at the gate, had now crossed the threshold as in Sir Luke Strett's person and quite on such a scale as to fill out the whole precinct. Densher's nerves, absolutely his heartbeats too, had measured the change before he on this occasion moved away.

The facts of physical suffering, of incurable pain, of the chance grimly narrowed, had been made, at a stroke, intense, and this was to be the way he was now to feel them. The clearance of the air, in short, making vision not only possible but inevitable, the one thing left to be thankful for was the breadth of Sir Luke's shoulders, which, should one be able to keep in line with them, might in some degree interpose. It was, however, far from plain to Densher for the first day or two that he was again to see his distinguished friend at all. That he couldn't, on any basis actually serving, return to the palace – this was as solid to him, every whit, as the other feature of his case, the fact of the publicity attaching to his proscription through his not having taken himself off. He had been seen often enough in the Leporelli gondola. As, accordingly, he was not on any presumption destined to meet Sir Luke about the town, where the latter would have neither time nor taste to lounge, nothing more would occur between them unless the great man should surprisingly wait upon him. His doing that, Densher further reflected, wouldn't even simply depend on Mrs Stringham's having decided to – as they might say – turn him on. It would depend as well – for there would be practically some difference to her – on her actually attempting it; and it would depend above all on what Sir Luke would make of such an overture. Densher had for that matter his own view of the amount, to say nothing of the particular sort, of response it might expect from him. He had his own view of the ability of such a personage even to understand such an appeal. To what extent could he be prepared, and what importance in fine could he attach? Densher asked himself these questions, in truth, to put his own position at the worst. He should miss the great man completely unless the great man should come to see him, and the great man could only come to see him for a purpose unsupposable. Therefore he wouldn't come at all, and consequently there was nothing to hope.

It wasn't in the least that Densher invoked this violence to all probability; but it pressed on him that there were few possible diversions he could afford now to miss. Nothing in his predicament was so odd as that, incontestably afraid of himself, he was not afraid of Sir Luke. He had an impression, which he clung to, based on a previous taste of the visitor's company, that *he* would somehow let him off. The truth about Milly perched on his shoulders and sounded in his tread, became by the fact of his presence the name and the form, for the time, of everything in the place; but it didn't, for the difference, sit in his face, the face so squarely and easily turned to Densher at the earlier season. His presence on the first occasion, not as the result of a summons, but as a friendly whim of his own, had had quite another value; and though our young man could scarce regard that value as recoverable he yet reached out in imagination to a renewal of the old contact. He didn't propose, as he privately and forcibly phrased the matter, to be a hog; but there was something he after all did want for himself. It was something – this stuck to him – that Sir Luke would have had for him if it hadn't been impossible. These were his worst days, the two or three; those on which even the sense of the tension at the palace didn't much help him not to feel that his destiny made but light of him. He had never been, as he judged it, so down. In mean conditions, without books, without society, almost without money, he had nothing to do but to wait. His main support really was his original idea, which didn't leave him, of waiting for the deepest depth his predicament could sink him to. Fate would invent, if he but gave it time, some refinement of the horrible. It was just inventing meanwhile this suppression of Sir Luke. When the third day came without a sign he knew what to think. He had given Mrs Stringham during her call on him no such answer as would have armed her faith, and the ultimatum she had described as ready for him when *he* should be ready was therefore – if on no other ground than her want of this power to answer for him – not to be presented. The presentation, heaven knew, was not what he desired.

That was not, either, we hasten to declare – as Densher then soon enough saw – the idea with which Sir Luke finally stood before him again. For stand before him again he finally did; just when our friend had gloomily embraced the belief that the limit of his power to absent himself from London obligations would have been reached. Four or five days, exclusive of journeys, represented the largest supposable sacrifice – to a head not crowned – on the part of one of the highest medical lights in the world; so that really when the personage in question, following up a tinkle of the bell, solidly rose in the doorway, it was to impose on Densher a vision that for the instant cut like a knife. It spoke, the fact, and in a single dreadful word, of the magnitude – he shrank from calling it anything else – of Milly's case. The great man had not gone then, and an immense surrender to her immense need was so expressed in it that some effect, some help, some hope, were flagrantly part of the expression. It was for Densher, with his reaction from disappointment, as if he were conscious of ten things at once – the foremost being that just conceivably, since Sir Luke *was* still there, she had been saved. Close upon its heels, however, and quite as sharply, came the sense that the crisis – plainly even now to be prolonged for him – was to have none of that sound simplicity. Not only had his visitor not dropped in to gossip about Milly, he hadn't dropped in to mention her at all; he had dropped in fairly to show that during the brief remainder of his stay, the end of which was now in sight, as little as possible of that was to be looked for. The demonstration, such as it was, was in the key of their previous acquaintance, and it was their previous acquaintance that had made him come. He was not to stop longer than the Saturday next at hand, but there were things of interest he should like to see again meanwhile. It was for these things of interest, for Venice and the opportunity of Venice, for a prowl or two, as he called it, and a turn about, that he had looked his young man up – producing on the latter's part, as soon as the case had, with the lapse of a further twenty-four hours, so defined itself, the most incongruous, yet most beneficent revulsion. Nothing could in fact have been more monstrous on the surface – and Densher was well aware of it – than the relief he found during this short period in the tacit drop of all reference to the palace, in neither hearing news nor asking for it. That was what had come out for him, on his visitor's entrance, even in the very seconds of suspense that were connecting the fact also directly and intensely with Milly's state. He had come to say he had saved her – he had come, as from Mrs Stringham, to say how she might *be* saved – he had come, in spite of Mrs Stringham, to say she was lost: the distinct throbs of hope, of fear, simultaneous for all their distinctness, merged their identity in a bound of the heart just as immediate and which remained after they had passed. It simply did wonders for him – this was the truth – that Sir Luke was, as he would have said, quiet.

The result of it was the oddest consciousness as of a blest calm after a storm. He had been trying for weeks, as we know, to keep superlatively still, and trying it largely in solitude and silence; but he looked back on it now as on the heat of fever. The real, the right stillness was this particular form of society. They walked together and they talked, looked up pictures again and recovered impressions – Sir Luke knew just what he wanted; haunted a little the dealers in old wares; sat down at Florian's for rest and mild drinks; blessed above all the grand weather, a bath of warm air, a pageant of autumn light. Once or twice while they rested the great man closed his eyes – keeping them so for some minutes while his companion, the more easily watching his face for it, made private reflexions on the subject of lost sleep. He had been up at night with her – he in person, for hours; but this was all he showed of it and was apparently to remain his nearest approach to an allusion. The extraordinary thing was that Densher could take it in perfectly as evidence, could turn cold at the image looking out of it; and yet that he could at the same time not intermit a throb of his response to

241

accepted liberation. The liberation was an experience that held its own, and he continued to know why, in spite of his deserts, in spite of his folly, in spite of everything, he had so fondly hoped for it. He had hoped for it, had sat in his room there waiting for it, because he had thus divined in it, should it come, some power to let him off. He was *being* let off; dealt with in the only way that didn't aggravate his responsibility. The beauty was also that this wasn't on system or on any basis of intimate knowledge; it was just by being a man of the world and by knowing life, by feeling the real, that Sir Luke did him good. There had been in all the case too many women. A man's sense of it, another man's, changed the air; and he wondered what man, had he chosen, would have been more to his purpose than this one. He was large and easy – that was the benediction; he knew what mattered and what didn't; he distinguished between the essence and the shell, the just grounds and the unjust for fussing. One was thus – if one were concerned with him or exposed to him at all – in his hands for whatever he should do, and not much less affected by his mercy than one might have been by his rigour. The grand thing – it did come to that – was the way he carried off, as one might fairly call it, the business of making odd things natural. Nothing, if they hadn't taken it so, could have exceeded the unexplained oddity, between them, of Densher's now complete detachment from the poor ladies at the palace; nothing could have exceeded the no less marked anomaly of the great man's own abstentions of speech. He made, as he had done when they met at the station, nothing whatever of anything; and the effect of it, Densher would have said, was a relation with him quite resembling that of doctor and patient. One took the cue from him as one might have taken a dose – except that the cue was pleasant in the taking.

That was why one could leave it to his tacit discretion, why for the three or four days Densher again and again did so leave it; merely wondering a little, at the most, on the eve of Saturday, the announced term of the episode. Waiting once more on this latter occasion, the Saturday morning, for Sir Luke's reappearance at the station, our friend had to recognise the drop of his own borrowed ease, the result, naturally enough, of the prospect of losing a support. The difficulty was that, on such lines as had served them, the support was Sir Luke's personal presence. Would he go without leaving some substitute for that? – and without breaking, either, his silence in respect to his errand? Densher was in still deeper ignorance than at the hour of his call, and what was truly prodigious at so supreme a moment was that – as had immediately to appear – no gleam of light on what he had been living with for a week found its way out of him. What he had been doing was proof of a huge interest as well as of a huge fee; yet when the Leporelli gondola again, and somewhat tardily, approached, his companion, watching from the water-steps, studied his fine closed face as much as ever in vain. It was like a lesson, from the highest authority, on the subject of the relevant, so that its blankness affected Densher of a sudden almost as a cruelty, feeling it quite awfully compatible, as he did, with Milly's having ceased to exist. And the suspense continued after they had passed together, as time was short, directly into the station, where Eugenio, in the field early, was mounting guard over the compartment he had secured. The strain, though probably lasting, at the carriage-door, but a couple of minutes, prolonged itself so for our poor gentleman's nerves that he involuntarily directed a long look at Eugenio, who met it, however, as only Eugenio could. Sir Luke's attention was given for the time to the right bestowal of his numerous effects, about which he was particular, and Densher fairly found himself, so far as silence could go, questioning the representative of the palace. It didn't humiliate him now; it didn't humiliate him even to feel that that personage exactly knew how little he satisfied him. Eugenio resembled to that extent Sir Luke – to the extent of the extraordinary things with which his facial habit was compatible. By the time, however, that Densher had taken from it all its possessor intended Sir Luke was free and with a hand out for farewell. He offered the hand at first without speech; only on meeting his eyes could our young man see that they had never yet so completely looked at him. It was never, with Sir Luke, that they looked harder at one time than at another; but they looked longer, and this, even a shade of it, might mean on his part everything. It meant, Densher for ten seconds believed, that Milly Theale was dead; so that the word at last spoken made him start.

'I shall come back.'

'Then she's better?'

'I shall come back within the month,' Sir Luke repeated without heeding the question. He had dropped Densher's hand, but he held him otherwise still. 'I bring you a message from Miss Theale,' he said as if they hadn't spoken of her. 'I'm commissioned to ask you from her to go and see her.'

Densher's rebound from his supposition had a violence that his stare betrayed. '*She* asks me?'

Sir Luke had got into the carriage, the door of which the guard had closed; but he spoke again as he stood at the window, bending a little but not leaning out. 'She told me she'd like it, and I promised that, as I expected to find you here, I'd let you know.'

Densher, on the platform, took it from him, but what he took brought the blood into his face quite as what he had

244

had to take from Mrs Stringham. And he was also bewildered. 'Then she can receive—?'

'She can receive you.'

'And you're coming back—?'

'Oh because I must. She's not to move. She's to stay. I come to her.'

'I see, I see,' said Densher, who indeed did see – saw the sense of his friend's words and saw beyond it as well. What Mrs Stringham had announced, and what he had yet expected not to have to face, *had* then come. Sir Luke had kept it for the last, but there it was, and the colourless compact form it was now taking – the tone of one man of the world to another, who, after what had happened, would understand – was but the characteristic manner of his appeal. Densher was to understand remarkably much; and the great thing certainly was to show that he did. 'I'm particularly obliged, I'll go today.' He brought that out, but in his pause, while they continued to look at each other, the train had slowly creaked into motion. There was time but for one more word, and the young man chose it, out of twenty, with intense concentration. 'Then she's better?'

Sir Luke's face was wonderful. 'Yes, she's better.' And he kept it at the window while the train receded, holding him with it still. It was to be his nearest approach to the utter reference they had hitherto so successfully avoided. If it stood for everything; never had a face had to stand for more. So Densher, held after the train had gone, sharply reflected; so he reflected, asking himself into what abyss it pushed him, even while conscious of retreating under the maintained observation of Eugenio.

FREDERICK ROLFE
BARON CORVO

From

THE DESIRE AND PURSUIT
OF THE WHOLE

XVII

CALIBAN TO CRABBE: "Oh why will you be so crabby?
Don't you understand that mother and father only hadn't
written because, knowing your troubles and being unable to
help, they found it hard to find anything to say. But you took
offence at their silence, and when they did their best to oblige
you, you rear up and tear them into tatters with your awful
talons and make them your bitter enemies. It's very hard on
me. However, here's another proposition for you; and I do
hope you'll be sensible enough to accept it. If you do, there'll
be no difficulty about funds for your first-class journey with
every comfort. I'm afraid you'll have to make a discreet
departure and leave your things behind, but as you only took
a few things when you left home which must be worn out
by now, you won't mind losing them. Bobugo says come
back and live with him and do that book about *Saint Thomas
of Canterbury*. He will not insult you by offering to take you
in out of charity, but says that he'll consider it an equivalent
for board, lodging, and washing if you'll do such work about
the house and poultry-yard and putting his gardens in order
as he may require. He promises not to speak to you except
on business, and the book can be done in your spare time.
Now there you have an offer of exactly what you want, viz.
an open-air life and a chance of writing in peace where your
creditors can't get at you. So I send you the proverbial guinea,

which I want you to use like this. Go and have a good dinner for a change, for I guess you're starving yourself as usual when things don't go quite as you like. After that, swear violently at and tip heavily a cheap gondoliere. And wire me your consent with the balance. I'll instantly instruct Cook to secretly give you the necessary tickets, etc.   I.T.SS.S."

Crabbe to Caliban: "You do make me smile. Your parents wrote to me as to a merely casual acquaintance, and an undesirable one at that. It was stupefying: but, not being slow at taking hints, I sent them the kind of answers they seemed to want. And you say they're coughing horribly. Well, I say that they must be comical people: for it does strike me as extremely comical when people say that they don't know what to say to a most intimate friend in trouble, being unable to help him – and not being either asked or expected to help him, mind you. (Damn you.) Of course, I, being peculiar (thank Heaven and The Black Cat), think that the moment when a partner and most intimate friend is in trouble is just the very moment of all others when kind consoling encouraging words are far more suitable than stony silence. But your people (who used to pretend that they were mine too) 'found it hard to find anything to say.' Quite so. Admirable. Delicious. That clears up mysteries. Do you know why they f.i.h.t.f.a.t.s.? I'll tell you. They haven't got it, my dear. That's all. And one knows precisely what sort of people people are who f.i.h.t.f.a.t.s. to a friend in trouble. They are people who have most magnificently mucked the most gorgeous opportunity of their lives. No doubt they're biting with rage. But – are they raging wholly at me? Archbishop Laud bless Your Splendour, no! Ha-ha! Ha-ha! And, no, thank you very much, I will not run away from Venice, at your expense, and leave my debts unpaid. And I will not on any account go and live with your Bobugo. It's ridiculous (and perhaps sinful) to use a razor for chopping stone: but I haven't the slightest objection to polishing his boots and emptying his pails, and scrubbing his floors and creating his capons, and trenching his celery and manuring his marrows, in certain circumstances. And it's not that I altogether refuse to write a book for him to sign. No. I won't go and live with him for another reason. You just sit down while papa tickles your toes at tea-time, and read Bobugo's book *The Sensiblist* over again. You'll find my reason there (in the character of his 'Mr Rhodes') for refusing the offer of which his sadimaniac effrontery makes your blank ineptitude the medium. That is a character which he invented – he thinks it like God (Who said, 'Come unto Me, all ye that are weary and heavy-laden, and I will refresh you') and got an archbishop's widow to think so too – he also thinks it himself, and lives and labours to make himself it. No, thank you: I will not incarcerate myself in the lonely country-house dungeon of a despot, whose fixed idea is to break in pieces men's minds and natures by physical torment and mental torture, so that he may gum them together again on a model of his own and exhibit them on crimson carpets at garden-parties as perfect cures, all for his own greater glory. No, thank you, and your Bobugo. This is Century XX; and this fly will not walk into the parlour of that spider. Think of something else. But, by the by, why not stick to the matter in hand? Why not fulfil Your Splendid promise that You wouldn't let me suffer in honour, person, or property? Why not reclaim Morlaix and Sartor from their evil courses? Yes, why not? And, haven't you received *Sieur René* yet? Then why haven't you sent (or seen sent) the remittance promised for it? Eh? By the by, here's your infernal guinea.   I.T.SS.S."

The plump face of Parrucchiero became longer and

longer. Crabbe, invited to conferences and aware that the envelopes of his correspondence were not unnaturally scrutinized before they reached him, had no news of pleasing nature to bestow. A sort of indignant serenity encased him: he was indignant that his torment should be prolonged by his own consideration for an imbecile: but he was serene, with the two types of serenity produced respectively from the conviction that one's facts are substantial, and from the consciousness of merit gained in the attempt to win a man from dishonour by confiding in his honour. But indignant serenity on the part of a debtor doesn't prevent his creditor from baying him; and Parrucchiero's became strained with the apparently insusceptible Crabbe.

Caliban wrote by return: "I wish I'd never heard of Bobugo. And I'm getting quite uneasy about you. For goodness' sake do something. You can't go on running up a bill at your hotel, you know. No one suggests that you should do anything dishonourable: but I do wish you'd run away – I suppose you move about Venice as you like and could slip off from the station without a row – and go somewhere into the mountains just across the frontier. There are heaps of villages in the Austrian Tyrol where you could live on nothing. And, once safe out of Italy, write and tell your landlord that you'll pay him when you can. There is nothing dishonourable in that. Pray do it. I have sent your manuscript of *De Burgh's Delusion* to friend Wallace for an opinion and revision, which he says he'll gladly give. When he has trimmed it, mother shall type it. You know it's ripping to get a man like Wallace to do this for us: his last book, which I suppose you haven't seen, *Annals of an Individual of Condition*, is selling like hot cakes, and that's just what we want ours to do. I say – please take my advice for once.   I.T.SS.S."

Crabbe instantly replied: "Your jests (or gests) are

becoming clumsier than ever, my Caliban. My purely personal opinion is that jesting hardly is opportune. As sovereign of the Order, You can claim my obedience to Your mandates – if You dare to issue mandates: but I utterly refuse even to ponder such requests and such advice as you lately have seen fit to spue upon me. I just toss them back at you. Once for all, be it known that I won't leave Venice till I've paid my debts – if then. They don't amount to a couple of hundred sterling; and it's inconceivable why such a fuss should be made about so paltry a sum. Make those treacherous Judases who keep my bag render the last two half-years' accounts; and let's see how I stand. If they've been mismanaging, put my property in the hands of someone who'll manage better. If You, my Sovereign – one of 'em, anyhow – hadn't made me stop action on Your spontaneous promise that I shouldn't suffer, I could have got things straight by myself weeks and weeks ago. As for sending my MS. of *De Burgh's Delusion* to Wallace, I don't think I ever heard of anything so truly and lusciously fat. Fancy letting a Quaker go rooting and snouting in my lovely catholic garden! Man alive! Why, he'll tusk up every single flower which I so artfully planted and brought to bloom there! Ajuto! Take it away from him at once; and send it, with *The Weird*, to Shortmans. You yourself said, in January, that there was our only way of getting ready money; and here we are at the end of March; and still you play the giddy – Lieutenant. And, what about *Sieur René*? My dear, I'm becoming a bit tired. I.T.SS.S."

You'll admit, o most affable reader, that Crabbe had sufficient cause for boredom. His overdrafts, amounting to about twenty-five sterling, went entirely in tobacco and postage of the shoals of night-born manuscripts which he secretly was sowing in England. For living expenses, he went in debt to his landlord; and denied himself everything else. But nothing was coming in. He had no certain knowledge of when anything was likely to come in. And he was convinced that delay in bringing his agents to book confirmed them in their position while it weakened his. But the experiment was fascinating to his temperament; and he resolved to bear these intolerable conditions till he had completed *Sebastian Archer*, but not a moment longer. Once let that book be safely and secretly sent direct to a decent publisher, and then he would discomfit several and stop all hanky-panky. So he worked on, harder than ever. Luckily his bedroom had electric light, and abnormal consumption of it (not being separately registered) did not betray him. The diminution of his meals (for which he actually had a conscientious motive) excited remarks – he refused the various courses of the table d'hôte, and ate one plate only at luncheon and dinner: but he explained that the work which everyone saw him do (on the book of Mr Exeter Warden) necessitated a brain unimpeded by the functions of a delightfully-employed interior. Little Piero of the squirrel eyes offered to steal walnuts for him, all the same; and Arthur the Blond saw that he never lacked bread and butter. And, of course, a certain wan anxiety in his gaze did not pass unnoticed: but it was generally known now, in the hotel, that something was wrong; and, on the whole, he was rather admired and pitied than suspected. The fierce and banausic Venetians have the most tender heart-commoving pity for misfortune, and are not a bit ashamed of shewing it. But gentle pity only excited Crabbe to fury. He went in most horrible and ghastly fear of suspicion. The bare idea of it goaded him into frenzied activity at night, when the rest of Venice slept; and the customary quaking of the mud, on which the miraculous city is poised – not a proper earthquake, but a gentle ripple as of a swayed jelly or (if one must be literary) the pleasured sighing of a maiden breast – gave him a most wonderful understanding of that ever-moving instability of human things, an infinitesimal morsel of which (now and again) some persistent genius contrives to consolidate and to crystallize for all time by the force of irreversibly resolute human will. But he need not have feared. He was not suspected then. Your regular swindler doesn't deny himself kinematographs and society. And Crabbe shewed a shell-like adamant to all diversions. He went for an hour sometimes to Mactavish's Mondays, sitting and smoking and listening, sometimes speaking with incisiveness, but making no friends, and acquiring the reputation of a swordstick. That was his sole dissipation. And then, one sunny spring day, La Pash pounced upon him.

He had been rowing infirmary people on the lagoon throughout the afternoon, and the nurses offered a quiet cup of tea when he returned. La Pash, they said, had been and was gone, taking the bibbling directress with her to do some shopping. The nurses' room was in the garden at the back of the hall: one door opened in the kitchen corridor, the other in the paved court at the beginning of the garden. And Crabbe, thinking the coast clear, was just drawing up his chair when Her Ladyship pranced in from the corridor, ostensibly to neigh farewell at the nurse who was pouring tea. The open garden door was but a step behind him: but escape in full face he could not. Incivility was not one of his habits. He merely reared while the nurse lisped a presentation. La Pash bridled: she was charmed, gracious, and suppliant. Her nephew, young Hoste, staying with her, was mad on learning to row in the mode Venetian. She had borrowed the sandolo of the infirmary for him; and (curvetting) could Mr Crabbe be so kind as to send a nice boy, expert with the oar, to act as his instructor. Crabbe didn't like the look of the white of her eye, and remained all shell, with enormous pincers tidily disposed but visible. He would try. What would she pay? Anything which he thought right: if he would send the boy to Ca' Pachello, with a card saying what, that would be enough and admirable. Crabbe said that a boy would appear on the following morning. And he whispered to himself that that boy would not be Zildo, no matter what La Pash's little game was. On the whole, he was rather pleased. He saw that she was vicious: he guessed that she hadn't forgotten his thwacking 'Please leave me alone': he fully intended to avoid her as carefully as ever; and the notion of bows (now obligatory) from a distance (minimum 15 metres) did not perturb him unduly. For he had scooped two points. He had gained a chance of making one of these aliens (who treated their gondolieri so meanly) pay handsomely by way of a change. And he had gained a chance of giving a job to one of a crowd of delightful, capable, but (perforce) idle youngsters, always hanging about the door of the club in the hope of being taken into the service of the English, whose former gondolieri were reported to have wallowed in illimitable luxury.

At 8 o'clock the next day, the only idler at the Bucintoro was a leggy lissome creature of fifteen, all pink and white with a round black poll and comic chinese eyes, who called himself Richard of the Knights.

'Ciò, toso,' cried Nicholas, 'would it please you to serve an English?'

'Sìssiorsì, but willingly.'

The job was explained to him; and he was armed with a card inscribed 'This is Riccardo Cavalieri. Engagement for one month at least. Payment L. 21 a week, with handsel (according to merit) up to L. 25.'

Zildo observed these proceedings with his usual gentle imperturbability. When the stranger had dashed eagerly off to Ca' Pachello, 'Sior,' he said, 'will it not please you to use the pupparin this morning: for my young-lady American voyaged to her place yesterday?'

Nicholas surveyed the tempting water. It was one of those shouting spring days which offer celestial bliss in the open sunlight. He was sick of indoor. Oh, to get out – to go far –

'Yes,' he said, 'let us go to Burano, where I had much pleasure last year.'

The two swirled through the city, entering by Rio della Canonica, rocking and ramping through little canals, with Zildo's clanging bell-like 'E-oe,' and 'Pre-i' or 'Sta-i' booming at the turnings; and emerged, by the Rio dei Mendicanti, on the northern lagoon. They swept at full speed along the cemetery-islands of Sammichele and Sancristoforo, and through the Canale Ordello by the glass-making island of Murano to the long stretch of the Canale di Giustizia beyond. At the islet of Saint James in the Marsh, where Madonna sits in her altar-shrine on the sea-wall, Nicholas called for a halt. The pace had been terrific: but his magnificent strength (sapped though it was by night-work and by the strain of making and wearing a dauntless defiant front to the world), and perhaps also his unconquerable sense of superiority which answered to every call and kept him taut and erect, enabled him not to shew signs of distress before the boy. As for Zildo, flushed and beaming, his fair head bare and crowned with its waving plume, he exulted in using the force of his insuperable youth.

'Sior,' he said, roping to the stake by the shrine, 'many banners have been gained for courses of a quarter of our speed and a half of our length.'

'Do you desire to gain a banner?'

'Nòssior – not without His Sioria.'

'But I do not wish to gain banners from the Venetians.'

'Also me: the banner of the English contents me.'

Nicholas went to the prow, and twisted straight the little Red Ensign which a breeze was wrapping round the shining brazen flagstaff. He was flying England now, in place of the Bucintoro vexillo, because Venice simply creeps with Germans in late spring. Then he sank into the cane arm-chair amidships, and began to roll a cigarette.

A hand curved from the poop behind him, laying four notes of ten lire each with three silver lire and five pajanche in copper on his lap.

'Còssa xe?' he blankly demanded.

'Sior,' answered a voice of infinite young jubilation, 'that is the price of three collars of pomegranates, in silver beads on pearls, in pearl beads on silver, and in silver beads on gold, which I wove for my young-lady American. And here, also, is a design' (shewing a paper) 'for a new collar of tiny feathers of peacocks, which tomorrow I shall weave in gold beads with green and blue, for sending to America to the same.'

'Benissimo.' He folded the coins in the notes, and, turning round, placed them in the boy's hand.

'But – Sior—'

'Put your deniers in your pocket.'

'Nòssior.'

'I am not disputing. I am telling you.'

'Sior, listen' (gabbling hurriedly), 'I wove the collars with beads which I bought with your deniers which I took from Sior Caloprin of the Cassa di Risparmio—'

'Zildo, listen. There are no deniers of mine in the Cassa di Risparmio. – The deniers which you take from Sior Caloprin are your earned wages. – You have woven collars of beads bought with your own deniers, not with mine. Bravo, my Zildo. Do it again. I am very contented with you. Make some more, and yet some more. Fill your pockets with deniers while you can. Good auguries to you. That is all. Understand? Good. And, now, do me the pleasure of rowing me to Burano: for I wish to repose myself with my thoughts—'

Tears welled in unchecked flood from the boy's frank wistful innocent eyes. Nicholas felt like a perfect beast: but he set his teeth against any sort of putrid foolery. Better feel like one than be one; and he shuddered to think how near to the verge of an embrace his heart had so suddenly thrust him. He hardened, and struck a match for his cigarette.

Zildo blinked a bit, without wile, that he might see his way to cast off; and his ripe young lips closed courageously against so ruthlessly bitter and cruel a disappointment. But he obeyed his master implicitly, saying not another word. In half a minute the bark was flying on, driven by the long regular sweeps of his oar. He says that this was when he first knew that he must wait and wait.

Nicholas remained rigid, facing prow-ward, thankful that only his back was visible to his servant: for certain emotions were beginning to play a fierce game with him. The love and the leaky, the gentle delicate honour, the unswerving faith and trust, the grave deliberate singleness of purpose, of the exquisite soul which inhabited that splendidly young and vigorous and alluring form behind him, rang echoing through every secret cavern of his being. Zildo was minded to give. For his own part, he also yearned to give. But he yearned to take as well. And Zildo! Light of light! What would be the unravelling of this tangle, in which he had involved himself and Zildo? Why had Zildo so conclusively refused to leave him. Why had he, with such unusual weakness, acquiesced in that refusal? What portended this content

with the position – this content – this – no, not content –
this suppressed consuming longing to take and to give, to
give and to take all, all, to mingle and dissolve in as one?
What was this hunger, this thirst, this ravenous sense of
desire for the χτημα ες αει of that soul and body? It was not
mere everyday lust: his admiration was as great for the naïve
spring-like soul, for the mind as gently and firmly bright as
a star, as for the long lithe limbs, the soft firm fragrant flesh,
the noble features, the stalwart grace, the virginal freshness
(all once seen, and never for a moment forgotten); and his
admiration (for beauty pure and simple) was refrained by
impregnable virtue proclaiming its object sacrosanct and
inviolable. Nor was it mere vulgar recognition, in the
humble manner of Christians (that latebrosa et lucifuga,
natio, as Minucius Felix calls them) of any inferiority in his
own soul or in his own body. He was ware of his own distinction and force and untainted excellence of form and feature,
of his own inexhaustible youth and strength. He knew himself to be capable of thoughts and deeds as worthy as Zildo's,
fine and rare and cardinal as those undoubtedly were. Was
it, then, only the effect of the shock, the appulse, the thun-
derclap of joy, at the knowledge that he had (actually in his
hand and devoted to him) one so completely sympathetic,
so precisely resembling the majestic eternal primaveral ideal
which he formed for his own attainment? His friends – never,
in all his life, had he had such a friend – never had he even
seen anyone capable of being such a friend as Zildo seemed
to wish to be, and might be – one and all of them had taken
the most hideous and egregious tosses at the very first
approach to his ideal. Sympathy – oh yes, they said that they
sympathized with him. They roared it. But they knew no
Greek: they hadn't the faintest notion of what they were saying. Asked to define, they whimpered that they felt for him.

Felt for him – yes, they felt feelings of their own; and expected him to feel them too. The idea of feeling his feelings never entered their fat heads. They felt for, not with, him; and, what they thought was sym-pathy, actually was dys-pathy. No one had ever felt with him. No one had ever been able to take his part. What heaps of miawling minnocks thought themselves so beastly virtuose for taking – and one admits that they took it with both hands – was, not his part but, that which they thought ought to be his part; and their precious taking of it was their gain and his loss. Bobugo, whom he had really wished to love – pheuph! – the stench of his shame! – Caliban, monstrous farcical buffoon, victim of inordinate vanity and the foot disease called Talipes Plantaris! – And now, here, was an ideal friend, whose form and thought and word and deed and very being were as his own: whom all laws, divine and human, forbade him to have for a friend. Human law held Zildo out of his reach. Nor did he really want Zildo for his friend. That slim strong brave-breasted athlete, aloft there in blue trousers and white guernsey, was his servant, inadmissible to friendship. Co-operation is a different relation from union. But, after all, Zildo was not Zildo – not-Zildo. And honour and reverence forbade him to begin to think of taking not-Zildo for his friend. – What had Caliban spluttered, 'marry some nice girl – instead of sneezing at them all – heaps would jump at you, if you would condescend to ask them nicely, as you can, if you choose.' Ouph! 'Marry some nice girl with money!' – some 'nice girl' – some 'fille repugnante, la femelle du male, un chose horrible, tout en tignasse, en pattes rougeaudes, yeux ravages, bouche défraichie, talons écules – ci-devant provinciale, nippé comme une Hottentot – puis bonne a tout faire, feignante, voleuse, sale – brrr!' – Some coarse, raucous, short-legged hockey – or hunting – female hideous in hairy felt – some bulgy kallipyg with swung skirts and cardboard waist and glass-balled hat-pins and fat open-work stockings and isosceles shoes – something pink-nosed and round-eyed and frisky, as inane and selfish and snappy-mannered as a lap-dog – some leek-shaped latest thing, heaving herself up from long tight lambrequins to her own bursting bosom and bonneted with a hearse-plumed jungle-crowned bath – some pretentious pompadoured image trailing satin, moving (apparently leglessly) in society – all of the mental and physical consistency of parrots crossed with jelly-fish. O god of Love, never! Infinitely far better to marry not-Zildo – if not-Zildo would. But – would not-Zildo? Well, why not? 'He, who dispenses with woman, lives in sin,' said Maimonides.

He stood up; and turned round, as though to look back at Venice. Zildo, poised, swaying at the oar in the centre of vision, looked down, straight at him, as he turned, with the usual gentle persuasive welcoming smile. There must have been, in the aspect of Nicholas at that moment, something of the aspect of a conquistador sampling a spoil of damsels: for the boy flushed vividly, and returned his bright gaze to the dancing prow to keep it straight with infinitesimally-calculated wrist-turns, pushing or feathering the oar. Nicholas attentively observed him, from the proudly-floating panache of his hair like candle-flames, to the rosy tips of his arching honey-hued feet – the candid wistful visage, the long lovely form full of promise, full of joy, the slim magnificent membrature, all alive, all supple, all indefectible, all without trace of sex. Oh, to take! – Marry? Rather than anything else in this world. Oh, to take the offered bud, which taking would bring to bloom. Buds neglected wither. Was so halcyon a bud to be left – to wither?

Yes: he must leave it, to wither: because he might not take

it. He might not take it against its will. And – sordid horror – he dared not to ask leave to take it: for he had no garden wherein to plant it. O fool, to dally thus!

He threw himself headlong down again to the world of things as they were – to the staggering priest scheming to batten on his brains – to the coxcomb, catarrhic with incompetence, who juggled with his trust – to the agents squalling stolidly on his means – to his creditors, his empty purse, his empty hungry heart, his empty lonely life. These, these, were what he had to face. He might not indulge in dreams. – His mind was still ecclesiastically tinged. – He was still very very young.

He picked up his oar; and began to row, as the pupparin approached the canal which enters the islet of Mazzorbo. 'Sta-i,' he commanded.

Zildo steered to the right, along the sea-wall painted with a lace-maker's advertisement; and would have turned sharply to the left, into the canal where a long wooden bridge connects Mazzorbo with Burano.

'No,' cried his master, 'keep straight on.'

'Sior, there is no canal across this lagoon; and we shall be stranded.' (Gondolieri are dreadfully nervous about leaving the staked waterways for short cuts across tempting but unmarked expanses.)

'It is true that there is no canal: but I will not go in dry. Do me the pleasure of obeying me.'

'Sissior.'

They struck a more or less diagonal course toward their nearing goal. Nicholas kept vigilant watch on the shallows at the end of his own oar, and held the bark in depths just out of reach of them with shouts of 'Pre-i,' or 'Sta-i,' to the steersman; and, so, slightly zigzagging along the short-cut used by fishermen, they came to the south end of the canal which penetrates Burano. Zildo's panting anxiety, lest his Paron's prepotence should have run the bark aground, gave place to an admiring smile worth millions. Nicholas shipped his oar; and went to the prow to shove aside barks impeding the way, the canal being narrow and crowded.

As they went under the iron bridge, a sturdy islander (of the Re Galantuomo type) saluted from the quay. Nicholas recognized him as one who used to take a modest nightly potion at the inn where he had often stayed in the previous autumn. They glided on, turning the corner, and going under the second bridge, tying up the bark at the Albergo di Roma. Nicholas went in; and was welcomed by all, from the pursy paron to shock-headed Scimiotto the waiter: he ordered luncheon – something fortunately fried and a flask of white chianti.

Zildo remained at the door, shewing his teeth, keeping an eye like a knife on the pupparin. The quay swarmed with ragamuffins, cubs, cinderellas, and slubberdegullions, eager to snatch from the well-known English. 'All the Buranelli, who are not mendicants, are brigands,' said the boy, citing the aristocratic opinion of serene Venice, when his master came out to lounge beside him.

'And the Buranelle?'

'Mah! Like this like that, and all verminous (pidocchiose)': he said with disgusted indifference.

Now the girls of Burano really are wonderfully handsome. ('O che beo biondo!' screamed a jade in Zildo's ear. 'Go away, Blessed She,' growled that Beautiful Fair-He). Of course they're as bold as brass, as they spadge about the quays of their tiny island-city, arm in arm, with clattering of clogs; and their taste in dress is alarming and vulgar beyond words. But Nicholas had not investigated their personal cleanliness.

Judging from the density of the population and the stench of their canals, possibly Zildo's sentence was just.

'See that fisher-boy with the black eyes, who walks on his hands for our diversion?' asked Nicholas abruptly.

'Sissior.'

'Go and say to him, like this, "Emilio, the paron wishes you to guard his bark."'

Zildo stepped across the quay; and delivered the message. Active-footed Emilio vaulted upright, brown-gleaming thighs bare, mud-green trunks, black shirt open, arms to shoulders and breast to waist bare and brown as a cigar, brown face, sparkling eyes, glittering teeth – a wicked merry mercurial muscular slip of tatterdemalion, clean because amphibious, prompt to do anything (blessed or damned) for tenpence, a born slave. His naked arms and legs whirled: there were shrieks, yells, thuds, a patter of feet, as he cleared away the rabble of riff-raff. Nicholas laughed: and chucked him a couple of cigarettes. He deftly caught and stuck them over his ears; and, bounding to a post-top, sat there to smoke on guard, legs open, one ankle laid on the other knee and one leg dangling down, in the exact pose of the fine bronze called *Intervallo* which a Venetian sculptor, Ugo Bottassi, once exhibited to unappreciative London. Nicholas wondered where that bronze was now.

While they ate their luncheon, the sturdy citizen (who saluted their arrival) passed through the inn to imbibe at the back. Catching a glance, he paused at their table: and presented a black-bordered visiting-card. 'With permission, Siore,' he said, 'seeing that gentility leads you to revisit this island, I affright myself to demand the honour of shewing you some pictures.'

'You will give me a pleasure,' Nicholas replied: 'but

I ought to say that I am that strange thing called a poor English, who cannot afford to buy pictures.'

'That is of no import, Siore: I only wish to give you a pleasure.'

'And I accept it with many thanks.'

'Then, when you are ready, I will conduct you to my little house.'

'Permit me, meanwhile, to offer you calcosa a bere.'

'Grazienò, Siore,' with a noble retiring gesture worthy of a renunciating exarkh.

Nicholas read on the card 'Novello Ermenegildo,' as he paid his bill. 'Here is a namesake of yours, who is going to shew you some pictures,' he said to his servant.

'Sior, he is a brave, and very beneficent; and, as for me, I am appassionated for pictures.'

Nicholas sat up. 'What do you know about pictures?'

'Much, Sior: for, always when I spy a painter, I creep near to peep over his shoulder: but I forget all those pictures: though I never have forgotten certain pictures, which I used to see on festivals, while Bastian my father had life, before I went into Calabria.'

'And those?'

The boy's big long blue eyes explored past memories. 'Sior, there was, in a corridor of the Accademia, a very celestial azure picture of an angel – o be-o! – And, in a hall – yes – a picture of ten thousand martyrs – o be-issimi!' – He became rapt in mental contemplation.

Nicholas knew the Ten Thousand Crucified Martyrs of Mount Ararat by Carpaccio, a myriad of the ordinary stalwart Venetian nudes who adorn all time, dilated in divers demeanours on the trees of wooded hills. 'Why did that picture please you?' he inquired.

266

'Because, Sior, the martyrs were so amiable; and I wished them alive to hug me, I being then an infant. And also, Sior, there was a picture with his patron of my father, Sambastian, very sane and vegete, very sedate and noble, with an arrow in his left belly and another in his left calf.' (This, no doubt, was the Giambellini.) – 'Then, Sior, there was a picture of Sancristoforo in the church of Sanzancristostom: but my father said he was a Buranello, being of that type, but beautiful – and, also, I remember a picture of a toso, amiable, amiable, amiable and brave like my Paron, at Santamaria Odorifera, on the wall by the altar of Sanlorenzo—'

Sior Novello reappeared, and led them along the quays to his house, Emilio following (at a beckon) with the bark.

It was a tiny three-floored cottage, one of a row, entered (from the quay) to a room which was parlour and cobbler's shop. On the right, were Sior Novello's bench and apron and tools of trade with a medley of finished and unfinished cobbling. Three walls were covered with religious or national chromos and family photographs. Furniture and ornament were of the most undistinguished taste imaginable. On the left wall was a very large oblong curtain. The cobbler drew it aside. He was as sober and as staid a respectability as one could find anywhere.

Nicholas gasped; and stared. He never praised anything without a but: but this was astounding. It was a finely framed picture of a perfectly feminine female nude asleep, simply and grandly depicted by a master. No accessories jumped or buzzed. Nothing disturbed your unique impression. You were struck (with one blow) unconscious of anything but her.

'Ma che!' Zildo ejaculated. He glared: went gradually hot and red; and, turning his back, picked up a waxed thread from the bench to twiddle.

'Who – who – is the painter?' Nicholas demanded.

'Siore, my dead brother, Luigi Novello, professor of the Roman Academy, to serve you,' superbly said the cobbler.

He led them over the three floors of his little house. Every foot of wall, of stair and landing and room was covered with pictures and studies – a Dead Christ watched by Modern Maries embellished the stair. Everywhere was exquisite imagination, singular insight, noble taste, masterly skill. Portfolios full of sketches, early and prime and late, were extracted from bureaux and dowry-chests. It was a most astonishing revelation of the dead painter's talented personality. And to be lost here, unknown, in this poor cottage! – This was the first intimate view which Crabbe had had of a humble Venetian dwelling, the delicious cleanliness of bareness, of embroidered sheets, of polished pewter and copper and glass and linen, the airy windows, the sweet-scented beds, the decent homely necessaries which are the luxuries of simple people. 'How did these valuable objects of art come here?' he inquired.

'Siore, I was my brother's heir, to serve you. And I thank you, Siore, for the honour of your visit.'

As they rowed away into the sunny gold of afternoon, Zildo had several things to say. If only the gondolieri of Venice knew of that picture gallery, what mountains of deniers might be gained. How? Most simply, like this. When rich English and Americans went to see the lace-makers of Burano, their gondolieri (to divert them) would say, like this, Here, also, is another little thing, and most antique. Sior Ermenegildo Novello would display his squares. The forestiers naturally would buy them, paying (let us say) three thousand franchi for the veiled picture, whereof eight hundred and fifty would go to the gondolieri for their handsel, leaving two thousand and one hundred and fifty for Sior Ermenegildo. But, what a good combination!'

'But Sir Ermenegildo does not want to sell.'

'Otherwise, Sior, otherwise, I assure you. One will always sell anything for deniers in cash.'

'It's not true. There are many things of mine which I will not sell. And you, Zildo – have you nothing which you will not sell?'

The boy, posed, rowed silently. Nicholas looked round at him. 'Speak,' he said.

'Sior, with permission, I wish first to examine my thoughts.'

'Good. Think. And, when you have finished thinking, tell me what you think. But, at this moment, tell me whether the pictures pleased you.'

'Moderately. And you, Sior?'

'They are well done.'

'Sìssior. And, Mrs Bare?'

Nicholas gave a snort of laughter. 'La Siora Ignua? Oh, she was very well done.'

'Mah! But who would be painted like that, for all to see, for ever.'

'And why not?'

'It would not please me. It would cause me much shame.'

'Now why? What have you of which to be ashamed? Are you dirty, or wicked, or hunchbacked, or distorted, or deformed, or diseased?'

'Nòssiornò! Nonòsior! No-nò! I am none of these bad things. But, nothing of me belongs to me which I could give away. And it would cause me shame, Sior, to be like that, asleep, unknowing, for all to see, at their will, for ever, taking little views of my aspect away from me. Sior, I do not wish to be observed by strangers, by persons (brutti individui) whom I do not even know, but – but only – only by whom I – trust—'

Nicholas saw the red danger-signal of the masculine pronoun; and put the brake full on. So Zildo deemed him like that grand athletic young Saint Vincent (or was it Saint Lawrence) at the church of Madonna del Orto, amiable, amiable, amiable and brave. And Zildo was saving himself – reserving himself – offering—. O Lord!

'Well, now that you know of these pictures, tell your next Signorina Americana of them; and gain your mound of deniers,' said Nicholas, hurriedly and bleakly.

'Nòssior. I am not as other gondolieri. Also, with permission, I belong to my Paron.' And not another word would he say, even when they touched Venice in a marvellous sunset of streaks of lilac edged with silver on fawn colour about a disk of boiling blood.

This indeed was desire. But, what whole was he pursuing? Priesthood? Or marriage? Neither: till able to choose.

XVIII

THE BLUBBER-LIPPED professor of Greek had the blazing face to write: 'Dear Crabbe, I must congratulate you on *Terribile la Femmina*, Yours Richard Macpawkins'; and set him rearing in two tantrums. How dared that unutterable one congratulate him? What in the world did the screed mean?

Crabbe was frightfully worried that morning: his mask of serenity cost an effort to bear: his conscience had been giving him beans on the score of yesterday's idiotic (and almost criminal) dalliance; and he cursed himself anew for his crab-like habit of sidling and for his unconquerable predilection for larking on verges of giddy precipices. It was sinful, too, to play with temptation, specially when another's peace was concerned. After Mass, he came across the square of the little porphyry lions in front of the patriarchal palace to drink his coffee, case-hardened anew, freshly resolved not to let himself go any more in regard to Zildo – till his way was clear. Even then, a problem would confront him – the question of continued celibacy as proof of priestly vocation: twenty years had been the measure of his vow which was to lapse at Easter – it was not an ungenerous slice of mortal life to sacrifice: it was a rather huge pearl to cast before three totally stolid archbishops one after another. He had inward warnings of the exhaustibility of human patience.

And, at this point, came the Macpawkins note, or gibe.

He took it with him when he went to the club; and racked his brains for its signification. Looking over the balcony, he saw Zildo below, in the Rio, bare-legged, bare-armed, with the bark half-full of water, and its floor-boards out to be scrubbed. Active happiness was this boy's portion when he had plenty of polishing to do.

Yes: of course! *Terribile la Femmina* was the title of one of that bundle of manuscripts sent to Lord Arthur Baliol Kingsbury, the editor of *The Lykeion*, at the beginning of the year, by request of the incredible Bobugo. Ha-ha! Here, then was some money. And Crabbe instantly wrote his news to Caliban, telling to collect and send the sum due. He added something else. As the Lieutenant had forbidden personal communication with Bobugo, Crabbe wished that priest to know that refusal of the Rite of Benediction had barred him from the Sacraments for three months: Easter was at hand, and it must be clearly understood that he considered himself prevented from his Easter duties as things were. It was a trick of intimidation which had been tried before, by another sacerdotal bully whom resistance had brought crashing to the ground. So he now gave Bobugo warning. No law of God or Man empowered a priest to sin in this hole-and-corner way. Formal excommunication would be welcomed, and instantly and unconditionally submitted to. But, excommunication required a bishop and a trial; and a furtive little priest, who dared to deprive of Sacraments by refusing a Rite, couldn't find a tame bishop on every bush to assist his nefarious prostitution of spiritualities for purely temporal coercive purposes. Labels are more lethal than libels.

Satisfaction, at this neat presentment of a dilemma, mitigated annoyance at Parrucchiero's uneasiness which took concrete form when he went back to the hotel for luncheon. The usual spring visitors were flocking to Venice: Crabbe occupied a desirable room: would he either change it, or pay his bill? He moved his things to the room which Zildo had occupied, No. 27, two steps across the landing, a tiny closet with a couple of windows over a narrow alley pervaded (all night long) by raucous night-birds and tipsy songsters.

Here, the final touches were put to *Sebastian Archer*; and the fair copy of it went through Cook to Messieurs Ferrer Senior in England. Maintaining his plan of secrecy, Crabbe gave the Bucintoro Club as his address; and instructed the marangon, who mended oars all day by the letter-box, to look after communications which might come for him.

Next, he nerved himself anew to make a clean sweep of the Warden's book. He returned a batch of revised proof-sheets, one evening, when the worthy man and his Wardeness came back from La Pash's weekly reception.

They had the mean little sidelong air and the solicitous feeble but attempting gait of peachicks afflicted with gapes.

The pair, toothy, pregnant, and gleaming, perched themselves by him in the hall, with the evident intention of talking with tedious concentration. The long cardboard-tipped cigarettes were lighted; and the lady began. 'We bring you,' she said, 'a message from Lady Pash—'

'And,' the Thiasarkh burst to interrupt, 'we do so sincerely hope—'

'No, Exeter,' she patted him, 'let me. Lady Pash,' she continued to Crabbe, 'has been speaking about you all the evening; and she wants us to ask you to consent – wait – let her put you on the infirmary committee – listen – because, she says, you're the only Englishman who has ever been of any real practical service to it!'

'Of course I can't do anything of the kind,' Crabbe promptly snapped.

'Oh! But why?'

'My good people – I'm not addressing Lady Pash, I'm addressing you – will you try to give your serious attention to the following considerations. I'm almost certain that I'm ruined. I'm next door to certain that I am ruined for this year at least. I really am, now. Consequently, I'm not fit to associate with comfortable people; and I'm certainly not fit to take an official position in the infirmary. I'm an undesirable, and I know it. And I have the decency, or the devilry (which you please), to take the wind out of everyone else's sails by proclaiming the damaging fact first myself.'

'But, dear person, are you so certain? Don't you think that, if you'd take us just a little bit into your confidence, we might – is it quite sure that we couldn't perhaps hit on some—'

'It's not a matter of confidence. Anyone can know everything. I only kept quiet because I do so detest a bore—'

'Oh, do then tell us what the difficulty really is.'

On this invitation, and in the sure and certain hope of a joyful riddance of rotters, he briefly and concisely told his tale, making it as black and unprepossessing and hopeless as possible, of Bobugo's treacherous breach of agreement and his attempt to get a book for next to nothing, of Morlaix and Sartor's breach of agreement in stopping allowances and refusing an account of five years' management of his property, of Caliban's authoritative assumption of responsibility for rectification and his neglect of the two books entrusted to him. 'The point is that my own hands,' he concluded, 'are tied, by command of my Lieutenant, and by want of about two hundred sterling to work with apart from him. I'm convinced that Peary-Buthlaw is a pompous palavering turncoat, that Morlaix and Sartor are stupid old fools who've omitted their duty and are ashamed to confess it, that Bonsen has adroitly used my agents and my friend for his own questionable ends, and that I'm quite comfortably embroiled with all three of 'em.'

'But do you think that a priest would—'

'Yes: a banausic one like Bobugo certainly would. You "other sheep" don't know half about the lovely lot of baa-lambs who caper inside the fold.'

'And yet, you remain—'

'Inside? Rather. And for jolly good reason. Run away and read Boccaccio's tale of the Jew. A church, which continues to flourish with criminals for its ministers, must be divine, don't you know? Beside, wasn't there a Judas among the apostles?'

'Oh! How you pain me! But – I also had just a little something to say to you. Would you mind if I made a suggestion? May I? Thank you so much. I have such a dear friend, a member of my congregation (a communicant), living at the Grand Hotel. He's a retired financier, who used to do Rothschild's most intimate and confidential work. I can tell you, from personal experience, that he's simply a magician in unravelling money-tangles. Indeed I don't know what we should do without him. We certainly shan't possibly be able to go to England unless—'

'Then you are going? When?'

'At the end of May. But we leave the hotel after Easter.'

'For your own palace?'

'Oh no! We shall be packing up there: so we're going to be the guest of dear Mrs—'

'But, you see, I don't know your financier.'

'A word from me—'

'Thank you: no.'

'I assure you – may I speak quite plainly? Thank you so much. I wanted to say that, if you'd let me speak to Mr

Sappytower, you'd place him under such an obligation to you. He does so enjoy arranging money difficulties. It's his art, you see; and he takes quite an artist's joy in it. Our own case seemed absolutely hopeless; and now – dear person, do let me just name—'

'No: I can't. I detest the notion of talking to strangers about money affairs. It gives one a kind of name. And, after all, there's the bare chance that I'm exciting myself unnecessarily.'

'Do promise me – I shall be so unhappy – promise me to think it over.'

'Very well: I'll bear it in mind.'

'But – if you'd only let me speak now, I could guarantee that your worries would be ended in a week. Ours were.'

'No: I'll think it over.'

Crabbe did think it over, with tingling talons; and worried himself properly, I promise you.

What did this man really mean? Why couldn't people spit it all out straight at once? Why, with triumphant and kindly and interested demonstrations, bring these two particular propositions simultaneously? What was the connection between La Pash's command to join her infirmary committee, and the assurance that money difficulties could be solved in a week by the magic of this financier of Rothschild's – if there was a connection? And, could anything be more distracting than the dropping of Rothschild's name, of all other names, among his present circumstances?

Crabbe knew that he was (as they said) the only Englishman who had ever been of any real practical service to the infirmary. He wasn't inclined to complacency about it: because the job really amused him and made him happy, and his virtue was its own (and his only) reward. But he knew, too – oh, jolly well he knew – that he could and would be infinitely more useful to the institution in an official capacity. He would have an English medical man on the premises all the time, for one thing. And, now that the new English law forbade the shipping of pneumonic and phthisical sailors at English ports for shedding in Italy and the marine patients were consequently much reduced in number, it would be well to develop the nursing-home department to provide the private treatment for which Venetian doctors howled. Also, nurses (and directresses too), who invoked La Pash against doctors whenever they felt a little hysterical, should be sacked on the spot for insubordination and unprofessional conduct, instead of compelling medical resignations and aiding the invasion of Venice by German hospitallers. Efficiency and discipline should be introduced, and rigorously maintained. Accounts should be rendered weekly, and not laboriously cooked by gas and guess for annual reports issued eight months late. And, there should be a resident steward, with charge of servants and stores, instead of the sloppy venal huggermuggery which bought through the cook from such of his friends as would tip him. Yes: Crabbe well knew how to organize the Universal Infirmary, redeeming it from its reputation in the city as an amateurish hen-roost, and from its reputation on the Island of Spinalonga as an English sort of maniacal café-chantant or casino rivalling the Sailors' Institute by the Papadopoli Gardens. And, if La Pash liked to pay the bill, she could continue to absorb the credit: but one does not take credit for charity; and, as public begging for funds went on, and, as patients paid a printed tariff, the infirmary should not sail under false pretences any longer as a charity. He had plenty of views on the place, and willingly would sacrifice time and money to carry them into effect. And, was it really a fact – for he had openly expounded these views, drumming them into the ears of the Wardens and the

Portingall Jew and the bibbling directress and donnish Mactavish, scores of times – that La Pash, the supreme proprietress, actually did wish him to carry them into effect? If so, he had been doing that curvetting equine-faced female a gross injustice. If not, why did she want him on her committee? He was a nobody, possessed of no name embellishing to a prospectus; he was known to be hard-up; and he had given unmistakable tokens that he was not at all the sort of marionette whose wires can be moved by anybody. So much for La Pash's command. Next, why this sudden cut and dried offer of Sappytower to straighten his pecuniary tangles within a week? What could Rothschild's most confidential agent do – what could Rothschild (magical colossal name) himself do – which Crabbe himself could not do, were he free to move – free, from the fetters of obedience to the Lieutenant of his Order, from the shackles of his empty pockets, from the gyves of his exhausted overdraft? Was this proposal (he whispered) meant to herald the advent of a new Mæcenas? No doubt Mæcenas could do much. Even a common friend, if such a commodity appertained, could do all which was necessary, could see him through a trouble which (after all) was but of trumpery magnitude and quite temporary. Touching the matter of Mæcenas, however (he suddenly sat up and told himself out loud), it would be essential to regard the creature with great caution. Mæcenas was apt to presume: had to be taught his place and kept there, to prevent him from becoming a most infernal nuisance; and, as an axiom of purely ordinary sagacity, it was just as well not to have anything to do with him, at least till he had made a very humble access on his knees licking a substantial length of pavement in token of abjection and subjection. Yes: on the whole, Crabbe fancied that he had met the Wardens and their propositions very appropriately.

'Maaah! You dear thing!' the directress mouthed at him, when he went on Palm Sunday to the infirmary, 'so you've heard from Lady Pash that you're to come on our committee! Isn't it sweet of her?'

'I came to say that you mustn't expect me this week, because I want to go to church,' he answered, touching his cap; and rowed away.

It was Holy Week; and he promised his soul a debauch of attention. 'Si uis felicitas, terram excede' is a very good rule on these occasions. At such times, he was generally happy, away from this world, embosomed so deep and obscure in stately immemorial symbol that he approached quite close to the other. They were the times when he suspended his soul in far diviner air, to be winnowed and purged of chaff and husk – times of purification, invigoration, fortification, which he took, as he took sun-baths, and light-baths and his daily swim from Sanzorzi to La Grazia and back for the health of his body. But, this year, the result was faint. Undoubtedly the prince of darkness had leave to torment him for a season. Mass left him cold. Stations of the Cross were the most inartistically dismal of all dull dronings. The tedium of Tenebrae dried and tired him to extinction. And his meditations failed to carry him out of his valley to the higher peak and view of the city celestial. Once, indeed, he thought to have won there. It was the night of the exposition of great relics in Saint Mark's. He stood, in the thick of the crowd; and watched the procession of seven canons, in crimson copes, go, through the gloom, as of caverns, with a galaxy of torches and a wonderful song, to the treasury. Wedged in the crowd, a head above all, he watched the return of that starry throng, turning, as they turned. He watched, in the twinkling host, the seven crimson canons carrying

279

marvellous reliquaries, shrine-shaped, cross-shaped, frames of gold and silver with cylinders or slabs of rock-crystal incrusted with gems, and the great basilican reliquary held in two hands. He watched the seven canons ascending the enormous pulpit, violet and crimson and orange and silver and yellow and scarlet and gold in the rich brown gloom as of caverns, while a forest of lofty tapers and torches held by white-robed singers amassed in a ring below, silver and primrose and mauve and lemon and daffodil yellow and snow, pale vivid pointed flamelets flickering on snow, swaying like catenas of myriads of fire-flies in the cavernous gloom. He watched the mystic circle of seven crimson canons moving round and round aloft in the pulpit, nimbused with glory, when the greatest there, stripped of his glory, simple in rochet and stole, emerging alone from the ring, to the sound of the wonderful long-drawn song, took the greatest relic of all, holding it high above the starry blaze below, and blessed the world with The Sign. He felt the lilt and the lift of soul-ascension, then, from the world of brown gloom – felt his soul gently soaring away, from heaving crowd, clustered flames, long-drawn wonderful song, splendour of crimson and primrose and silver and gold and snow – through the high golden haze splashed with golden slabs of light among the mosaics of the domes, beyond – beyond all these, up to a realm of darkness, empty, imperscutable, where he waited, waited to soar higher, or to see his way to soar. There he stayed, stayed, in a place of no joy and no pain, a place of nothingness, just out of reach of trouble, not in sight of bliss. There, with effort, he held himself, till he should have word to come up higher. On Holy Saturday, at the first Mass of Easter, again his form stood in the crowd beneath the golden domes, acutely sensible, while his soul aloft waited dryly in a dark void. Came the liturgical moment when grief is banished by joy. The deacon intoned the first Alleluias of Easter. The Easter-candle flamed. Lanthorns and lamps and tapers and torches on all sides blossomed with light. Violet veils fell from images and pictures. Violet vestments were changed for tissues of silver and gold. Violet curtains swept aside, disclosing golden altar and pala d'oro blazing with enamels and precious stones. And all the bells and organs in basilica and city rang and sounded at the chaunt of the Gloria Angelical. Now, if ever, his soul would be summoned ad audiendum verbum, would have leave to rise with its Lord in newness of perfect joy. But, under his eyes, in the crowd, just within reach of his fist, a self-unpriested oratorian – Scotch, of course – smartly and fashionably dressed as a lay-man by Bond Street and Savile Row, giggled, decorously flirting with an aged Erastian gossip nodding, nodding in a flower-bed of a hat. And down came Crabbe's soul, crashing, Ikaros-like, on the crags of this world of ugly horror and gloom. 'Nor knowest thou what argument Thy life to thy neighbour's creed hath lent.' The only consolation which he got was from his ruthless immitigable faith, his defiant unconquerable trust. Etiam si occiderit me, in Ipso sperabo: ueruntamen uias meas in Conspectu Eius arguam, expressed his mind. He spent his Easter in picking up the little pieces of his soul and putting them miserably but undauntedly together. 'God, Who, to enlighten the darkness of the world, didst deign to mount upon the holy cross, grant that, in my darkness, I may see Thy light, and, by it, mount upon what-ever cross Thou deignst to me, and, having mounted, rise from it triumphantly to Thee, Who, with The Father and The Spirit, livest and reignest, ever, one God: Amen.' Thus, he prayed, or tried to pray, among the fierce bitter moanings of his soul. But he saw no light, tasted no Easter joy.

Zildo, clean, fed with Bread of angels, radiant in happiness unalloyed, met him after Mass on Easter day. 'Sior,' he said, 'I augur for you a good Easter.'

'And I for you.'

'Sior, you are not quite content. Tell me why. For, with permission, that does me harm.'

'You wouldn't understand.'

'Sior, with excuses and the greatest possible respect to your blessed and valorous face, I should understand everything perfectly.'

'I am content with you. What more do you want? Che cossa vuol de più de Domeniddio?'

'Va ben. Sior, you are master: I am servant. I say no more now. But the pupparin is polished and ready, with the two banners of England and the Vexillo of the Bucintoro in honour of the festival.'

On flood-tide, the bark glided along the canal of Zuecca without effort. All the ships anchored in the Basin of Saint Mark, and the Istrian firewood trabaccoli at the Zattere, with the coal-tramps and cotton-ships and grain-ships, were bright with bunting as Nicholas went by, sitting in his cane arm-chair to read a neglected letter of Holy Week. Caliban wrote: "I sent a copy of your last to Bobugo; and he commissions me to confer upon you his New Year's Benediction: which I now do by these presents. I hope this will solve your religious difficulty. As for what is to happen, I am at a loss. Why don't you get a job of some kind? I can't make anything of Morlaix and Sartor, though I have had letters from and four interviews with them of which you know nothing. They don't seem to want to treat with me. Bobugo says that you haven't been hammered enough yet by Olympos, and hammered you will be till you give in. I've applied to *The Lykeion*: your story appeared in the issue of Jan. 23rd; and they'll send me your cheque at the end of the month. You know you really are most unjust about Wallace. Although he is a Quaker, he's incapable of rooting and snouting in any lovely catholic garden. He has only made certain suggestions, which I think it wise to adopt. Don't you understand that Wallace is a successful novelist, whose novels sell ten thousand to a thousand of yours? Surely you ought to be glad of his help, wanting money as we do. We have decided that generals of the Order and their provinces are to be called priors and priories in future, like the Templars. And We have done the Latin office for Our incoronation next June Ourself as you don't seem willing to oblige Us. Do try to get a job. I.T.SS.S."

A job? Yes. Why not make a job, a picric job, a violently dynamic job, for example? Crabbe wrote: "Kindly convey this message from me to your blessed Bobugo – Received, through a Freemason, one New Year's Benediction, three months and more after date, and too late, and not regarded as valid. – Kindly answer the following questions: 1. As *Terribile la Femmina* was printed in *The Lykeion* in Jan., the cheque was due at end of Jan.: Why have you not got it for me in Apr., with author's copies of that journal and an explanation of its surreptitious publication of my story? 2. Why don't you tell me what you've been doing with *The Weird* these nine months? 3. What have you done with *Sieur René*; and where is the remittance promised (as you alleged) by Morlaix and Sartor on condition of my sending you its proofs? 4. What are you going to do about Morlaix and Sartor, and about Bobugo, after keeping me from writing to them during four months while you have been embroiling me further with them? 5. What of your oath that no harm should touch me in my honour or my person or my property? 6. Mark this well: I refuse any of Wallace's intervention in *De Burgh's Delusion*; and I want to know what you're going to do about it? 7. Will you let me see the proper Form of Defiance, to be used by a knight of the Order wishing (on account of treachery) to withdraw his faith pledged to the Lieutenant of the Grandmagistracy of the Order? 8. Are you my friend, or my enemy? Illuminet te Sanctissima Sapientia."

In the days ensuing, Crabbe nourished himself in patience, hardening his carapax, closing the joints of his mail for defence, sharpening his awful pincers, for dreadfully offensive operations on a large scale.

Caliban wrote: "Strictly private. As you seem to wish to leave the Order, We hereby return you your faith and release you from all oaths and obligations: but, in view of your past most eminent services, We, in Our Own name and in the name of the curial council and indeed of the whole Order, hereby stablish your right to resume your rank and precedence in the said Order when it shall seem good to you so to do. Please burn Rule and return your Badge, as (in case you are in danger of publicity) it will be well to have removed all traces of your connection with the Order beforehand. Of course I am your friend though you do seem to think me your enemy. Don't be a fool. I have been again to *The Lykeion*, and they say that the manager who is absent will go into the question of remuneration on his return at the end of next week. I can't make out why Morlaix and Sartor haven't sent you what I swear they promised on receipt of *Sieur René*. You'd better write to them yourself. They are not quite so evil as you think – they repeated to me that they won't touch the profits of *Sieur René*, which should go to your credit entirely. About *The Weird* and *De Burgh's Delusion*, if you won't be mixed up with Wallace's revisions, I'll get both books published at once, either under my own name alone or 'by C. H. C. Peary-Buthlaw and Another,' of course sending you your half of the profits, but you must assign me the right of altering titles and contents of both books in any way I consider desirable at my own discretion. I enclose duplicate bonds to this effect. You will see that I have signed them with father as my witness. All you have to do is to sign them, getting someone to witness your signature, and send me one copy while you keep the other. I really have done my best to help you though I suppose you won't believe it. Here is a coupon which you can change at the post-office for a stamp worth twopence-halfpenny, as I am most anxious to have your Badge and acknowledgments of what I say about the Order.   I.T.SS.S."

Crabbe wrote: "The headlong eager precipitancy with which Your Splendour has been pleased to abuse my request for the Form of Defiance shews me that my dismissal from the Order (at a time when I am in trouble through Your grievous fault) is precisely what is most greedily desired. But I will not submit to the secret dismissal, which Y.S. so timorously has sent me, with twopence-halfpenny: such hole-and-corner work being contrary to the spirit of chivalry. Therefore, I myself (in accordance with apostolic precept, which directs that all things should be done decently and in order) do here renounce my allegiance to Y.S., and defy You, for the reasons following: First, because Y.S. secretly entered into alliance with two externs, Bonsen and Macpawkins, both my declared enemies, and the former notoriously guilty of treachery against me, submitting Y.S. to their conditions in my despite, which conditions were dishonouring to me, Your faithful knight: Second, because I utterly abhor from Y.S.'s interpretation of the law of chivalry regarding the treatment due to a knight fallen on evil times. Further, I reject the secret encomiums sent by Y.S. (in the name of the curial council and indeed of the whole Order) in Your secret breve, seeing that the said encomiums are not countersigned by the chancellor or by any curial officer or by any knight. Furthermore, I refuse and spit upon Y.S.'s secret stablishment of my right to resume my rank and precedence in the Order, seeing that (in the words of the Sage) 'It is not I who have lost the Athenians, but it is the Athenians who have lost me.' And my rentrance into the Order forms the subject of a question which could only be discussed when the Order and Y.S. very humbly have made amends for the treachery and injustice with which You have afflicted me. And I will not burn the Rule of the Order, but will hold it (with my other documents) at the disposition of the Quæstor of Venice in case of necessity. And I cannot return my Badge, which is (with many of my other valuables) at the Mount of Piety of Venice. And regarding other evidences of my connection with the Order, I refuse to incur any further suffering by destroying them so that the imbecility and infidelity and cowardice of Your Splendour might (if possible) be concealed. And I denounce Y.S. as a craven braggart and perjured traitor, false to your oath of defending my honour and my person and my property. This is the Defiance of me, Nicholas, Knight-Founder and Knight-Magnate and sometime Provost of the Order of Sanctissima Sophia, hurled at the face of Harricus, Lieutenant of the Grandmagistracy of the same Order, and written with my own hand in the Sexter of Saint Mark at Venice, and sealed with my own seal of Herakles and the Hydra in the octave of The Lord's Resurrection, m c m viiii. – My dear Enemy: no friend could behave as you (and your people) behave, in spasms, in sulky silence, always and exactly contrary to my expressed will. So I say, My dear Enemy: please do nothing further with *The Lykeion*. You only complicate a very simple matter. I myself have written to the editor. I will not consent to the revision of my *De*

Burgh's Delusion on the lines of your Quaker, or to the alteration of a single word, at least till after my manuscript has been submitted to and rejected by Shortmans, Ferrer, Macmartin, Albemarle, Dr Wright, and perhaps some others. As for your beastly bonds, I have no intention of helping you (and your father) to commit villainy in your rages. So I refuse to sign the enclosed: the other copy, bearing your and your father's signatures, I shall keep. Please understand that I decline to be the 'Ghost' of a Fool, as you and your father have tried to make me. I'm shocked at you both. You ought to be ashamed of yourselves. I hope this is plain. The notion of your intermittent playing with the magnum opus of a man in peril is more than I can stand. It is positively awful to see you treating my pearl as animals with a preference for acorns generally treat such gems. How (in Heaven's Name) does your Quaker make a successful book? By writing a book different from anybody else's book? And do you, Caliban, think that you, tyro, can make a successful book by assimilating my already-unique book to Wallace's books? Tush! Your only sensible and practical and honourable course – if you lied to me in Jan., when you said that Shortmans had promised to take *The Weird* and *De Burgh's Delusion* on sight – is to send my manuscripts of both books round the publishers, beginning with my own publishers, until they are accepted, and (meanwhile) not to cease for an instant from collaborating further works either to follow them or to replace them – that is, if Life and Death and Honour and Truth and Justice mean anything to you. Apparently they don't. So I say, My dear Enemy: please do nothing further about *Sieur René*. It was bad enough to get the proofs from me on the false pretence that my retention of them was the only thing which prevented my agents from paying my usual income. And, even now, you won't tell me what you have done with my

287

proofs. For Goodness' Sake, if you're going to belie your sovereign oath, if you won't straighten or help me to straighten my affairs, do have the decency at least not to muck them any more. For four months you have capered goatishly, entirely disregarding me. You will neither get my dues for me, nor let me get them for myself. O Friend! Please leave me alone. And don't blame me if I disown your shatterpated muddle-headed fatwitted anile inept bœotian actions now. O Enemy."

Three thunderclaps followed these fulgurations. One, to Lord Arthur Baliol Kingsbury, stated that Crabbe had no representative in England; and asked for the four-months' overdue fee for *Terribile la Femmina*. Another, to Morlaix and Sartor, repudiated Caliban; and requested them to resume direct communication with their principal. And a third went to the publisher of *Sieur René* forbidding the issue of that work before its author had seen (and passed) not only proofs of text but also proofs of illustrations and binding.

The fact is that Crabbe was very much amazed indeed at being so studiously kept in ignorance of the whereabouts of *Sieur René*. The whole of Caliban's behaviour, however, was so staggering that Crabbe (on reviewing it) debated with himself whether to use his old magic arts, or the simple sortes, for obtaining hints on the appropriate method of dealing with it. He was always a great one for concentrating every possible sidelight with the central illumination of knowledge and instinct on problems which bothered him. He got out his *Tempest* and tried, as a beginning, the sortes. And he went no further. The book opened and the blind finger indicated instantly this astounding passage:

> "*Caliban* (*loq.*) ... Remember
> First to possess his books, for without them
> He's but a sot as I am."

It chimed in so accurately with the instinct which was leading him to suspect that Caliban (nerved by the example of Bobugo's persistent efforts to acquire a book for a benediction) was trying similar cantrips with the three entrusted to him, and even apeing Bobugo's appetite for witnessed bonds, that Crabbe saw that he would have to make up his mind to face another disgusting disillusionment. The sovereign of the Order of Sanctissima Sophia was a false scoundrel. Crabbe thought that enough had been done for the protection of *Sieur René* for the moment. He had a half-matured plan at the back of his brain for guarding his rights in *The Weird* and *De Burgh's Delusion*: but a state of penurious uncertainty as to the attitude of his agents after Caliban's capering among them forced him to move deliberately, without weakness, and without undue precipitancy. This does not mean that he was meek and mild; on the contrary, it signified the steady stoking of the fiery furnace of devouring and dangerous and utterly ruthless anger.

Fierce the ordeal of the One who fares forth to fight with the Many: how should he ride, and array, who is Half and not One?

MARCEL PROUST

SOJOURN IN VENICE

From

IN SEARCH OF LOST TIME

Translated by C. K. Scott Moncrieff and Terence Kilmartin

MY MOTHER HAD taken me to spend a few weeks in Venice, and – as beauty may exist in the most precious as well as in the humblest things – I received there impressions analogous to those which I had felt so often in the past at Combray, but transposed into a wholly different and far richer key. When, at ten o'clock in the morning, my shutters were thrown open, I saw blazing there, instead of the gleaming black marble into which the slates of Saint-Hilaire used to turn, the golden angel on the campanile of St Mark's. Glittering in a sunlight which made it almost impossible to keep one's eyes upon it, this angel promised me, with its outstretched arms, for the moment when I appeared on the Piazzetta half an hour later, a joy more certain than any that it could ever in the past have been bidden to announce to men of good will. I could see nothing else so long as I remained in bed, but as the whole world is merely a vast sundial, a single sunlit segment of which enables us to tell what time it is, on the very first morning I was reminded of the shops in the Place de l'Eglise at Combray, which, on Sunday mornings, were always on the point of shutting when I arrived for mass, while the straw in the marketplace smelt strongly in the already hot sunlight. But on the second morning, what I saw on awakening, what made me get out of bed (because they had taken the place in my memory and in my desire of the recollections of Combray), were the impressions of my first morning stroll in Venice, in Venice where everyday life was no less real than in Combray, where as in Combray on Sunday mornings one had the pleasure of stepping down into a festive street, but where that street was entirely paved with sapphire-blue water, cooled by warm breezes and of a colour so durable that my tired eyes might rest their gaze upon it in search of relaxation without fear of its blenching. Like the good folk of the Rue de l'Oiseau at Combray, so also in this strange town, the inhabitants actually emerged from houses lined up side by side along the main street, but the role played there by houses of casting a patch of shade at their feet was entrusted in Venice to palaces of porphyry and jasper, above the arched doors of which the head of a bearded god (breaking the alignment, like the knocker on a door at Combray) had the effect of darkening with its shadow, not the brownness of the earth, but the splendid blueness of the water. On the Piazza, the shadow that would have been produced at Combray by the awning over the draper's shop and the barber's pole was a carpet of little blue flowers strewn at its feet upon the desert of sun-scorched flagstones by the relief of a Renaissance façade, which is not to say that, when the sun beat down, one was not obliged, in Venice as at Combray, to pull down the blinds, even beside the canal, but they hung between the quatrefoils and foliage of Gothic windows. Of this sort was the window in our hotel behind the balusters of which my mother sat waiting for me, gazing at the canal with a patience which she would not have displayed in the old days at Combray, at a time when, cherishing hopes for my future which had never been realised, she was unwilling to let me see how much she loved me. Nowadays she was well aware that an apparent coldness on her part would alter nothing, and the affection she lavished upon me was like those forbidden foods which are no longer withheld from invalids when it is certain that they are past recovery. True,

the humble details which gave an individuality to the window of my aunt Léonie's bedroom seen from the Rue de
l'Oiseau, the impression of asymmetry caused by its unequal
distance from the windows on either side of it, the excep-
tional height of its wooden ledge, the angled bar which
served to open the shutters, the two curtains of glossy blue
satin tied back with loops – the equivalent of all these things
existed in this hotel in Venice where I could hear also those
words, so distinctive and so eloquent, which enable us to
recognise from a distance the dwelling to which we are going
home to lunch, and afterwards remain in our memory as
testimony that, for a certain period of time, that dwelling
was ours; but the task of uttering them had, in Venice,
devolved not, as at Combray and most other places, upon
the simplest, not to say the ugliest things, but upon the ogive,
still half Arab, of a façade which is reproduced in all the
architectural museums and all the illustrated art books as one
of the supreme achievements of the domestic architecture of
the Middle Ages; from a long way away and when I had
barely passed San Giorgio Maggiore, I caught sight of this
ogival window which had already seen me, and the thrust of
its pointed arches added to its smile of welcome the distinction of a loftier, scarcely comprehensible gaze. And because,
behind its multi-coloured marble balusters, Mamma was sitting reading while she waited for me to return, her face
shrouded in a tulle veil as heart-rending in its whiteness as
her hair to me who sensed that, hiding her tears, she had
pinned it to her straw hat not so much with the idea of
appearing 'dressed' in the eyes of the hotel staff as in order
to appear to me to be less in mourning, less sad, almost con-
soled for the death of my grandmother; because, not having
recognised me at first, as soon as I called to her from the
gondola, she sent out to me, from the bottom of her heart,

a love which stopped only where there was no longer any corporeal matter to sustain it, on the surface of her impassioned gaze which she brought as close to me as possible, which she tried to thrust forward to the advanced post of her lips, in a smile which seemed to be kissing me, within the frame and beneath the canopy of the more discreet smile of the arched window lit up by the midday sun – because of this, that window has assumed in my memory the precious quality of things that have had, simultaneously with us, side by side with us, their share in a certain hour that struck, the same for us and for them; and however full of admirable tracery its mullions may be, that illustrious window retains in my eyes the intimate aspect of a man of genius with whom we have spent a month in some holiday resort, where he has acquired a friendly regard for us; and if, ever since then, whenever I see a cast of that window in a museum, I am obliged to hold back my tears, it is simply because it says to me the thing that touches me more than anything else in the world: 'I remember your mother so well.'

And as I went indoors to join my mother who by now had left the window, on leaving the heat of the open air I had the same sensation of coolness that I experienced long ago at Combray when I went upstairs to my room; but in Venice it was a breeze from the sea that kept the air cool, and no longer on a little wooden staircase with narrow steps, but on the noble surfaces of marble steps continually splashed by shafts of blue-green sunlight, which, to the valuable instruction in the art of Chardin acquired long ago, added a lesson in that of Veronese. And since, in Venice, it is works of art, things of priceless beauty, that are entrusted with the task of giving us our impressions of everyday life, it is to falsify the character of that city, on the grounds that the Venice of certain painters is coldly aesthetic in its most celebrated parts (let us make an exception of the superb studies of Maxime Dethomas), to represent only its poverty-stricken aspects, in the districts where nothing of its splendour is to be seen, and, in order to make Venice more intimate and more genuine, to give it a resemblance to Aubervilliers. It has been the mistake of some very great artists, from a quite natural reaction against the artificial Venice of bad painters, to concentrate exclusively on the Venice of the more humble *campi*, the little deserted *rü*, which they found more real.

It was this Venice that I used often to explore in the afternoon, when I did not go out with my mother. The fact was that it was easier to find there women of the people, match-sellers, pearl-stringers, glass or lace makers, young seamstresses in black shawls with long fringes, whom there was nothing to prevent me from loving, because I had to a large extent forgotten Albertine, and who seemed to me more desirable than others, because I still remembered her a little. Who, in any case, could have told me precisely, in this passionate quest of mine for Venetian women, how much there was of themselves, how much of Albertine, how much of my old, long-cherished desire to visit Venice? Our slightest desire, though unique as a chord, nevertheless includes the fundamental notes on which the whole of our life is built. And sometimes, if we were to eliminate one of them, even one that we do not hear, that we are not aware of, one that has no connexion with the object of our quest, we would nevertheless see our whole desire for that object disappear. There were many things that I made no attempt to identify in the excitement I felt as I went in search of Venetian women.

My gondola followed the course of the small canals; like the mysterious hand of a genie leading me through the maze of this oriental city, they seemed, as I advanced, to be cutting a path for me through the heart of a crowded quarter which they bisected, barely parting, with a slender furrow arbitrarily traced, the tall houses with their tiny Moorish windows; and as though the magic guide had been holding a candle in his hand and were lighting the way for me, they kept casting ahead of them a ray of sunlight for which they cleared a route. One felt that between the mean dwellings which the canal had just parted, and which otherwise would have formed a compact whole, no open space had been reserved; so that a campanile or a garden trellis vertically overhung the *rio*, as in a flooded city. But, for both churches and gardens, thanks to the same transposition as in the Grand Canal, the sea so readily served as means of communication, as substitute for street or alley, that on either side of the *canaletto* the belfries rose from the water in this poor and populous district like those of humble and much-frequented parish churches bearing the stamp of their necessity, of their use by crowds of simple folk, the gardens traversed by the canal cutting trailed their startled leaves and fruit in the water, and on the ledges of the houses whose crudely cut stone was still rough as though it had only just been sawn, urchins surprised by the gondola sat back trying to keep their balance and allowing their legs to dangle vertically, like sailors seated upon a swing-bridge the two halves of which have been swung apart, allowing the sea to pass between them. Now and again would appear a handsomer building that happened to be there like a surprise in a box which one has just opened, a little ivory temple with its Corinthian columns and an allegorical statue on its pediment, somewhat out of place among the ordinary surroundings in the midst of which, for all that we tried to make space for it, the peristyle with which the canal had provided it retained the look of a landing-stage for market gardeners. I had the impression, which my desire strengthened further, of not being outside, but of entering more and more into the depths of something secret, because each time I found something new which came to place itself on one side of me or the other, a small monument or an unexpected *campo*, keeping the surprised expression of beautiful things which one sees for the first time and of which one doesn't yet perfectly understand the intended purpose or the utility.

I returned on foot through narrow lanes; I accosted plebeian girls as Albertine perhaps had done, and I should have liked to have her with me. Yet these could not be the same girls; at the time when Albertine had been in Venice, they would have been children still. But, after having been unfaithful in the past, in a basic sense and out of cowardice, to each of the desires that I had conceived as unique – since I had sought an analogous object and not the same one, which I despaired of finding again – now I systematically sought women whom Albertine had not known, just as I no longer sought those that I had desired in the past. True, it often happened to me to recall, with an extraordinary violence of desire, some wench of Méséglise or Paris, or the milk-girl I had seen early in the morning at the foot of a hill during my first journey to Balbec. But alas! I remembered them as they were then, that is to say as they certainly would not be now. So that if in the past I had been led to qualify my impression of the uniqueness of a desire by seeking, in place of a convent-girl I had lost sight of, a similar convent-girl, now, in order to recapture the girls who had troubled my adolescence or that of Albertine, I had to consent to a further departure from the principle of the individuality of desire: what I must look for was not those who were sixteen then, but those who were sixteen today, for now, in the absence of that which was most distinctive in the person and which eluded me, what I loved was youth. I knew that the youth of those I had known existed no longer except in my impassioned recollection, and that it was not them, however anxious I might be to make contact with them when my memory recalled them to me, that I must cull if I really wished to harvest the youth and the blossom of the year.

The sun was still high in the sky when I went to meet my mother on the Piazzetta. We would call for a gondola. 'How your poor grandmother would have loved this simple grandeur!' Mamma would say to me, pointing to the Doges' Palace which stood contemplating the sea with the thoughtful expression that had been bequeathed to it by its architect and that it faithfully retained in its mute attendance on its vanished lords. 'She would even have loved those soft pink tints, because they are unmawkish. How she would have loved the whole of Venice, and what informality, worthy of nature itself, she would have found in all these beauties, this plethora of objects that seem to need no formal arrangement but present themselves just as they are – the Doges' Palace with its cubic shape, the columns which you say are those of Herod's palace, slap in the middle of the Piazzetta, and, even less deliberately placed, put there as though for want of anywhere better, the pillars from Acre, and those horses on the balcony of St Mark's! Your grandmother would have had as much pleasure seeing the sun setting over the Doges' Palace as over a mountain.' And there was indeed an element of truth in what my mother said, for, as the gondola brought us back along the Grand Canal, we watched the double line of palaces between which we passed reflect the light and angle of the sun upon their pink flanks, and alter with them, seeming not so much private habitations and historic buildings as a chain of marble cliffs at the foot of which one goes out in the evening in a boat to watch the sunset. Seen thus, the buildings arranged along either bank of the canal made one think of objects of nature, but of a nature which seemed to have created its works with a human imagination. But at the same time (because of the always urban character of the impressions which Venice gives almost in the open sea, on those waters whose ebb and flow makes itself felt twice daily, and which alternately cover at high tide and uncover at low tide the splendid outside stairs of the palaces), as we should have done in Paris on the boulevards, in the Champs-Elysées, in the Bois, in any wide and fashionable avenue, we passed the most elegant women in the hazy evening light, almost all foreigners, who, languidly reclining against the cushions of their floating carriages, followed one another in procession, stopped in front of a palace where they had a friend to call on, sent to inquire whether she was at home, and while, as they waited for the answer, they prepared to leave a card just in case, as they would have done at the door of the Hôtel de Guermantes, turned to their guide-books to find out the period and the style of the palace, being shaken the while, as though upon the crest of a blue wave, by the wash of the glittering, swirling water, which took alarm on finding itself pent between the dancing gondola and the resounding marble. And thus any outing, even when it was only to pay calls or to leave visiting-cards, was threefold and unique in this Venice where the simplest social coming and going assumed at the same time the form and the charm of a visit to a museum and a trip on the sea.

Several of the palaces on the Grand Canal had been converted into hotels, and for the sake of a change or out of hospitality towards Mme Sazerat whom we had encountered – the unexpected and inopportune acquaintance whom one invariably meets when one travels abroad – and whom Mamma had invited to dine with us, we decided one evening to try a hotel which was not our own and in which we had been told that the food was better. While my mother was paying the gondolier and taking Mme Sazerat to the drawing-room which she had engaged, I slipped away to inspect the great hall of the restaurant with its fine marble pillars and walls and ceiling that were once entirely covered with frescoes, recently and badly restored. Two waiters were conversing in an Italian which I translate:

'Are the old people going to dine in their room? They never let us know. It's annoying; I never know whether I ought to keep their table for them (*non so se bisogna conserva loro la tavola*). Serve them right if they come down and find it's been taken! I don't understand how they can take in *forestieri* (foreigners) like that in such a smart hotel. They're not our sort of people.'

Notwithstanding his scorn, the waiter was anxious to know what action he was to take with regard to the table, and was about to send the lift-boy upstairs to inquire when, before he had had time to do so, he received his answer: he had just caught sight of the old lady who was entering the room. I had no difficulty, despite the air of melancholy and weariness that comes with the weight of years, and despite a sort of eczema, of red leprosy that covered her face, in recognising beneath her bonnet, in her black jacket made by W— but to the untutored eye exactly like that of an old concierge, the Marquise de Villeparisis. The place where I was standing, engaged in studying the remains of a fresco between two of the beautiful marble panels, happened by chance to be immediately behind the table at which Mme de Villeparisis had just sat down.

'Then M. de Villeparisis won't be long. They've been here a month now, and they've only once not eaten together,' said the waiter.

I was wondering who could be the relative with whom she

was travelling and who was named M. de Villeparisis, when a few moments later I saw her old lover, M. de Norpois, advance towards the table and sit down beside her.

His great age had weakened the resonance of his voice, but had in compensation imparted to his speech, formerly so reserved, a positive intemperance. The cause of this was perhaps to be sought in ambitions for the realisation of which he felt that little time remained to him and which filled him with all the more vehemence and ardour; perhaps in the fact that, cut off from a world of politics to which he longed to return, he imagined, in the naïvety of his desire, that he could turn out of office, by the savage criticisms which he launched at them, the men he was determined to replace. Thus do we see politicians convinced that the Cabinet of which they are not members cannot hold out for three days. It would, however, be an exaggeration to suppose that M. de Norpois had entirely forgotten the traditions of diplomatic speech. Whenever 'important matters' were at issue, he became once more, as we shall see, the man whom we remember in the past, but for the rest of the time he would inveigh against this man and that with the senile violence which makes certain octogenarians hurl themselves at women to whom they are no longer capable of doing any serious damage.

Mme de Villeparisis preserved, for some minutes, the silence of an old woman who in the exhaustion of age finds it difficult to rise from recollection of the past to consideration of the present. Then, turning to one of those eminently practical questions that indicate the survival of a mutual affection:

'Did you call at Salviati's?'

'Yes.'

'Will they send it tomorrow?'

'I brought the bowl back myself. You shall see it after dinner. Let us look at the menu.'

'Did you send instructions about my Suez shares?'

'No; at the present moment the Stock Exchange is entirely taken up with oil shares. But there's no hurry, in view of the propitious state of the market. Here is the menu. As a first course there is red mullet. Shall we try them?'

'I shall, but you are not allowed them. Ask for a risotto instead. But they don't know how to cook it.'

'Never mind. Waiter, some mullet for Madame and a risotto for me.'

A fresh and prolonged silence.

'Here, I've brought you the papers, the *Corriere della Sera*, the *Gazzetta del Popolo*, and all the rest of them. Did you know that there is a strong likelihood of a diplomatic reshuffle in which the first scapegoat will be Paléologue, who is notoriously inadequate in Serbia. He may perhaps be replaced by Lozé, and there will be a vacancy at Constantinople. But,' M. de Norpois hastened to add in a biting tone, 'for an Embassy of such scope, in a capital where it is obvious that Great Britain must always, whatever happens, occupy the chief place at the council-table, it would be prudent to turn to men of experience better equipped to counter the subterfuges of the enemies of our British ally than are diplomats of the modern school who would walk blindfold into the trap.' The angry volubility with which M. de Norpois uttered these last words was due principally to the fact that the newspapers, instead of suggesting his name as he had recommended them to do, named as a 'hot favourite' a young minister of Foreign Affairs. 'Heaven knows that the men of years and experience are far from eager to put themselves forward, after all manner of tortuous manoeuvres, in the place of more or less incapable recruits. I have known many of these self-styled diplomats of the empirical school who centred all their hopes in flying a kite which it didn't take me long to shoot down. There can be no question that if the Government is so lacking in wisdom as to entrust the reins of state to unruly hands, at the call of duty any conscript will always answer "Present!" But who knows' (and here M. de Norpois appeared to know perfectly well to whom he was referring) 'whether it would not be the same on the day when they came in search of some veteran full of wisdom and skill. To my mind, though everyone may have his own way of looking at things, the post at Constantinople should not be accepted until we have settled our existing difficulties with Germany. We owe no man anything, and it is intolerable that every six months they should come and demand from us, by fraudulent machinations and under protest, some full discharge or other which is invariably advocated by a venal press. This must cease, and naturally a man of high distinction who has proved his merit, a man who would have, if I may say so, the Emperor's ear, would enjoy greater authority than anyone else in bringing the conflict to an end.'

A gentleman who was finishing his dinner bowed to M. de Norpois.

'Why, there's Prince Foggi,' said the Marquis.

'Ah, I'm not sure that I know who you mean,' muttered Mme de Villeparisis.

'But, of course you do – Prince Odo. He's the brother-in-law of your cousin Doudeauville. Surely you remember that I went shooting with him at Bonnétable?'

'Ah! Odo, is he the one who went in for painting?'

'Not at all, he's the one who married the Grand Duke N—'s sister.'

M. de Norpois uttered these remarks in the cross tone of a schoolmaster who is dissatisfied with his pupil, and stared fixedly at Mme de Villeparisis out of his blue eyes.

When the Prince had drunk his coffee and was leaving his table, M. de Norpois rose, hastened towards him and with a majestic sweep of his arm, stepping aside himself, presented him to Mme de Villeparisis. And during the few minutes that the Prince was standing beside their table, M. de Norpois never ceased for an instant to keep his azure pupils trained on Mme de Villeparisis, with the mixture of indulgence and severity of an old lover, but principally from fear of her committing one of those verbal solecisms which he had relished but which he dreaded. Whenever she said anything to the Prince that was not quite accurate he corrected her mistake and stared into the eyes of the abashed and docile Marquise with the steady intensity of a hypnotist.

A waiter came to tell me that my mother was waiting for me. I went to join her and made my apologies to Mme Sazerat, saying that I had been amused to see Mme de Villeparisis. At the sound of this name, Mme Sazerat turned pale and seemed about to faint. Controlling herself with an effort: 'Mme de Villeparisis who was Mlle de Bouillon?' she inquired.

'Yes.'

'Couldn't I just get a glimpse of her for a moment? It has been the dream of my life.'

'Then there's no time to lose, Madame, for she will soon have finished her dinner. But how do you come to take such an interest in her?'

'Because Mme de Villeparisis was, before her second marriage, the Duchesse d'Havré, beautiful as an angel, wicked as a demon, who drove my father to distraction, ruined him and then abandoned him immediately. Well, she may have behaved to him like the lowest prostitute, she may have been the cause of our having had to live, my family and myself, in humble circumstances at Combray, but now that my father is dead, my consolation is to think that he loved the most beautiful woman of his generation, and as I've never set eyes on her, it will be a sort of solace in spite of everything . . .'

I escorted Mme Sazerat, trembling with emotion, to the restaurant and pointed out Mme de Villeparisis.

But, like a blind person who looks everywhere but in the right direction, Mme Sazerat did not bring her eyes to rest upon the table at which Mme de Villeparisis was dining, but, looking towards another part of the room, said:

'But she must have gone, I don't see her where you say she is.'

And she continued to gaze round the room in quest of the loathed, adored vision that had haunted her imagination for so long.

'Yes, there she is, at the second table.'

'Then we can't be counting from the same point. At what I count as the second table there's only an old gentleman and a little hunchbacked, red-faced, hideous woman.'

'That's her!'

Meanwhile, Mme de Villeparisis having asked M. de Norpois to invite Prince Foggi to sit down, a friendly conversation ensued among the three of them. They discussed politics, and the Prince declared that he was indifferent to the fate of the Cabinet and would spend another week at least in Venice. He hoped that by that time all risk of a ministerial crisis would have been avoided. Prince Foggi thought for a few moments that these political topics did not interest M. de Norpois, for the latter, who until then had been expressing himself with such vehemence, had become suddenly absorbed in an almost angelic silence which seemed capable of blossoming, should his voice return, only into some innocent and tuneful melody by Mendelssohn or César Franck. The Prince supposed also that this silence was due to the reserve of a Frenchman who naturally would not wish to discuss Italian affairs in the presence of an Italian. Now in this the Prince was completely mistaken. Silence and an air of indifference had remained, in M. de Norpois, not a sign of reserve but the habitual prelude to an intervention in important affairs. The Marquis had his eye upon nothing less (as we have seen) than Constantinople, after the prior settlement of the German question, with a view to which he hoped to force the hand of the Rome Cabinet. He considered, in fact, that an action on his part of international significance might be the worthy consummation of his career, perhaps even a prelude to fresh honours, to difficult tasks to which he had not relinquished his pretensions. For old age makes us incapable of doing but not, at first, of desiring. It is only in a third period that those who live to a very great age relinquish desire, as they have already had to forgo action. They no longer even present themselves as candidates in futile elections where they have so often tried to win success, such as that for the Presidency of the Republic. They content themselves with taking the air, eating, reading the newspapers; they have outlived themselves.

The Prince, to put the Marquis at his ease and to show him that he regarded him as a compatriot, began to speak of the possible successors to the Prime Minister then in office. Successors who would have a difficult task before them. When Prince Foggi had mentioned more than twenty names of politicians who seemed to him suitable for office, names to which the ex-Ambassador listened with his eyelids drooping over his blue eyes and without moving a muscle, M. de Norpois broke his silence at length to utter the words which were to provide the chancelleries with food for conversation for many years to come, and afterwards, when they had been forgotten, would be exhumed by some personage signing himself 'One Who Knows' or 'Testis' or 'Machiavelli' in a newspaper in which the very oblivion into which they had fallen enabled them to create a fresh sensation. So, Prince Foggi had mentioned more than twenty names to the diplomat who remained as motionless and silent as a deaf-mute, when M. de Norpois raised his head slightly, and, in the form in which his most pregnant and far-reaching diplomatic interventions had been couched, albeit this time with greater audacity and less brevity, shrewdly inquired: 'And has no one mentioned the name of Signor Giolitti?' At these words the scales fell from Prince Foggi's eyes; he could hear a celestial murmur. Then at once M. de Norpois began to speak about one thing and another, no longer afraid to make a noise, as, when the last note of a sublime aria by Bach has died away, the audience are no longer afraid to talk aloud, to go and look for their hats and coats in the cloakroom. He made the break even more marked by begging the Prince to pay his most humble respects to Their Majesties the King and Queen when next he should see them, a farewell phrase corresponding to the shout for a coachman at the end of a concert: 'Auguste, from the Rue de Belloy.' We cannot say what exactly were Prince Foggi's impressions. He must certainly have been delighted to have heard the gem: 'And has no one mentioned Signor Giolitti's name?' For M. de Norpois, in whom age had extinguished or deranged his most outstanding qualities, had on the other hand, as he grew older, perfected his bravura, as certain aged musicians, who in all other respects have declined, acquire and retain until the end, in the field of chamber-music, a perfect virtuosity which they did not formerly possess.

However that may be, Prince Foggi, who had intended to spend a fortnight in Venice, returned to Rome that very night and was received a few days later in audience by the King in connexion with certain properties which, as we may perhaps have mentioned already, the Prince owned in Sicily. The Cabinet hung on for longer than might have been expected. When it fell, the King consulted various statesmen as to the most suitable leader of a new Cabinet. Then he sent for Signor Giolitti, who accepted. Three months later a newspaper reported Prince Foggi's meeting with M. de Norpois. The conversation was reported as we have given it here, with the difference that, instead of: 'M. de Norpois shrewdly inquired,' one read: 'M. de Norpois said with that shrewd and charming smile which is so characteristic of him.' M. de Norpois considered that 'shrewdly' had in itself sufficient explosive force for a diplomat and that this addition was, to say the least, excessive. He had even asked the Quai d'Orsay to issue an official denial, but the Quai d'Orsay did not know which way to turn. For, ever since the conversation had been made public, M. Barrère had been telegraphing several times hourly to Paris complaining of this unofficial ambassador to the Quirinal and describing the indignation with which the incident had been received throughout the whole of Europe. This indignation was non-existent, but the other ambassadors were too polite to contradict M. Barrère's assertion that everyone was up in arms. M. Barrère, guided only by his own reaction, mistook this courteous silence for assent. Immediately he telegraphed to Paris: 'I have just had an hour's conversation with the Marchese Visconti-Venosta,' and so forth. His secretaries were worn out.

M. de Norpois, however, had at his disposal a French newspaper of very long standing, which already in 1870, when he was French Minister in a German capital, had been of great service to him. This paper (especially its leading article, which was unsigned) was admirably written. But the paper became a thousand times more interesting whenever this leading article (styled 'premier-Paris' in those far-off days and now, no one knows why, 'editorial') was on the contrary badly expressed, with endless repetitions of words. Everyone sensed then, with great excitement, that the article had been 'inspired.' Perhaps by M. de Norpois, perhaps by some other man of the hour. To give an anticipatory idea of the Italian incident, let us show how M. de Norpois made use of this paper in 1870, to no purpose, it may be thought, since war broke out nevertheless, but most efficaciously, according to M. de Norpois, whose axiom was that one ought first and foremost to prepare public opinion. His articles, every word in which was weighted, resembled those optimistic bulletins which are at once followed by the death of the patient. For instance, on the eve of the declaration of war in 1870, when mobilisation was almost complete, M. de Norpois (remaining, of course, in the background) had felt it his duty to send to this famous newspaper the following 'editorial':

'The opinion seems to prevail in authoritative circles that, since the afternoon hours of yesterday, the situation, without of course being of an alarming nature, might well be envisaged as serious and even, from certain angles, as susceptible of being regarded as critical. M. le Marquis de Norpois would appear to have had several conversations with the Prussian Minister, with a view to examining, in a firm and conciliatory spirit, and in a wholly concrete fashion, the various existing causes of friction, if one may so put it. Unfortunately, we have not yet heard, at the time of going to press, whether Their Excellencies have been able to agree upon a formula that may serve as the basis for a diplomatic instrument.'

Stop press: 'It has been learned with satisfaction in well-informed circles that a slight slackening of tension seems to have occurred in Franco-Prussian relations. Particular importance would appear to be attached to the fact that M. de Norpois is reported to have met the British Minister "unter den Linden" and to have conversed with him for fully twenty minutes. This report is regarded as highly satisfactory.' (There was added, in brackets, after the word 'satisfactory' its German equivalent '*befriedigend*.') And on the following day one read in the editorial: 'It would appear that, notwithstanding all the dexterity of M. de Norpois, to whom everyone must hasten to render homage for the skill and energy with which he has defended the inalienable rights of France, a rupture is now, one might say, virtually inevitable.'

The newspaper could not refrain from following an editorial couched in this vein with a selection of comments, furnished of course by M. de Norpois. The reader may perhaps have observed in these last pages that the conditional was one of the Ambassador's favourite grammatical forms in the literature of diplomacy. ('Particular importance would appear to be attached' for 'Particular importance is attached.') But the present indicative employed not in its usual sense but in that of the old 'optative' was no less dear to M. de Norpois. The comments that followed the editorial were as follows:

'Never has the public shown itself so admirably calm' (M. de Norpois would have liked to believe that this was true but feared that it was precisely the opposite of the truth). 'It is weary of fruitless agitation and has learned with satisfaction that the Government of His Majesty the Emperor would assume their responsibilities whatever the eventualities that might occur. The public asks' (optative) 'nothing more. To its admirable composure, which is in itself a token of success, we shall add a piece of intelligence eminently calculated to reassure public opinion, were there any need of that. We are assured that M. de Norpois who, for reasons of health, was ordered long ago to return to Paris for medical treatment, would appear to have left Berlin where he considered that his presence no longer served any purpose.'

Stop press: 'His Majesty the Emperor left Compiègne this morning for Paris in order to confer with the Marquis de Norpois, the Minister for War and Marshal Bazaine in whom public opinion has especial confidence. H. M. the Emperor has cancelled the banquet which he was to give for his sister-in-law the Duchess of Alba. This action created everywhere, as soon as it became known, a particularly favourable impression. The Emperor has held a review of his troops, whose enthusiasm is indescribable. Several corps, by virtue of a mobilisation order issued immediately upon the Sovereign's arrival in Paris, are, in any contingency, ready to move in the direction of the Rhine.'

Sometimes at dusk as I returned to the hotel I felt that the Albertine of long ago, invisible to my eyes, was nevertheless enclosed within me as in the lead-covered cells of an inner Venice, the tight lid of which some incident occasionally lifted to give me a glimpse of that past.

Thus for instance one evening a letter from my stock-broker reopened for me for an instant the gates of the prison in which Albertine dwelt within me, alive, but so remote, so profoundly buried that she remained inaccessible to me. Since her death I had ceased to indulge in the speculations that I had made in order to have more money for her. But time had passed; the wisest judgments of the previous generation had been belied by the next, as had occurred in the past to M. Thiers who had said that railways could never prove successful; and the stocks of which M. de Norpois had said to us: 'The income from them may not be very great, but at least the capital will never depreciate,' were, more often than not, those which had declined most in value. In the case of my English Consols and Raffineries Say shares alone, I had to pay out such considerable sums in brokers' commissions, as well as interest and contango fees, that in a rash moment I decided to sell out everything and found that I now possessed barely a fifth of what I had inherited from my grandmother and still possessed when Albertine was alive. This became known at Combray among the surviving members of our family and their friends who, knowing that I went about with the Marquis de Saint-Loup and the Guermantes family, said to themselves: 'Pride goes before a fall!' They would have been greatly astonished to learn that it was for a girl of Albertine's modest background, almost a protégée of my grandmother's former piano-teacher, Vinteuil, that I had made these speculations. Besides, in that Combray world in which everyone is classified for ever, as in an Indian caste, according to the income he is known to enjoy, no one would have been capable of imagining the great freedom that prevailed in the world of the Guermantes, where no importance was attached to wealth and where poverty was regarded as being as disagreeable as, but no more degrading, having no more effect on a person's social position, than a stomach-ache. Doubtless people at Combray imagined, on the contrary, that Saint-Loup and M. de Guermantes must be ruined aristocrats with heavily mort-gaged estates, to whom I had been lending money, whereas if I had been ruined they would have been the first to offer, unavailingly, to come to my assistance. As for my compara-tive penury, it was all the more awkward at the moment, inasmuch as my Venetian interests had been concentrated for some little time past on a young vendor of glassware whose blooming complexion offered to the delighted eye a whole range of orange tones and filled me with such a longing to see her daily that, realising that my mother and I would soon be leaving Venice, I had made up my mind to try to create some sort of position for her in Paris which would save me from being parted from her. The beauty of her seventeen years was so noble, so radiant, that it was like acquiring a genuine Titian before leaving the place. But would the scant remains of my fortune be enough to tempt her to leave her native land and come to live in Paris for my sole convenience?

But as I came to the end of the stockbroker's letter, a passage in which he said: 'I shall look after your credits' reminded me of a scarcely less hypocritically professional expression which the bath-attendant at Balbec had used in speaking to Aimé of Albertine: 'It was I who looked after her,' she had said. And these words which had never recurred to my mind acted like an 'Open sesame!' upon the hinges of the prison door. But a moment later the door closed once more upon the immured victim – whom I was not to blame for not wishing to join since I was no longer able to see her, to call her to mind, and since other people exist for us only through the idea that we have of them – but who for a moment had been rendered more touching by my desertion of her, albeit she was unaware of it, so that for the duration of a lightning-flash I had thought with longing of the time, already remote, when I used to suffer night and day from the companionship of her memory. Another time, in San Giorgio degli Schiavoni, an eagle accompanying one of the Apostles, and conventionalised in the same manner, revived the memory and almost the suffering caused by the two rings the similarity of which Françoise had revealed to me, and as to which I had never learned who had given them to Albertine.

One evening, however, an incident occurred of such a nature that it seemed as though my love must revive. No sooner had our gondola stopped at the hotel steps than the porter handed me a telegram which the messenger had already brought three times to the hotel, for owing to the inaccurate rendering of the addressee's name (which I recognised nevertheless, through the corruptions introduced by the Italian clerks, as my own) the post-office required a signed receipt certifying that the telegram was indeed for me. I opened it as soon as I was in my room, and, glancing through the message which was filled with inaccurately transmitted words, managed nevertheless to make out: 'My dear friend, you think me dead, forgive me, I am quite alive, I long to see you, talk about marriage, when do you return? Affectionately. Albertine.' Then there occurred in me in reverse order a process parallel to that which had occurred in the case of my grandmother. When I had learned the fact of my grandmother's death, I had not at first felt any grief. And I had been really grieved by her death only when certain involuntary memories had brought her alive again for me. Now that Albertine no longer lived for me in my thoughts, the news that she was alive did not cause me the joy that I might have expected. Albertine had been no more to me than a bundle of thoughts, and she had survived her physical death so long as those thoughts were alive in me; on the other hand, now that those thoughts were dead, Albertine did not rise again for me with the resurrection of her body. And when I realised that I felt no joy at the thought of her being alive, that I no longer loved her, I ought to have been more shattered than a man who, looking at his reflexion in a mirror, after months of travel or sickness, discovers that he has white hair and a different face, that of a middle-aged or an old man. This is shattering because its message is: 'the man that I was, the fair-haired young man, no longer exists, I am another person.' And yet, was not the impression that I now felt the proof of as profound a change, as total a death of my former self and of the no less complete substitution of a new self for that former self, as the sight of a wrinkled face topped with a white wig instead of the face of long ago? But one is no more distressed at having become another person, after a lapse of years and in the natural sequence of time, than one is at any given moment by the fact of being, one after another, the incompatible persons, malicious, sensitive, refined, caddish, disinterested, ambitious which one can be, in turn, every day of one's life. And the reason why one is not distressed is the same, namely that the self which has been eclipsed – momentarily in this latter case and when it is a question of character, permanently in the former case and when the passions are involved – is not there to deplore the other, the other which is for the moment, or from then onwards, one's whole self; the caddish self laughs at his caddishness because one is the cad, and the forgetful self does not grieve about his forgetfulness precisely because he has forgotten.

I should have been incapable of resuscitating Albertine because I was incapable of resuscitating myself, of resuscitating the self of those days. Life, in accordance with its habit which is, by unceasing, infinitesimal labours, to change the face of the world, had not said to me on the morrow of Albertine's death: 'Become another person,' but, by changes too imperceptible for me to be conscious even that I was changing, had altered almost everything in me, with the result that my mind was already accustomed to its new master – my new self – when it became aware that it had changed; it was to this new master that it was attached. My feeling for Albertine, my jealousy, stemmed, as we have seen, from the irradiation, by the association of ideas, of certain pleasant or painful impressions, the memory of Mlle Vinteuil at Montjouvain, the precious good-night kisses that Albertine used to give me on the neck. But in proportion as these impressions had grown fainter, the vast field of impressions which they coloured with a hue that was agonising or sooth-ing reverted to neutral tones. As soon as oblivion had taken hold of certain dominant points of suffering and pleasure, the resistance offered by my love was overcome, I no longer loved Albertine. I tried to recall her image to my mind. I had been right in my presentiment when, a couple of days after Albertine's flight, I was appalled by the discovery that I had been able to live for forty-eight hours without her. It had been the same as when I wrote to Gilberte long ago saying to myself: 'If this goes on for a year or two, I shall no longer love her.' And if, when Swann asked me to come and see Gilberte again, this had seemed to me as embarrassing as greeting a dead woman, in Albertine's case death – or what I had supposed to be death – had achieved the same result as a prolonged breach in Gilberte's. Death merely acts in the same way as absence. The monster at whose apparition my love had trembled, oblivion, had indeed, as I had feared, ended by devouring that love. Not only did the news that she was alive fail to revive my love, not only did it enable me to realise how far I had already proceeded along the road towards indifference, it at once and so abruptly accelerated that process that I wondered retrospectively whether the opposite report, that of Albertine's death, had not, con-versely, by completing the effect of her departure, rekindled my love and delayed its decline. Yes, now that the knowledge that she was alive and the possibility of our reunion made her suddenly cease to be so precious to me, I wondered whether Françoise's insinuations, our rupture itself, and even her death (imaginary, but believed to be real) had not prolonged my love, to such an extent do the efforts of third persons, and even those of fate, to separate us from a woman succeed only in attaching us to her. Now it was the contrary process that had occurred. Anyhow, I tried to recall her image and perhaps because I had only to raise a finger for her to be mine once more, the memory that came to me was that of a somewhat stout and mannish-looking girl from whose faded features protruded already, like a sprouting seed, the profile of Mme Bontemps. What she might or might not have done with Andrée or with other girls no longer interested me. I no longer suffered from the malady which I had so long thought to be incurable, and really I might have foreseen this. Certainly, regret for a lost mistress and surviving jealousy are physical maladies fully as much as tuberculosis or leukaemia. And yet among physical maladies it is possible to distinguish those which are caused by a purely physical agency, and those which act upon the body only through the medium of the intelligence. Above all, if the part of the mind which serves as carrier is the memory – that is to say if the cause is obliterated or remote – however agonising the pain, however profound the disturbance to the organism may appear to be, it is very seldom (the mind having a capacity for renewal or rather an incapacity for conservation which the tissues lack) that the prognosis is not favourable. At the end of a given period after which someone who has been attacked by cancer will be dead, it is very seldom that the grief of an inconsolable widower or father is not healed. Mine was healed. Was it for this girl whom I saw in my mind's eye so bloated and who had certainly aged, as the girls whom she had loved had aged – was it for her that I must renounce the dazzling girl who was my memory of yesterday, my hope for tomorrow, to whom I could no longer give a sou, any more than to any other, if I married Albertine, that I must renounce this 'new Albertine' whom I loved 'not as Hades had beheld her ... but faithful, but proud, and even rather shy'? It was she who was now what Albertine had been in the past: my love for Albertine had been but a transitory form of my devotion to youth. We think that we are in love with a girl, whereas we love in her, alas! only that dawn the glow of which is momentarily reflected on her face.

The night went by. In the morning I gave the telegram back to the hotel porter explaining that it had been brought to me by mistake and that it was not for me. He told me that now it had been opened he might get into trouble, that it would be better if I kept it; I put it back in my pocket, but made up my mind to behave as though I had never received it. I had finally ceased to love Albertine. So that this love, after departing so greatly from what I had anticipated on the basis of my love for Gilberte, after obliging me to make so long and painful a detour, had ended too, after having proved an exception to it, by succumbing, like my love for Gilberte, to the general law of oblivion.

But then I thought to myself: I used to value Albertine more than myself; I no longer value her now because for a certain time past I have ceased to see her. My desire not to be parted from myself by death, to rise again after my death – that desire was not like the desire never to be parted from Albertine; it still persisted. Was this due to the fact that I valued myself more highly than her, that when I loved her I loved myself more? No, it was because, having ceased to see her, I had ceased to love her, whereas I had not ceased to love myself because my everyday links with myself had not been severed like those with Albertine. But if my links with my body, with myself, were severed also . . .? Obviously, it would be the same. Our love of life is only an old liaison of which we do not know how to rid ourselves. Its strength lies in its permanence. But death which severs it will cure us of the desire for immortality.

After lunch, when I was not going to roam about Venice by myself, I went up to my room to get ready to go out with my mother and to collect the exercise books in which I would take notes for some work I was doing on Ruskin. In the abrupt angles of the walls I sensed the restrictions imposed by the sea, the parsimony of the soil. And when I went downstairs to join Mamma who was waiting for me, at that hour when at Combray it was so pleasant to feel the sun close at hand in the darkness preserved by the closed shutters, here, from top to bottom of the marble staircase where one could no more tell than in a Renaissance picture whether it was in a palace or on a galley, the same coolness and the same sense of the splendour of the scene outside were imparted thanks to the awnings which stirred outside the ever-open windows through which, upon an incessant stream of air, the warm shade and the greenish sunlight flowed as if over a liquid surface and suggested the mobile proximity, the glitter, the shimmering instability of the sea.

As often as not we would set off for St Mark's, with all the more pleasure because, since one had to take a gondola to go there, the church represented for me not simply a monument but the terminus of a voyage on these vernal, maritime waters, with which, I felt, St Mark's formed an indivisible and living whole. My mother and I would enter the baptistery, treading underfoot the marble and glass mosaics of the paving, in front of us the wide arcades whose curved pink surfaces have been slightly warped by time, thus giving the church, wherever the freshness of this colouring has been preserved, the appearance of having been built of a soft and malleable substance like the wax in a giant honeycomb, and, where on the contrary time has shrivelled and hardened the material and artists have embellished it with gold tracery, of being the precious binding, in the finest Cordoba leather, of the colossal Gospel of Venice. Seeing that I needed to spend some time in front of the mosaics representing the Baptism of Christ, and feeling the icy coolness that pervaded the baptistery, my mother threw a shawl over my shoulders. When I was with Albertine at Balbec, I felt that she was revealing one of those insubstantial illusions which clutter the minds of so many people who do not think clearly, when she used to speak of the pleasure – to my mind baseless – that she would derive from seeing works of art with me. Today I am sure that the pleasure does exist, if not of seeing, at least of having seen, a beautiful thing with a particular person. A time has now come when, remembering the baptistery of St Mark's – contemplating the waters of the Jordan in which St John immerses Christ, while the gondola awaited us at the landing-stage of the Piazzetta – it is no longer a matter of indifference to me that, beside me in that cool penumbra, there should have been a woman draped in her mourning with the respectful and enthusiastic fervour of the old woman in Carpaccio's *St Ursula* in the Accademia, and that that woman, with her red cheeks and sad eyes and in her black veils, whom nothing can ever remove from that softly lit sanctuary of St Mark's where I am always sure to find her because she has her place reserved there as immutably as a mosaic, should be my mother.

Carpaccio, as it happens, who was the painter we visited most readily when I was not working in St Mark's, almost succeeded one day in reviving my love for Albertine. I was seeing for the first time *The Patriarch of Grado exorcising a demoniac.* I looked at the marvellous rose-pink and violet sky and the tall encrusted chimneys silhouetted against it, their flared stacks, blossoming like red tulips, reminiscent of so many Whistlers of Venice. Then my eyes travelled from the old wooden Rialto to that fifteenth-century Ponte Vecchio with its marble palaces decorated with gilded capitals, and returned to the canal on which the boats are manoeuvred by adolescents in pink jackets and plumed toques, the spitting image of those avowedly inspired by Carpaccio in that dazzling *Legend of Joseph* by Sert, Strauss and Kessler. Finally, before leaving the picture, my eyes came back to the shore, swarming with the everyday Venetian life of the period. I looked at the barber wiping his razor, at the negro humping his barrel, at the Muslims conversing, at the noblemen in wide-sleeved brocade and damask robes and hats of cerise velvet, and suddenly I felt a slight gnawing at my heart. On the back of one of the *Compagni della Calza* identifiable from the emblem, embroidered in gold and pearls on their sleeves or their collars, of the merry confraternity to which they were affiliated, I had just recognised the cloak which Albertine had put on to come with me to Versailles in an open carriage on the evening when I so little suspected that scarcely fifteen hours separated me from the moment of her departure from my house. Always ready for anything, when I had asked her to come out with me on that melancholy occasion which she was to describe in her last letter as 'a double twilight since night was falling and we were about to part,' she had flung over her shoulders a Fortuny cloak which she had taken away with her next day and which I had never thought of since. It was from this Carpaccio picture that that inspired son of Venice had taken it, it was from the shoulders of this *Compagno della Calza* that he had removed it in order to drape it over the shoulders of so many Parisian women who were

323

certainly unaware, as I had been until then, that the model for it existed in a group of noblemen in the foreground of the *Patriarch of Grado* in a room in the Accademia in Venice. I had recognised it down to the last detail, and, that forgotten cloak having restored to me as I looked at it the eyes and the heart of him who had set out that evening with Albertine for Versailles, I was overcome for a few moments by a vague and soon dissipated feeling of desire and melancholy.

There were days when my mother and I were not content with visiting the museums and churches of Venice only, and once, when the weather was particularly fine, in order to see the 'Virtues' and 'Vices' of which M. Swann had given me reproductions that were probably still hanging on the wall of the schoolroom at Combray, we went as far afield as Padua. After walking across the garden of the Arena in the glare of the sun, I entered the Giotto chapel, the entire ceiling of which and the background of the frescoes are so blue that it seems as though the radiant daylight has crossed the threshold with the human visitor in order to give its pure sky a momentary breather in the coolness and shade, a sky merely of a slightly deeper blue now that it is rid of the glitter of the sunlight, as in those brief moments of respite when, though no cloud is to be seen, the sun has turned its gaze elsewhere and the azure, softer still, grows deeper. This sky transplanted on to the blue-washed stone was peopled with flying angels which I was seeing for the first time, for M. Swann had given me reproductions only of the Vices and Virtues and not of the frescoes depicting the life of the Virgin and of Christ. Watching the flight of these angels, I had the same impression of actual movement, literally real activity, that the gestures of Charity and Envy had given me. For all the celestial fervour, or at least the childlike obedience and application, with which their minuscule hands are joined, they are represented in the Arena chapel as winged creatures of a particular species that had really existed, that must have figured in the natural history of biblical and apostolic times. Constantly flitting about above the saints whenever the latter walk abroad, these little beings, since they are real creatures with a genuine power of flight, can be seen soaring upwards, describing curves, 'looping the loop,' diving earthwards head first, with the aid of wings which enable them to support themselves in positions that defy the laws of gravity, and are far more reminiscent of an extinct species of bird, or of young pupils of Garros practising gliding, than of the angels of the Renaissance and later periods whose wings have become no more than emblems and whose deportment is generally the same as that of heavenly beings who are not winged.

On returning to the hotel I would meet young women, mainly Austrians, who came to Venice to spend the first fine days of this flowerless spring. There was one in particular whose features did not resemble Albertine's but who attracted me by the same fresh complexion, the same gay, light-hearted look. Soon I became aware that I was beginning to say the same things to her as I had said to Albertine at the start, that I concealed the same misery when she told me she would not be seeing me the following day because she was going to Verona, and that I immediately wanted to go to Verona too. It did not last – she was soon to leave for Austria and I would never see her again – but already, vaguely jealous as one is when one begins to fall in love, looking at her charming and enigmatic face I wondered whether she too loved women, whether what she had in common with Albertine, that clear complexion, that bright-eyed look, that air of friendly candour which charmed everyone and which stemmed more from the fact that she was not in the least interested in knowing about other people's actions, which interested her not at all, than that she was confessing her own, which on the contrary she concealed beneath the most puerile lies – I wondered whether all this constituted the morphological characteristics of the woman who loves other women. Was it this about her that, without my being able rationally to grasp why, exercised its attraction upon me, caused my anxieties (perhaps a deeper cause of my attraction towards her by virtue of the fact that we are drawn towards that which will make us suffer), gave me when I saw her so much pleasure and sadness, like those magnetic elements in the air of certain places which we do not see but which cause us such physical discomfort? Alas, I should never know. I should have liked, when I tried to read her face, to say to her: 'You really should tell me, it would interest me as an example of human natural history,' but she would never tell me. She professed an especial loathing for anything that resembled that vice, and was extremely distant towards her women friends. Perhaps indeed this was proof that she had something to hide, perhaps that she had been mocked or reviled for it, and the air that she assumed in order that people should not think such things of her was like an animal's instinctive and revealing recoil from someone who has beaten it. As for my finding out about her life, it was impossible; even in the case of Albertine, how long it had taken me to get to know anything! It had taken her death to loosen people's tongues, such prudent circumspection had Albertine, like this young woman, observed in all her con- duct. And in any case, could I be certain that I had discovered anything about Albertine? Moreover, just as the conditions of life that we most desire become a matter of indifference to us if we cease to love the person who, without our realising it, made us desire them because they enabled us to be close to her, to be in a position to please her, so it is with certain kinds of intellectual curiosity. The scientific importance which I attached to knowing the particular kind of desire that lay hidden beneath the delicate pink petals of those cheeks, in the brightness, a sunless brightness as at daybreak, of those pale eyes, in those days that were never accounted for, would doubtless subside when I had entirely ceased to love Albertine or when I had entirely ceased to love this young woman.

After dinner, I went out alone, into the heart of the enchanted city where I found myself in the middle of strange purlieus like a character in the *Arabian Nights*. It was very seldom that, in the course of my wanderings, I did not come across some strange and spacious *piazza* of which no guide-book, no tourist had ever told me. I had plunged into a network of little alleys, or *calli*. In the evening, with their high bell-mouthed chimneys on which the sun throws the brightest pinks, the clearest reds, it is a whole garden blossoming above the houses, its shades so various that you would have said it was the garden of some tulip lover of Delft or Haarlem, planted on top of the town. Moreover, the extreme proximity of the houses made of every casement a frame from which a day-dreaming cook gazed out, or in which a seated girl was having her hair combed by an old woman whose face in the dark looked like a witch's – made of each humble quiet house, so close because of the narrowness of the *calli*, a display of a hundred Dutch paintings placed side by side. Packed tightly together, these *calli* divided in all directions with their furrows a chunk of Venice carved out between a canal and the lagoon, as if it had crystallised in accordance with these innumerable, tenuous and minute patterns. Suddenly, at the end of one of these alleys, it seemed as though a distension had occurred in the crystallised matter. A vast and splendid *campo* of which, in this network of little streets, I should never have guessed the scale, or even found room for it, spread out before me surrounded by charming palaces silvery in the moonlight. It was one of those architectural ensembles towards which, in any other town, the streets converge, lead you and point the way. Here it seemed to be deliberately concealed in an interlacement of alleys, like those palaces in oriental tales whither mysterious agents convey by night a person who, brought back home before daybreak, can never find his way back to the magic dwelling which he ends by believing that he visited only in a dream.

The next day, I set out in quest of my beautiful nocturnal *piazza*, following *calle* after *calle* which were exactly like one another and refused to give me the smallest piece of information, except such as would lead me further astray. Sometimes a vague landmark which I seemed to recognise led me to suppose that I was about to see appear, in its seclusion, solitude and silence, the beautiful exiled *piazza*. At that moment, some evil genie which had assumed the form of a new *calle* made me unwittingly retrace my steps, and I found myself suddenly brought back to the Grand Canal. And as there is no great difference between the memory of a dream and the memory of a reality, I finally wondered whether it was not during my sleep that there had occurred, in a dark patch of Venetian crystallisation, that strange mirage which offered a vast *piazza* surrounded by romantic palaces to the meditative eye of the moon.

But, far more than certain places, it was the desire not to lose for ever certain women that kept me while in Venice in a state of agitation which became febrile when, towards the end of the day on which my mother had decided that we should leave, and our luggage was already on the way to the station in a gondola, I read in the register of guests expected at the hotel: 'Mme Putbus and attendants.' At once, the thought of all the hours of casual pleasure of which our departure would deprive me raised this desire, which existed in me in a chronic state, to the level of a feeling, and drowned it in a vague melancholy. I asked my mother to put off our departure for a few days, and her air of not for a moment taking my request into consideration, of not even listening to it seriously, reawakened in my nerves, exacerbated by the Venetian springtime, that old desire to rebel against an imaginary plot woven against me by my parents, who imagined that I would be forced to obey them, that defiant spirit which drove me in the past to impose my will brutally upon the people I loved best in the world, though finally conforming to theirs after I had succeeded in making them yield. I told my mother that I would not leave Venice, but she, thinking it wiser not to appear to believe that I was saying this seriously, did not even answer. I went on to say that she would soon see whether I was serious or not. The porter brought us three letters, two for her, and one for me which I put in my wallet among several others without even looking at the envelope. And when the hour came at which, accompanied by all my belongings, she set off for the station, I ordered a drink to be brought out to me on the terrace overlooking the canal, and settled down there to watch the sunset, while from a boat that had stopped in front of the hotel a musician sang *O sole mio*.

The sun continued to sink. My mother must be nearing the station. Soon she would be gone, and I should be alone in Venice, alone with the misery of knowing that I had distressed her, and without her presence to comfort me. The hour of the train's departure was approaching. My irrevocable solitude was so near at hand that it seemed to me to have begun already and to be complete. For I felt myself to be alone; things had become alien to me; I no longer had calm enough to break out of my throbbing heart and introduce into them a measure of stability. The town that I saw before me had ceased to be Venice. Its personality, its name, seemed to me to be mendacious fictions which I no longer had the will to impress upon its stones. I saw the palaces reduced to their basic elements, lifeless heaps of marble with nothing to choose between them, and the water as a combination of hydrogen and oxygen, eternal, blind, anterior and exterior to Venice, oblivious of the Doges or of Turner. And yet this unremarkable place was as strange as a place at which one has just arrived, which does not yet know one, or a place which one has left and which has forgotten one already. I could no longer tell it anything about myself, I could leave nothing of myself imprinted upon it; it contracted me into myself until I was no more than a beating heart and an attention strained to follow the development of *O sole mio*. In vain might I fix my mind despairingly upon the beautiful and distinctive curve of the Rialto, it seemed to me, with the mediocrity of the obvious, a bridge not merely inferior to but as alien to the notion I had of it as an actor of whom, in spite of his blond wig and black garments, we know quite well that in his essence he is not Hamlet. So it was with the palaces, the canal, the Rialto, divested of the idea that constituted their reality and dissolved into their vulgar material elements. But at the same time this mediocre place seemed distant to me. In the dock basin of the Arsenal, because of an element which itself also was scientific, namely latitude, there was that singularity in things whereby, even when similar in appearance to those of our own land, they reveal themselves to be alien, in exile beneath other skies; I felt that that horizon so close at hand, which I could have reached in an hour by boat, was a curvature of the earth quite different from that of France, a distant curvature which, by the artifice of travel, happened to be moored close to where I was; so that the dock basin of the Arsenal, at once insignificant and remote, filled me with that blend of distaste and alarm which I had felt as a child when I first accompanied my mother to the Deligny baths, where, in that weird setting of a pool of water reflecting neither sky nor sun, which nevertheless amid its fringe of cabins one felt to be in communication with invisible depths crowded with human bodies in swimming-trunks, I had asked myself whether those depths, concealed from mortal eyes by hutments which made their existence impossible to divine from the street, were not the entry to arctic seas which began at that point, in which the poles were comprised, and whether that narrow space was not indeed the open water that surrounds the pole; and in this lonely, unreal, icy, unfriendly setting in which I was going to be left alone, the strains of *O sole mio*, rising like a dirge for the Venice I had known, seemed to bear witness to my misery. No doubt I ought to have ceased to listen to it if I wished to be able to join my mother and take the train with her; I ought to have made up my mind to leave without losing another second. But this was precisely what I was powerless to do; I remained motionless, incapable not merely of rising, but even of deciding that I would rise from my chair. My mind, no doubt in order not to have to consider the decision I had to take, was entirely occupied in following the course of the successive phrases of *O sole mio*, singing them to myself with the singer, anticipating each surge of melody, soaring aloft with it, sinking down with it once more.

No doubt this trivial song which I had heard a hundred times did not interest me in the least. I could give no pleasure to myself or anyone else by listening to it religiously to the end. After all, none of the already familiar phrases of this

sentimental ditty was capable of furnishing me with the resolution I needed; what was more, each of these phrases, when
it came and went in its turn, became an obstacle in the way
of my putting that resolution into effect, or rather it forced
me towards the contrary resolution not to leave Venice, for
it made me too late for the train. Wherefore this occupation,
devoid of any pleasure in itself, of listening to *O sole mio* was
charged with a profound, almost despairing melancholy.
I was well aware that in reality it was the resolution not to
go that I was making by remaining there without stirring,
but to say to myself 'I'm not going,' which in that direct form
was impossible, became possible in this indirect form: 'I'm
going to listen to one more phrase of *O sole mio*'; but the
practical significance of this figurative language did not
escape me and, while I said to myself: 'After all, I'm only listening to one more phrase,' I knew that the words meant:
'I shall remain by myself in Venice.' And it was perhaps this
melancholy, like a sort of numbing cold, that constituted
the despairing but hypnotic charm of the song. Each
note that the singer's voice uttered with a force and ostent-
ation that were almost muscular stabbed me to the heart.
When the phrase was completed down below and the song
seemed to be at an end, the singer had still not had enough
and resumed at the top as though he needed to proclaim once
more my solitude and despair.

My mother must by now have reached the station. In a
little while she would be gone. I was gripped by the anguish
that was caused me by the sight of the Canal which had
become diminutive now that the soul of Venice had fled
from it, of that commonplace Rialto which was no longer
the Rialto, and by the song of despair which *O sole mio* had
become and which, bellowed thus beside the insubstantial
palaces, finally reduced them to dust and ashes and

completed the ruin of Venice; I looked on at the slow realisation of my distress, built up artistically, without haste, note by note, by the singer as he stood beneath the astonished gaze of the sun arrested in its course beyond San Giorgio Maggiore, with the result that the fading light was to combine for ever in my memory with the shiver of my emotion and the bronze voice of the singer in an equivocal, unalterable and poignant alloy.

Thus I remained motionless, my will dissolved, no decision in sight. Doubtless at such moments our decision has already been made: our friends can often predict it, but we ourselves are unable to do so, otherwise we should be spared a great deal of suffering.

But suddenly, from caverns darker than those from which flashes the comet which we can predict – thanks to the unsuspected defensive power of inveterate habit, thanks to the hidden reserves which by a sudden impulse it hurls at the last moment into the fray – my will to action arose at last; I set off in hot haste and arrived, when the carriage doors were already shut, but in time to find my mother flushed with emotion and with the effort to restrain her tears, for she thought that I was not coming. 'You know,' she said, 'your poor grandmother used to say: It's curious, there's nobody who can be as unbearable or as nice as that child.' Then the train started and we saw Padua and Verona come to meet us, to speed us on our way, almost on to the platforms of their stations, and, when we had drawn away from them, return – they who were not travelling and were about to resume their normal life – one to its plain, the other to its hill.

The hours went by. My mother was in no hurry to read her two letters, which she had merely opened, and tried to prevent me from pulling out my pocket-book at once to take from it the letter which the hotel porter had given me. She was always afraid of my finding journeys too long and too tiring, and put off as long as possible, so as to keep me occupied during the final hours, the moment at which she would seek fresh distractions for me, bring out the hard-boiled eggs, hand me the newspapers, untie the parcel of books which she had bought without telling me. We had long passed Milan when she decided to read the first of her two letters. At first I sat watching her, as she read it with an air of astonishment, then raised her head, her eyes seeming to come to rest upon a succession of distinct and incompatible memories which she could not succeed in bringing together. Meanwhile I had recognised Gilberte's handwriting on the envelope which I had just taken from my pocket-book. I opened it. Gilberte wrote to inform me that she was marrying Robert de Saint-Loup. She told me that she had sent me a telegram about it to Venice but had had no reply. I remembered that I had been told that the telegraphic service there was inefficient. I had never received her telegram. Perhaps she would refuse to believe this. All of a sudden I felt in my brain a fact, which was installed there in the guise of a memory, leave its place and surrender it to another fact. The telegram that I had received a few days earlier, and had supposed to be from Albertine, was from Gilberte. As the somewhat laboured originality of Gilberte's handwriting consisted chiefly, when she wrote a line, in introducing into the line above it the strokes of her *t*'s which appeared to be underlining the words, or the dots over her *i*'s which appeared to be punctuating the sentence above them, and on the other hand in interspersing the line below with the tails and flourishes of the words immediately above, it was quite natural that the clerk who dispatched the telegram should have read the loops of *s*'s or *y*'s in the line above as an '-ine' attached to the word 'Gilberte.' The dot over the *i* of Gilberte had climbed

334

up to make a suspension point. As for her capital *G*, it resembled a Gothic *A*. The fact that, in addition to this, two or three words had been misread, had dovetailed into one another (some of them indeed had seemed to me incomprehensible), was sufficient to explain the details of my error and was not even necessary. How many letters are actually read into a word by a careless person who knows what to expect, who sets out with the idea that the message is from a certain person? How many words into the sentence? We guess as we read, we create; everything starts from an initial error; those that follow (and this applies not only to the reading of letters and telegrams, not only to all reading), extraordinary as they may appear to a person who has not begun at the same place, are all quite natural. A large part of what we believe to be true (and this applies even to our final conclusions) with an obstinacy equalled only by our good faith, springs from an original mistake in our premises.

DAPHNE DU MAURIER

DON'T LOOK NOW

'DON'T LOOK NOW,' John said to his wife, 'but there are a couple of old girls two tables away who are trying to hypnotise me.'

Laura, quick on cue, made an elaborate pretence of yawning, then tilted her head as though searching the skies for a non-existent aeroplane.

'Right behind you,' he added. 'That's why you can't turn round at once – it would be much too obvious.'

Laura played the oldest trick in the world and dropped her napkin, then bent to scrabble for it under her feet, sending a shooting glance over her left shoulder as she straightened once again. She sucked in her cheeks, the first tell-tale sign of suppressed hysteria, and lowered her head.

'They're not old girls at all,' she said. 'They're male twins in drag.'

Her voice broke ominously, the prelude to uncontrolled laughter, and John quickly poured some more chianti into her glass.

'Pretend to choke,' he said, 'then they won't notice. You know what it is – they're criminals doing the sights of Europe, changing sex at each stop. Twin sisters here on Torcello. Twin brothers tomorrow in Venice, or even tonight, parading arm-in-arm across the Piazza San Marco. Just a matter of switching clothes and wigs.'

'Jewel thieves or murderers?' asked Laura.

'Oh, murderers, definitely. But why, I ask myself, have they picked on me?'

The waiter made a diversion by bringing coffee and bearing away the fruit, which gave Laura time to banish hysteria and regain control.

'I can't think,' she said, 'why we didn't notice them when we arrived. They stand out to high heaven. One couldn't fail.'

'That gang of Americans masked them,' said John, 'and the bearded man with a monocle who looked like a spy. It wasn't until they all went just now that I saw the twins. Oh God, the one with the shock of white hair has got her eye on me again.'

Laura took the powder compact from her bag and held it in front of her face, the mirror acting as a reflector.

'I think it's me they're looking at, not you,' she said. 'Thank heaven I left my pearls with the manager at the hotel.' She paused, dabbing the sides of her nose with powder. 'The thing is,' she said after a moment, 'we've got them wrong. They're neither murderers nor thieves. They're a couple of pathetic old retired schoolmistresses on holiday, who've saved up all their lives to visit Venice. They come from some place with a name like Walabanga in Australia. And they're called Tilly and Tiny.'

Her voice, for the first time since they had come away, took on the old bubbling quality he loved, and the worried frown between her brows had vanished. At last, he thought, at last she's beginning to get over it. If I can keep this going, if we can pick up the familiar routine of jokes shared on holiday and at home, the ridiculous fantasies about people at other tables, or staying in the hotel, or wandering in art galleries and churches, then everything will fall into place, life will become as it was before, the wound will heal, she will forget.

'You know,' said Laura, 'that really was a very good lunch. I did enjoy it.'

Thank God, he thought, thank God. ... Then he leant forward, speaking low in a conspirator's whisper. 'One of them is going to the loo,' he said. 'Do you suppose he, or she, is going to change her wig?'

'Don't say anything,' Laura murmured. 'I'll follow her and find out. She may have a suitcase tucked away there, and she's going to switch clothes.'

She began to hum under her breath, the signal, to her husband, of content. The ghost was temporarily laid, and all because of the familiar holiday game, abandoned too long, and now, through mere chance, blissfully recaptured.

'Is she on her way?' asked Laura.

'About to pass our table now,' he told her.

Seen on her own, the woman was not so remarkable. Tall, angular, aquiline features, with the close-cropped hair which was fashionably called an Eton crop, he seemed to remember, in his mother's day, and about her person the stamp of that particular generation. She would be in her middle sixties, he supposed, the masculine shirt with collar and tie, sports jacket, grey tweed skirt coming to mid-calf. Grey stockings and laced black shoes. He had seen the type on golf-courses and at dog-shows – invariably showing not sporting breeds but pugs – and if you came across them at a party in somebody's house they were quicker on the draw with a cigarette-lighter than he was himself, a mere male, with pocket-matches. The general belief that they kept house with a more feminine, fluffy companion was not always true. Frequently they boasted, and adored, a golfing husband. No, the striking point about this particular individual was that there were two of them. Identical twins cast in the same mould. The only difference was that the other one had whiter hair.

'Supposing,' murmured Laura, 'when I find myself in the *toilette* beside her she starts to strip?'

'Depends on what is revealed,' John answered. 'If she's hermaphrodite, make a bolt for it. She might have a hypodermic syringe concealed and want to knock you out before you reached the door.'

Laura sucked in her cheeks once more and began to shake. Then, squaring her shoulders, she rose to her feet. 'I simply must not laugh,' she said, 'and whatever you do, don't look at me when I come back, especially if we come out together.' She picked up her bag and strolled self-consciously away from the table in pursuit of her prey.

John poured the dregs of the chianti into his glass and lit a cigarette. The sun blazed down upon the little garden of the restaurant. The Americans had left, and the monocled man, and the family party at the far end. All was peace. The identical twin was sitting back in her chair with her eyes closed. Thank heaven, he thought, for this moment at any rate, when relaxation was possible, and Laura had been launched upon her foolish, harmless game. The holiday could yet turn into the cure she needed, blotting out, if only temporarily, the numb despair that had seized her since the child died.

'She'll get over it,' the doctor said. 'They all get over it, in time. And you have the boy.'

'I know,' John had said, 'but the girl meant everything. She always did, right from the start, I don't know why. I suppose it was the difference in age. A boy of school age, and a tough one at that, is someone in his own right. Not a baby of five. Laura literally adored her. Johnnie and I were nowhere.'

'Give her time,' repeated the doctor, 'give her time. And anyway, you're both young still. There'll be others. Another daughter.'

So easy to talk. . . . How replace the life of a loved lost child with a dream? He knew Laura too well. Another child, another girl, would have her own qualities, a separate identity, she might even induce hostility because of this very fact. A usurper in the cradle, in the cot, that had been Christine's. A chubby, flaxen replica of Johnnie, not the little waxen dark-haired sprite that had gone.

He looked up, over his glass of wine, and the woman was staring at him again. It was not the casual, idle glance of someone at a nearby table, waiting for her companion to return, but something deeper, more intent, the prominent, light blue eyes oddly penetrating, giving him a sudden feeling of discomfort. Damn the woman! All right, bloody stare, if you must. Two can play at that game. He blew a cloud of cigarette smoke into the air and smiled at her, he hoped offensively. She did not register. The blue eyes continued to hold his, so that he was obliged to look away himself, extinguish his cigarette, glance over his shoulder for the waiter and call for the bill. Settling for this, and fumbling with the change, with a few casual remarks about the excellence of the meal, brought composure, but a prickly feeling on his scalp remained, and an odd sensation of unease. Then it went, as abruptly as it had started, and stealing a furtive glance at the other table he saw that her eyes were closed again, and she was sleeping, or dozing, as she had done before. The waiter disappeared. All was still.

Laura, he thought, glancing at his watch, is being a hell of a time. Ten minutes at least. Something to tease her about, anyway. He began to plan the form the joke would take. How the old dolly had stripped to her smalls, suggesting that Laura should do likewise. And then the manager had burst in upon them both, exclaiming in horror, the reputation of the restaurant damaged, the hint that unpleasant consequences might follow unless ... The whole exercise turning out to be a plant, an exercise in blackmail. He and Laura and the twins taken in a police launch back to Venice for questioning. Quarter of an hour. ... Oh, come on, come on. ...

There was a crunch of feet on the gravel. Laura's twin walked slowly past, alone. She crossed over to her table and stood there a moment, her tall, angular figure interposing itself between John and her sister. She was saying something, but he couldn't catch the words. What was the accent, though – Scottish? Then she bent, offering an arm to the seated twin, and they moved away together across the garden to the break in the little hedge beyond, the twin who had stared at John leaning on her sister's arm. Here was the difference again. She was not quite so tall, and she stooped more – perhaps she was arthritic. They disappeared out of sight, and John, becoming impatient, got up and was about to walk back into the hotel when Laura emerged.

'Well, I must say, you took your time,' he began, and then stopped, because of the expression on her face.

'What's the matter, what's happened?' he asked.

He could tell at once there was something wrong. Almost as if she were in a state of shock. She blundered towards the table he had just vacated and sat down. He drew up a chair beside her, taking her hand.

'Darling, what is it? Tell me – are you ill?'

She shook her head, and then turned and looked at him. The dazed expression he had noticed at first had given way to one of dawning confidence, almost of exaltation.

'It's quite wonderful,' she said slowly, 'the most wonderful thing that could possibly be. You see, she isn't dead, she's still with us. That's why they kept staring at us, those two sisters. They could see Christine.'

344

Oh God, he thought. It's what I've been dreading. She's going off her head. What do I do? How do I cope?

'Laura, sweet,' he began, forcing a smile, 'look, shall we go? I've paid the bill, we can go and look at the cathedral and stroll around, and then it will be time to take off in that launch again for Venice.'

She wasn't listening, or at any rate the words didn't penetrate.

'John, love,' she said, 'I've got to tell you what happened. I followed her, as we planned, into the *toilette* place. She was combing her hair and I went into the loo, and then came out and washed my hands in the basin. She was washing hers in the next basin. Suddenly she turned and said to me, in a strong Scots accent, "Don't be unhappy any more. My sister has seen your little girl. She was sitting between you and your husband, laughing." Darling, I thought I was going to faint. I nearly did. Luckily, there was a chair, and I sat down, and the woman bent over me and patted my head. I'm not sure of her exact words, but she said something about the moment of truth and joy being as sharp as a sword, but not to be afraid, all was well, but the sister's vision had been so strong they knew I had to be told, and that Christine wanted it. Oh John, don't look like that. I swear I'm not making it up, this is what she told me, it's all true.'

The desperate urgency in her voice made his heart sicken. He had to play along with her, agree, soothe, do anything to bring back some sense of calm.

'Laura, darling, of course I believe you,' he said, 'only it's a sort of shock, and I'm upset because you're upset. ...'

'But I'm not upset,' she interrupted. 'I'm happy, so happy that I can't put the feeling into words. You know what it's been like all these weeks, at home and everywhere we've been on holiday, though I tried to hide it from you. Now it's lifted,

because I know, I just know, that the woman was right. Oh
Lord, how awful of me, but I've forgotten their name – she
did tell me. You see, the thing is that she's a retired doctor,
they come from Edinburgh, and the one who saw Christine
went blind a few years ago. Although she's studied the occult
all her life and been very psychic, it's only since going blind
that she has really seen things, like a medium. They've had
the most wonderful experiences. But to describe Christine
as the blind one did to her sister, even down to the little blue-
and-white dress with the puff sleeves that she wore at her
birthday party, and to say she was smiling happily. ...
Oh, darling, it's made me so happy I think I'm going
to cry.'

No hysteria. Nothing wild. She took a tissue from her bag
and blew her nose, smiling at him. 'I'm all right, you see, you
don't have to worry. Neither of us need worry about anything
any more. Give me a cigarette.'

He took one from his packet and lighted it for her. She
sounded normal, herself again. She wasn't trembling. And if
this sudden belief was going to keep her happy he couldn't
possibly begrudge it. But ... but ... he wished, all the same,
it hadn't happened. There was something uncanny about
thought-reading, about telepathy. Scientists couldn't
account for it, nobody could, and this is what must have
happened just now between Laura and the sisters. So the one
who had been staring at him was blind. That accounted for
the fixed gaze. Which somehow was unpleasant in itself,
creepy. Oh hell, he thought, I wish we hadn't come here for
lunch. Just chance, a flick of a coin between this, Torcello,
and driving to Padua, and we had to choose Torcello.

'You didn't arrange to meet them again or anything, did
you?' he asked, trying to sound casual.

'No, darling, why should I?' Laura answered. 'I mean,

there was nothing more they could tell me. The sister had had her wonderful vision, and that was that. Anyway, they're moving on. Funnily enough, it's rather like our original game. They *are* going round the world before returning to Scotland. Only I said Australia, didn't I? The old dears. . . . Anything less like murderers and jewel thieves.'

She had quite recovered. She stood up and looked about her. 'Come on,' she said. 'Having come to Torcello we must see the cathedral.'

They made their way from the restaurant across the open piazza, where the stalls had been set up with scarves and trinkets and postcards, and so along the path to the cathedral. One of the ferry-boats had just decanted a crowd of sightseers, many of whom had already found their way into Santa Maria Assunta. Laura, undaunted, asked her husband for the guidebook, and, as had always been her custom in happier days, started to walk slowly through the cathedral, studying mosaics, columns, panels from left to right, while John, less interested, because of his concern at what had just happened, followed close behind, keeping a weather eye alert for the twin sisters. There was no sign of them. Perhaps they had gone into the church of Santa Fosca close by. A sudden encounter would be embarrassing, quite apart from the effect it might have upon Laura. But the anonymous, shuffling tourists, intent upon culture, could not harm her, although from his own point of view they made artistic appreciation impossible. He could not concentrate, the cold clear beauty of what he saw left him untouched, and when Laura touched his sleeve, pointing to the mosaic of the Virgin and Child standing above the frieze of the Apostles, he nodded in sympathy yet saw nothing, the long, sad face of the Virgin infinitely remote, and turning on sudden impulse stared back over the heads of the tourists towards the door,

347

where frescoes of the blessed and the damned gave themselves to judgment.

The twins were standing there, the blind one still holding on to her sister's arm, her sightless eyes fixed firmly upon him. He felt himself held, unable to move, and an impending sense of doom, of tragedy, came upon him. His whole being sagged, as it were, in apathy, and he thought, 'This is the end, there is no escape, no future.' Then both sisters turned and went out of the cathedral and the sensation vanished, leaving indignation in its wake, and rising anger. How dare those two old fools practise their mediumistic tricks on him? It was fraudulent, unhealthy; this was probably the way they lived, touring the world making everyone they met uncomfortable. Give them half a chance and they would have got money out of Laura – anything.

He felt her tugging at his sleeve again. 'Isn't she beautiful? So happy, so serene.'

'Who? What?' he asked.

'The Madonna,' she answered. 'She has a magic quality. It goes right through to one. Don't you feel it too?'

'I suppose so. I don't know. There are too many people around.'

She looked up at him, astonished. 'What's that got to do with it? How funny you are. Well, all right, let's get away from them. I want to buy some postcards anyway.'

Disappointed, she sensed his lack of interest, and began to thread her way through the crowd of tourists to the door.

'Come on,' he said abruptly, once they were outside, 'there's plenty of time for postcards, let's explore a bit,' and he struck off from the path, which would have taken them back to the centre where the little houses were, and the stalls, and the drifting crowd of people, to a narrow way amongst uncultivated ground, beyond which he could see a sort of cutting, or canal. The sight of water, limpid, pale, was a soothing contrast to the fierce sun above their heads.

'I don't think this leads anywhere much,' said Laura. 'It's a bit muddy, too, one can't sit. Besides, there are more things the guidebook says we ought to see.'

'Oh, forget the book,' he said impatiently, and, pulling her down beside him on the bank above the cutting, put his arms round her.

'It's the wrong time of day for sight-seeing. Look, there's a rat swimming there the other side.'

He picked up a stone and threw it in the water, and the animal sank, or somehow disappeared, and nothing was left but bubbles.

'Don't,' said Laura. 'It's cruel, poor thing,' and then suddenly, putting her hand on his knee, 'Do you think Christine is sitting here beside us?'

He did not answer at once. What was there to say? Would it be like this forever?

'I expect so,' he said slowly, 'if you feel she is.'

The point was, remembering Christine before the onset of the fatal meningitis, she would have been running along the bank excitedly, throwing off her shoes, wanting to paddle, giving Laura a fit of apprehension. 'Sweetheart, take care, come back . . .'

'The woman said she was looking so happy, sitting beside us, smiling,' said Laura. She got up, brushing her dress, her mood changed to restlessness. 'Come on, let's go back,' she said.

He followed her with a sinking heart. He knew she did not really want to buy postcards or see what remained to be seen; she wanted to go in search of the women again, not necessarily to talk, just to be near them. When they came to the open place by the stalls he noticed that the crowd of tourists had thinned, there were only a few stragglers left, and the sisters were not amongst them. They must have joined the main body who had come to Torcello by the ferry-service. A wave of relief seized him.

'Look, there's a mass of postcards at the second stall,' he said quickly, 'and some eye-catching head scarves. Let me buy you a head scarf.'

'Darling, I've so many!' she protested. 'Don't waste your lire.'

'It isn't a waste. I'm in a buying mood. What about a basket? You know we never have enough baskets. Or some lace. How about lace?'

She allowed herself, laughing, to be dragged to the stall. While he rumpled through the goods spread out before them, and chatted up the smiling woman who was selling her wares, his ferociously bad Italian making her smile the more, he knew it would give the body of tourists more time to walk to the landing-stage and catch the ferry-service, and the twin sisters would be out of sight and out of their life.

'Never,' said Laura, some twenty minutes later, 'has so much junk been piled into so small a basket,' her bubbling laugh reassuring him that all was well, he needn't worry any more, the evil hour had passed. The launch from the Cipriani that had brought them from Venice was waiting by the landing-stage. The passengers who had arrived with them, the Americans, the man with the monocle, were already assembled. Earlier, before setting out, he had thought the price for lunch and transport, there and back, decidedly steep. Now he grudged none of it, except that the outing to Torcello itself had been one of the major errors of this particular holiday in Venice. They stepped down into the launch, finding a place in the open, and the boat chugged away down the canal and into the lagoon. The ordinary ferry had gone before, steaming towards Murano, while their own craft headed past San Francesco del Deserto and so back direct to Venice.

He put his arm around her once more, holding her close, and this time she responded, smiling up at him, her head on his shoulder.

'It's been a lovely day,' she said. 'I shall never forget it, never. You know, darling, now at last I can begin to enjoy our holiday.'

He wanted to shout with relief. It's going to be all right, he decided, let her believe what she likes, it doesn't matter, it makes her happy. The beauty of Venice rose before them, sharply outlined against the glowing sky, and there was still so much to see, wandering there together, that might now be perfect because of her change of mood, the shadow having lifted, and aloud he began to discuss the evening to come, where they would dine – not the restaurant they usually went to, near the Fenice theatre, but somewhere different, somewhere new.

'Yes, but it must be cheap,' she said, falling in with his mood, 'because we've already spent so much today.'

Their hotel by the Grand Canal had a welcoming, comforting air. The clerk smiled as he handed over their key. The bedroom was familiar, like home, with Laura's things arranged neatly on the dressing-table, but with it the little festive atmosphere of strangeness, of excitement, that only a holiday bedroom brings. This is ours for the moment, but no more. While we are in it we bring it life. When we have gone it no longer exists, it fades into anonymity. He turned on both taps in the bathroom, the water gushing into the bath, the steam rising. 'Now,' he thought afterwards, 'now at last is the moment to make love,' and he went back into the bedroom, and she understood, and opened her arms

351

and smiled. Such blessed relief after all those weeks of restraint.

'The thing is,' she said later, fixing her ear-rings before the looking-glass, 'I'm not really terribly hungry. Shall we just be dull and eat in the dining-room here?'

'God, no!' he exclaimed. 'With all those rather dreary couples at the other tables? I'm ravenous. I'm also gay. I want to get rather sloshed.'

'Not bright lights and music, surely?'

'No, no . . . some small, dark, intimate cave, rather sinister, full of lovers with other people's wives.'

'H'm,' sniffed Laura, 'we all know what *that* means. You'll spot some Italian lovely of sixteen and smirk at her through dinner, while I'm stuck high and dry with a beastly man's broad back.'

They went out laughing into the warm soft night, and the magic was about them everywhere. 'Let's walk,' he said, 'let's walk and work up an appetite for our gigantic meal,' and inevitably they found themselves by the Molo and the lapping gondolas dancing upon the water, the lights everywhere blending with the darkness. There were other couples strolling for the same sake of aimless enjoyment, backwards, forwards, purposeless, and the inevitable sailors in groups, noisy, gesticulating, and dark-eyed girls whispering, clicking on high heels.

'The trouble is,' said Laura, 'walking in Venice becomes compulsive once you start. Just over the next bridge, you say, and then the next one beckons. I'm sure there are no restaurants down here, we're almost at those public gardens where they hold the Biennale. Let's turn back. I know there's a restaurant somewhere near the church of San Zaccaria, there's a little alley-way leading to it.'

'Tell you what,' said John, 'if we go down here by the

Arsenal, and cross that bridge at the end and head left, we'll come upon San Zaccaria from the other side. We did it the other morning.'

'Yes, but it was daylight then. We may lose our way, it's not very well lit.'

'Don't fuss. I have an instinct for these things.'

They turned down the Fondamenta dell'Arsenale and crossed the little bridge short of the Arsenal itself, and so on past the church of San Martino. There were two canals ahead, one bearing right, the other left, with narrow streets beside them. John hesitated. Which one was it they had walked beside the day before?

'You see,' protested Laura, 'we shall be lost, just as I said.'

'Nonsense,' replied John firmly. 'It's the left-hand one, I remember the little bridge.'

The canal was narrow, the houses on either side seemed to close in upon it, and in the daytime, with the sun's reflection on the water and the windows of the houses open, bedding upon the balconies, a canary singing in a cage, there had been an impression of warmth, of secluded shelter. Now, ill-lit, almost in darkness, the windows of the houses shuttered, the water dank, the scene appeared altogether different, neglected, poor, and the long narrow boats moored to the slippery steps of cellar entrances looked like coffins.

'I swear I don't remember this bridge,' said Laura, pausing, and holding on to the rail, 'and I don't like the look of that alley-way beyond.'

'There's a lamp halfway up,' John told her. 'I know exactly where we are, not far from the Greek quarter.'

They crossed the bridge, and were about to plunge into the alley-way when they heard the cry. It came, surely, from one of the houses on the opposite side, but which one it was impossible to say. With the shutters closed each one of them

353

seemed dead. They turned, and stared in the direction from which the sound had come.

'What was it?' whispered Laura.

'Some drunk or other,' said John briefly. 'Come on.'

Less like a drunk than someone being strangled, and the choking cry suppressed as the grip held firm.

'We ought to call the police,' said Laura.

'Oh, for heaven's sake,' said John. Where did she think she was – Piccadilly?

'Well, I'm off, it's sinister,' she replied, and began to hurry away up the twisting alley-way. John hesitated, his eye caught by a small figure which suddenly crept from a cellar entrance below one of the opposite houses, and then jumped into a narrow boat below. It was a child, a little girl – she couldn't have been more than five or six – wearing a short coat over her minute skirt, a pixie hood covering her head. There were four boats moored, line upon line, and she proceeded to jump from one to the other with surprising agility, intent, it would seem, upon escape. Once her foot slipped and he caught his breath, for she was within a few feet of the water, losing balance; then she recovered, and hopped on to the furthest boat. Bending, she tugged at the rope, which had the effect of swinging the boat's after-end across the canal, almost touching the opposite side and another cellar entrance, about thirty feet from the spot where John stood watching her. Then the child jumped again, landing upon the cellar steps, and vanished into the house, the boat swinging back into mid-canal behind her. The whole episode could not have taken more than four minutes. Then he heard the quick patter of feet. Laura had returned. She had seen none of it, for which he felt unspeakably thankful. The sight of a child, a little girl, in what must have been near danger, her fear that the scene he had just witnessed was in some way a sequel to the alarming cry, might have had a disastrous effect on her overwrought nerves.

'What are you doing?' she called. 'I daren't go on without you. The wretched alley branches in two directions.'

'Sorry,' he told her. 'I'm coming.'

He took her arm and they walked briskly along the alley, John with an apparent confidence he did not possess.

'There were no more cries, were there?' she asked.

'No,' he said, 'no, nothing. I tell you, it was some drunk.'

The alley led to a deserted *campo* behind a church, not a church he knew, and he led the way across, along another street and over a further bridge.

'Wait a minute,' he said. 'I think we take this right-hand turning. It will lead us into the Greek quarter – the church of San Georgio is somewhere over there.'

She did not answer. She was beginning to lose faith. The place was like a maze. They might circle round and round forever, and then find themselves back again, near the bridge where they had heard the cry. Doggedly he led her on, and then surprisingly, with relief, he saw people walking in the lighted street ahead, there was a spire of a church, the surroundings became familiar.

'There, I told you,' he said. 'That's San Zaccaria, we've found it all right. Your restaurant can't be far away.'

And anyway, there would be other restaurants, somewhere to eat, at least here was the cheering glitter of lights, of movement, canals beside which people walked, the atmosphere of tourism. The letters 'Ristorante', in blue lights, shone like a beacon down a left-hand alley.

'Is this your place?' he asked.

'God knows,' she said. 'Who cares? Let's feed there anyway.'

And so into the sudden blast of heated air and hum of

voices, the smell of pasta, wine, waiters, jostling customers, laughter. 'For two? This way, please.' Why, he thought, was one's British nationality always so obvious? A cramped little table and an enormous menu scribbled in an indecipherable mauve biro, with the waiter hovering, expecting the order forthwith.

'Two very large camparis, with soda,' John said. '*Then* we'll study the menu.'

He was not going to be rushed. He handed the bill of fare to Laura and looked about him. Mostly Italians – that meant the food would be good. Then he saw them. At the opposite side of the room. The twin sisters. They must have come into the restaurant hard upon Laura's and his own arrival, for they were only now sitting down, shedding their coats, the waiter hovering beside the table. John was seized with the irrational thought that this was no coincidence. The sisters had noticed them both, in the street outside, and had followed them in. Why, in the name of hell, should they have picked on this particular spot, in the whole of Venice, unless ... unless Laura herself, at Torcello, had suggested a further encounter, or the sister had suggested it to her? A small restaurant near the church of San Zaccaria, we go there sometimes for dinner. It was Laura, before the walk, who had mentioned San Zaccaria ....

She was still intent upon the menu, she had not seen the sisters, but any moment now she would have chosen what she wanted to eat, and then she would raise her head and look across the room. If only the drinks would come. If only the waiter would bring the drinks, it would give Laura something to do.

'You know, I was thinking,' he said quickly, 'we really ought to go to the garage tomorrow and get the car, and do

356

that drive to Padua. We could lunch in Padua, see the cathedral and touch St Antony's tomb and look at the Giotto frescoes, and come back by way of those various villas along the Brenta that the guidebook cracks up.'

It was no use, though. She was looking up, across the restaurant, and she gave a little gasp of surprise. It was genuine. He could swear it was genuine.

'Look,' she said. 'how extraordinary! How really amazing!'

'What?' he said sharply.

'Why, there they are. My wonderful old twins. They've seen us, what's more. They're staring this way.' She waved her hand, radiant, delighted. The sister she had spoken to at Torcello bowed and smiled. False old bitch, he thought. I know they followed us.

'Oh, darling, I must go and speak to them,' she said impulsively, 'just to tell them how happy I've been all day, thanks to them.'

'Oh, for heaven's sake!' he said. 'Look, here are the drinks. And we haven't ordered yet. Surely you can wait until later, until we've eaten?'

'I won't be a moment,' she said, 'and anyway I want scampi, nothing first. I told you I wasn't hungry.'

She got up, and, brushing past the waiter with the drinks, crossed the room. She might have been greeting the loved friends of years. He watched her bend over the table and shake them both by the hand, and because there was a vacant chair at their table she drew it up and sat down, talking, smiling. Nor did the sisters seemed surprised, at least not the one she knew, who nodded and talked back, while the blind sister remained impassive.

'All right,' thought John savagely, 'then I *will* get sloshed,' and he proceeded to down his campari and soda and order

357

another, while he pointed out something quite unintelligible on the menu as his own choice, but remembered scampi for Laura. 'And a bottle of Soave,' he added, 'with ice.'

The evening was ruined anyway. What was to have been an intimate, happy celebration would now be heavy-laden with spiritualistic visions, poor little dead Christine sharing the table with them, which was so damned stupid when in earthly life she would have been tucked up hours ago in bed. The bitter taste of the campari suited his mood of sudden self-pity, and all the while he watched the group at the table in the opposite corner, Laura apparently listening while the more active sister held forth and the blind one sat silent, her formidable sightless eyes turned in his direction.

'She's phoney,' he thought, 'she's not blind at all. They're both of them frauds, and they could be males in drag after all, just as we pretended at Torcello, and they're after Laura.'

He began on his second campari and soda. The two drinks, taken on an empty stomach, had an instant effect. Vision became blurred. And still Laura went on sitting at the other table, putting in a question now and again, while the active sister talked. The waiter appeared with the scampi, and a companion beside him to serve John's own order, which was totally unrecognisable, heaped with a livid sauce.

'The signora does not come?' enquired the first waiter, and John shook his head grimly, pointing an unsteady finger across the room.

'Tell the signora,' he said carefully, 'her scampi will get cold.'

He stared down at the offering placed before him, and prodded it delicately with a fork. The pallid sauce dissolved, revealing two enormous slices, rounds, of what appeared to be boiled pork, bedecked with garlic. He forked a portion to his mouth and chewed, and yes, it was pork, steamy, rich, the spicy sauce having turned it curiously sweet. He laid down his fork, pushing the plate away, and became aware of Laura, returning across the room and sitting beside him. She did not say anything, which was just as well, he thought, because he was too near nausea to answer. It wasn't just the drink, but reaction from the whole nightmare day. She began to eat her scampi, still not uttering. She did not seem to notice he was not eating. The waiter, hovering at his elbow, anxious, seemed aware that John's choice was somehow an error, and discreetly removed the plate. 'Bring me a green salad,' murmured John, and even then Laura did not register surprise, or, as she might have done in more normal circumstances, accuse him of having had too much to drink. Finally, when she had finished her scampi and was sipping her wine, which John had waved away, to nibble at his salad in small mouthfuls like a sick rabbit, she began to speak.

'Darling,' she said, 'I know you won't believe it, and it's rather frightening in a way, but after they left the restaurant in Torcello the sisters went to the cathedral, as we did, although we didn't see them in that crowd, and the blind one had another vision. She said Christine was trying to tell her something about us, that we should be in danger if we stayed in Venice. Christine wanted us to go away as soon as possible.'

So that's it, he thought. They think they can run our lives for us. This is to be our problem from henceforth. Do we eat? Do we get up? Do we go to bed? We must get in touch with the twin sisters. They will direct us.

'Well?' she said. 'Why don't you say something?'

'Because,' he answered, 'you are perfectly right, I don't believe it. Quite frankly, I judge your old sisters as being a couple of freaks, if nothing else. They're obviously unbalanced, and I'm sorry if this hurts you, but the fact is they've found a sucker in you.'

'You're being unfair,' said Laura. 'They are genuine, I know it. I just know it. They were completely sincere in what they said.'

'All right. Granted. They're sincere. But that doesn't make them well-balanced. Honestly, darling, you meet that old girl for ten minutes in a loo, she tells you she sees Christine sitting beside us – well, anyone with a gift for telepathy could read your unconscious mind in an instant – and then, pleased with her success, as any old psychic expert would be, she flings a further mood of ecstasy and wants to boot us out of Venice. Well, I'm sorry, but to hell with it.'

The room was no longer reeling. Anger had sobered him. If it would not put Laura to shame he would get up and cross to their table, and tell the old fools where they got off.

'I knew you would take it like this,' said Laura unhappily. 'I told them you would. They said not to worry. As long as we left Venice tomorrow everything would come all right.'

'Oh, for God's sake,' said John. He changed his mind, and poured himself a glass of wine.

'After all,' Laura went on, 'we have really seen the cream of Venice. I don't mind going on somewhere else. And if we stayed – I know it sounds silly, but I should have a nasty nagging sort of feeling inside me, and I should keep thinking of darling Christine being unhappy and trying to tell us to go.'

'Right,' said John with ominous calm, 'that settles it. Go we will. I suggest we clear off to the hotel straight away and warn the reception we're leaving in the morning. Have you had enough to eat?'

'Oh dear,' sighed Laura, 'don't take it like that. Look, why not come over and meet them, and then they can explain about the vision to you? Perhaps you would take it seriously then. Especially as you are the one it most concerns. Christine is more worried over you than me. And the extraordinary thing is that the blind sister says you're psychic and don't know it. You are somehow *en rapport* with the unknown, and I'm not.'

'Well, that's final,' said John. 'I'm psychic, am I? Fine. My psychic intuition tells me to get out of this restaurant now, at once, and we can decide what we do about leaving Venice when we are back at the hotel.'

He signalled to the waiter for the bill and they waited for it, not speaking to each other, Laura unhappy, fiddling with her bag, while John, glancing furtively at the twins' table, noticed that they were tucking into plates piled high with spaghetti, in very un-psychic fashion. The bill disposed of, John pushed back his chair.

'Right. Are you ready?' he asked.

'I'm going to say goodbye to them first,' said Laura, her mouth set sulkily, reminding him instantly, with a pang, of their poor lost child.

'Just as you like,' he replied, and walked ahead of her out of the restaurant, without a backward glance.

The soft humidity of the evening, so pleasant to walk about in earlier, had turned to rain. The strolling tourists had melted away. One or two people hurried by under umbrellas. This is what the inhabitants who live here see, he thought. This is the true life. Empty streets by night, the dank stillness of a stagnant canal beneath shuttered houses. The rest is a bright façade put on for show, glittering by sunlight.

Laura joined him and they walked away together in silence, and emerging presently behind the ducal palace came out into the Piazza San Marco. The rain was heavy now, and they sought shelter with the few remaining stragglers under the colonnades. The orchestras had packed up for the evening. The tables were bare. Chairs had been turned upside down.

The experts are right, he thought, Venice is sinking. The whole city is slowly dying. One day the tourists will travel here by boat to peer down into the waters, and they will see pillars and columns and marble far, far beneath them, slime and mud uncovering for brief moments a lost underworld of stone. Their heels made a ringing sound on the pavement and the rain splashed from the gutterings above. A fine ending to an evening that had started with brave hope, with innocence.

When they came to their hotel Laura made straight for the lift, and John turned to the desk to ask the night-porter for the key. The man handed him a telegram at the same time. John stared at it a moment. Laura was already in the lift. Then he opened the envelope and read the message. It was from the headmaster of Johnnie's preparatory school.

> Johnnie under observation suspected
> appendicitis in city hospital here.
> No cause for alarm but surgeon thought
> wise advise you.
> Charles Hill

He read the message twice, then walked slowly towards the lift where Laura was waiting for him. He gave her the telegram. 'This came when we were out,' he said. 'Not awfully good news.' He pressed the lift button as she read the telegram. The lift stopped at the second floor, and they got out.

'Well, this decides it, doesn't it?' she said. 'Here is the proof. We have to leave Venice because we're going home. It's Johnnie who's in danger, not us. This is what Christine was trying to tell the twins.'

The first thing John did the following morning was to put a call through to the headmaster at the preparatory school. Then he gave notice of their departure to the reception manager, and they packed while they waited for the call. Neither of them referred to the events of the preceding day, it was not necessary. John knew the arrival of the telegram and the foreboding of danger from the sisters was coincidence, nothing more, but it was pointless to start an argument about it. Laura was convinced otherwise, but intuitively she knew it was best to keep her feelings to herself. During breakfast they discussed ways and means of getting home. It should be possible to get themselves, and the car, on to the special car train that ran from Milan through to Calais, since it was early in the season. In any event, the headmaster had said there was no urgency.

The call from England came while John was in the bathroom. Laura answered it. He came into the bedroom a few minutes later. She was still speaking, but he could tell from the expression in her eyes that she was anxious.

'It's Mrs Hill,' she said. 'Mr Hill is in class. She says they reported from the hospital that Johnnie had a restless night and the surgeon may have to operate, but he doesn't want to unless it's absolutely necessary. They've taken X-rays and the appendix is in a tricky position, it's not awfully straightforward.'

'Here, give it to me,' he said.

The soothing but slightly guarded voice of the headmaster's wife came down the receiver. 'I'm so sorry this may spoil your plans,' she said, 'but both Charles and I felt you ought to be told, and that you might feel rather easier if you were on the spot. Johnnie is very plucky, but of course he has some fever. That isn't unusual, the surgeon says, in the circumstances. Sometimes an appendix can get displaced, it appears, and this makes it more complicated. He's going to decide about operating this evening.'

'Yes, of course, we quite understand,' said John.

'Please do tell your wife not to worry too much,' she went on. 'The hospital is excellent, a very nice staff, and we have every confidence in the surgeon.'

'Yes,' said John, 'yes,' and then broke off because Laura was making gestures beside him.

'If we can't get the car on the train, I can fly,' she said. 'They're sure to be able to find me a seat on a plane. Then at least one of us would be there this evening.'

He nodded agreement. 'Thank you so much, Mrs Hill,' he said, 'we'll manage to get back all right. Yes, I'm sure Johnnie is in good hands. Thank your husband for us. Goodbye.'

He replaced the receiver and looked round him at the tumbled beds, suitcases on the floor, tissue-paper strewn. Baskets, maps, books, coats, everything they had brought with them in the car. 'Oh God,' he said, 'what a bloody mess. All this junk.' The telephone rang again. It was the hall porter to say he had succeeded in booking a sleeper for them both, and a place for the car, on the following night.

'Look,' said Laura, who had seized the telephone, 'could you book one seat on the midday plane from Venice to London today, for me? It's imperative one of us gets home this evening. My husband could follow with the car tomorrow.'

'Here, hang on,' interrupted John. 'No need for panic

364

stations. Surely twenty-four hours wouldn't make all that difference?'

Anxiety had drained the colour from her face. She turned to him, distraught.

'It mightn't to you, but it does to me,' she said. 'I've lost one child, I'm not going to lose another.'

'All right, darling, all right ...' He put his hand out to her but she brushed it off, impatiently, and continued giving directions to the porter. He turned back to his packing. No use saying anything. Better for it to be as she wished. They could, of course, both go by air, and then when all was well, and Johnnie better, he could come back and fetch the car, driving home through France as they had come. Rather a sweat, though, and the hell of an expense. Bad enough Laura going by air and himself with the car on the train from Milan.

'We could, if you like, both fly,' he began tentatively, explaining the sudden idea, but she would have none of it. 'That really *would* be absurd,' she said impatiently. 'As long as I'm there this evening, and you follow by train, it's all that matters. Besides, we shall need the car, going backwards and forwards to the hospital. And our luggage. We couldn't go off and just leave all this here.'

No, he saw her point. A silly idea. It was only – well, he was as worried about Johnnie as she was, though he wasn't going to say so.

'I'm going downstairs to stand over the porter,' said Laura. 'They always make more effort if one is actually on the spot. Everything I want tonight is packed. I shall only need my overnight case. You can bring everything else in the car.' She hadn't been out of the bedroom five minutes before the telephone rang. It was Laura. 'Darling,' she said, 'it couldn't have worked out better. The porter has got me on a charter flight that leaves Venice in less than an hour. A special motor-launch takes the party direct from San Marco in about ten minutes. Some passenger on the charter flight cancelled. I shall be at Gatwick in less than four hours.'

'I'll be down right away,' he told her.

He joined her by the reception desk. She no longer looked anxious and drawn, but full of purpose. She was on her way. He kept wishing they were going together. He couldn't bear to stay on in Venice after she had gone, but the thought of driving to Milan, spending a dreary night in a hotel there alone, the endless dragging day which would follow, and the long hours in the train the next night, filled him with intolerable depression, quite apart from the anxiety about Johnnie. They walked along to the San Marco landing-stage, the Molo bright and glittering after the rain, a little breeze blowing, the postcards and scarves and tourist souvenirs fluttering on the stalls, the tourists themselves out in force, strolling, contented, the happy day before them.

'I'll ring you tonight from Milan,' he told her. 'The Hills will give you a bed, I suppose. And if you're at the hospital they'll let me have the latest news. That must be your charter party. You're welcome to them!'

The passengers descending from the landing-stage down into the waiting launch were carrying hand-luggage with Union Jack tags upon them. They were mostly middle-aged, with what appeared to be two Methodist ministers in charge. One of them advanced towards Laura, holding out his hand, showing a gleaming row of dentures when he smiled. 'You must be the lady joining us for the homeward flight,' he said. 'Welcome aboard, and to the Union of Fellowship. We are all delighted to make your acquaintance. Sorry we hadn't a seat for hubby too.'

Laura turned swiftly and kissed John, a tremor at the

366

corner of her mouth betraying inward laughter. 'Do you think they'll break into hymns?' she whispered. 'Take care of yourself, hubby. Call me tonight.'

The pilot sounded a curious little toot upon his horn, and in a moment Laura had climbed down the steps into the launch and was standing amongst the crowd of passengers, waving her hand, her scarlet coat a gay patch of colour amongst the more sober suiting of her companions. The launch tooted again and moved away from the landing-stage, and he stood there watching it, a sense of immense loss filling his heart. Then he turned and walked away, back to the hotel, the bright day all about him desolate, unseen.

There was nothing, he thought, as he looked about him presently in the hotel bedroom, so melancholy as a vacated room, especially when the recent signs of occupation were still visible about him. Laura's suitcases on the bed, a second coat she had left behind. Traces of powder on the dressing-table. A tissue, with a lipstick smear, thrown in the waste-paper basket. Even an old tooth-paste tube squeezed dry, lying on the glass shelf above the wash-basin. Sounds of the heedless traffic on the Grand Canal came as always from the open window, but Laura wasn't there any more to listen to it, or to watch from the small balcony. The pleasure had gone. Feeling had gone.

John finished packing, and leaving all the baggage ready to be collected he went downstairs to pay the bill. The reception clerk was welcoming new arrivals. People were sitting on the terrace overlooking the Grand Canal reading newspapers, the pleasant day waiting to be planned.

John decided to have an early lunch, here on the hotel terrace, on familiar ground, and then have the porter carry the baggage to one of the ferries that steamed direct between San Marco and the Porta Roma, where the car was garaged.

The fiasco meal of the night before had left him empty, and he was ready for the trolley of hors d'oeuvres when they brought it to him, around midday. Even here, though, there was change. The head-waiter, their especial friend, was off-duty, and the table where they usually sat was occupied by new arrivals, a honeymoon couple, he told himself sourly, observing the gaiety, the smiles, while he had been shown to a small single table behind a tub of flowers.

'She's airborne now,' John thought, 'she's on her way,' and he tried to picture Laura seated between the Methodist ministers, telling them, no doubt, about Johnnie ill in hospital, and heaven knows what else besides. Well, the twin sisters anyway could rest in psychic peace. Their wishes would have been fulfilled.

Lunch over, there was no point in lingering with a cup of coffee on the terrace. His desire was to get away as soon as possible, fetch the car, and be en route for Milan. He made his farewells at the reception desk, and, escorted by a porter who had piled his baggage on to a wheeled trolley, made his way once more to the landing-stage of San Marco. As he stepped on to the steam-ferry, his luggage heaped beside him, a crowd of jostling people all about him, he had one momentary pang to be leaving Venice. When, if ever, he wondered, would they come again? Next year ... in three years. ... Glimpsed first on honeymoon, nearly ten years ago, and then a second visit, *en passant*, before a cruise, and now this last abortive ten days that had ended so abruptly.

The water glittered in the sunshine, buildings shone, tourists in dark glasses paraded up and down the rapidly receding Molo, already the terrace of their hotel was out of sight as the ferry churned its way up the Grand Canal. So many impressions to seize and hold, familiar loved façades, balconies, windows, water lapping the cellar steps of decaying palaces, the little red house where d'Annunzio lived, with its garden – our house, Laura called it, pretending it was theirs – and too soon the ferry would be turning left on the direct route to the Piazzale Roma, so missing the best of the Canal, the Rialto, the further palaces.

Another ferry was heading downstream to pass them, filled with passengers, and for a brief foolish moment he wished he could change places, be amongst the happy tourists bound for Venice and all he had left behind him. Then he saw her. Laura, in her scarlet coat, the twin sisters by her side, the active sister with her hand on Laura's arm, talking earnestly, and Laura herself, her hair blowing in the wind, gesticulating, on her face a look of distress. He stared, astounded, too astonished to shout, to wave, and anyway they would never have heard or seen him, for his own ferry had already passed and was heading in the opposite direction.

What the hell had happened? There must have been a holdup with the charter flight and it had never taken off, but in that case why had Laura not telephoned him at the hotel? And what were those damned sisters doing? Had she run into them at the airport? Was it coincidence? And why did she look so anxious? He could think of no explanation. Perhaps the flight had been cancelled. Laura, of course, would go straight to the hotel, expecting to find him there, intending, doubtless, to drive with him after all to Milan and take the train the following night. What a blasted mix-up. The only thing to do was to telephone the hotel immediately his ferry reached the Piazzale Roma and tell her to wait – he would return and fetch her. As for the damned interfering sisters, they could get stuffed.

The usual stampede ensued when the ferry arrived at the landing-stage. He had to find a porter to collect his baggage, and then wait while he discovered a telephone. The fiddling with change, the hunt for the number, delayed him still more. He succeeded at last in getting through, and luckily the reception clerk he knew was still at the desk.

'Look, there's been some frightful muddle,' he began, and explained how Laura was even now on her way back to the hotel – he had seen her with two friends on one of the ferry-services. Would the reception clerk explain and tell her to wait? He would be back by the next available service to collect her. 'In any event, detain her,' he said. 'I'll be as quick as I can.' The reception clerk understood perfectly, and John rang off.

Thank heaven Laura hadn't turned up before he had put through his call, or they would have told her he was on his way to Milan. The porter was still waiting with the baggage, and it seemed simplest to walk with him to the garage, hand everything over to the chap in charge of the office there and ask him to keep it for an hour, when he would be returning with his wife to pick up the car. Then he went back to the landing-station to await the next ferry to Venice. The minutes dragged, and he kept wondering all the time what had gone wrong at the airport and why in heaven's name Laura hadn't telephoned. No use conjecturing. She would tell him the whole story at the hotel. One thing was certain: he would not allow Laura and himself to be saddled with the sisters and become involved with their affairs. He could imagine Laura saying that they also had missed a flight, and could they have a lift to Milan?

Finally the ferry chugged alongside the landing-stage and he stepped aboard. What an anti-climax, thrashing back past the familiar sights to which he had bidden a nostalgic farewell such a short while ago! He didn't even look about him this time, he was so intent on reaching his destination. In

San Marco there were more people than ever, the afternoon crowds walking shoulder to shoulder, every one of them on pleasure bent.

He came to the hotel and pushed his way through the swing door, expecting to see Laura, and possibly the sisters, waiting in the lounge to the left of the entrance. She was not there. He went to the desk. The reception clerk he had spoken to on the telephone was standing there, talking to the manager.

'Has my wife arrived?' John asked.

'No, sir, not yet.'

'What an extraordinary thing. Are you sure?'

'Absolutely certain, sir. I have been here ever since you telephoned me at a quarter to two. I have not left the desk.'

'I just don't understand it. She was on one of the vaporettos passing by the Accademia. She would have landed at San Marco about five minutes later and come on here.'

The clerk seemed nonplussed. 'I don't know what to say. The signora was with friends, did you say?'

'Yes. Well, acquaintances. Two ladies we had met at Torcello yesterday. I was astonished to see her with them on the vaporetto, and of course I assumed that the flight had been cancelled, and she had somehow met up with them at the airport and decided to return here with them, to catch me before I left.'

Oh hell, what was Laura doing? It was after three. A matter of moments from San Marco landing-stage to the hotel.

'Perhaps the signora went with her friends to their hotel instead. Do you know where they are staying?'

'No,' said John, 'I haven't the slightest idea. What's more, I don't even know the names of the two ladies. They were sisters, twins, in fact – looked exactly alike. But anyway, why go to their hotel and not here?'

The swing-door opened but it wasn't Laura. Two people staying in the hotel.

The manager broke into the conversation. 'I tell you what I will do,' he said. 'I will telephone the airport and check about the flight. Then at least we will get somewhere.' He smiled apologetically. It was not usual for arrangements to go wrong.

'Yes, do that,' said John. 'We may as well know what happened there.'

He lit a cigarette and began to pace up and down the entrance hall. What a bloody mix-up. And how unlike Laura, who knew he would be setting off for Milan directly after lunch – indeed, for all she knew he might have gone before. But surely, in that case, she would have telephoned at once, on arrival at the airport, had the flight been cancelled? The manager was ages telephoning, he had to be put through on some other line, and his Italian was too rapid for John to follow the conversation. Finally he replaced the receiver.

'It is more mysterious than ever, sir,' he said. 'The charter flight was not delayed, it took off on schedule with a full complement of passengers. As far as they could tell me, there was no hitch. The signora must simply have changed her mind.' His smile was more apologetic than ever.

'Changed her mind,' John repeated. 'But why on earth should she do that? She was so anxious to be home tonight.'

The manager shrugged. 'You know how ladies can be, sir,' he said. 'Your wife may have thought that after all she would prefer to take the train to Milan with you. I do assure you, though, that the charter party was most respectable, and it was a Caravelle aircraft, perfectly safe.'

'Yes, yes,' said John impatiently, 'I don't blame your arrangements in the slightest. I just can't understand what induced her to change her mind, unless it was meeting with these two ladies.'

The manager was silent. He could not think of anything to say. The reception clerk was equally concerned. 'Is it possible,' he ventured, 'that you made a mistake, and it was not the signora that you saw on the vaporetto?'

'Oh no,' replied John, 'it was my wife, I assure you. She was wearing her red coat, she was hatless, just as she left here. I saw her as plainly as I can see you. I would swear to it in a court of law.'

'It is unfortunate,' said the manager, 'that we do not know the name of the two ladies, or the hotel where they were staying. You say you met these ladies at Torcello yesterday?'

'Yes ... but only briefly. They weren't staying there. At least, I am certain they were not. We saw them at dinner in Venice later, as it happens.'

'Excuse me....' Guests were arriving with luggage to check in, the clerk was obliged to attend to them. John turned in desperation to the manager. 'Do you think it would be any good telephoning the hotel in Torcello in case the people there knew the name of the ladies, or where they were staying in Venice?'

'We can try,' replied the manager. 'It is a small hope, but we can try.'

John resumed his anxious pacing, all the while watching the swing-door, hoping, praying, that he would catch sight of the red coat and Laura would enter. Once again there followed what seemed an interminable telephone conversation between the manager and someone at the hotel in Torcello.

'Tell them two sisters,' said John, 'two elderly ladies dressed in grey, both exactly alike. One lady was blind,' he added. The manager nodded. He was obviously giving a detailed description. Yet when he hung up he shook his head.

'The manager at Torcello says he remembers the two ladies well,' he told John, 'but they were only there for lunch. He never learnt their names.'

'Well, that's that. There's nothing to do now but wait.'

John lit his third cigarette and went out on to the terrace, to resume his pacing there. He stared out across the canal, searching the heads of the people on passing steamers, motorboats, even drifting gondolas. The minutes ticked by on his watch, and there was no sign of Laura. A terrible fore-boding nagged at him that somehow this was prearranged, that Laura had never intended to catch the aircraft, that last night in the restaurant she had made an assignation with the sisters. Oh God, he thought, that's impossible, I'm going paranoiac. . . . Yet why, why? No, more likely the encounter at the airport was fortuitous, and for some incredible reason they had persuaded Laura not to board the aircraft, even pre-vented her from doing so, trotting out one of their psychic visions, that the aircraft would crash, that she must return with them to Venice. And Laura, in her sensitive state, felt they must be right, swallowed it all without question.

But granted all these possibilities, why had she not come to the hotel? What was she doing? Four o'clock, half-past four, the sun no longer dappling the water. He went back to the reception desk.

'I just can't hang around,' he said. 'Even if she does turn up, we shall never make Milan this evening. I might see her walking with these ladies, in the Piazza San Marco, any-where. If she arrives while I'm out, will you explain?'

The clerk was full of concern. 'Indeed, yes,' he said. 'It is very worrying for you, sir. Would it perhaps be prudent if we booked you in here tonight?'

John gestured, helplessly. 'Perhaps, yes, I don't know. Maybe . . .'

He went out of the swing-door and began to walk towards the Piazza San Marco. He looked into every shop up and down the colonnades, crossed the piazza a dozen times, threaded his way between the tables in front of Florian's, in front of Quadri's, knowing that Laura's red coat and the distinctive appearance of the twin sisters could easily be spotted, even amongst this milling crowd, but there was no sign of them. He joined the crowd of shoppers in the Merceria, shoulder to shoulder with idlers, thrusters, window-gazers, knowing instinctively that it was useless, they wouldn't be here. Why should Laura have deliberately missed her flight to return to Venice for such a purpose? And even if she had done so, for some reason beyond his imagining, she would surely have come first to the hotel to find him.

The only thing left to him was to try to track down the sisters. Their hotel could be anywhere amongst the hundreds of hotels and pensions scattered through Venice, or even across the other side at the Zattere, or further again on the Giudecca. These last possibilities seemed remote. More likely they were staying in a small hotel or pension somewhere near San Zaccaria handy to the restaurant where they had dined last night. The blind one would surely not go far afield in the evening. He had been a fool not to have thought of this before, and he turned back and walked quickly away from the brightly lighted shopping district towards the narrower, more cramped quarter where they had dined last evening. He found the restaurant without difficulty, but they were not yet open for dinner, and the waiter preparing tables was not the one who had served them. John asked to see the *padrone*, and the waiter disappeared to the back regions, returning after a moment or two with the somewhat dishevelled-looking proprietor in shirt-sleeves, caught in a slack moment, not in full tenue.

'I had dinner here last night,' John explained. 'There were two ladies sitting at that table there in the corner.' He pointed to it.

'You wish to book that table for this evening?' asked the proprietor.

'No,' said John. 'No, there were two ladies there last night, two sisters, due sorelle, twins, gemelle' – what was the right word for twins? – 'Do you remember? Two ladies, sorelle vecchie . . .'

'Ah,' said the man, 'si, si, signore, la povera signorina.' He put his hands to his eyes to feign blindness. 'Yes, I remember.'

'Do you know their names?' asked John. 'Where they were staying? I am very anxious to trace them.'

The proprietor spread out his hands in a gesture of regret. 'I am ver' sorry, signore, I do not know the names of the signorine, they have been here once, twice, perhaps for din-ner, they do not say where they were staying. Perhaps if you come again tonight they might be here? Would you like to book a table?'

He pointed around him, suggesting a whole choice of tables that might appeal to a prospective diner, but John shook his head.

'Thank you, no. I may be dining elsewhere. I am sorry to have troubled you. If the signorine should come . . .' he paused, 'possibly I may return later,' he added. 'I am not sure.'

The proprietor bowed, and walked with him to the entrance. 'In Venice the whole world meets,' he said smiling. 'It is possible the signore will find his friends tonight. Arri-verderci, signore.'

Friends? John walked out into the street. More likely kid-nappers. . . . Anxiety had turned to fear, to panic. Something had gone terribly wrong. Those women had got hold of

Laura, played upon her suggestibility, induced her to go with them, either to their hotel or elsewhere. Should he find the Consulate? Where was it? What would he say when he got there? He began walking without purpose, finding himself, as they had done the night before, in streets he did not know, and suddenly came upon a tall building with the word 'Questura' above it. This is it, he thought. I don't care, something has happened, I'm going inside. There were a number of police in uniform coming and going, the place at any rate was active, and, addressing himself to one of them behind a glass partition, he asked if there was anyone who spoke English. The man pointed to a flight of stairs and John went up, entering a door on the right where he saw that another couple were sitting, waiting, and with relief he recognised them as fellow-countrymen, tourists, obviously a man and his wife, in some sort of predicament.

'Come and sit down,' said the man. 'We've waited half an hour but they can't be much longer. What a country! They wouldn't leave us like this at home.'

John took the proffered cigarette and found a chair beside them.

'What's your trouble?' he asked.

'My wife had her handbag pinched in one of those shops in the Merceria,' said the man. 'She simply put it down one moment to look at something, and you'd hardly credit it, the next moment it had gone. I say it was a sneak thief, she insists it was the girl behind the counter. But who's to say? These Ities are all alike. Anyway, I'm certain we shan't get it back. What have you lost?'

'Suitcase stolen,' John lied rapidly. 'Had some important papers in it.'

How could he say he had lost his wife? He couldn't even begin . . .

377

The man nodded in sympathy. 'As I said, these Ities are all alike. Old Musso knew how to deal with them. Too many Communists around these days. The trouble is, they're not going to bother with our troubles much, not with this murderer at large. They're all out looking for him.'

'Murderer? What murderer?' asked John.

'Don't tell me you've not heard about it?' The man stared at him in surprise. 'Venice has talked of nothing else. It's been in all the papers, on the radio, and even in the English papers. A grizzly business. One woman found with her throat slit last week – a tourist too – and some old chap discovered with the same sort of knife wound this morning. They seem to think it must be a maniac, because there doesn't seem to be any motive. Nasty thing to happen in Venice in the tourist season.'

'My wife and I never bother with the newspapers when we're on holiday,' said John. 'And we're neither of us much given to gossip in the hotel.'

'Very wise of you,' laughed the man. 'It might have spoilt your holiday, especially if your wife is nervous. Oh well, we're off tomorrow anyway. Can't say we mind, do we, dear?' He turned to his wife. 'Venice has gone downhill since we were here last. And now this loss of the handbag really is the limit.'

The door of the inner room opened, and a senior police officer asked John's companion and his wife to pass through.

'I bet we don't get any satisfaction,' murmured the tourist, winking at John, and he and his wife went into the inner room. The door closed behind them. John stubbed out his cigarette and lighted another. A strange feeling of unreality possessed him. He asked himself what he was doing here, what was the use of it? Laura was no longer in Venice but had disappeared, perhaps forever, with those diabolical sisters. She would never be traced. And just as the two of them had made up a fantastic story about the twins, when they first spotted them in Torcello, so, with nightmare logic, the fiction would have basis in fact; the women were in reality disguised crooks, men with criminal intent who lured unsuspecting persons to some appalling fate. They might even be the murderers for whom the police sought. Who would ever suspect two elderly women of respectable appearance, living quietly in some second-rate pension or hotel? He stubbed out his cigarette, unfinished.

'This,' he thought, 'is really the start of paranoia. This is the way people go off their heads.' He glanced at his watch. It was half-past six. Better pack this in, this futile quest here in police headquarters, and keep to the single link of sanity remaining. Return to the hotel, put a call through to the prep school in England, and ask about the latest news of Johnnie. He had not thought about poor Johnnie since sighting Laura on the vaporetto.

Too late, though. The inner door opened, the couple were ushered out.

'Usual clap-trap,' said the husband sotto voce to John. 'They'll do what they can. Not much hope. So many foreigners in Venice, all of 'em thieves! The locals all above reproach. Wouldn't pay 'em to steal from customers. Well, I wish you better luck.'

He nodded, his wife smiled and bowed, and they had gone. John followed the police officer into the inner room.

Formalities began. Name, address, passport. Length of stay in Venice, etc., etc. Then the questions, and John, the sweat beginning to appear on his forehead, launched into his interminable story. The first encounter with the sisters, the meeting at the restaurant, Laura's state of suggestibility because of the death of their child, the telegram about Johnnie, the decision to take the chartered flight, her departure, and her sudden inexplicable return. When he had finished he felt as exhausted as if he had driven three hundred miles non-stop after a severe bout of 'flu. His interrogator spoke excellent English with a strong Italian accent.

'You say,' he began, 'that your wife was suffering the after-effects of shock. This had been noticeable during your stay here in Venice?'

'Well, yes,' John replied, 'she had really been quite ill. The holiday didn't seem to be doing her much good. It was only when she met these two women at Torcello yesterday that her mood changed. The strain seemed to have gone. She was ready, I suppose, to snatch at every straw, and this belief that our little girl was watching over her had somehow restored her to what appeared normality.'

'It would be natural,' said the police officer, 'in the circum-stances. But no doubt the telegram last night was a further shock to you both?'

'Indeed, yes. That was the reason we decided to return home.'

'No argument between you? No difference of opinion?'

'None. We were in complete agreement. My one regret was that I could not go with my wife on this charter flight.'

The police officer nodded. 'It could well be that your wife had a sudden attack of amnesia, and meeting the two ladies served as a link, she clung to them for support. You have described them with great accuracy, and I think they should not be too difficult to trace. Meanwhile, I suggest you should return to your hotel, and we will get in touch with you as soon as we have news.'

At least, John thought, they believed his story. They did not consider him a crank who had made the whole thing up and was merely wasting their time.

'You appreciate,' he said, 'I am extremely anxious. These

women may have some criminal design upon my wife. One has heard of such things . . . .'

The police officer smiled for the first time. 'Please don't concern yourself,' he said. 'I am sure there will be some satisfactory explanation.'

All very well, thought John, but in heaven's name, what?

'I'm sorry,' he said, 'to have taken up so much of your time. Especially as I gather the police have their hands full hunting down a murderer who is still at large.'

He spoke deliberately. No harm in letting the fellow know that for all any of them could tell there might be some connection between Laura's disappearance and this other hideous affair.

'Ah, that,' said the police officer, rising to his feet. 'We hope to have the murderer under lock and key very soon.'

His tone of confidence was reassuring. Murderers, missing wives, lost handbags were all under control. They shook hands, and John was ushered out of the door and so downstairs. Perhaps, he thought, as he walked slowly back to the hotel, the fellow was right. Laura had suffered a sudden attack of amnesia, and the sisters happened to be at the airport and had brought her back to Venice, to their own hotel, because Laura couldn't remember where she and John had been staying. Perhaps they were even now trying to track down his hotel. Anyway, he could do nothing more. The police had everything in hand, and, please God, would come up with the solution. All he wanted to do right now was to collapse upon a bed with a stiff whisky, and then put through a call to Johnnie's school.

The page took him up in the lift to a modest room on the fourth floor at the rear of the hotel. Bare, impersonal, the shutters closed, with a smell of cooking wafting up from a courtyard down below.

'Ask them to send me up a double whisky, will you?' he said to the boy. 'And a ginger-ale,' and when he was alone he plunged his face under the cold tap in the wash-basin, relieved to find that the minute portion of visitor's soap afforded some measure of comfort. He flung off his shoes, hung his coat over the back of a chair and threw himself down on the bed. Somebody's radio was blasting forth an old popular song, now several seasons out of date, that had been one of Laura's favourites a couple of years ago. 'I love you, Baby ...' He reached for the telephone, and asked the exchange to put through the call to England. Then he closed his eyes, and all the while the insistent voice persisted, 'I love you, Baby ... I can't get you out of my mind.'

Presently there was a tap at the door. It was the waiter with his drink. Too little ice, such meagre comfort, but what desperate need. He gulped it down without the ginger-ale, and in a few moments the ever-nagging pain was eased, numbed, bringing, if only momentarily, a sense of calm. The telephone rang, and now, he thought, bracing himself for ultimate disaster, the final shock, Johnnie probably dying, or already dead. In which case nothing remained. Let Venice be engulfed ....

The exchange told him that the connection had been made, and in a moment he heard the voice of Mrs Hill at the other end of the line. They must have warned her that the call came from Venice, for she knew instantly who was speaking.

'Hullo?' she said. 'Oh, I am so glad you rang. All is well. Johnnie has had his operation, the surgeon decided to do it at midday rather than wait, and it was completely successful. Johnnie is going to be all right. So you don't have to worry any more, and will have a peaceful night.'

'Thank God,' he answered.

'I know,' she said, 'we are all so relieved. Now I'll get off the line and you can speak to your wife.'

John sat up on the bed, stunned. What the hell did she mean? Then he heard Laura's voice, cool and clear.

'Darling? Darling, are you there?'

He could not answer. He felt the hand holding the receiver go clammy cold with sweat. 'I'm here,' he whispered.

'It's not a very good line,' she said, 'but never mind. As Mrs Hill told you, all is well. Such a nice surgeon, and a very sweet Sister, on Johnnie's floor, and I really am happy about the way it's turned out. I came straight down here after landing at Gatwick – the flight O.K., by the way, but such a funny crowd, it'll make you hysterical when I tell you about them – and I went to the hospital, and Johnnie was coming round. Very dopey, of course, but so pleased to see me. And the Hills are being wonderful, I've got their spare room, and it's only a short taxi-drive into the town and the hospital. I shall go to bed as soon as we've had dinner, because I'm a bit fagged, what with the flight and the anxiety. How was the drive to Milan? And where are you staying?'

John did not recognise the voice that answered as his own. It was the automatic response of some computer.

'I'm not in Milan,' he said. 'I'm still in Venice.'

'Still in Venice? What on earth for? Wouldn't the car start?'

'I can't explain,' he said. 'There was a stupid sort of mix-up . . . .'

He felt suddenly so exhausted that he nearly dropped the receiver, and, shame upon shame, he could feel tears pricking behind his eyes.

'What sort of mix-up?' Her voice was suspicious, almost hostile. 'You weren't in a crash?'

'No ... no ... nothing like that.'

A moment's silence, and then she said, 'Your voice sounds very slurred. Don't tell me you went and got pissed.'

Oh Christ ... If she only knew! He was probably going to pass out any moment, but not from the whisky.

'I thought,' he said slowly, 'I thought I saw you, in a vaporetto, with those two sisters.'

What was the point of going on? It was hopeless trying to explain.

'How could you have seen me with the sisters?' she said. 'You knew I'd gone to the airport. Really, darling, you are an idiot. You seem to have got those two poor old dears on the brain. I hope you didn't say anything to Mrs Hill just now.'

'No.'

'Well, what are you going to do? You'll catch the train at Milan tomorrow, won't you?'

'Yes, of course,' he told her.

'I still don't understand what kept you in Venice,' she said. 'It all sounds a bit odd to me. However ... thank God Johnnie is going to be all right and I'm here.'

'Yes,' he said, 'yes.'

He could hear the distant boom-boom sound of a gong from the headmaster's hall.

'You had better go,' he said. 'My regards to the Hills, and my love to Johnnie.'

'Well, take care of yourself, darling, and for goodness' sake don't miss the train tomorrow, and drive carefully.'

The telephone clicked and she had gone. He poured the remaining drop of whisky into his empty glass, and sousing it with ginger-ale drank it down at a gulp. He got up, and crossing the room threw open the shutters and leant out of the window. He felt light-headed. His sense of relief, enormous, overwhelming, was somehow tempered with a curious feeling of unreality, almost as though the voice speaking from England had not been Laura's after all but a fake, and she was still in Venice, hidden in some furtive pension with the two sisters.

The point was, he *had* seen all three of them on the vaporetto. It was not another woman in a red coat. The women *had* been there, with Laura. So what was the explanation? That he was going off his head? Or something more sinister? The sisters, possessing psychic powers of formidable strength, had seen him as their two ferries had passed, and in some inexplicable fashion had made him believe Laura was with them. But why, and to what end? No, it didn't make sense. The only explanation was that he had been mistaken, the whole episode an hallucination. In which case he needed psychoanalysis, just as Johnnie had needed a surgeon.

And what did he do now? Go downstairs and tell the management he had been at fault and had just spoken to his wife, who had arrived in England safe and sound from her charter flight? He put on his shoes and ran his fingers through his hair. He glanced at his watch. It was ten minutes to eight. If he nipped into the bar and had a quick drink it would be easier to face the manager and admit what had happened. Then, perhaps, they would get in touch with the police. Profuse apologies all round for putting everyone to enormous trouble.

He made his way to the ground floor and went straight to the bar, feeling self-conscious, a marked man, half-imagining everyone would look at him, thinking, 'There's the fellow with the missing wife.' Luckily the bar was full and there wasn't a face he knew. Even the chap behind the bar was an underling who hadn't served him before. He downed his whisky and glanced over his shoulder to the reception hall. The desk was momentarily empty. He could see the

385

manager's back framed in the doorway of an inner room, talking to someone within. On impulse, coward-like, he crossed the hall and passed through the swing-door to the street outside.

'I'll have some dinner,' he decided, 'and then go back and face them. I'll feel more like it once I've some food inside me.'

He went to the restaurant nearby where he and Laura had dined once or twice. Nothing mattered any more, because she was safe. The nightmare lay behind him. He could enjoy his dinner, despite her absence, and think of her sitting down with the Hills to a dull, quiet evening, early to bed, and on the following morning going to the hospital to sit with Johnnie. Johnnie was safe, too. No more worries, only the awkward explanations and apologies to the manager at the hotel.

There was a pleasant anonymity sitting down at a corner table alone in the little restaurant, ordering vitello alla Marsala and half a bottle of Merlot. He took his time, enjoying his food but eating in a kind of haze, a sense of unreality still with him, while the conversation of his nearest neighbours had the same soothing effect as background music.

When they rose and left, he saw by the clock on the wall that it was nearly half-past nine. No use delaying matters any further. He drank his coffee, lighted a cigarette and paid his bill. After all, he thought, as he walked back to the hotel, the manager would be greatly relieved to know that all was well.

When he pushed through the swing-door, the first thing he noticed was a man in police uniform, standing talking to the manager at the desk. The reception clerk was there too. They turned as John approached, and the manager's face lighted up with relief.

'Eccolo!' he exclaimed. 'I was certain the signore would not be far away. Things are moving, signore. The two ladies have been traced, and they very kindly agreed to accompany the police to the Questura. If you will go there at once, this agente di polizia will escort you.'

John flushed. 'I have given everyone a lot of trouble,' he said. 'I meant to tell you before going out to dinner, but you were not at the desk. The fact is that I have contacted my wife. She did make the flight to London after all, and I spoke to her on the telephone. It was all a great mistake.'

The manager looked bewildered. 'The signora is in London?' he repeated. He broke off, and exchanged a rapid conversation in Italian with the policeman. 'It seems that the ladies maintain they did not go out for the day, except for a little shopping in the morning,' he said, turning back to John. 'Then who was it the signore saw on the vaporetto?'

John shook his head. 'A very extraordinary mistake on my part which I still don't understand,' he said. 'Obviously, I did not see either my wife or the two ladies. I really am extremely sorry.'

More rapid conversation in Italian. John noticed the clerk watching him with a curious expression in his eyes. The manager was obviously apologising on John's behalf to the policeman, who looked annoyed and gave tongue to this effect, his voice increasing in volume, to the manager's concern. The whole business had undoubtedly given enormous trouble to a great many people, not least the two unfortunate sisters.

'Look,' said John, interrupting the flow, 'will you tell the agente I will go with him to headquarters and apologise in person both to the police officer and to the ladies?'

The manager looked relieved. 'If the signore would take the trouble,' he said. 'Naturally, the ladies were much distressed when a policeman interrogated them at their hotel, and they offered to accompany him to the Questura only because they were so distressed about the signora.'

John felt more and more uncomfortable. Laura must never learn any of this. She would be outraged. He wondered if there were some penalty for giving the police misleading information involving a third party. His error began, in retrospect, to take on criminal proportions.

He crossed the Piazza San Marco, now thronged with after-dinner strollers and spectators at the cafés, all three orchestras going full blast in harmonious rivalry, while his companion kept a discreet two paces to his left and never uttered a word.

They arrived at the police station and mounted the stairs to the same inner room where he had been before. He saw immediately that it was not the officer he knew but another who sat behind the desk, a sallow-faced individual with a sour expression, while the two sisters, obviously upset – the active one in particular – were seated on chairs nearby, some underling in uniform standing behind them. John's escort went at once to the police officer, speaking in rapid Italian, while John himself, after a moment's hesitation, advanced towards the sisters.

'There has been a terrible mistake,' he said. 'I don't know how to apologise to you both. It's all my fault, mine entirely, the police are not to blame.'

The active sister made as though to rise, her mouth twitching nervously, but he restrained her.

'We don't understand,' she said, the Scots inflection strong. 'We said goodnight to your wife last night at dinner, and we have not seen her since. The police came to our pension more than an hour ago and told us your wife was missing and you had filed a complaint against us. My sister is not very strong. She was considerably disturbed.'

'A mistake. A frightful mistake,' he repeated.

He turned towards the desk. The police officer was

addressing him, his English very inferior to that of the previous interrogator. He had John's earlier statement on the desk in front of him, and tapped it with a pencil.

'So?' he queried. 'This document all lies? You not speaka the truth?'

'I believed it to be true at the time,' said John. 'I could have sworn in a court of law that I saw my wife with these two ladies on a vaporetto in the Grand Canal this afternoon. Now I realise I was mistaken.'

'We have not been near the Grand Canal all day,' protested the sister, 'not even on foot. We made a few purchases in the Merceria this morning, and remained indoors all afternoon. My sister was a little unwell. I have told the police officer this a dozen times, and the people at the pension would corroborate our story. He refused to listen.'

'And the signora?' rapped the police officer angrily. 'What happen to the signora?'

'The signora, my wife, is safe in England,' explained John patiently. 'I talked to her on the telephone just after seven. She did join the charter flight from the airport, and is now staying with friends.'

'Then who you see on the vaporetto in the red coat?' asked the furious police officer. 'And if not these signorine here, then what signorine?'

'My eyes deceived me,' said John, aware that his English was likewise becoming strained. 'I think I see my wife and these ladies but no, it was not so. My wife in aircraft, these ladies in pension all the time.'

It was like talking stage Chinese. In a moment he would be bowing and putting his hands in his sleeves.

The police officer raised his eyes to heaven and thumped the table. 'So all this work for nothing,' he said. 'Hotels and pensiones searched for the signorine and a missing signora inglese, when here we have plenty, plenty other things to do. You maka a mistake. You have perhaps too much vino at mezzo giorno and you see hundred signore in red coats in hundred vaporetti.' He stood up, rumpling the papers on his desk. 'And you, signorine,' he said, 'you wish to make complaint against this person?' He was addressing the active sister.

'Oh no,' she said, 'no, indeed. I quite see it was all a mistake. Our only wish is to return at once to our pension.'

The police officer grunted. Then he pointed at John. 'You very lucky man,' he said. 'These signorine could file complaint against you – very serious matter.'

'I'm sure,' began John, 'I'll do anything in my power . . .'

'Please don't think of it,' exclaimed the sister, horrified. 'We would not hear of such a thing.' It was her turn to apologise to the police officer. 'I hope we need not take up any more of your valuable time,' she said.

He waved a hand of dismissal and spoke in Italian to the underling. 'This man walk with you to the pension,' he said. 'Buona sera, signorine,' and, ignoring John, he sat down again at his desk.

'I'll come with you,' said John. 'I want to explain exactly what happened.'

They trooped down the stairs and out of the building, the blind sister leaning on her twin's arm, and once outside she turned her sightless eyes to John.

'You saw us,' she said, 'and your wife too. But not today. You saw us in the future.'

Her voice was softer than her sister's, slower, she seemed to have some slight impediment in her speech.

'I don't follow,' replied John, bewildered.

He turned to the active sister and she shook her head at him, frowning, and put her finger on her lips.

'Come along, dear,' she said to her twin. 'You know you're very tired, and I want to get you home.' Then, sotto voce to John, 'She's psychic. Your wife told you, I believe, but I don't want her to go into trance here in the street.'

God forbid, thought John, and the little procession began to move slowly along the street, away from police headquarters, a canal to the left of them. Progress was slow, because of the blind sister, and there were two bridges. John was completely lost after the first turning, but it couldn't have mattered less. Their police escort was with them, and anyway, the sisters knew where they were going.

'I must explain,' said John softly. 'My wife would never forgive me if I didn't,' and as they walked he went over the whole inexplicable story once again, beginning with the telegram received the night before and the conversation with Mrs Hill, the decision to return to England the following day, Laura by air, and John himself by car and train. It no longer sounded as dramatic as it had done when he had made his statement to the police officer, when, possibly because of his conviction of something uncanny, the description of the two vaporettos passing one another in the middle of the Grand Canal had held a sinister quality, suggesting abduction on the part of the sisters, the pair of them holding a bewildered Laura captive. Now that neither of the women had any further menace for him he spoke more naturally, yet with great sincerity, feeling for the first time that they were somehow both in sympathy with him and would understand.

'You see,' he explained, in a final endeavour to make amends for having gone to the police in the first place, 'I truly believed I had seen you with Laura, and I thought ...' he hesitated, because this had been the police officer's suggestion and not his, 'I thought that perhaps Laura had some sudden loss of memory, had met you at the airport, and you had brought her back to Venice to wherever you were staying.'

They had crossed a large square and were approaching a house at one end of it, with a sign 'Pensione' above the door. Their escort paused at the entrance.

'Is this it?' asked John.

'Yes,' said the sister. 'I know it is nothing much from the outside, but it is clean and comfortable, and was recommended by friends.' She turned to the escort. 'Grazie,' she said to him, 'grazie tanto.'

The man nodded briefly, wished them 'Buona notte,' and disappeared across the campo.

'Will you come in?' asked the sister. 'I am sure we can find you some coffee, or perhaps you prefer tea?'

'No, really,' John thanked her, 'I must get back to the hotel. I'm making an early start in the morning. I just want to make quite sure you do understand what happened, and that you forgive me.'

'There is nothing to forgive,' she replied. 'It is one of the many examples of second sight that my sister and I have experienced time and time again, and I should very much like to record it for our files, if you will permit it.'

'Well, as to that, of course,' he told her, 'but I myself find it hard to understand. It has never happened to me before.'

'Not consciously, perhaps,' she said, 'but so many things happen to us of which we are not aware. My sister felt you had psychic understanding. She told your wife. She also told your wife, last night in the restaurant, that you were to experience trouble, danger, that you should leave Venice. Well, don't you believe now that the telegram was proof of this? Your son was ill, possibly dangerously ill, and so it was necessary for you to return home immediately. Heaven be praised your wife flew home to be by his side.'

'Yes, indeed,' said John, 'but why should I see her on the vaporetto with you and your sister when she was actually on her way to England?'

'Thought transference, perhaps,' she answered. 'Your wife may have been thinking about us. We gave her our address, should you wish to get in touch with us. We shall be here another ten days. And she knows that we would pass on any message that my sister might have from your little one in the spirit world.'

'Yes,' said John awkwardly, 'yes, I see. It's very good of you.' He had a sudden rather unkind picture of the two sisters putting on headphones in their bedroom, listening for a coded message from poor Christine. 'Look, this is our address in London,' he said. 'I know Laura will be pleased to hear from you.'

He scribbled their address on a sheet torn from his pocket-diary, even, as a bonus thrown in, the telephone number, and handed it to her. He could imagine the outcome. Laura springing it on him one evening that the 'old dears' were passing through London on their way to Scotland, and the least they could do was to offer them hospitality, even the spare-room for the night. Then a seance in the living-room, tambourines appearing out of thin air.

'Well, I must be off,' he said. 'Goodnight, and apologies, once again, for all that has happened this evening.' He shook hands with the first sister, then turned to her blind twin. 'I hope,' he said, 'that you are not too tired.'

The sightless eyes were disconcerting. She held his hand fast and would not let it go. 'The child,' she said, speaking in an odd staccato voice, 'the child . . . I can see the child . . .'

and then, to his dismay, a bead of froth appeared at the corner of her mouth, her head jerked back, and she half-collapsed in her sister's arms.

'We must get her inside,' said the sister hurriedly. 'It's all right, she's not ill, it's the beginning of a trance state.'

Between them they helped the twin, who had gone rigid, into the house, and sat her down on the nearest chair, the sister supporting her. A woman came running from some inner room. There was a strong smell of spaghetti from the back regions. 'Don't worry,' said the sister, 'the signorina and I can manage. I think you had better go. Sometimes she is sick after these turns.'

'I'm most frightfully sorry . . .' John began, but the sister had already turned her back, and with the signorina was bending over her twin, from whom peculiar choking sounds were proceeding. He was obviously in the way, and after a final gesture of courtesy, 'Is there anything I can do?', which received no reply, he turned on his heel and began walking across the square. He looked back once, and saw they had closed the door.

What a finale to the evening! And all his fault. Poor old girls, first dragged to police headquarters and put through an interrogation, and then a psychic fit on top of it all. More likely epilepsy. Not much of a life for the other sister, but she seemed to take it in her stride. An additional hazard, though, if it happened in a restaurant or in the street. And not particularly welcome under his and Laura's roof should the sisters ever find themselves beneath it, which he prayed would never happen.

Meanwhile, where the devil was he? The square, with the inevitable church at one end, was quite deserted. He could not remember which way they had come from police headquarters, there had seemed to be so many turnings.

Wait a minute, the church itself had a familiar appearance. He drew nearer to it, looking for the name which was sometimes on notices at the entrance. San Giovanni in Bragora, that rang a bell. He and Laura had gone inside one morning to look at a painting by Cima da Conegliano. Surely it was only a stone's throw from the Riva degli Schiavoni and the open wide waters of the San Marco lagoon, with all the bright lights of civilisation and the strolling tourists? He remembered taking a small turning from the Schiavoni and they had arrived at the church. Wasn't that the alley-way ahead? He plunged along it, but halfway down he hesitated. It didn't seem right, although it was familiar for some unknown reason.

Then he realised that it was not the alley they had taken the morning they visited the church, but the one they had walked along the previous evening, only he was approaching it from the opposite direction. Yes, that was it, in which case it would be quicker to go on and cross the little bridge over the narrow canal, and he would find the Arsenal on his left and the street leading down to the Riva degli Schiavoni to his right. Simpler than retracing his steps and getting lost once more in the maze of back streets.

He had almost reached the end of the alley, and the bridge was in sight, when he saw the child. It was the same little girl with the pixie-hood who had leapt between the tethered boats the preceding night and vanished up the cellar steps of one of the houses. This time she was running from the direction of the church the other side, making for the bridge. She was running as if her life depended on it, and in a moment he saw why. A man was in pursuit, who, when she glanced backwards for a moment, still running, flattened himself against a wall, believing himself unobserved. The child came on, scampering across the bridge, and John, fearful of alarming her further, backed into an open doorway that led into a small court.

He remembered the drunken yell of the night before which had come from one of the houses near where the man was hiding now. This is it, he thought, the fellow's after her again, and with a flash of intuition he connected the two events, the child's terror then and now, and the murders reported in the newspapers, supposedly the work of some madman. It could be coincidence, a child running from a drunken relative, and yet, and yet ... His heart began thumping in his chest, instinct warning him to run himself, now, at once, back along the alley the way he had come – but what about the child? What was going to happen to the child?

Then he heard her running steps. She hurtled through the open doorway into the court in which he stood, not seeing him, making for the rear of the house that flanked it, where steps led presumably to a back entrance. She was sobbing as she ran, not the ordinary cry of a frightened child, but the panic-stricken intake of breath of a helpless being in despair. Were there parents in the house who would protect her, whom he could warn? He hesitated a moment, then followed her down the steps and through the door at the bottom, which had burst open at the touch of her hands as she hurled herself against it.

'It's all right,' he called. 'I won't let him hurt you, it's all right,' cursing his lack of Italian, but possibly an English voice might reassure her. But it was no use – she ran sobbing up another flight of stairs, which were spiral, twisting, leading to the floor above, and already it was too late for him to retreat. He could hear sounds of the pursuer in the courtyard behind, someone shouting in Italian, a dog barking. This is it, he thought, we're in it together, the child and I. Unless we can bolt some inner door above he'll get us both.

He ran up the stairs after the child, who had darted into a room leading off a small landing, and followed her inside and slammed the door, and, merciful heaven, there was a bolt which he rammed into its socket. The child was crouching by the open window. If he shouted for help someone would surely hear, someone would surely come before the man in pursuit threw himself against the door and it gave, because there was no one but themselves, no parents, the room was bare except for a mattress on an old bed, and a heap of rags in one corner.

'It's all right,' he panted, 'it's all right,' and held out his hand, trying to smile.

The child struggled to her feet and stood before him, the pixie-hood falling from her head on to the floor. He stared at her, incredulity turning to horror, to fear. It was not a child at all but a little thick-set woman dwarf, about three feet high, with a great square adult head too big for her body, grey locks hanging shoulder-length, and she wasn't sobbing any more, she was grinning at him, nodding her head up and down.

Then he heard the footsteps on the landing outside and the hammering on the door, and a barking dog, and not one voice but several voices, shouting, 'Open up! Police!' The creature fumbled in her sleeve, drawing a knife, and as she threw it at him with hideous strength, piercing his throat, he stumbled and fell, the sticky mess covering his protecting hands.

And he saw the vaporetto with Laura and the two sisters steaming down the Grand Canal, not today, not tomorrow, but the day after that, and he knew why they were together and for what sad purpose they had come. The creature was gibbering in its corner. The hammering and the voices and the barking dog grew fainter, and, 'Oh God,' he thought, 'what a bloody silly way to die. . . .'

JEANETTE WINTERSON

THE QUEEN OF SPADES

From

THE PASSION

THERE IS A CITY surrounded by water with watery alleys that do for streets and roads and silted up back ways that only the rats can cross. Miss your way, which is easy to do, and you may find yourself staring at a hundred eyes guarding a filthy palace of sacks and bones. Find your way, which is easy to do, and you may meet an old woman in a doorway. She will tell your fortune, depending on your face.

This is the city of mazes. You may set off from the same place to the same place every day and never go by the same route. If you do so, it will be by mistake. Your bloodhound nose will not serve you here. Your course in compass reading will fail you. Your confident instructions to passers-by will send them to squares they have never heard of, over canals not listed in the notes.

Although wherever you are going is always in front of you, there is no such thing as straight ahead. No as the crow flies short cut will help you to reach the café just over the water. The short cuts are where the cats go, through the impossible gaps, round corners that seem to take you the opposite way. But here, in this mercurial city, it is required you do awake your faith.

With faith, all things are possible.

Rumour has it that the inhabitants of this city walk on water. That, more bizarre still, their feet are webbed. Not all feet, but the feet of the boatmen whose trade is hereditary.

This is the legend.

When a boatman's wife finds herself pregnant she waits until the moon is full and the night empty of idlers. Then she takes her husband's boat and rows to a terrible island where the dead are buried. She leaves her boat with rosemary in the bows so that the limbless ones cannot return with her and hurries to the grave of the most recently dead in her family. She has brought her offerings: a flask of wine, a lock of hair from her husband and a silver coin. She must leave the offerings on the grave and beg for a clean heart if her child be a girl and boatman's feet if her child be a boy. There is no time to lose. She must be home before dawn and the boat must be left for a day and a night covered in salt. In this way, the boatmen keep their secrets and their trade. No newcomer can compete. And no boatman will take off his boots, no matter how you bribe him. I have seen tourists throw diamonds to the fish, but I have never seen a boatman take off his boots.

There was once a weak and foolish man whose wife cleaned the boat and sold the fish and brought up their children and went to the terrible island as she should when her yearly time was due. Their house was hot in summer and cold in winter and there was too little food and too many mouths. This boatman, ferrying a tourist from one church to another, happened to fall into conversation with the man and the man brought up the question of the webbed feet. At the same time he drew a purse of gold from his pocket and let it lie quietly in the bottom of the boat. Winter was approaching, the boatman was thin and he thought what harm could it do to unlace just one boot and let this visitor see what there was. The next morning, the boat was picked up by a couple of priests on their way to Mass. The tourist was babbling incoherently and pulling at his toes with his fingers. There was no boatman. They took the tourist to the

402

madhouse, San Servelo, a quiet place that caters for the well-off and defective. For all I know, he's still there.

And the boatman?

He was my father.

I never knew him because I wasn't born when he disappeared.

A few weeks after my mother had been left with an empty boat she discovered she was pregnant. Although her future was uncertain and she wasn't strictly speaking married to a boatman any more, she decided to go ahead with the gloomy ritual, and on the appropriate night she rowed her way silently across the lagoon. As she fastened the boat, an owl flew very low and caught her on the shoulder with its wing. She was not hurt but she cried out and stepped back and, as she did so, dropped the sprig of rosemary into the sea. For a moment she thought of returning straight away but, crossing herself, she hurried to her father's grave and placed her offerings. She knew her husband should have been the one, but he had no grave. How like him, she thought, to be as absent in death as he was in life. Her deed done, she pushed off from the shore that even the crabs avoided and later covered the boat in so much salt that it sank.

The Blessed Virgin must have protected her. Even before I was born she had married again. This time, a prosperous baker who could afford to take Sundays off.

The hour of my birth coincided with an eclipse of the sun and my mother did her best to slow down her labour until it had passed. But I was as impatient then as I am now and I forced my head out while the midwife was downstairs heating some milk. A fine head with a crop of red hair and a pair of eyes that made up for the sun's eclipse.

A girl.

It was an easy birth and the midwife held me upside down

by the ankles until I bawled. But it was when they spread me out to dry that my mother fainted and the midwife felt forced to open another bottle of wine.

My feet were webbed.

There never was a girl whose feet were webbed in the entire history of the boatmen. My mother in her swoon had visions of rosemary and blamed herself for her carelessness. Or perhaps it was her carefree pleasure with the baker she should blame herself for? She hadn't thought of my father since his boat had sunk. She hadn't thought of him much while it was afloat. The midwife took out her knife with the thick blade and proposed to cut off the offending parts straight away. My mother weakly nodded, imagining I would feel no pain or that pain for a moment would be better than embarrassment for a lifetime. The midwife tried to make an incision in the translucent triangle between my first two toes but her knife sprang from the skin leaving no mark. She tried again and again in between all the toes on each foot. She bent the point of the knife, but that was all.

'It's the Virgin's will,' she said at last, finishing the bottle. 'There's no knife can get through that.'

My mother started to weep and wail and continued in this way until my stepfather came home. He was a man of the world and not easily put off by a pair of webbed feet.

'No one will see so long as she wears shoes and when it comes to a husband, why it won't be the feet he'll be interested in.'

This comforted my mother somewhat and we passed the next eighteen years in a normal family way.

Since Bonaparte captured our city of mazes in 1797, we've more or less abandoned ourselves to pleasure. What else is there to do when you've lived a proud and free life and suddenly you're not proud and free any more? We became an enchanted island for the mad, the rich, the bored, the perverted. Our glory days were behind us but our excess was just beginning. That man demolished our churches on a whim and looted our treasures. That woman of his has jewels in her crown that come out of St Mark's. But of all sorrows, he has our living horses cast by men who stretched their arms between the Devil and God and imprisoned life in a brazen form. He took them from the Basilica and has thrown them up in some readymade square in that tart of towns, Paris.

There were four churches that I loved, which stood looking out across the lagoon to the quiet islands that lie about us. He tore them down to make a public garden. Why did we want a public garden? And if we had and if we had chosen it ourselves we would never have filled it with hundreds of pines laid out in regimental rows. They say Joséphine's a botanist. Couldn't she have found us something a little more exotic? I don't hate the French. My father likes them. They've made his business thrive with their craving for foolish cakes.

He gave me a French name too.

Villanelle. It's pretty enough.

I don't hate the French. I ignore them.

When I was eighteen I started to work the Casino. There aren't many jobs for a girl. I didn't want to go into the bakery and grow old with red hands and forearms like thighs. I couldn't be a dancer, for obvious reasons, and what I would have most liked to have done, worked the boats, was closed to me on account of my sex.

I did take a boat out sometimes, rowing alone for hours up and down the canals and out into the lagoon. I learned the secret ways of boatmen, by watching and by instinct.

If ever I saw a stern disappearing down a black, inhospitable-looking waterway, I followed it and discovered the city within the city that is the knowledge of a few. In this inner city are thieves and Jews and children with slant eyes who come from the eastern wastelands without father or mother. They roam in packs like the cats and the rats and they go after the same food. No one knows why they are here or on what sinister vessel they arrived. They seem to die at twelve or thirteen and yet they are always replaced. I've watched them take a knife to each other for a filthy pile of chicken.

There are exiles too. Men and women driven out of their gleaming palaces that open so elegantly on to shining canals. Men and women who are officially dead according to the registers of Paris. They're here, with the odd bit of gold plate stuffed in a bag as they fled. So long as the Jews will buy the plate and the plate holds out, they survive. When you see the floating corpses belly upwards, you know the gold is ended.

One woman who kept a fleet of boats and a string of cats and dealt in spices lives here now, in the silent city. I cannot tell how old she may be, her hair is green with slime from the walls of the nook she lives in. She feeds on vegetable matter that snags against the stones when the tide is sluggish. She has no teeth. She has no need of teeth. She still wears the curtains that she dragged from her drawing-room window as she left. One curtain she wraps round herself and the other she drapes over her shoulders like a cloak. She sleeps like this.

I've spoken to her. When she hears a boat go by her head pokes out of her nook and she asks you what time of day it might be. Never what time it is; she's too much of a philosopher for that. I saw her once, at evening, her ghoulish hair lit by a lamp she has. She was spreading pieces of rancid meat on a cloth. There were wine goblets beside her.

'I'm having guests to dinner,' she shouted, as I glided past on the other side. 'I would have invited you, but I don't know your name.'

'Villanelle,' I shouted back.

'You're a Venetian, but you wear your name as a disguise. Beware the dice and games of chance.'

She turned back to her cloth and, although we met again, she never used my name, nor gave any sign that she recognised me.

I went to work in the Casino, raking dice and spreading cards and lifting wallets where I could. There was a cellarful of champagne drunk every night and a cruel dog kept hungry to deal with anyone who couldn't pay. I dressed as a boy because that's what the visitors liked to see. It was part of the game, trying to decide which sex was hidden behind tight breeches and extravagant face-paste ...

It was August. Bonaparte's birthday and a hot night. We were due for a celebration ball in the Piazza San Marco, though what we Venetians had to celebrate was not clear. In keeping with our customs, the ball was to be fancy dress and the Casino was arranging outdoor gaming tables and booths of chance. Our city swarmed with French and Austrian pleasure-seekers, the usual bewildered stream of English and even a party of Russians intent on finding satisfaction. Satisfying our guests is what we do best. The price is high but the pleasure is exact.

I made up my lips with vermilion and overlaid my face with white powder. I had no need to add a beauty spot, having one of my own in just the right place. I wore my yellow Casino breeches with the stripe down each side of the leg and a pirate's shirt that concealed my breasts. This was required, but the moustache I added was for my own amusement. And perhaps for my own protection. There are too many dark alleys and too many drunken hands on festival nights.

Across our matchless square that Bonaparte had contemptuously called the finest drawing-room in Europe, our engineers had rigged a wooden frame alive with gunpowder. This was to be triggered at midnight and I was optimistic that, with so many heads looking up, so many pockets would be vulnerable.

The ball began at eight o'clock and I began my night drawing cards in the booth of chance.

Queen of spades you win, Ace of clubs you lose. Play again. What will you risk? Your watch? Your house? Your mistress? I like to smell the urgency on them. Even the calmest, the richest, have that smell. It's somewhere between fear and sex. Passion I suppose.

There's a man who comes to play Chance with me most nights at the Casino. A large man with pads of flesh on his palms like baker's dough. When he squeezes my neck from behind, the sweat on his palms makes them squeak. I always carry a handkerchief. He wears a green waistcoat and I've seen him stripped to that waistcoat because he can't let the dice roll without following it. He has funds. He must have. He spends in a moment what I earn in a month. He's cunning though, for all his madness at the table. Most men wear their pockets or their purses on their sleeves when they're drunk. They want everyone to know how rich they are, how fat with gold. Not him. He has a bag down his trousers and he dips into it with his back turned. I'll never pick that one.

I don't know what else might be down there.

He wonders the same thing about me. I catch him staring at my crotch and now and again I wear a codpiece to taunt him. My breasts are small, so there's no cleavage to give me away, and I'm tall for a girl, especially a Venetian.

I wonder what he'd say to my feet.

Tonight, he's wearing his best suit and his moustache gleams. I fan the cards before him; close them, shuffle them, fan them again. He chooses. Too low to win. Choose again. Too high. Forfeit. He laughs and tosses a coin across the counter.

'You've grown a moustache since two days ago.'

'I come from a hairy family.'

'It suits you.' His eyes stray as usual, but I am firmly behind the booth. He takes out another coin. I spread. The Jack of hearts. An ill-omened card but he doesn't think so, he promises to return and taking the Jack with him for luck moves over to the gaming table. His bottom strains his jacket. They're always taking the cards. I wonder whether to get out another pack or just cheat the next customer. I think that will depend on who the next customer might be.

I love the night. In Venice, a long time ago, when we had our own calendar and stayed aloof from the world, we began the days at night. What use was the sun to us when our trade and our secrets and our diplomacy depended on darkness? In the dark you are in disguise and this is the city of disguises. In those days (I cannot place them in time because time is to do with daylight), in those days when the sun went down we opened our doors and slid along the eely waters with a hooded light in our prow. All our boats were black then and left no mark on the water where they sat. We were dealing in perfume and silk. Emeralds and diamonds. Affairs of State. We didn't build our bridges simply to avoid walking on water. Nothing so obvious. A bridge is a meeting place. A neutral place. A casual place. Enemies will choose to meet on a bridge and end their quarrel in that void. One will cross to the other side. The other will not return. For lovers, a bridge is a possibility, a metaphor of their chances. And for the traffic in whispered goods, where else but a bridge in the night?

We are a philosophical people, conversant with the nature of greed and desire, holding hands with the Devil and God. We would not wish to let go of either. This living bridge is tempting to all and you may lose your soul or find it here.

And our own souls?

They are Siamese.

Nowadays, the dark has more light than in the old days. There are flares everywhere and soldiers like to see the streets lit up, like to see some reflection on the canals. They don't trust our soft feet and thin knives. None the less, darkness can be found; in the under-used waterways or out on the lagoon. There's no dark like it. It's soft to the touch and heavy in the hands. You can open your mouth and let it sink into you till it makes a close ball in your belly. You can juggle with it, dodge it, swim in it. You can open it like a door.

The old Venetians had eyes like cats that cut the densest night and took them through impenetrable ways without stumbling. Even now, if you look at us closely you will find that some of us have slit eyes in the daylight.

I used to think that darkness and death were probably the same. That death was the absence of light. That death was nothing more than the shadow-lands where people bought and sold and loved as usual but with less conviction. The night seems more temporary than the day, especially to lovers, and it also seems more uncertain. In this way it sums up our lives, which are uncertain and temporary. We forget about that in the day. In the day we go on for ever. This is the city of uncertainty, where routes and faces look alike and are not. Death will be like that. We will be forever recognising people we have never met.

But darkness and death are not the same.

The one is temporary, the other is not.

Our funerals are fabulous affairs. We hold them at night, returning to our dark roots. The black boats skim the water and the coffin is crossed with jet. From my upper window that overlooks two intersecting canals, I once saw a rich man's cortège of fifteen boats (the number must be odd) glide out to the lagoon. At the same moment, a pauper's boat, carrying a coffin not varnished but covered in pitch, floated out too, rowed by an old woman with scarcely enough strength to drag the oars. I thought they would collide, but the rich man's boatmen pulled away. Then his widow motioned with her hand and the cortège opened the line at the eleventh boat and made room for the pauper, tossing a rope round the prow so that the old woman had only to guide her craft. They continued thus towards the terrible island of San Michele and I lost sight of them.

For myself, if I am to die, I would like to do it alone, far from the world. I would like to lie on the warm stone in May until my strength is gone, then drop gently into the canal. Such things are still possible in Venice.

Nowadays, the night is designed for the pleasure-seekers and tonight, by their reckoning, is a *tour de force*. There are fire-eaters frothing at the mouth with yellow tongues. There is a dancing bear. There is a troupe of little girls, their sweet bodies hairless and pink, carrying sugared almonds in copper dishes. There are women of every kind and not all of them are women. In the centre of the square, the workers on Murano have fashioned a huge glass slipper that is constantly filled and re-filled with champagne. To drink from it you must lap like a dog and how these visitors love it. One has already drowned, but what is one death in the midst of so much life?

From the wooden frame above where the gunpowder waits there are also suspended a number of nets and trapezes. From here acrobats swing over the square, casting grotesque shadows on the dancers below. Now and again, one will dangle by the knees and snatch a kiss from whoever is standing below. I like such kisses. They fill the mouth and leave the body free. To kiss well one must kiss solely. No groping hands or stammering hearts. The lips and the lips alone are the pleasure. Passion is sweeter split strand by strand. Divided and re-divided like mercury then gathered up only at the last moment.

You see, I am no stranger to love.

It's getting late, who comes here with a mask over her face? Will she try the cards?

She does. She holds a coin in her palm so that I have to pick it out. Her skin is warm. I spread the cards. She chooses. The ten of diamonds. The three of clubs. Then the Queen of spades.

'A lucky card. The symbol of Venice. You win.'

She smiled at me and pulling away her mask revealed a pair of grey-green eyes with flecks of gold. Her cheekbones were high and rouged. Her hair, darker and redder than mine.

'Play again?'

She shook her head and had a waiter bring over a bottle of champagne. Not any champagne. Madame Clicquot. The only good thing to come out of France. She held the glass in a silent toast, perhaps to her own good fortune. The Queen of spades is a serious win and one we are usually careful to avoid. Still she did not speak, but watched me through the crystal and suddenly draining her glass stroked the side of my face. Only for a second she touched me and then she was gone and I was left with my heart smashing at my chest and three-quarters of a bottle of the best champagne. I was careful to conceal both.

I am pragmatic about love and have taken my pleasure with both men and women, but I have never needed a guard for my heart. My heart is a reliable organ.

At midnight the gunpowder was triggered and the sky above St Mark's broke into a million coloured pieces. The fireworks lasted perhaps half an hour and during that time I was able to finger enough money to bribe a friend to take over my booth for a while. I slipped through the press towards the still bubbling glass slipper looking for her.

She had vanished. There were faces and dresses and masks and kisses to be had and a hand at every turn but she was not there. I was detained by an infantryman who held up two glass balls and asked if I would exchange them for mine. But I was in no mood for charming games and pushed past him, my eyes begging for a sign.

The roulette table. The gaming table. The fortune tellers. The fabulous three-breasted woman. The singing ape. The double-speed dominoes and the tarot.

She was not there.

She was nowhere.

My time was up and I went back to the booth of chance full of champagne and an empty heart.

'There was a woman looking for you,' said my friend. 'She left this.'

On the table was an earring. Roman by the look of it, curiously shaped, made of that distinct old yellow gold that these times do not know.

I put it in my ear and, spreading the cards in a perfect

413

fan, took out the Queen of spades. No one else should win tonight. I would keep her card until she needed it.

Gaiety soon ages.

By three o'clock the revellers were drifting away through the arches around St Mark's or lying in piles by the cafés, opening early to provide strong coffee. The gaming was over. The Casino tellers were packing away their gaudy stripes and optimistic baize. I was off-duty and it was almost dawn. Usually, I go straight home and meet my stepfather on his way to the bakery. He slaps me about the shoulder and makes some joke about how much money I'm making. He's a curious man; a shrug of the shoulders and a wink and that's him. He's never thought it odd that his daughter cross-dresses for a living and sells second-hand purses on the side. But then, he's never thought it odd that his daughter was born with webbed feet.

'There are stranger things,' he said.

And I suppose there are.

This morning, there's no going home. I'm bolt upright, my legs are restless and the only sensible thing is to borrow a boat and calm myself in the Venetian way; on the water.

The Grand Canal is already busy with vegetable boats. I am the only one who seems intent on recreation and the others eye me curiously, in between steadying a load or arguing with a friend. These are my people, they can eye me as much as they wish.

I push on, under the Rialto, that strange half-bridge that can be drawn up to stop one half of this city warring with the other. They'll seal it eventually and we'll be brothers and mothers. But that will be the doom of paradox.

Bridges join but they also separate.

* * *

Out now, past the houses that lean into the water. Past the Casino itself. Past the money-lenders and the churches and the buildings of state. Out now into the lagoon with only the wind and the seagulls for company.

There is a certainty that comes with the oars, with the sense of generation after generation standing up like this and rowing like this with rhythm and ease. This city is littered with ghosts seeing to their own. No family would be complete without its ancestors.

Our ancestors. Our belonging. The future is foretold from the past and the future is only possible because of the past. Without past and future, the present is partial. All time is eternally present and so all time is ours. There is no sense in forgetting and every sense in dreaming. Thus the present is made rich. Thus the present is made whole. On the lagoon this morning, with the past at my elbow, rowing beside me, I see the future glittering on the water. I catch sight of myself in the water and see in the distortions of my face what I might become.

If I find her, how will my future be?

I will find her.

Somewhere between fear and sex passion is.

Passion is not so much an emotion as a destiny. What choice have I in the face of this wind but to put up sail and rest my oars?

Dawn breaks.

I spent the weeks that followed in a hectic stupor.

Is there such a thing? There is. It is the condition that most resembles a particular kind of mental disorder. I have seen ones like me in San Servelo. It manifests itself as a compulsion to be forever doing something, however meaningless. The body must move but the mind is blank.

415

I walked the streets, rowed circles around Venice, woke up in the middle of the night with my covers in impossible knots and my muscles rigid. I took to working double shifts at the Casino, dressing as a woman in the afternoon and a young man in the evenings. I ate when food was put in front of me and slept when my body was throbbing with exhaustion.

I lost weight.

I found myself staring into space, forgetting where I was going.

I was cold.

I never go to confession; God doesn't want us to confess, he wants us to challenge him, but for a while I went into our churches because they were built from the heart. Improbable hearts that I had never understood before. Hearts so full of longing that these old stones still cry out with their ecstasy. These are warm churches, built in the sun.

I sat at the back, listening to the music or mumbling through the service. I'm never tempted by God but I like his trappings. Not tempted but I begin to understand why others are. With this feeling inside, with this wild love that threatens, what safe places might there be? Where do you store gunpowder? How do you sleep at night again? If I were a little different I might turn passion into something holy and then I would sleep again. And then my ecstasy would be my ecstasy but I would not be afraid.

My flabby friend, who has decided I'm a woman, has asked me to marry him. He has promised to keep me in luxury and all kinds of fancy goods, provided I go on dressing as a young man in the comfort of our own home. He likes that. He says he'll get my moustaches and codpieces specially made and a rare old time we'll have of it, playing games and getting drunk. I was thinking of pulling a knife on him right there in the middle of the Casino, but my Venetian pragmatism stepped in and I thought I might have a little game myself. Anything now to relieve the ache of never finding her.

I've always wondered where his money comes from. Is it inherited? Does his mother still settle his bills?

No. He earns his money. He earns his money supplying the French army with meat and horses. Meat and horses he tells me that wouldn't normally feed a cat or mount a beggar.

How does he get away with it?

There's no one else who can supply so much so fast, any-where; as soon as his orders arrive, the supplies are on their way.

It seems that Bonaparte wins his battles quickly or not at all. That's his way. He doesn't need quality, he needs action. He needs his men on their feet for a few days' march and a few days' battle. He needs horses for a single charge. That's enough. What does it matter if the horses are lame and the men are poisoned so long as they last so long as they're needed?

I'd be marrying a meat man.

I let him buy me champagne. Only the best. I hadn't tasted Madame Clicquot since the hot night in August. The rush of it along my tongue and into my throat brought back other memories. Memories of a single touch. How could anything so passing be so pervasive?

But Christ said, 'Follow me,' and it was done.

Sunk in these dreams, I hardly felt his hand along my leg, his fingers on my belly. Then I was reminded vividly of squid and their suckers and I shook him off shouting that I'd never marry him, not for all the Veuve Clicquot in France nor a

Venice full of codpieces. His face was always red so it was hard to tell what he felt about these insults. He got up from where he'd been kneeling and straightened his waistcoat. He asked me if I wanted to keep my job.

'I'll keep my job because I'm good at it and clients like you come through the door every day.'

He hit me then. Not hard but I was shocked. I'd never been hit before. I hit him back. Hard.

He started to laugh and coming towards me squashed me flat against the wall. It was like being under a pile of fish. I didn't try to move, he was twice my weight at least and I'm no heroine. I'd nothing to lose either, having lost it already in happier times.

He left a stain on my shirt and threw a coin at me by way of goodbye.

What did I expect from a meat man?

I went back to the gaming floor.

November in Venice is the beginning of the catarrh season. Catarrh is part of our heritage like St Mark's. Long ago, when the Council of Three ruled in mysterious ways, any traitor or hapless one done away with was usually announced to have died of catarrh. In this way, no one was embarrassed. It's the fog that rolls in from the lagoon and hides one end of the Piazza from another that brings on our hateful congestion. It rains too, mournfully and quietly, and the boatmen sit under sodden rags and stare helplessly into the canals. Such weather drives away the foreigners and that's the only good thing that can be said of it. Even the brilliant water-gate at the Fenice turns grey.

On an afternoon when the Casino didn't want me and I didn't want myself, I went to Florian's to drink and gaze at the Square. It's a fulfilling pastime.

I had been sitting perhaps an hour when I had the feeling of being watched. There was no one near me, but there was someone behind a screen a little way off. I let my mind retreat again. What did it matter? We are always watching or watched. The waiter came over to me with a packet in his hand.

I opened it. It was an earring. It was the pair.

And she stood before me and I realised I was dressed as I had been that night because I was waiting to work. My hand went to my lip.

'You shaved it off,' she said.

I smiled. I couldn't speak.

She invited me to dine with her the following evening and I took her address and accepted.

In the Casino that night I tried to decide what to do. She thought I was a young man. I was not. Should I go to see her as myself and joke about the mistake and leave gracefully? My heart shrivelled at this thought. To lose her again so soon. And what was myself? Was this breeches and boots self any less real than my garters? What was it about me that interested her?

You play, you win. You play, you lose. You play.

I was careful to steal enough to buy a bottle of the best champagne.

Lovers are not at their best when it matters. Mouths dry up, palms sweat, conversation flags and all the time the heart is threatening to fly from the body once and for all. Lovers have been known to have heart attacks. Lovers drink too much from nervousness and cannot perform. They eat too little and faint during their fervently wished consummation. They do not stroke the favoured cat and their face-paint comes loose. This is not all. Whatever you have set store by, your dress, your dinner, your poetry, will go wrong.

* * *

Her house was gracious, standing on a quiet waterway, fashionable but not vulgar. The drawing-room, enormous with great windows at either end and a fireplace that would have suited an idle wolfhound. It was simply furnished; an oval table and a *chaise-longue*. A few Chinese ornaments that she liked to collect when the ships came through. She had also a strange assortment of dead insects mounted in cases on the wall. I had never seen such things before and wondered about this enthusiasm.

She stood close to me as she took me through the house, pointing out certain pictures and books. Her hand guided my elbow at the stairs and when we sat down to eat she did not arrange us formally but put me beside her, the bottle in between.

We talked about the opera and the theatre and the visitors and the weather and ourselves. I told her that my real father had been a boatman and she laughed and asked could it be true that we had webbed feet?

'Of course,' I said and she laughed the more at this joke.

We had eaten. The bottle was empty. She said she had married late in life, had not expected to marry at all being stubborn and of independent means. Her husband dealt in rare books and manuscripts from the east. Ancient maps that showed the lairs of griffins and the haunts of whales. Treasure maps that claimed to know the whereabouts of the Holy Grail. He was a quiet and cultured man of whom she was fond.

He was away.

We had eaten, the bottle was empty. There was nothing more that could be said without strain or repetition. I had been with her more than five hours already and it was time to leave. As we stood up and she moved to get something

I stretched out my arm, that was all, and she turned back into my arms so that my hands were on her shoulder blades and hers along my spine. We stayed thus for a few moments until I had courage enough to kiss her neck very lightly. She did not pull away. I grew bolder and kissed her mouth, biting a little at the lower lip.

She kissed me.

'I can't make love to you,' she said.

Relief and despair.

'But I can kiss you.'

And so, from the first, we separated our pleasure. She lay on the rug and I lay at right angles to her so that only our lips might meet. Kissing in this way is the strangest of distractions. The greedy body that clamours for satisfaction is forced to content itself with a single sensation and, just as the blind hear more acutely and the deaf can feel the grass grow, so the mouth becomes the focus of love and all things pass through it and are re-defined. It is a sweet and precise torture.

When I left her house some time later, I did not set off straight away, but watched her moving from room to room extinguishing the lights. Upwards she went, closing the dark behind her until there was only one light left and that was her own. She said she often read into the small hours while her husband was away. Tonight she did not read. She paused briefly at the window and then the house was black.

What was she thinking?

What was she feeling?

I walked slowly through the silent squares and across the Rialto, where the mist was brooding above the water. The boats were covered and empty apart from the cats that make their homes under the seat boards. There was no one, not even the beggars who fold themselves and their rags into any doorway.

How is it that one day life is orderly and you are content, a little cynical perhaps but on the whole just so, and then without warning you find the solid floor is a trapdoor and you are now in another place whose geography is uncertain and whose customs are strange?

Travellers at least have a choice. Those who set sail know that things will not be the same as at home. Explorers are prepared. But for us, who travel along the blood vessels, who come to the cities of the interior by chance, there is no preparation. We who were fluent find life is a foreign language. Somewhere between the swamp and the mountains. Somewhere between fear and sex. Somewhere between God and the Devil passion is and the way there is sudden and the way back is worse.

I'm surprised at myself talking in this way. I'm young, the world is before me, there will be others. I feel my first streak of defiance since I met her. My first upsurge of self. I won't see her again. I can go home, throw aside these clothes and move on. I can move out if I like. I'm sure the meat man can be persuaded to take me to Paris for a favour or two.

Passion, I spit on it.

I spat into the canal.

Then the moon came visible between the clouds, a full moon, and I thought of my mother rowing her way in faith to the terrible island.

The surface of the canal had the look of polished jet. I took off my boots slowly, pulling the laces loose and easing them free. Enfolded between each toe were my own moons. Pale and opaque. Unused. I had often played with them but

I never thought they might be real. My mother wouldn't even tell me if the rumours were real and I have no boating cousins. My brothers are gone away.

Could I walk on that water?

Could I?

I faltered at the slippery steps leading into the dark. It was November, after all. I might die if I fell in. I tried balancing my foot on the surface and it dropped beneath into the cold nothingness.

Could a woman love a woman for more than a night?

I stepped out and in the morning they say a beggar was running round the Rialto talking about a young man who'd walked across the canal like it was solid.

I'm telling you stories. Trust me.

When we met again I had borrowed an officer's uniform. Or, more precisely, stolen it.

This is what happened.

At the Casino, well after midnight, a soldier had approached me and suggested an unusual wager. If I could beat him at billiards he would make me a present of his purse. He held it up before me. It was round and nicely padded and there must be some of my father's blood in me because I have never been able to resist a purse.

And if I lost? I was to make him a present of my purse. There was no mistaking his meaning.

We played, cheered on by a dozen bored gamblers and, to my surprise, the soldier played well. After a few hours at the Casino nobody plays anything well.

I lost.

We went to his room and he was a man who liked his women face down, arms outstretched like the crucified Christ. He was able and easy and soon fell asleep. He was

423

also about my height. I left him his shirt and boots and took the rest.

She greeted me like an old friend and asked me straight away about the uniform.

'You're not a soldier.'

'It's fancy dress.'

I began to feel like Sarpi, that Venetian priest and diplomat, who said he never told a lie but didn't tell the truth to everyone. Many times that evening as we ate and drank and played dice I prepared to explain. But my tongue thickened and my heart rose up in self-defence.

'Feet,' she said.

'What?'

'Let me stroke your feet.'

Sweet Madonna, not my feet.

'I never take off my boots away from home. It's a nervous habit.'

'Then take off your shirt instead.'

Not my shirt, if I raised my shirt she'd find my breasts.

'In this inhospitable weather it would not be wise. Everyone has catarrh. Think of the fog.'

I saw her eyes stray lower. Did she expect my desire to be obvious?

What could I allow; my knees?

Instead I leaned forward and began to kiss her neck. She buried my head in her hair and I became her creature. Her smell, my atmosphere, and later when I was alone I cursed my nostrils for breathing the everyday air and emptying my body of her.

As I was leaving she said, 'My husband returns tomorrow.'

Oh.

As I was leaving she said, 'I don't know when I will see you again.'

Does she do this often? Does she walk the streets, when her husband goes away, looking for someone like me? Everyone in Venice has their weakness and their vice. Perhaps not only in Venice. Does she invite them to supper and hold them with her eyes and explain, a little sadly, that she can't make love? Perhaps this is her passion. Passion out of passion's obstacles. And me? Every game threatens a wild card. The unpredictable, the out of control. Even with a steady hand and a crystal ball we couldn't rule the world the way we wanted it. There are storms at sea and there are other storms inland. Only the convent windows look serenely out on both.

I went back to her house and banged on the door. She opened it a little. She looked surprised.

'I'm a woman,' I said, lifting up my shirt and risking the catarrh.

She smiled. 'I know.'

I didn't go home. I stayed.

The churches prepared for Christmas. Every Madonna was gilded and every Jesus re-painted. The priests took out their glorious golds and scarlets and the incense was especially sweet. I took to going to service twice a day to bask in the assurance of Our Lord. I've never had a conscience about basking. In summer I do it against the walls or I sit like the lizards of the Levant on top of our iron wells. I love the way wood holds heat, and if I can I take my boat and lie directly in the path of the sun for a day. My body loosens then, my mind floats away and I wonder if this is what holy men feel when they talk about their trances? I've seen holy men come from the eastern lands. We had an exhibit of them once to make up for the law prohibiting bull-baiting. Their bodies were loose but I have heard it's to do with the food they eat.

Basking can't be called holy, but if it achieves the same results will God mind? I don't think so. In the Old Testament the end always justified the means. We understand that in Venice, being a pragmatic people.

The sun is gone now and I must do my basking in other ways. Church basking is taking what's there and not paying for it. Taking the comfort and joy and ignoring the rest. Christmas but not Easter. I never bother with church at Easter. It's too gloomy, and besides the sun's out by then.

If I went to confession, what would I confess? That I cross-dress? So did Our Lord, so do the priests.

That I steal? So did Our Lord, so do the priests.

That I am in love?

The object of my love has gone away for Christmas. That's what they do at this time of year. He and she. I thought I'd mind, but since the first few days, when my stomach and chest were full of stones, I've been happy. Relieved almost. I've seen my old friends and walked by myself with almost the same sure-footedness that I used to. The relief comes from no more clandestine meetings. No more snatched hours. There was a particular week when she ate two breakfasts every day. One at home and one with me. One in the drawing-room and one in the Square. After that her lunches were a disaster.

She is much prone to going to the theatre, and because he does not enjoy the stage she goes alone. For a time she only saw one act of everything. In the interval she came to me.

Venice is full of urchins who will carry notes from one eager palm to another. In the hours we could not meet we sent messages of love and urgency. In the hours we could meet our passion was brief and fierce.

She dresses for me. I have never seen her in the same clothes twice.

Now, I am wholly given over to selfishness. I think about myself, I get up when I like, instead of at the crack of dawn just to watch her open the shutters. I flirt with waiters and gamblers and remember that I enjoy that. I sing to myself and I bask in churches. Is this freedom delicious because rare? Is any respite from love welcome because temporary? If she were gone for ever these days of mine would not be lit up. Is it because she will return that I take pleasure in being alone?

Hopeless heart that thrives on paradox; that longs for the beloved and is secretly relieved when the beloved is not there. That gnaws away at the night-time hours desperate for a sign and appears at breakfast so self-composed. That longs for certainty, fidelity, compassion, and plays roulette with anything precious.

Gambling is not a vice, it is an expression of our humanness.

We gamble. Some do it at the gaming table, some do not. You play, you win, you play, you lose. You play.

The Holy child has been born. His mother is elevated. His father forgotten. The angels are singing in the choir stalls and God sits on the roof of each church and pours his blessing on to those below. What a wonder, joining yourself to God, pitting your wits against him, knowing that you win and lose simultaneously. Where else could you indulge without fear the exquisite masochism of the victim? Lie beneath his lances and close your eyes. Where else could you be so in control? Not in love, certainly.

His need for you is greater than your need for him because

he knows the consequences of not possessing you, whereas you, who know nothing, can throw your cap in the air and live another day. You paddle in the water and he never crosses your mind, but he is busy recording the precise force of the flood around your ankles.

Bask in it. In spite of what the monks say, you can meet God without getting up early. You can meet God lounging in the pew. The hardship is a man-made device because man cannot exist without passion. Religion is somewhere between fear and sex. And God? Truly? In his own right, without our voices speaking for him? Obsessed I think, but not passionate.

In our dreams we sometimes struggle from the oceans of desire up Jacob's ladder to that orderly place. Then human voices wake us and we drown.

On New Year's Eve, a procession of boats alive with candles stretched down the Grand Canal. Rich and poor shared the same water and harboured the same dreams that next year, in its own way, would be better. My mother and father in their bakery best gave away loaves to the sick and the dispossessed. My father was drunk and had to be stopped from singing verses he had learnt in a French bordello.

Farther out, hidden away in the inner city, the exiles had their own observation. The dark canals were as dark as ever but a closer look revealed tattered satin on yellow bodies, the glint of a goblet from some subterranean hole. The slant-eyed children had stolen a goat and were solemnly slitting its throat when I rowed past. They stopped their red knives for a moment to watch me.

My philosopher friend was on her balcony. That is, a couple of crates fastened to the iron rings on either side of her nook. She was wearing something on her head, a circle, dark and heavy. I slid past her and she asked me what time it might be.

'Almost New Year.'

'I know it. It smells.'

She went back to dipping her cup into the canal and taking deep swigs. Only when I had gone on did I realise that her crown was made out of rats tied in a circle by their tails.

I saw no Jews. Their business is their own tonight.

It was bitterly cold. No wind but the icy air that freezes the lungs and bites at the lips. My fingers were numb about the oars and I almost thought of tying up my boat and hurrying to join the crowd pushing into St Mark's. But this was not a night for basking. Tonight the spirits of the dead are abroad speaking in tongues. Those who may listen will learn. She is at home tonight.

I rowed by her house, softly lit, and hoped to catch sight of her shadow, her arm, any sign. She was not visible, but I could imagine her seated, reading, a glass of wine by her side. Her husband would be in his study, poring over some new and fabulous treasure. The whereabouts of the Cross or the secret tunnels that lead to the centre of the earth where the fire dragons are.

I stopped by her water-gate, and climbing up the railing looked in through the window. She was alone. Not reading but staring at the palms of her hands. We had compared hands once, mine are very lined and hers, though they have been longer in this world, have the innocence of a child. What was she trying to see? Her future? Another year? Or was she trying to make sense of her past? To understand how the past had led to the present. Was she searching for the line of her desire for me?

I was about to tap on the window when her husband entered the room, startling her. He kissed her forehead and she smiled. I watched them together and saw more in a moment than I could have pondered in another year. They did not live in the fiery furnace she and I inhabited, but they had a calm and a way that put a knife to my heart.

I shivered with cold, suddenly realising that I was two storeys in mid-air. Even a lover is occasionally afraid.

The great clock in the Piazza struck a quarter to twelve. I hurried to my boat and rowed without feeling my hands or feet into the lagoon. In that stillness, in that quiet, I thought of my own future and what future there could be meeting in cafés and always dressing too soon. The heart is so easily mocked, believing that the sun can rise twice or that roses bloom because we want them to.

In this enchanted city all things seem possible. Time stops. Hearts beat. The laws of the real world are suspended. God sits in the rafters and makes fun of the Devil and the Devil pokes Our Lord with his tail. It has always been so. They say the boatmen have webbed feet and a beggar says he saw a young man walk on water.

If you should leave me, my heart will turn to water and flood away.

The Moors on the great clock swing back their hammers and strike in turn. Soon the Square will be a rush of bodies, their warm breath ascending and shaping little clouds above their heads. My breath shoots out straight in front of me like the fire dragon's. The ancestors cry from about the water and in St Mark's the organ begins. In between freezing and melting. In between love and despair. In between fear and sex, passion is. My oars lie flat on the water. It is New Year's Day, 1805.

ACKNOWLEDGMENTS

CAMILLO BOITO: "Senso", translation copyright © Christine Donougher 1993. First published in *Senso (and other stories)* by Camillo Boito, translated by Christine Donougher. Dedalus, 1993.

GIACOMO CASANOVA: Excerpt from *History of My Life*, by Giacomo Casanova, translated by William R. Trask. English translation copyright © 1966, renewed 1994 by Houghton Mifflin Harcourt Publishing Company. Reprinted by permission of Houghton Mifflin Harcourt Publishing Company. All rights reserved.

DAPHNE DU MAURIER: "Don't Look Now" reproduced with permission of Curtis Brown Group Limited, London on behalf of The Chichester Partnership. Copyright © The Chichester Partnership, 1971.

MARCEL PROUST: From *In Search of Lost Time* by *Marcel Proust,* translated by C. K. Scott Moncrieff & Terence Kilmartin with revisions by D. J. Enright. Published by Chatto & Windus. Reprinted by permission of The Random House Group Limited. © 1992.

From *In Search of Lost Time* by *Marcel Proust,* translated by C. K. Scott Moncrieff & Terence Kilmartin with revisions by D. J. Enright.

"Sojourn in Venice" from IN SEARCH OF LOST TIME, VOLUME 5: THE CAPTIVE, THE FUGITIVE by Marcel Proust, translated by C.K. Scott Moncrieff and Terence Kilmartin, revised by D.J. Enright, translation copyright © 1981